Everyone hated Jerrold Willet.
But that was no reason to murder him...

"Ellie," Vanessa gasped, out of breath, "you've got to come quick. I can't look....It's awful. Oh, God, I think I'm going to be sick."

She pointed to the corner where the untidy pile of wood was flanked by a flower bed on one side and a lilac bush on the other. But something else was there too. A man's legs in gray trousers were sticking out from behind the shrubbery.

Poor Vanessa had a body in her backyard, and I'd been summoned to find out whose. Not especially delighted that my unique accomplishments made me the natural choice for this unenviable task, I edged reluctantly toward the prone figure.

The man was lying face down with his head half buried in a clump of crushed petunias, one arm flung awkwardly to the side. His hairpiece had fallen forward, leaving a pathetically bald pate visible. I steeled myself to check his pulse. There was none. His wrist was cold to the touch, stiff with what I assumed was rigor mortis. Then I saw the bullet holes...

FALSE IMPRESSIONS

A MYSTERY BY

KARIN BERNE

POPULAR LIBRARY

An Imprint of Warner Books, Inc.

A Warner Communications Company

The characters and events described in this book are entirely fictitious. Any resemblance to any actual persons or events is purely coincidental.

POPULAR LIBRARY EDITION

Popular Library® is a registered trademark of Warner Books, Inc.

Popular Library Books are published by
Warner Books, Inc.
666 Fifth Avenue
New York, N.Y. 10103

 A Warner Communications Company

Printed in the United States of America

First Printing: November, 1986

10   9   8   7   6   5   4   3   2   1

Dedicated to

Gideon
Julie
David
Sarah

Acknowledgments: Dr. Robert L. Karp, Eugene Adler, Lane W. Vance, Meike Kerper, Elizabeth Ortiz, Robert Lauer, Harry Tipton, Mary Mahoney, Janice Caudill, Elaine Kramer, Bryna Gollin, Joseph A. Robles, Dr. Richard D. McCleary, Albuquerque Balloon Fiesta.

— *Prologue* —

May 25

Dear Ellie,

Everything is wonderful. My divorce is final, the art gallery is opening in July, and Santa Fe is just as fantastic as I thought it would be. So how about spending your vacation here fraternizing with the elite—writers, movie stars, dethroned kings and out-of-favor politicians? You'll fit right in.

I keep inviting you to New Mexico and you keep saying you're too busy. Bull crap. No excuses this time. You've got pull with your boss. Use it, and I'll show you the most exciting two weeks of your life. Or at least as much fun as you had in Mazatlán last year.

Say yes.

Love,
Vanessa

P.S. Have I got a man for you!

–1–

Chapter
1

"Stomach-churning, isn't it? A Conchita unoriginal would have much more aesthetic merit if it were done in disappearing ink, so at least the paper could be recycled. Too bad she wasted such effort using a dry-brush technique when no brush would have been an improvement."

"You don't care for the artist's execution?"

"Her execution would be very appropriate." The dapper man with the winged eyebrows and matching toupee favored me with a puff of smoke from his cigar. "But you really don't think this is art? Sorry, my dear, the Discriminating Palette has sent engraved invitations to view cartoons, jokes. You can rest assured this drivel will never desecrate the walls of the Louvre. These sentimental effusions are pathetic examples of what happens when a classical medium is debased for the sake of mass consumption."

"How do you feel about paint by numbers?" I asked politely.

"He calls it a blessed distraction for the great unwashed. Am I right, Jerrold?" an impatient voice cut in from behind me.

"Ah, Conchita herself." He grimaced. "The mistress of kitsch in the grand style. And to what do I owe the honor of your personal attention? Could it be for auld lang syne or worry that I'll talk this attractive lady into putting her checkbook away?"

The young woman glared at him. "Don't flatter yourself. The only reason I'm not totally ignoring you is that disgusting cigar. You're stinking up the whole gallery. Take that thing outside and bury it."

"Afraid I might mar the finish on your lyrical landscapes," he expelled another cloud of smoke, "or perhaps tarnish the bloom on the cheeks of your doe-eyed moppets?"

"Why did you bother coming?" she hissed over my shoulder. "You could have written your usual bloodthirsty review without seeing the show—unless panning me in print isn't as much fun as insulting me in person?"

"Insulting you is enjoyable, but manifestly redundant," he said with a sneer. "Your paintings do that quite adequately without my help."

"Excuse me." I tried to inch myself away from the firing line, but Conchita gripped my upper arm.

"Don't run off. I'd like you to meet the publisher of *Insight,* Santa Fe's third-rate magazine of the arts. Jerrold Willet, this is Ellie Gordon, a distinguished visitor from California."

"From California and distinguished." He looked down his nose at me as if the two words were a contradiction in terms. "Beckoned all the way to New Mexico by the thrill of attending tonight's reception, I take it."

"My, you do have insight." My guileless smile didn't fool him for a moment.

Unsure whether to aim his next thrust at the upstart from the Coast or the more familiar object of his cutting sarcasm, he took a swipe at both. "Then may I offer my condolences on a wasted airplane ticket, Ms. Gordon. You'd have been just as satisfied with a trip to Disneyland. Mesdames." He bowed.

As soon as he turned his back, my companion let loose a string of expletives. "Pig! Fucking bastard," was her closing endorsement.

"He's a charmer, all right," I agreed, rubbing the spot where Conchita's sharp fingernails had dug into my skin. "Who put him on the guest list? An evil genie?"

"No, your friend Vanessa. I warned her Jerrold was one critic it would be safer to ignore, but she thought the omission would make him even more malicious. As you can tell, that would be impossible," she said, tight-lipped. "Never mind. Another group of people are coming in, and I should be over there welcoming them with a smile, if I can manage one." Her frown deepened. "Listen. Do you hear that? Fireworks. Why can't those damn kids wait until tomorrow?" Still grumbling to herself, she smoothed her blue-black chignon, then strode across the polished brick floor, the wide skirt of her Mexican fiesta dress swirling around her legs.

The third of July and my introduction to Santa Fe; so far the experience was proving to be as colorful as promised. I glanced down at the pink welts on my arm. The lady hadn't meant to disfigure me for life. Between opening night jitters and that pompous pedant who could blow more hot air without a cigar, anyone would be driven to distraction, even if Willet's attack hadn't been a surprise assault. Apparently, they'd been at each other's throats for quite some time, which was a shame considering how much they had in common. A critic with fake hair and an artist with a fake name ought to be a perfect match.

Conchita, the featured star of the evening, was really Melinda Morrison, an undiscovered commodity until she refashioned herself into an "authentic" Southwestern artist. Maybe the giveaway was the freckles on her upturned nose, but I couldn't help feeling that her native Kansas had left an indelible stamp no amount of black hair dye or ethnic embroidery could camouflage.

Nevertheless, her work with its Hispanic flavor had captured the public's fancy as well as the interest of a major greeting-card company. Some purists might cry "what price glory?", but for any occasion, including Bar Mitzvahs, miniature reprints of expensive Conchita originals with color-coordinated envelopes were available at gloriously affordable prices. The display rack prominently located at the front of the gallery was brimming with every conceivable variety. Her simplistically sweet *niños*, a trademark by now, could be found sitting on gentle burros, peeking shyly from behind a thornless cactus, or merely staring dreamily into a pastel version of a desert sunset.

I called it bunny rabbit art. That reflected my personal taste, mind you, and was not a total indictment like Willet's, or even a criticism of Conchita's draftsmanship. She drew rabbits very well.

Innovative, no. Her style was more insipid than inspired. Of course, the fact that it inspired people to buy was enough to make Willet's toupee stand on end. By his standards, commercial success lowered the ideal of art for art's sake to painting for profit; although if Van Gogh had been so lucky, he might have died rich and with two ears.

Anyway, nobody around here cared if Conchita bedecked herself in borrowed finery. This was Santa Fe, the "city different," filled with people different and not all of them artists, though it was hard to tell which ones painted only by number. When the next crew of exalted invitees made a grand entrance into the long white-walled room, I retreated to a corner where I could gape without being disturbed.

As a born-and-bred Californian, I'd seen my fair share of the fashionably outlandish, but this was the *haut ton* of quaint. Santa Feans lived in quaint adobe mansions, drove on winding streets that could scarcely accommodate two

Mercedes passing each other. They also wore quaint little get-ups like the one across the room . . . a deerskin camisole studded with coral. Clearly, I was out of place in my basic black evening frock bought especially for this party. Might as well have hung a sign around my neck that said tourist and been done with it. Vanessa should have warned me; I would have borrowed beaded moccasins for the occasion.

Actually, there were some people in trite designer label cocktail dresses and plain old Brooks Brothers suits, but they were outnumbered, and outshone, and not nearly as much fun to watch as the walking turquoise mine in lizard-skin cowboy boots. When a satin blouse topped by a fringed headdress began to seem tame, I wondered if there were any literary lions lurking among all the glitter. Santa Fe was a writers' colony, as well as a home away from home for some famous Hollywood actors who retreated here periodically for a few weeks of peace and quiet. Vanessa bragged that there would be at least one Pulitzer Prize winner wandering around, though I wouldn't recognize James Michener unless he flashed an American Express card in my face. Still, I looked.

A few minutes later, Vanessa found me. "What did he say?" she asked anxiously.

"I presume you don't mean James."

"James? No, Jerrold Willet, the art critic." She brushed a wayward strand of red hair off her face. "I saw you talking to him."

"Oh, the man with insight. He didn't say much. We were discussing Disneyland."

"That's all? Then why was Conchita so upset?"

"The fireworks." My answer was punctuated by the sound of a cherry bomb going off outside. "She's not in the mood for so much patriotism."

"Maybe I shouldn't have planned the opening for this weekend," Vanessa fretted for the umpteenth time. "Suppose hardly anyone comes? We sent only three hundred invitations."

"A paltry number, granted, but you sent them to the cream of Santa Fe society, and rich people don't go out of town on national holidays. They wait until the traffic is less congested."

A smile tugged at her lips. "Couldn't they just stay home?"

"What for? So the butler can toss some hot dogs on the grill and light a few sparklers for them? Believe me, Nessa, all three hundred will be here. You're providing the upper crust with upper-class entertainment tonight."

"Oh, Ellie, you're such a pragmatic idiot," she said with a laugh, pressing a soft, perfumed cheek to mine. "I would have fallen apart without you here today."

Since I had been whisked from airport to gallery a mere five hours earlier, Vanessa's gratitude was as exaggerated as her lavish claim that I hadn't changed a bit in ten years. But then, to a brunette with gray eyes who'd metamorphosed into a green-eyed redhead, someone who'd kept her original coloring might seem unchanged. So what if my baby browns were now delicately trimmed with crow's feet and the curves in my figure had dropped an inch closer to the ground? If Vanessa Harper could insist that Ellie Gordon still looked twenty-nine, then I could lie about the Louvre.

"Where is Willet now?" She scanned the room.

"Taking his stogie for a walk. So why don't you stop worrying and go sell something expensive to that lady in the conservative white suit?"

"I plan to, but first things first." Nessa grabbed me by the wrist. "See that man coming in the door? Well, keep your curly head turned in his direction and get ready for the match of a lifetime I promised. He's it."

"I don't want to be fixed up, Nessa. I told you. . . . That's him?"

"In the flesh," she said triumphantly. "You like?"

Did I like? The vision across the room was the most magnificent specimen of manhood I'd ever had the privilege of drooling over. Then Nessa told me who he was. That I had missed seeing Adam Montgomery's gorgeous face on the back of his book jackets was as inexcusable as not having read any of his six bestsellers. Unfortunately, spy thrillers had never appealed to me until that very minute.

But when Nessa suggested I put my best foot forward, best and second best suddenly got cold and glued themselves to the ground. "I know opposites are supposed to attract, but that hunk won't be interested in me. I'm too old . . . too short . . . too ordinary. It's okay. I'll admire from afar."

"Don't be silly," she snorted, towing me through the crowd. "Dating younger men is in, and you've never been ordinary. Besides, tall men always love petite women. Oh, Adam," she said enthusiastically, "this is Ellie Gordon. The friend I told you about who solves real murders, just for fun."

"I don't do it for fun," I protested, feeling a blush creep up my neck.

"Then you're serious and successful," the deep voice soothed my embarrassment. "And I'm very impressed."

"It's nothing." I shrugged awkwardly. "Nothing to boast of, I mean."

"As modest as she is lovely." He took my hand. He could have kept it forever as far as I was concerned.

After searching for a scintillating remark that would charm the boots off this bona fide member of the literati, I came up with a clever "oh."

Let me explain that under normal circumstances I am not an inarticulate boob. If anything, I usually talk too much, especially when I have nothing to say. But since meeting internationally acclaimed authors wasn't an everyday occurrence in my humdrum life, having the Adonis of category fiction request the pleasure of my company certainly deserved a moment of reverent silence.

He flashed a dazzling view of perfect white teeth. "We can go see some Indian ruins, if that appeals to you."

"It appeals," Vanessa answered for me while I smiled fatuously and wondered if his sports jackets had to be specially tailored to fit those broad shoulders.

"In return," his blue eyes teased, "you can tell me all about your fearless exploits."

"Fearful is more like it," I said, finding my voice at last. "But thank you. I'd love a guided tour, although I ought to warn you that I'm really not at home on the range."

"Meaning you'd rather go by car than mule train."

"If that wouldn't be inconvenient," I said warily.

"Not at all." He laughed. "Once was enough, and I was doing some research at the time."

"You remember, Ellie." Nessa poked me. "The mule ride in *Desert Intrigue*."

"How could anyone forget." I nodded, vowing to begin a crash course on Adam Montgomery's books no later than dawn tomorrow.

"Except that Ellie and I won't be scaling the mountainside in the dark or dodging gunfire," he said reassuringly. "Ours will be strictly a pleasure jaunt. We'll go the civilized way," he winked at me, "by Maserati."

A hit, a very palpable hit. I sighed as he squeezed my fingers once more and said I'd be hearing from him later in the week. That gave me approximately seventy-two hours to lose five pounds, though if he called after I'd lost only four, I'd just suck in my gut and go anyway.

"There. Did I lie or is that man ideal for you?" Vanessa chortled, shepherding me over to the bar for a restorative glass of champagne.

"Since when isn't tall, tanned, and devastating every sane woman's ideal?"

"Dolt. I mean on an intellectual plane."

"He has one of those too, huh?"

"Very funny. I told him you're brilliant, so you better live up to the recommendation."

"Is that how you arranged this match? Touting my mental prowess, which, by the way, you overrated and overstated."

"Don't quibble. Adam thought you sounded fascinating. Now all you have to do is keep him thinking it."

"How? Are you going to murder someone so I can show-off by solving the crime?"

"That won't be necessary. You'll wow him with your erudition as a classical scholar."

With a self-satisfied smile, Nessa patted me on the shoulder and sallied forth to work her wiles on some other unsuspecting customers, though Adam Montgomery had been sold the biggest bill of goods. He'd probably ask for a refund when he discovered my claim to genius was a B.A. in English literature. But Vanessa always did believe the ability to read unannotated Shakespeare was a greater achievement than knowing how to tell the difference between a Titian and a Tintoretto, as she jokingly summed up her art history studies. I thought they were both useless talents. Besides, a modern writer wouldn't be impressed because I could recite ten soliloquies from memory. Better if I could quote a line from *Publishers Weekly*.

A timely volley of firecrackers seemed to second that opinion, although the noise passed almost unnoticed on top of the chattering voices in here. If anyone did complain about the rockets' red glare, Vanessa could always say she'd ordered the star-spangled celebration outside to match the one going on inside. Sort of an all-American twenty-one hundred gun salute in honor of her distinguished guests. It was an unusual way to promote the opening of a new gallery, but far more suited to this gathering than a "buy one, get an all-occasion card free" gambit. Not that Nessa would dare try anything so crass. Formal exhibits were supposed to be elegant, exude a certain dignity. The only flashy give-away permitted was serving champagne and hors d'oeuvres on the house, an acceptable freebie judging from the horde around the buffet table.

Proper surroundings have always been an important fac-tor when merchandising art. People who shop for high-priced paintings are enticed by an atmosphere of luxury. In fact, they're more inclined to buy when the showplace is grander than what it shows. In Santa Fe, though, no one expected neo-Corinthian columns. The environmental stan-dard for a gallery here was that it look like an old adobe whether it was or not, and that it be located on Canyon Road. So far, so good. Vanessa and her partner had started on a winning note, but as Ruth Metcalf said to me earlier, it was this notable throng who'd decide if the Discriminating Palette could please the most exacting taste.

"Refill?" The bartender held up a bottle.

"Just half a glass. I've recovered my equilibrium, and am now on a strict diet. Nothing fattening will cross my lips until after my date with Adam Montgomery. Come on, Frank, don't tempt me with tostados. Take it away."

He obligingly moved the bowl, then wiped down the counter with a damp cloth. "I'd'a thought a big time gal from the Coast like you was used to hobnobbing with celeb-rities."

"Hey, my address isn't Rodeo Drive. I'm a simple ex-housewife from suburbia who's biggest move was from a family-sized split-level to a condo for one on the other side of the same small town. Hollywood is not my stamping grounds."

"Yeah? Well, I hail from a pissant place in Tennessee where four farmers rubbing shoulders is a regular hoedown, but these hotshots around here don't impress me none."

Frank Ott might have sounded like a country boy, even

looked the part with his aw-shucks blond cowlick and cornflower blue eyes, but he didn't get that tattoo on the back of his hand while chopping cotton. Based on the anchor, I guessed he spent a few years as a seafaring man since leaving home. Maybe that's where he learned to swing a hammer, repairing the deck on a freighter bound for Shanghai. A landlubber now, he'd been hired to do the remodeling on Vanessa's adobe hacienda, turning the front of the rambling house into a showroom and the back into snug living quarters. For tonight, though, the carpenter had put away his tools to pour drinks, another skill he probably acquired on his travels. When I was helping him unpack the cases of domestic bubbly this afternoon, he said all that stuff did was tickle your nose. One of these days he'd fix me a Singapore Sling "that'll make you come home in the morning singing with the cows."

That would be some sunrise serenade, but if the accompanying hangover didn't scare me off, the calories did. Five pounds, I reminded myself, noting the underfed couple sauntering up to the bar. Sure, they probably lived on celery sticks and caviar. As I stepped aside to make room for them, though they didn't need much, a cloud of cigar smoke drifted by my head.

So he was back. Mr. Malice disguised as wit, with a new Havana and a fresh supply of poisoned puns. What a nasty man. No question he had come here to bury Conchita, not to praise her. But then, critics feel obliged to live up to their titles. People who say nice things are called press agents. No one could mistake Willet for a purveyor of PR. He'd choke on the first syllable if he had to spread the good word, which was no doubt why he joined the ranks of chronic complainers.

How else would you describe a profession that's dedicated to looking for the worst? Critics get paid to find fault. They're nothing but salaried cynics with a by-line and a literary license to go on search-and-destroy missions. This wouldn't be so terrible if they didn't take themselves so seriously. But when a hired misanthrope writes a thumbs-down review, he expects it to be read as evidence of superior perception.

Too bad my Aunt Sophie wasn't still around. She would have been perfect for the job. Nothing ever pleased her. The brisket was always underdone, the kugel only fit for the dog. To her, even the bride was too pretty. What a connoisseur, though in my family we called it being a *kvetch*.

I still did, and since I'd taken a hearty dislike to Willet at first gripe, another whiff of tobacco was my signal to leave or lend him my ear. Now, in the old days, escaping my aunt was as simple as hiding under the dining room table. She might have stooped to a lot of things, but her corset kept her from bending over that far. However, in the wide open but rapidly filling spaces of Vanessa's gallery my only recourse was to duck behind a post. Unfortunately, I forgot that all respectable adobes are infested with little brick steps at every turn. With the grace of Frank's cows, I stumbled off the first step, skipped right over the second, and landed smack in the arms of a raving prohibitionist.

He looked more like a bearded bohemian than an ax-wielding member of the Temperance Union. Before I could stammer out an apology or make a self-deprecating joke about being felled by a Santa Fe pitfall, he plucked me off his chest, set me on my feet, and whipped the champagne glass from my hand.

"This stuff should be outlawed."

Retaliating instinctively, I snatched his cigar. "Only after smoking is banned."

Momentarily stymied in his fight against demon rum, he glared at me from beneath bushy eyebrows. "Give that back."

"You first." We reformers have such mature bargaining methods.

Without considering the consequences, either to himself or to the local plant life, the lunatic dumped what was left of my drink into a potted cactus that still had its congratulatory note attached. Then he held up the empty glass. "Why don't you trade this in on a sobering cup of coffee?"

"You are definitely crazy," I informed him, in case he thought his behavior was normal, "but I hope you're not insinuating that I'm drunk."

"No insinuation intended. You came reeling into me as if a herd of stampeding pink elephants were at your heels."

"Obviously, you were blinded by smoke. I merely tripped on the steps."

"Naturally." Even though his mouth was obscured by an overgrown crop of brown bristles, there was no mistaking the disdainful twist of his lips or the double meaning in his answer. "Now may I have my cigar?"

Ignoring his outstretched hand, I leaned over the inebriated cactus and doused the lit cheroot in a puddle of my champagne. "Compliments of a redeemed sot." I offered him the dripping butt. "You were kind enough to show me the error of my ways, and I'd like to return the favor by helping you break a filthy habit. Oh, please, don't thank me." I forestalled his nonexistent gratitude.

"Thank you? Lady, the cigar you just destroyed cost three dollars," he growled.

"Wonderful. At that rate, you'll soon save enough to pay for a shave and haircut."

And a new wardrobe, I wanted to add. In a faded T-shirt and jeans cut off above his knobby knees, this nondrinking, nonconformist was dressed like some bum who'd wandered in off the street to get his first decent hors d'oeuvre of the day. On the other hand, he could be an eccentric millionaire, and I'd just mortally offended one of Vanessa's preferred customers.

But apparently, he wasn't that offended. With a crafty gleam in his beady hazel eyes, he reached into his pocket and exposed the tip of another cigar. "And don't you dare touch it," he warned.

Deciding that discretion was the better part of good business practices, I didn't. It hurt to let him have the last word, but I turned on my heel and left him grinning after me. Hypocrite. He and Willet could both go smoke themselves into oblivion. The room was full of pleasant company, and for the rest of the evening I enjoyed it.

Chapter 2

As the last happy guests were being ushered out the door, I tottered back to Vanessa's sitting room and collapsed on the couch. I fully intended to pitch in with the postparty cleanup, but after standing around in heels for over three hours, I couldn't resist taking a moment to prop my stockinged feet on the armrest and wiggle my toes in sublime relief. My eyelids drooped shut entirely of their own accord.

They probably would have stayed that way, too, if Nessa hadn't jarred them open by poking me in the ribs. "Wake up, sluggard. It's time for a gabfest." Kicking off her sandals, she flopped down on the rug and rested her chin on her hands. "So? What's the verdict?"

"Tonight was a rip-roaring success." I yawned. "The chili dip was spicy, and the bite-sized tacos no bigger than a mouthful. Congratulations. You're a true entrepreneur."

"We even sold a few paintings," she bragged. "And what about the entrepreneur's new image? Now that you've seen me in action, you gotta admit the old gray mare was pretty smart to change what she used to be, huh?"

"A stroke of genius." I rolled over on my side and fixed her with a groggy squint. "Becoming a horse of many colors definitely shows your artistic flair. But why red and green? Inspired by a traffic light?"

The cushion beneath my head was yanked out and tossed into my face. "Auburn and emerald, you clod. Don't you think it's stunning?"

I calmly tucked the velvet pillow back in place. "If you can see a rose-colored world through emerald-tinted contact lenses, it's not only stunning, it's chromatically magnificent."

"Does that translate into a compliment?" she asked suspiciously.

"Yes. You're dazzling," I answered in all truth.

"Good. I wanted a complete change from Nessa the bore. She was such a wimp, her favorite shade was plaid. I think red hair fits my new life." She swept a bright strand off her forehead.

"Picture perfect. Almost as much a statement as that artsy-fartsy creation you're wearing."

Nessa denied that the handwoven batik with the fringed skirt was at all exotic. In fact, she claimed it was on the conservative side, though she didn't say of what. True, it wasn't as flamboyant as Conchita's magenta and gold embroidery, but compared to anything in my wardrobe, both of their outfits qualified as tax-deductible promotional expenses. Of course, in the law office I managed, no one expected me to be a walking advertisement for the trade, which was just as well, since a white curly wig and a long black robe would dwarf me. Vanessa had the height to carry off a *grande toilette,* and the figure to wear a shawl draped around the waist. It added a few flattering pounds to the slender frame that had honed down to near boniness since I'd seen her last.

Her partner made up for that deficit, and she wasn't much of a clothes horse either. In contrast to the colorful Vanessa, Ruth Metcalf's evening attire was a sensible skirt and blouse that cut her full figure into two large halves. Either she felt a woman of fifty should try to look older, or, as the one in charge of the financial end of the business, Ruth was dressed for her role, with black and white representing the ledger books.

Standing in the doorway, she announced that Frank was ready to go home. "The garbage is sacked and he'll haul it away tomorrow when he returns the portable bar to U-Rent-It. Is that okay with you?" she asked Nessa.

"Sure. Tell him thanks again. He's been a doll and I know we can count on him to see that everything is in shape for the public on Monday morning."

When Ruth nodded and left to release Frank officially from duty, as if the decision required a majority vote, we could hear the murmur of voices, then the sound of the front door being shut and locked.

"Sorry. I didn't mean to sleep through KP duty." I smothered another yawn. "What time is it, anyway?"

"About ten after twelve. Not late."

"Then it's only eleven in California, so what's making me so tired?" I complained.

"The altitude. It does that to the unacclimated. We're at seven thousand feet, you know." Then she gave a sly little smile. "Or you might still be reacting to the devastating effects of Adam Montgomery."

That subject certainly generated some animation. I even sat up. "Do you think he'll really call me?"

"Absolutely. He's a man of honor, unless you indicate he can behave otherwise. Hey, stop!" she squealed, laughing when I tickled her bare foot. "No fair hitting below the belt." Prudently, I tucked my own shoeless feet under me, but she was sidetracked by a trip down memory lane. "Do you realize this could be a replay of our college days?"

"Uh-uh. I never got this sleepy until after three in the morning."

"No, idiot. I mean the way we used to sit around and talk about men. Look at us, children grown and gone, husbands shed, leaving us both single and fancy-free again. Doesn't that give you a sense of déjà vu?"

"Yes, and what I'm remembering is your generosity some twenty years ago in a similar situation."

"Carlos Rozetti," she guessed immediately.

"Right. Now tell me what's Adam's hidden flaw."

"Not ten pairs of hands." She shook her head.

"There has to be some reason he's unattached and available to little old me, courtesy of little old you. Rich, famous, handsome men are not exactly a glut on the market. Why aren't you telling me the line forms to the rear?"

Ruth came back and plunked herself down on the easy chair. "If you're talking about that writer, Vanessa's not interested."

"So I gather."

"Aside from the fact that Adam and I have a platonic relationship, it's a matter of priorities," Nessa explained. "Ruth and I have taken a vow that the gallery comes first, at least until the books show a profit. We've sunk every penny into this joint venture. If it fails, my partner will have to go be an accountant again, which she hates, and I'm back to square one. Yuck." She shuddered.

"For you, I presume, square one is Malcolm."

Ruth snorted. "Vanessa thinks he's the snake that crawled from under."

Knowing better than to defend a former husband to his ex-wife, I simply said that it was very nice of her to have invited him to the reception.

"Are you kidding? I didn't ask him to come. He was just checking to see how I'm spending my half of the property settlement."

"Are you sure? Malcolm told me he was lonesome up there in Los Alamos all by himself."

"Don't believe it." Vanessa took a handful of nuts from the silver dish on the coffee table. "He didn't even notice I was gone until he ran out of brown socks. But when the black ones were dirty too, then you should have heard him." She crunched down on a cashew ferociously. "That's when he decided I was behaving like a fool. An unused degree in art history didn't qualify me to run a gallery. I should come home before I fell on my fanny, as if life with him weren't the pits already. Trust me, Ellie, Malcolm's only interest in this world is his damn laboratory and those stupid computers. I was just background noise to him . . . static mostly." She passed me the dish. "He never appreciated how emotionally starved I was in that cultural wasteland they call a scientific community. But Malcolm's a typical physicist. All brains, no soul. Beauty to him is a government research project."

There wasn't much point in reminding her that both Los Alamos and Malcolm, whether soulless or not, had suited her for a good long time. I knew from personal experience that a marriage could be a haven for eighteen years, then suddenly seem like a cage. Though in my case, it had been the husband who flew the coop, which was probably why I felt a certain empathy for Nessa's discarded spouse.

"Anyway," she brushed off her hands, "since Santa Fe has always been my escape route and I know so many people here, it seemed logical to try my wings where I could take advantage of the contacts I've made." She grinned impishly. "Sitting on the Chamber Music Festival Board can be so elevating."

"So that's where you found the affluent crowd who showed up this evening. While I was busy being the happy homemaker all those years, you were sneaking out at night to mingle with the elite. Lousy social climber." I sniffed. "I suppose you know Alan Alda, too."

"Eat your heart out."

"Oh, I will, don't worry. But out of respect for our long-standing friendship, next time invite him and spare me some of your more outrageous acquaintances. There was one obnoxious creep who should be dropped from your social register."

"Which one?" Ruth asked. "The barefoot girl who drives a Porsche or the dowager who'll only write checks in excess of five hundred dollars?" She shrugged a polyester-clad shoulder. "The Discriminating Palette can't afford to be *that* discriminating."

"No. This was a man. Medium height, stocky, forty-fiveish," I described my tormentor, "with a big, fat cigar growing out of his big, fat mouth."

"Jerrold Willet." Her square face twisted into an expression of distaste. "The authority's authority. I heard he was in top form this evening."

Vanessa looked worried. "Yes, Conchita assured me again that the next edition of *Insight* would feature a damning review of her show. Let's hope Jerrold will be a little nicer to the gallery that dared to show it."

"If you don't mind me asking a dumb question, why did you?"

"Because we needed to open the doors with a guaranteed winner, and Conchita's work sells," Nessa answered defensively. "It's popular, and not just locally, either. Those greeting cards have given her national exposure, name recognition. The tourists who trot down Canyon Road are looking for a souvenir to take back to Dubuque. Of course, only a few will spend the money for an original oil, but the signed lithographs are affordable. At the least, people will buy a personally autographed card, 'as suitable for framing as sending,'" she quoted the sign over the display.

That alone was enough to earn Willet's disapproval. Anything that appealed to the masses would get an automatic stamp of "mindless entertainment" from him. Art couldn't be for fun's sake. After all, if a painting was decorative instead of depressing, what was its value? Not pleasure, certainly.

"I don't see why you're both so concerned. Didn't tonight prove that the public's wants speak louder that Willet's words? Conchita doesn't need his endorsement," I comforted.

Ruth leaned forward and wagged an emphatic finger at me. "She doesn't, but the gallery sure could use it. We're the new kid on the block without a reputation yet, good or bad. Two months from now, when we're featuring an unknown artist, one who doesn't draw the crowds, Willet might still feel inclined to give us a no-star rating. His magazine is in every motel room in town, and if he says what we offer will only appeal to garbage collectors, who's going to bother checking us out for themselves?"

"Oh, come on. Most people aren't that gullible," I argued. "You might be presenting Santa Fe with a cultural coup."

Vanessa patted my knee. "Who do you think determines what's a cultural coup? The only reason everybody wants to buy a Gauguin today, for a million dollars no less, is that the critics have been telling us for decades that he's the greatest. The poor guy's contemporaries wouldn't give him two francs for those masterpieces. Oh, sure, people say they know what they like, but they really like what they know. Let something different come along, then watch the reaction. Sorry to disillusion you, champion of the underdog, but only a rare soul can recognize genius before it hits the cover of *Time* magazine."

"Maybe so," I gave in ungracefully, "except I've been to those art shows where collages of newspaper scraps are reviewed as significant and relevant, but no one buys them."

"And you think a bad review would make them sell like hotcakes."

"All right," I grumbled. "You win."

"If Willet lets us," Ruth remarked under her breath, as she got to her feet. "But in the meantime, I need some sleep. See you in the morning."

"Stick around awhile. I was just going to fix us some hot cocoa," Vanessa enticed.

Ruth said she was too tired, and I said enough was enough. I'd made four meals from the buffet table tonight, one tidbit at a time—and that was after my vow of abstinence. If I wanted to be in prime shape for whatever Adam Montgomery had in mind, from now on gluttony was out and calesthenics were in. I'd do two leg lifts a day faithfully.

While Nessa walked her partner across the patio, I retrieved my shoes from under the couch, and padded barefoot into the bedroom. Both women had assured me I wasn't evicting Ruth. Her apartment, an old garage that had been totally remodeled, was completely habitable, even if Frank hadn't finished putting in the cabinets around the bathroom sink, and everything still smelled of paint. Separate living quarters gave both owners some privacy. Even the best of friends could find twenty-four-hour togetherness a strain. If the two of them talked as much as Nessa and I did that night, they'd drop from exhaustion before the first week was over.

As we lay on twin beds with just a strip of moonlight illuminating the room, the only sound besides our voices was the occasional pop of another firecracker. When the neighborhood kids finally wound down, we were still at it.

"So anyway," Nessa continued her explanation, "right after I filed for divorce, I called Ruth. She was surprised, but delighted. How often do acquaintances chat about their dreams for the future at a cocktail party, then actually make them come true together? But since both of us wanted to move from Los Alamos and go into business, it made sense to join forces. That's why Malcolm's attitude kills me. I know about art and she knows how to manage money. Why shouldn't we succeed?"

"You will." I yawned.

"I wish I had your confidence, Ellie. You were never afraid of anything. Remember the time I locked you out of the dormitory on the roof and you just calmly sat on the drain pipe until I let you back in the window?"

"What kind of calm? I was too scared to move."

"Liar. I was the one who almost wet my pants in fear you'd fall off."

"Then why didn't you open the window sooner?"

"I was laughing too hard."

"Louse."

"No. I was laughing at Dan. He just stood down there on the lawn and yelled at you to get back inside." She recalled the moment gleefully. "I'll never forget the look on his face, and you wouldn't answer him. Now that's bravery."

"I was struck dumb with terror."

"Baloney. People who catch crooks aren't faint-hearted, and women who refuse to fall apart when their husbands leave them are not scaredy-cats. Dan's sorry now, isn't he?"

"Certainly. Any man would regret losing a gem like me. You're not the only laundress around. Except Dan's problem is too much starch in his shirts. He thinks I used to do them by hand."

"You didn't tell him the truth?"

"Why spoil his fond memories?"

"I bet he's jealous of all the men you go out with, too."

"I don't do their shirts."

"Come on, you know what I mean. He tossed you over for a younger woman, and now there's a line of males vying for your attention. How does Dan react?" she asked in curiosity. "There must still be a strong tie between people who've been married for years, even after they've separated."

"You might say that Dan takes a fatherly interest in my personal life: 'Who are you dating?' 'What does he do for a living?' 'Remember, you have a name to consider . . . mine.'"

"Sounds like Dan," she gave a sleepy giggle, "and it sounds as though you've forgiven him."

"Well, we do share a son, and anyone who could co-produce a kid like Michael can't be all bad. Of course, since I'm only twenty-nine, it does seem unusual that I'd have a child in college."

"You give me hope for the future, Ellie. There is life A.D.—after divorce. If it just took you a year and a half to get this far, it's barely possible that Malcolm and I will be able to work out a truce. Say in another decade or so." She wrapped her arms around the pillow. "Who knows? By then I might look twenty-nine and have men panting after me."

"I'm far from a swinging single, Nessa. There's no . . ." I stopped. She was already asleep. Oh, well, maybe there would be a line of men for me too in a decade or so.

That closing thought was more than enough to insure sweet dreams, which I had until the specter of Dan intruded. Probably it was all the bite-sized tacos I had consumed earlier, or sheer overtiredness, but there I was in the front seat of Adam's Maserati with my ex-husband playing gooseberry in the back. But even though my slumbers were plagued by nightmares, it wasn't my own scream that woke me.

The sound of a screen door slamming was followed by footsteps pounding down the hall. Unwillingly, I opened my eyes to a bright sunlit room and Vanessa, still in her baby-doll pajamas, bending over me.

"Ellie," she gasped, out of breath, "you've got to come quick. I can't . . . I can't go near it."

"A tarantula in the cornflakes?" I asked sleepily, familiar with her reaction to the mere sight of creepy crawlies.

"It's awful. Oh, God, I think I'm going to be sick." Gagging with more realism than I needed to hear this early in the morning, she put one hand over her mouth and clamped the other around my wrist. "Hurry," she begged.

Not that I had any choice. She pulled me out of bed and dragged me unceremoniously down the hall, my nightgown flapping behind me. "Hey, where are you going?" I demanded. "We just passed the bathroom."

Apparently we were headed directly for the source of the problem, no detours allowed. Flying into the kitchen, Nessa hauled me past the table laid for breakfast, out the back door, then shoved me pell-mell into the middle of the patio. "See?" she choked.

Hardly awake yet, I blinked in the sudden brightness and looked around. The brick courtyard was completely enclosed by a high adobe wall. One corner was filled by some tools and a messy stack of lumber while in the center a Russian olive tree provided some shade against the glare of the sun. In a sheer pink nightie, hair uncombed, teeth unbrushed, feet unshod, I felt rather ill equipped to deal with whatever horrendous denizen of the insect world had completely unhinged Vanessa. But she was whimpering so, it would have been heartless not to try.

Then I noticed Ruth poised beside the screen door of the converted garage. She was fully dressed in slacks and a cream oxford shirt. Shoes too, I noticed, though obviously she couldn't bring herself to use them. She simply stared at me, her normally ruddy cheeks ashen. More than one bug? I thought sardonically.

"I'm sorry to wake you," she said in a quavering voice, "but neither of us has any experience in dealing with this sort of thing."

"That's all right. I'm an old hand at fatal blows. Just toss me a shoe and I won't bring 'em back alive."

"No, I'm afraid you won't."

She pointed to the corner where the untidy pile of wood

was flanked by a flower bed on one side and a lilac bush on the other. Something else was there too. A pair of legs in gray trousers stuck out from behind the shrubbery.

So that was the problem. Nothing as simple as a couple of black widow spiders or an invasion of cockroaches. There was a body in the backyard and I'd been summoned to find out whose. Not especially delighted that my reputation gave me first crack at this unenviable task, I edged reluctantly toward the prone figure while the two women watched silently. It had to be a drunk from last night, I told myself, a champagne-laden guest who had wandered onto the patio for a breath of air, then passed out. When I got closer, that comforting supposition had to be abandoned.

The man was lying facedown with his head half-buried in a clump of crushed petunias, one arm flung awkwardly to the side. His hairpiece had fallen forward, leaving a pathetically bald pate visible. Trying not to be sick, I lifted the hem of my nightgown and stepped around the streaks of dried blood on the bricks, steeling myself to check his pulse. There was none. His wrist was cold, stiff. Then I saw the bullet holes.

I turned my eyes away from the sight on the ground and looked at Ruth. "Call the police."

"What should I say?" she asked inanely.

"You can start by telling them that Jerrold Willet has been shot. Then ask if they'll please come over and remove the body."

Chapter
3

Legal holiday or not, the police were prompt. Within minutes of Ruth's call—no longer than it took me to throw on a denim wrap skirt, tank top, and a dab of lipstick—a patrol car pulled up in front. Having been cast as production manager, more or less by default, I let the uniformed officer in, explained our predicament, then escorted him as far as the kitchen door, where I simply pointed to stage left. Needing no further direction, he assumed command from there, and by the time a black-garbed Vanessa emerged from the bathroom with a bottle of aspirin in her hand, the prologue was over. A police field supervisor had arrived, followed by medical examiner, criminalistics team, and Detective Ramon Chavez.

Thirtyish, dark-haired, and pleasantly soft-spoken, he'd drawn the short straw for Sunday duty, getting to the gallery shortly after the preliminary experts had notified violent crimes that one had taken place. In fact, his speed was commendable considering that he must have been summoned from his bed for this prebreakfast homicide call, although the only indication that he'd been caught with his shoes off were his socks: one was brown and one was black.

Nevertheless, he took charge with calm efficiency, first ordering the scene secured, which meant cordoning off the street to prevent any evidence from wandering in or out. Second was to coordinate the interdivisional efforts of fingerprint crew, police photographer, and other assorted officials so that they could do their thing with dispatch. Since their thing took some time to dispatch, it was a while before he could compare their accumulated data with our accumulated void of information.

Finally, the curtain came down on act one. A standing room only audience of neighbors had been waiting at the curb across the street in anticipation of this moment. These were the privileged few who lived within the boundary lines. They were curious but courteous, obeying the uniformed sentry's request to stay back, except for a couple of rambunctious children who scampered past him to get a closer view. As the stretcher bearing Willet's covered body was carried through the open side gate, the two paramedics were bombarded with questions, which they answered with monosyllabic grunts and one burst of, "Hey, kid, keep your hands off the sheet." That little ghoul must have been the same monster who was still exploding firecrackers at three A.M.

Though the ambulance left minus the fanfare of blazing sirens, since there was no need to break any speed limits rushing Willet to the morgue, the interested bystanders on the block must have raced back to their various push-button phones to digit dial everyone in town. It certainly didn't take long for news of the murder macabre on Canyon Road to spread.

First to verify the exclusive called in by his brother-in-law was an announcer from the classical music radio station. He wanted to check the rumor before playing Mozart's *Requiem*. Hot on his heels came a roving reporter from the local paper looking for a human-interest story. And last but not least, two of the three television network affiliates sent minicam crews to record the proceedings. Unfortunately, an error in communications sent them to the wrong address. When they finally found the right one, there was nothing to film except exterior shots of the gallery and the man next door, who was quite happy to describe the scene they had missed.

Detective Chavez should have been so lucky. He had three possible witnesses and all of us were total flame-outs. This was after we had claimed to be even more hopeless as suspects. One of the first requirements of the morning had been to establish, or at least swear to, our innocence. What a trio of angels. No, we didn't murder anyone last night, either singly or as a group effort. No, none of us owned a gun, or even knew how to fire one. But if so, there certainly wasn't any reason we would use it on Jerrold Willet. Who had, and why, we couldn't answer with the same degree of assurance. His disagreeable personality might have had something to do with his disagreeable demise, but that was just speculation.

So was hope of enlightenment. Ramon Chavez's face was a study in despondency when the three blind mice said we hadn't seen the deceased leave the party, much less noticed if anyone had gone with him. He became even gloomier when we also confessed to partial deafness. We had heard plenty of explosions last night, but no bursts of noise, gunshots or otherwise, that sounded closer to the house than the regular barrage of firecrackers. Ruth helpfully suggested that someone in the crowd might have more specific information, though anything would be more than nothing. But when she told Chavez how many had attended the gallery's grand opening, his elbow almost slipped off the armrest of Vanessa's favorite wingback chair.

"Almost three hundred?" he repeated, sounding dismayed.

"We have the guest book. Everyone was supposed to sign it, but whether they did, I'm not sure," Ruth added.

With a sigh, he jotted down the information. "But none of you ladies can remember when you last saw Mr. Willet alive?"

"There were so many people coming and going," Nessa said on a nervous hiccup. "Hardly anyone bothered to say good-bye. It's not as if they were visiting our home. The kind of reception we held was really a business entertainment." She smiled anxiously at that unnecessary reminder, trying to be charming but managing only to be rather twitchily ingratiating.

Charm wouldn't have worked on Chavez anyway. He needed more than a medical examiner's preliminary report that simply stated the obvious. It was fairly clear that Willet had been shot sometime during the latter part of the evening, if only because that fit between the hours he was lost and then found. Neither did it take an expert to judge that the four bullet holes in his body were not self-inflicted. The one in his back would have been tough for a person who wasn't amazingly double-jointed; though even if Willet had had that talent, it didn't seem likely he'd have come to the party for the joy of committing hara-kiri in the yard. Or that he could have dragged his own dead body from the patio to the petunias. In fact, how anyone got to the petunias became a matter of debate when Ruth claimed she had padlocked the side gate early yesterday afternoon and hadn't opened it until the police arrived this morning. The matter might not have been worth debating since the lock faced the patio rather than the street, and the wooden gate was set into the high adobe wall without an inch to spare on any side. However, my friend Vanessa didn't feel that would be an insurmountable barrier to a gymnast bent on murder.

"Probably Jerrold went through the house, but couldn't the killer have climbed over the wall?" she suggested hopefully.

"Okay. We'll check it out," Chavez agreed, scribbling a reminder in his spiral notebook. "What about this end? How many exits from the house to the patio?"

"Just one through the kitchen," Ruth answered, "but nobody should have gone in there. The only room open to the public on this end of the house is the bathroom."

"But people had to go down the hall to use it," Chavez confirmed.

"Yes, that's why we have 'private, do not enter' signs posted on the other doors along the hallway. This sitting room, our workroom, and kitchen are clearly marked off-limits."

"That's right," Nessa echoed. "Off-limits."

"Then maybe Willet wasn't the only one who didn't honor your request," the detective said mildly.

It was nice of him to exclude us from immediate speculation, since homeowners and out-of-town company certainly didn't need special clearance to enter restricted zones. Still, he must have realized we had nothing to hide or we wouldn't be doing such a poor job of it. After all, an art critic murdered at an art gallery is somewhat self-explanatory. But even removing myself from consideration, unless Chavez thought I was a professional hit woman imported for the caper, Ruth and Vanessa weren't very logical candidates. Inviting a guest at your own party to step outside for the purpose of shooting him at point-blank range was a foolish way to save on guacamole dip. It was also bad business. Besides, there were literally hundreds of avenues to explore before accusing the hostesses of unsociable conduct. Nessa just didn't like any of them.

"I'm sure Jerrold Willet's death had nothing to do with anybody who came to the reception," she insisted, not appreciating that being one out of three hundred suspects was better odds than being one out of three.

Detective Chavez assured her that he wasn't dismissing

the idea that an intruder had entered the property from the backyard, done his dirty deed, then left the way he came, over a twelve-foot-high adobe barricade. The wall-hurdler theory was definitely the most welcome suggestion of the morning, but I doubted if the police would discover rappel marks or telltale ladder prints to substantiate it. For one thing, very few murderers lug around heavy equipment when performing a crime. It impedes escape. Secondly, why would anyone go to so much trouble, and possible rental expense, on the off-chance that his prey would ignore a keep-out-of-the-kitchen notice? It was just as realistic to believe that an innocent gunman had been using the patio for target practice, and the four bullets that landed in Willet were merely random shots in the dark.

That was the kind of realism Vanessa wanted, though. Safe. At a distance. Implicating some stranger who had nothing to do with the gallery, except to bring it under the glare of publicity. She attached her mouth to her thumbnail and gnawed nervously while Chavez asked Ruth what might have lured Willet into the dark night. To meet somebody? To continue an argument? To retreat from one? They never resolved anything, but the detective kept tapping his pen against his teeth as if the motion would eventually jar loose an answer. He stopped only when the first solid piece of evidence came to light.

All during our uninformative postmortem session, police had been in the yard, combing the area for clues. Finally, an enterprising young officer attacked the pile of lumber against the wall and retrieved buried treasure. A small-caliber pistol was wedged inside the mound of two-by-fours. He put it in a plastic bag and brought the bundle directly to Chavez.

"What do you think?"

With an appreciative gleam in his eyes, Chavez held up the bag and studied the contents. "We probably won't get any prints, but check first, then send it to ballistics. The size is right, anyway. Wait." He got up to show us the gun at close view. "You ladies ever seen this before? A Beretta, .22-caliber. Semiautomatic." We shook our heads no. "It might not be the murder weapon," he said encouragingly. When that still didn't prompt cries of recognition from us, he gave it back to the policeman and began writing in his notebook again.

There was a long silence in the sitting room as ball-point pen glided noiselessly across paper. Vanessa's prized antique grandfather clock in the corner went from ten-twenty to ten-twenty-three before anyone said a word.

"Could the killer have dropped the gun during his escape?" Ruth asked hesitantly, meaning would someone who'd risk a broken leg to avoid signing the guest book at the front door be careless enough to leave such an identifiable calling card at the back?

Up to this point, I had kept a low profile, speaking only when spoken to and offering no opinion that might be construed as aiding and abetting the enemy. The enemy, naturally, was this pleasant police detective who wanted the name of everyone who had attended last night's bash. Already Nessa had switched to gnawing her index finger at the dire prospect. The only way to save the rest of her nails was for me to support the idea of a murderous trespasser, although it was more likely that the killer had tossed the gun away because he didn't want to take a smoking weapon back inside the house with him. Nevertheless, in the spirit of friendship, I promoted the farfetched.

"Maybe Ruth's on track. The murderer could have dropped the gun by accident while he was escaping over the wall. It might have fallen out of his pocket, or he could have discarded it in a panic when he heard someone coming. Frank, for instance. He carried out garbage bags several times in the course of the evening. Then too, we can't overlook the possibility that the Beretta was left behind on purpose, to cast suspicion on the people in the house."

Nessa removed her finger from her mouth. "Ellie is a detective too," she said by way of explanation, as if my monologue were only a slight variation of "just the facts, ma'am."

Ramon Chavez merely stared at me. "Who's Frank?"

"Frank?" I repeated. "Oh, Frank Ott. He's a carpenter."

"Then why was he taking garbage outside last night?" Chavez's eyes narrowed. "Or, more to the point, how far did he take it?"

This time Nessa attacked her nails with a frenzy, although I thought she was overreacting. We claimed having gone nowhere near the far end of the patio until this morning, and Detective Chavez wasn't accusing us of lying. He might have thought we were, but he didn't say it aloud. But when Frank told him, not fifteen minutes later, that he went only a few feet past the kitchen door, where the trash bags were still standing in a neat row, the response was entirely different.

For a man who had kindly filled in as bartender and sanitation crew, Frank was getting poor reward for being in the right place at the wrong time. But then, anytime after Willet's unseen departure and before Ruth's discovery was wrong. Even though Frank had legitimate reason for going out back during that period, it cast a guilty cloud over him.

After we three staunchly denied that anyone else had the right to go through the kitchen to the patio in the course of the evening, I suddenly and carelessly mentioned a fourth person who had permission to wander the premises at will. Not that others didn't wander too, but our previous silence about Frank now seemed suspicious. The minute he walked into the gallery, expecting to face nothing more alarming than dirty floors, he was under immediate interrogation. Chavez wanted a time schedule of his movements last night and a list of witnesses who could verify that he had simply stepped out the kitchen door, then come right back inside. Frank's work gloves also became a source of interest. They were found on his sawhorse, a sensible place for them to be, except that the sawhorse wasn't ten feet from the spot where Willet was murdered.

"They're not taking him away in handcuffs," I consoled a tearful Vanessa. "He and Detective Chavez just went into the gallery so they could talk privately. Besides, nothing's going to happen until the lab results are in, and even if they discover traces of gunpowder on Frank's gloves, that still doesn't prove anything. They were sitting out there in the open. Anyone could have used them. Are you listening?"

"Barely," she said, sniffing.

"Then listen harder. If Frank were the killer, do you think he'd leave evidence lying around? For that matter, why leave the body lying around? Instead of waiting until this morning, he could have hauled the garbage bags to the city dump last night, and dropped Willet off there, too."

"That's true." She wiped her nose before Ruth set her into high gear again.

"If you'd like to go look," Ruth said dryly, "almost every wall in this house is dusted for fingerprints, so don't panic about Frank yet. If anyone put their grubby hands where they had no business being, the police will investigate."

"Oh my God," Nessa wailed. "That means everybody who came here last night has to be fingerprinted. The mayor. The DePaulings."

"Not the DePaulings," I soothed.

"We'll be ruined. They'll never forgive us. No one will ever set foot in the gallery again." She flung herself on the couch.

Ruth, who had bowed to the inevitable with pragmatic resignation, handed me the guest book. "Here, Ellie. Give this to Detective Chavez. He left it on the table, and I'm sure he'll be needing it."

I took the "guilt-trimmed" catalogue of murder suspects while Vanessa buried her head in the same pillow she had tossed playfully in my face the night before. Silently, Ruth indicated that she would take care of her, though three more aspirin tablets weren't going to change the grim possibility that the Discriminating Palette's grand opening might just be a less-than-grand closing. Usually, it's only the murderer who has a penchant for returning to the scene of the crime.

Shutting the door of the sitting room behind me, I took a brief detour into the kitchen, where I could see what Ruth meant. The police had done quite a job in here. They had even sprayed their iodine-based solution on things people wouldn't touch, unless someone slipped away from the party to make eggs Benedict. When I glanced out the grimy window, my eye was caught by a policewoman standing near the chalk outline that had been drawn around Willet's body. She bent over and reached into the battered bed of petunias. When she stood up, there was the stub of a cigar in her hand. I turned away and continued toward the gallery, but when I was halfway down the hall, the sound of raised voices brought me to a halt.

"You're not gonna pin anything on me, Chavez, so quit trying."

"I might not have to try, Ott. You got a record that talks for you. Armed robbery, burglary, assault."

"So what?" Frank's fists were jammed in the pockets of his jeans. "I never killed nobody. And I never killed Willet neither."

"Okay. Then you won't mind if we check out your truck, your apartment. Nothing to hide, nothing to find."

The detective had his back to me, but a streak of sunlight

glared on Frank's stone-hard face. "I been clean for two years and you know it."

"Yeah? Or maybe you just haven't been caught for two years."

"Fuck you," Frank spat out.

"Cool it, Ott. I don't want to charge you with assaulting a police officer, so watch that temper." There was an ugly edge in Chavez's tone that he hadn't used on us. "When you come down to sign a statement later, keep an extra-tight lid on it. Your old pal Billy Wayne's going to be there, and he won't be too happy to see you again anyway."

Frank spun around and charged down the hall, heading for where I was trying to hide in the woodwork. Hoping he'd think I had just come along, I pasted a smile on my face and waved cheerily as he thundered by me. Then, still keeping up the pretense that I'd heard nothing, I sailed into the gallery and gave Detective Chavez the benefit of my inane grin.

"Yoo-hoo, don't run off without this." I handed him his forgotten package. "Might be evidence in these autographed pages."

"But you hope there isn't." He tucked the leather-bound volume under his arm.

"Well, I'd rather you prove the murderer lowered himself into the courtyard by helicopter."

"Yes, that would be nice," he agreed. "Art collectors are too valuable a commodity to put behind bars, where their checkbooks can't do any good. But what do you really believe? That is, if you've been able to maintain a professional distance."

"A professional distance?" I said blankly.

"I realize you're not on duty, but as a detective, surely you must know we're not going to find landing tracks on the patio."

So he didn't suspect me of being a hit woman from California. Wonderful. Thanks to Vanessa, he thought I was a bona fide cop, with a bona fide badge. I could have let him continue under that delusion, but even in Santa Fe, where dressing up and pretending to be something you're not is local custom, there must be a law against impersonating a police officer. Rather than find out firsthand how stiff a penalty it carried, I confessed the awful truth.

"Yes . . . well I . . . I'm not exactly a detective. At least not a police detective."

"Oh. When Mrs. Harper said that, I figured you worked for the LAPD. So you're a private eye, huh?"

"No, not that either." I flashed him my most engaging smile, hoping he'd stop now and just assume I was a secret agent for the FBI who couldn't talk about her work.

But, like a good sleuth, and a licensed one at that, Ramon Chavez was persistent. "So what are you?" he teased. "A house dick at Bloomingdale's?"

That was a big slide down the totem pole, I thought perversely. He could have guessed insurance investigator before reducing me to skulking through ladies' lingerie in pursuit of girdle snatchers. But after futilely searching my mind for a more auspicious nonjob-description than amateur snoop, I gave a hollow little laugh.

"Actually . . . I'm nothing."

"What do you mean, nothing. You're not a detective?" He frowned as if I'd just admitted to a fourth-degree felony.

"No, but some of my best friends are policemen," I joked feebly. "And I really have assisted in a couple of cases."

"In what capacity?"

Deciding not to tell him that Casa Grande's police chief described me as a home-grown Nancy Drew, since being equated with a fictional teenager wasn't exactly a status symbol, I claimed that my services fell into the volunteer category. Unlike Vanessa, Ramon Chavez did not think that made me a cornerstone of the criminal justice system.

"Sorry, I misunderstood," he said politely, beginning a backward shuffle to the door.

"Does that mean you don't want my opinion now?" I couldn't resist asking.

A gentleman to the core, he tried to spare my feelings, but when he glanced at his wrist, hoping to use the pressure of time as an excuse to stave me off, there was no watch to consult. It must have gone the way of his other black sock. "Certainly I want your ideas," he said handsomely, retreating with every word. "Any impressions you have would be welcome; but why don't you save them for your police statement later. See you and the other ladies at three, Mrs. Gordon." The door closed firmly behind him.

I'd been the recipient of more believable brush-offs, but anyone who could suggest a fly-by-night helicopter theory didn't deserve an Oscar-winning performance. Of course, I'd said it facetiously, but once Chavez discovered I didn't have the credentials of a school crossing guard, he wasn't taking any chances. He probably thought my next idea would be UFOs and little green men with .22-caliber laser beams. Still, I couldn't let him go on thinking I was a legitimate member of the constabulary. He might have divulged something earth-shattering, like the revelation that he'd narrowed the suspects to two hundred and eighty-seven art lovers plus one carpenter cum bartender cum ex-con.

That bit of history certainly explained why Frank was getting special treatment. Not because I had spoken out of turn, but because he had "a record that talked for him." Typical police logic. They had a thing about repeater statistics. And how much safer could a gamble be than laying your money on a man who once had a number under his name?

Frank had a chance to volunteer the information himself. But then Chavez hadn't asked to see anybody else's gloves.

I looked around the gallery and wondered if Frank would have the heart to finish cleaning it today. The buffet table had been cleared and pushed against the wall, under a picture of two children on a horse with ribbons entwined in its mane. There was a "sold" tag on the painting. Directly beneath, the proud new owners had discarded their paper plates on the floor. I gathered them into a pile with a few other tidbits, then started a new collection near the portable bar. It was shoved on end, ready for return to the rental agency, and behind it was a half-empty glass of champagne someone had hidden in the corner for safekeeping. I had to get on my knees to reach it. Just then the front door opened.

"Can't stay off the sauce, huh?"

The bearded boor looked even worse than he had last night, when he'd at least remembered to tie his tennis shoes. He did remember to wear the same cut-off shorts, although now they were glamorized by a T-shirt that said SKI TAOS.

"We are not open for business," I informed him, jumping to my feet and wishing I'd locked the door after Chavez left. "You may come back tomorrow."

Totally ignoring me, he tucked his hands into his grubby pockets and sauntered farther into the room. "What are you doing? Drinking up the leftovers?"

"I'm warning you, there are police on the premises. If you don't leave immediately, I'll have them evict you forcibly."

At that moment a loud wail came from the back of the house. Forgetting my threat at the sound of Vanessa's cry, I rushed from the gallery, with the intruder racing down the hall behind me.

"Get out of the way," he said gruffly, fighting me for possession of the doorknob.

"Don't you dare step inside." I blocked the entry to the sitting room. "This is private property!"

"Dimwit! Move!" He thrust open the door, bumping my elbow and sending the contents of the champagne glass splashing all over my shirt.

What my retaliatory move would have been was lost in the scene that followed. Ruth looked up with a grateful, "Thank goodness you're here," while Nessa jumped off the couch and raced into his arms.

"Oh, Jake," she sobbed.

Chapter

4

By the time I had changed into a dry shirt, one mystery was solved anyway. The case of mistaken identity had been cleared up, though not to everyone's satisfaction. At least, not to mine. Jake Siegel was introduced to me as Vanessa's close friend and neighbor, which might have explained why he felt entitled to barge into the house without a by-your-leave. However, nothing explained why Vanessa had let the relationship progress so far.

Even after he learned I wasn't a dedicated wino with one hand perpetually wrapped around a bottle, his combative attitude didn't change. Following a rather terse "appearances can be deceiving," a remark I couldn't help echoing under the circumstances, he asked me to leave the room while he spoke to Vanessa privately. I did so, more out of respect for the fact that she didn't override his peremptory order than because he actually escorted me to the door. But when I joined Ruth in the kitchen, where she was milking the last of the coffee from the once-full urn, I told her exactly what I thought of Jake Siegel's good-neighbor policy.

"That is the rudest, most obnoxious man I've ever met."

"He can be a bit gruff at times." She tipped the pot forward. "But it was nice of him to drop everything and come over the minute I called."

Nice was not the word I would have chosen, but remembering her relief when he finally burst through my protective barrier, I couldn't very well suggest it was misplaced. "Oh, you're the one who invited him here. Sorry. I didn't realize."

"Sorry for not realizing?" she asked with a humorous glance at my clean blouse. "Or sorry for not liking him anyway?"

"Do I have to?" I replied bluntly, wondering if she too were also an unaccountable member of his fan club.

"Not for my sake." She sat down at the table and shoveled two heaping teaspoons of sugar into her coffee. "But Nessa thinks he's the best psychiatrist since Freud."

Startled into emptying an entire packet of Sweet 'n Low into my own cup, I could only stare at her. "You're joking. He's a shrink?"

"That's not quite how he's listed in the medical register, but the term applies. Didn't you know?" She looked at me quizzically.

"Hardly. Now that I do, I still don't believe it. Are you sure we're talking about the same person, or did someone else come over while I was changing?"

"Here." Ruth passed me a plate of toast. "Maybe this will make the news easier to swallow."

It didn't. Not even after she assured me that the man in the next room was in reality one Jacob R. Siegel, M.D., Ph.D., a prominent and highly respected therapist with a thriving practice. I would have disputed the "thriving" if only because of his obvious lack of a wardrobe. But even if a poverty-stricken doctor was a contradiction in terms, that didn't mean the other adjectives applied. Based on my two brief but stormy sessions with him, Jake Siegel was better at giving emotional disorders than curing them, unless social dipsomaniacs weren't worthy of his consideration. He'd certainly shown me none last night when he thought I was three sheets to the wind. He hadn't even had the therapeutic decency to help me off the floor this morning, when he found me there, glass in hand. However misleadingly, I'd certainly presented the picture of a person in need of professional help. Not that I expected a free consultation under the bar, but he could have scheduled me for an office visit.

"Far be it from me to question Vanessa's more unusual associations," I said with an unguarded touch of irony in my voice, "but where did she find this one? Not on the Chamber Music Festival executive board."

"No, not exactly."

"A mud-wrestling contest?"

Ruth took a long time to spread one little dab of apricot jam on her toast. She studied it a moment, compared it to how much less I had on mine, then stuck her knife into the jar and lifted out another scoop. "Didn't she tell you anything about Jake when you both gabbed into the wee small hours?"

I didn't need to be hit on the head with a Rorschach inkblot to understand what Ruth was trying not to say. Then I remembered that during her tirade against Malcolm, Nessa had said something about seeking a miracle cure and it not curing the problem. Seeing that Ruth felt uncomfortable about letting half the cat out of the bag, I decided not to make her go for a third helping of jam.

"Vanessa didn't tell me she was consulting with Jake specifically, but I wouldn't brag either if I went to that nut for marriage counseling."

"No, I suppose you wouldn't." Ruth sighed, clearly relieved that she hadn't given away her partner's awful secret, but dipping into the jelly jar again anyway. "However, in case it escaped your attention, she gave 'that nut' a rather warm greeting when he came in."

"Meaning I should watch my Ph.D.s and keep my unflattering opinion of the man to myself."

"You don't have to bite your tongue every time his medical degree crops up in conversation," she said with a wry smile. "Just bear in mind that Vanessa credits him with giving her life new direction."

"How? By pointing her toward the divorce courts?"

Despite my sarcasm, I really couldn't blame Dr. Siegel for the Harpers' split. A once-a-week talk session can't turn marital misery into bliss unless both partners practice what's preached them, and Nessa herself admitted that she suffered from terminal apathy when it came to Malcolm. Still, accepting the divorce as her choice didn't mean I was ready to kneel at Jake Siegel's couch in worship. Only my mother believed doctors were entitled to their God complexes. I'd dated too many pre-med students in my college days to cherish such blind faith.

"All right," I conceded grudgingly. "If Vanessa thinks a beard is a sign of wisdom, I'll keep my trap shut. I won't even mention the social liability of being seen in public with a man whose glad rags really are rags. You have to admit, it wouldn't hurt his appearance any if he spent some of the money from his tax shelters and splurged on a decent pair of pants."

"From what I hear," Ruth said, "three ex-wives took the tax shelters with them."

"Three?" Already my trap was back open. "And with that track record he's got the nerve to bill himself a marriage counselor? No wonder his patients are single. The guy's a charlatan."

"Not according to his diploma. In fact, he has a pair of those, too. One from Johns Hopkins and another from Bellevue."

"Where he should have been committed," I grumbled. "Okay," I waved my hand at her raised brow, "that is truly my final word on the subject. No more berating Jake Siegel. From this moment forth, I will only disparage him silently."

"Are you sure?" she asked in mild amusement. "Not one last criticism while no one else is listening?"

"Positively." I leaned my elbows on the table. "Besides, I was beginning to sound like another critic we all knew, and look what happened to him."

"I don't think you have to fear for life and limb. Believe me, I heard Willet in action, and you're not even in the same league. The man was deadly."

"No doubt why someone returned the favor, but whoever it was sure would do the rest of us a bigger one if he'd trot on down to the police station and confess."

Ruth reached for another slice of toast. "If he doesn't, you could live up to Nessa's fond hopes and do something about it. Seems she already assigned you to the case."

"Yes, I noticed. But Chavez unassigned me, and that is where I'm staying. On the sidelines. An observer." Which naturally prompted me to make an observation. "There isn't much to go on yet, but it is interesting that Willet died on the job, presuming he really did earn a living insulting people."

"I don't know how much of a living. All he did was write a weekly column for the local paper. Theater reviews, gallery notes, tidbits like that. According to gossip, his money was inherited, and I imagine it was quite a bit because he published his magazine at a loss. Very few advertisements and no cover pr... *Insight* was a giveaway."

"At least he appreciated what it was worth. But didn't he have a family to support? A wife? Children? Even an extravagant lover?"

Ruth wiped her mouth with a napkin. "He was unmarried, had no kiddies that I heard of, and just a series of live-in girl friends who evidently had their own incomes. The latest left him several months ago, and if he had replaced her with a new flame, she didn't come with him last night."

Nor had anyone called here wondering where her sweetie

pie was at four A.M. when he should have been snuggled next to her. Skipping the personal angle for now, I went back to the natural assumption that his death was work-related. "Did Willet have a lot of enemies?"

"Every artist he ever panned in print," Ruth said dryly.

"How many of those legions were here last night?"

"Several. And I'm sure most of them exchanged a few harsh words with him. Willet enjoyed seeking out the least favored and reminding them of their status."

"Yes. I was there when he did that to Conchita."

Ruth snorted. "You should have heard what he said to Leon Yepa. I came close to belting him myself when he told one of the best Indian potters around that he did better work when he was a drunk."

"That's atrocious. And this Leon is on the wagon now, I take it?"

"For almost a year. He's doing beautifully too, or was." Ruth frowned. "I don't think he'll backslide over what happened, although he might have released some of his frustration if I'd actually let him punch Willet in the nose."

"You mean he tried?"

Ruth looked at me and decided she'd said enough for one day. I recognized the eyes shuttering, the mouth turned down in regret that so much had spewed out. Apparently, she felt the unfortunate Leon Yepa had been sufficiently traduced, first by Willet and now by her. All he needed was for the inquisitive Ellie Gordon to launch a one-woman investigation into such irresistible fare. I put her mind at ease.

"Don't worry. I can't see why one unhappy potter should be singled out from all the unhappy potters. Surely there were others Willet impugned."

"Plenty," Ruth granted, relieved some by my analysis.

"Besides, we're only guessing that a disgruntled artist committed murder in revenge. Jerrold Willet might have been shot in a jealous rage," I said, although I couldn't imagine a straying wife wandering in his direction. "Or maybe the beneficiary of his will didn't want to wait until the family legacy was squandered to keep *Insight* rolling off the presses."

"You're right," she agreed briskly. "There's no reason for the police to suspect Leon because of one incident." Meaning, there was no reason for me to doubt the gentleman because of an undelivered punch. "It's just that I'm very fond of him." Ruth stood up. "But as you said, we don't even know the motive behind Jerrold Willet's murder. I can tell you this much." She began stacking empty paper coffee cups left by the police. "If simply not liking him had anything to do with it, half of Santa Fe could be guilty."

So I was beginning to realize. In fact, from all I had heard about Jerrold Willet, nothing in his life became him like the leaving of it. I had no personal ambition to find out who had sped him on his way, but I hoped the matter would get settled before my departure, just so Nessa would stop apologizing for presenting me with a dead body on my very first morning in town. I told her it was more original than a flower arrangement on the dresser, but her remorse was inconsolable. She invited me to visit Santa Fe and our tour of the city was starting at the police station.

Ruth and I were wondering if we'd make our three o'clock appointment when Officer Gail Martinez came inside and set her blue police-issue totebag on the counter. The clue hunt was over. If we'd be kind enough to let her wash her hands, she was dropping her finds at headquarters, then going home to spank her kids. They must have done something to deserve it while she was gone. They always did.

"Have any luck out there?" I watched as she checked the plastic zip-lock bags of evidence before zipping up her carrying case.

"Probably not." She shrugged and said hers was just a

secondary search to make sure the advance crew didn't miss anything important. All she had were some more dirt samples, a few crushed petunia petals, and a cigar butt.

I had a feeling the last item was one-of-a-kind, though it probably would just verify that Jerrold Willet had had a smoke before leaving his bloody imprint on the flower garden. With any luck, at least from a police standpoint, a soil analysis might show some foreign matter in that little bag of desert dirt. Nothing as foreign as UFO oil drippings or moon dust, which would be Nessa's first choice, and mine too if only to see the expression on Ramon Chavez's face. The reality might be a bit less ethereal, like an earthly piece of lint from a dyed-in-the-suede jacket, or an identifiable strand of L'Oreal #5 tinted human hair.

If there was anything that tangible to be found, it had better be inside the vinyl totebag Officer Martinez was slinging over her shoulder, because the on-the-site investigation had just come to a close. The brick courtyard was now declared ready for hosing down or covering up, whichever suited the owners. The bloodstains would wash off easily enough, the experienced policewoman told us, but we'd need a wire brush for the chalk marks that had been drawn around the body. Plain old soap and water would remove fingerprint powder from walls and doorjambs.

Thanking her for the helpful household hints, Ruth walked her to the front door while I assigned myself the less gruesome task of kitchen patrol. There was an honest day's work in this one room alone, and from the murmur of voices coming through the closed door across the hall, I could tell Nessa wasn't ready for KP duty just yet. Superpsych couldn't be doing such a super job of bringing a smile to her face, which was about the same effect he had on me. Anyway, removing even one layer of carbon powder would be a service to my hostesses, though only after I began rummaging under the sink did I think of looking for Frank first. It wasn't that I minded tackling some serious scrubbing on my own, but I totally forgot about him until the bottle of Mr. Clean was in my hands.

Murder certainly is dirty business, and not even "all the perfumes of Arabia" could sweeten a finger pointed in accusation. Of course, Frank Ott hadn't been charged with any crime other than having a record of them, though the last I saw of him, he'd taken that reminder with the grace of a wounded bull. He might have gone home to nurse his grievances in private, but if he was still here, I, unlike the callous Dr. Siegel, would not withhold a little applied psychology, provided I could think of a way to offer Frank solace without letting on that I knew why he needed it.

As it turned out, I didn't have to feign ignorance. After checking to see if he'd locked himself in the bathroom, which was more a ladies' retreat than a men's bolthole since they don't have mascara streaks to wipe off their cheeks, I saw his truck in the driveway. Taking the front route instead of the back, I went through the gallery, then around the corner of the house to the open side gate, and found him loading last night's garbage into the rear of his pickup.

He wiped his hands on his jeans and glared at me truculently. "You heard, didn't you?"

I might have denied it, but since my charade hadn't fooled him before, it seemed silly to continue making an ass of myself. "Afraid so."

"And you're not scared of talking to me?" he asked, the chip on his shoulder perfectly visible in the bright sunlight.

"Should I be?"

"Some people think I killed Willet, you know."

"Small world." I shrugged. "Some people think I did too."

The chip started to crumble. "Doesn't seem mighty likely to me, but I make a lot better suspect than you or any of them well-heeled dudes who was here last night."

"Fine. You want first prize, be my guest."

Finding my charm hard to resist, he leaned against the sun-baked side of the Chevy and eyed me warily. "Maybe you don't think it means a damn that I'm an ex-con, but the cops ain't so casual about it. Every time something so much as a loaf a' bread gets stolen, they come around hassling me. Lemme tell you, they're going to be sitting on my tail pretty close after this. Murder ain't no loaf a' bread."

"No, but in some respects, it could have been a piece of cake. The other way to look at things is that someone with your experience wouldn't have left the corpus delicti behind to point a dead finger at you."

Now I'd really won him over. He reached inside the open window of the pickup to take a battered pack of cigarettes from the dashboard and, as an afterthought, offered me one. I shook my head and, he lit an unfiltered Camel for himself. "That's a real twist." He exhaled a long stream of smoke. "You think with my record, I got the know-how to cover my tracks better. You're some detective, all right."

Hearing my analysis rephrased, I didn't find it quite as convincing as it had seemed originally. If a four-page rap sheet was an indication of a crook's experience, it was also a testament to his stupidity in getting caught so many times. Building up credit hours in prison doesn't exactly count toward a degree in criminology. But now that I was having second thoughts, so was Frank, except his brought a flicker of amusement to his lips.

"I kind of like your reasoning, ma'am. Truth is, I'm plumb sorry I never figured the same thing out for myself."

"Glad to be of service. But, not having a motive to kill Jerrold Willet would help too," I suggested belatedly, the unasked question hanging off the end of my sentence like a dangling participle.

Twin streams of smoke issued from his nostrils. "No motive at all to harm the man. Fact is, he owed me money.

Now it don't seem likely I'll ever collect." He rubbed out the cigarette on the heel of his boot. "Well, I'd best be finishing up here. There's a few more bits a' trash I gotta load up before doing something about the patio. The police left a real mess behind."

Pensively, I walked to the front of the house and gazed down Canyon Road. Nothing stirred. The soft shapes of salmon-pink adobe walls looked half-melted in the dry heat, while cicadas whirred undisturbed in the cottonwood trees. No throngs of tourists were banging on shop doors, but maybe the stores didn't open here on Sunday.

Come on, Ellie, I chided myself. *Stop speculating. You've already asked too many nosy questions, and you're not even going to be here long enough to hear the answers. This is your vacation. Get inside and clean the kitchen.*

I started to, but the second I stepped over the threshold, who should come colliding into me but Jake Siegel. "How's Vanessa?" I asked before he could make a snide comment on how we always seemed to be bumping into each other.

"She's feeling better," he started off politely enough before reverting to type. "Just don't make too many demands on her, like going out for a big fancy dinner. Let her take it easy."

There's nothing more irritating than being ordered to do what you already intended, unless it's having someone assume that you lack any sensitivity whatsoever. Not wanting to engage in another round of "Mom, he touched me first," I held myself to an inoffensive, "Thank you for the prescription on human kindness, Doctor."

He cocked an eyebrow at me. "I could say that enlightening you is the least I can do. But you'd probably beat me over the head with your purse."

"What a wonderful idea. If you'll wait here, I'll go get it."

For a moment we just looked at each other, regrouping.

Then an opening appeared between moustache and beard, and, to my amazement, he smiled. "You realize, this could go on forever."

"Not that long. I'm leaving in two weeks. But we could always start a poison pen correspondence."

"I'm a lousy writer."

"An occasional postcard would suffice."

"Never." He grinned, taking my elbow and steering me over to the wooden bench in the far corner of the porch. "I might be forfeiting the greatest hate-mail opportunity of a lifetime, but for the sake of preventing World War Three, don't you think it's time we declared a truce?"

I sat down next to him. "Do you have a white flag in your pocket?"

"Not even a sword to beat into a plowshare. You'll just have to settle for my Hippocratic oath. Pax?" He extended his hand.

I hesitated a moment, then accepted his olive branch. *"Shalom."*

"So?" He flashed me a look of surprise. "You're a landsman? Funny, you don't look Jewish."

"Otherwise you would have labeled me a JAP instead of a lush."

"My apologies. I misjudged you, jumped to erroneous and unfounded conclusions, and cast aspersions on your obviously sterling character."

"Why stop there?"

"Because you took my cigar."

"A grievous crime."

"Damn right it is." He bent forward to swat a fly off his bare leg. "One of my ex-wives used to do the same thing. That's why she's an ex."

"A fitting punishment."

"I think so. But if it'll make you happy to hear, I went outside last night to smoke my other one."

"Outside?" I glanced at him sharply. "Where outside? On the patio?"

"No. Right here in front. Where everyone else went to light up. Don't you see all the butts lying around?"

"Disgusting habit." I frowned at the remains on the porch and across the gravel path. "And you, a medical man, yet."

"Don't worry. When I get to be surgeon general, I'll tell everybody else to quit."

"Yes. I can just picture you standing on the podium in black tie, tails, and that SKI TAOS T-shirt, lighting up a three-dollar stogie while you order people to put theirs out. In their drinks, no less."

"Never tried that approach, but you may have something there. One of my specialties is treating alcohol and drug abusers."

Since marriage counseling didn't work out, I thought to myself. But while I had no intention of voicing my skepticism aloud, I couldn't resist one little dig.

"I hope you treat them better than you treated me," I said, only then wondering if I'd put too much of a strain on our tenuous truce. But just when I had him pegged as irrepressibly brash and ready with a flip answer at all times, he turned humble on me.

"About our run-in," he rubbed his fuzzy jaw, "what you got was the brunt of a bad mood. I'd just been having a conversation with a former patient. Somebody who dropped out of therapy too soon. It wasn't a very fruitful conversation, and when you came barreling into me, I was feeling pretty frustrated."

"While I showed all the symptoms of being on an alcoholiday."

"That's very Freudian," he complimented, acknowledging both the source of the pun and its application.

I nodded wisely. "We all let emotions get the best of us at times."

"Thank you for the lesson on transferred aggressions, Doctor." His eyes twinkled mischievously as he returned my original serve, but with a little extra English on it. Oh, well. At least he was back to normal again. Very normal for him. Reaching into the side pocket of his shorts, he took out a fob watch, minus the chain, naturally. "I've got to get going."

"Another house call? Excuse me, crisis intervention?"

"Nope. I may be the friendly neighborhood shrink, but not during the Yankee–Red Sox game. Although," he stood up and bowed ridiculously, "it was worth missing the first inning for the pleasure of finally making your acquaintance. From the moment we met I thought you were a good-looking woman, even if you were a drunk."

"How sweet. And from the moment we met, I've almost been driven to drink."

He grinned and pulled me to my feet. "Do you mind if we continue this battle another time?"

"Why? Because I'm getting the best of you now?"

"No, I'd stay and fight, but I don't want to miss the second inning." He waved and jogged off, the laces of his untied shoes flapping in the breeze.

Chapter 5

By Monday morning, the shock of Willet's death had worn off, and reaction set in. Yesterday's ritual at the police station had been more a formality of repeating what we'd told Detective Chavez already than a probe for new information. But if our sketchy statements solved nothing, putting our signatures to the fact did make two things abundantly clear to Vanessa: my vacation had been ruined, and the Discriminating Palette might as well declare bankruptcy.

Tackling first before foremost, I assured her that police headquarters was always my first sightseeing stop wherever I traveled. Since I had forgotten to bring my camera along yesterday, I'd definitely be going back for snapshots. After all, what was a holiday without pictures of my favorite haunt? And where else but in Santa Fe would I find a pink stucco jail? It was so quaint.

"As quaint as having a going-out-of-business sale before going into business?" she moaned.

Understandably, breakfast was not a festive meal. The lox and bagels bought in my honor for the Sunday brunch we never had were presented as day-old atonement for involving me in a murder investigation. Feeling that this wasn't the moment to remind Nessa of my diet, I ate the stale offerings while she alternately shredded a napkin to bits and picked the polish off her fingernails. I did try to minimize her fears of imminent catastrophe, but one glance at the newspaper had convinced her that receivership loomed on the horizon. Featured directly under the banner story on creative and innovative Fourth of July displays was a boldface announcement of Jerrold Willet's murder and a photograph of the gallery where the art critic had met his muse.

"Don't tell me that after reading the front page, anyone will be tempted by our ad on page sixteen. So what if we're finally open to the public? Any tourists who happen to amble down Canyon Road will make sure to do their browsing from the other side of the street."

"Murder isn't exactly a contagious disease," I soothed, smearing one more dab of cream cheese on one more dab of bagel. "In fact, human nature being what it is, all the notoriety is liable to make this place ye olde curiosity shoppe."

"Ellie's right." Ruth tapped the headline that proclaimed PORTRAIT OF MURDER IN SANTA FE'S ARTIST COLONY. "This publicity is more likely to do us good than harm. If we don't have a houseful of gawkers every day this week, I'll eat my hat. So stop putting ridges in your fingernails and get busy. Ellie will excuse us, I'm sure."

I not only excused them, I decided to take myself off their hands for a while and go snap a few pictures of the local hoosegow, as promised. By the time I made my bed, took a shower, and selected what the practical camera-toting tourist should wear—a skirt with deep pockets for holding sunglasses, film, and money to buy more film—my perceptive analysis had been proved correct. There was a crowd of customers gathered around the card rack and several people flipping through the bin of unframed prints, no doubt in hopes of finding at least a copy of a corpse. But, whatever had lured them to the Discriminating Palette, Ruth wasn't complaining as she hovered hopefully over the cash box.

Neither was Vanessa, I presumed. She was off in a corner whispering to a young man.

"Oh, Ellie, there you are!" she interrupted herself and waved me over. "Did you meet Leon Yepa Saturday night? He's going to be showing his marvelous pots with us starting next month. Leon, Ellie was an absolute tower of strength yesterday morning. I would have collapsed without her, my genius friend. Would you believe, she solved a couple of murders in California that had the police utterly baffled. She'll probably solve this one too."

Out of concern for her nerves, though not a tremor showed at the moment, I restrained an urge to stuff a gag in Vanessa's mouth. Her insistence on giving a biographical sketch of me with every introduction was getting out of hand. Not that I objected to being labeled clever, brilliant, or any other overstated term of flattery, but her catalog of my abilities was growing faster than Pinocchio's nose. As God's gift to California's unenlightened law enforcement agencies, I was now going to use my cunning expertise on Santa Fe's latest crime wave and make the town safe for critics again.

Sublimely forgetting that only an hour ago she felt guilty about inviting me here for what seemed to be a busman's holiday, Nessa switched to wanting me in the driver's seat, but with her calling the signals.

"Leon has to go to the police station this morning and make a statement. Everyone will eventually." She sighed. "But apparently somebody who went earlier finked to Detective Chavez that Leon and Jerrold had a little argument at the party. It was nothing, and I'm sure there's no reason to worry, is there, Ellie?"

"Probably not," I agreed politely.

"Besides, Leon wasn't the only person who clashed with Jerrold. You had words with him too."

"Several of them."

"But Chavez doesn't consider you a prime suspect."

"Not that I'm aware of."

"See?" She beamed at Leon. "I told you she's a pro."

Leon had listened to this exchange without the proverbial bat of an eyelash. Whether that meant he found my illustrious reputation richly undeserved or was simply in awe of how I conducted a third-party third-degree, I couldn't tell. His large, dark eyes were expressionless, though the rest of him made a declaration of sorts. He had long black hair, tied back with a red bandanna, and was wearing faded jeans that didn't quite cover the heels of his scuffed cowboy boots. Judging by appearances, I could only assume that he wasn't a very successful potter, which might or might not have any bearing on the case. Since my interest was purely academic, I just wished him luck in his upcoming interview.

Leon thanked me gravely and said he really wasn't worried. "Willet made a crack and I answered. No big deal. I didn't deck him or anything like that."

I'd already recognized Leon, by name and association, as the hapless victim of Jerrold Willet's almost-final insult. This was the Indian craftsman who'd been told he produced better work when he was in an alcoholic stupor. That was an appalling remark, true or false, and it rated at least a punch in the mouth. But just because Leon didn't follow through with one at the time wasn't proof he had exercised self-control for the rest of the evening. As Ruth had said, it might have relieved his frustration if she'd let him cream the critic, although if she'd given everyone the same privilege, Leon would have had to wait his turn in line. I pretty much told him that, but Vanessa wasn't satisfied with his being just another indignant face in the crowd.

"I know Willet was obnoxious the other night," she allowed, "but Leon wouldn't have lifted a finger against him."

"Certainly not," I murmured. "A potter needs all his fingers intact."

"Besides, Leon isn't the violent type," she persisted, still pushing for my unauthoritative all-clear. "He certainly wouldn't kill anyone, no matter how much he was provoked."

Whereas I, by contrast, had been prodded into doing what I should have done in the first place. My friend didn't expect me to open a private inquiry into the case. She just wanted me to use the credentials she kindly gave me so that I could dispense instant exoneration on her say-so. Fine. I'd say so.

"Take it from the resident expert, folks. The police won't consider such a picayune spat a worthy murder motive. They'll be looking for a suspect with a more substantial grievance, and one established before Saturday night. Remember, the person who fired four bullets into the dear departed had to plan the crime in advance. He not only brought a gun with him to the party, but had to make sure he got his victim alone and away from any possible witnesses. He probably chose the Fourth of July weekend because the sound of gunshots would be camouflaged by fireworks."

"You think that's what happened?" Despite his calm demeanor, Leon was clearly relieved by that analysis.

"Seems logical to me." Determined to change the subject, since any minute Nessa might realize that getting Leon off the hook, however unofficially, put everyone else back on it, I asked the potter about his wares.

Leon smiled for the first time. "My techniques are traditional, I don't use a potter's wheel or a kiln, yet my work is modern too. In some ways, I feel I'm moving toward sculpture," he elaborated. "My newer pieces don't have a function as such. They just are."

"Are just beautiful," Nessa capped his explanation. "You'd appreciate them, Ellie. I'll take you over to a shop on the Plaza and show you some of Leon's earlier work so you can see where he's coming from."

"Sounds wonderful, but I don't know anything about Native American ceramics," I confessed, "so prepare to be my walking encyclopedia, Nessa."

"If Ellie's interested in learning some of the fundamentals of Indian crafts, how about showing her where I really come from?" Leon suggested. "The three of us could make a day of it, leave for Jemez in the morning and be back here for supper."

"Oh, Ellie, you'll love it," Nessa said, giving my hand a squeeze.

"I certainly will," I seconded. Though my knowledge of local Indian customs was limited, I appreciated that Leon was offering me a rare chance to go beyond the usual superficial tourist trip. "Could you start my crash culture course by explaining whether Jemez is a town or a tribe?"

"Both." His eyes lit up with warmth. "The name stands for a lot of things. A pueblo, a reservation, a place of red earth and mountains, a way of life."

"The pueblo itself is not only the village but the farm land around it," Nessa told me. "The term comes from Spanish for town."

We had just agreed that Thursday would be the best day to go when Ruth walked over and joined us. Temporarily out of customers, she could now spare a minute to announce that she had just sold two lithographs and six boxes of cards. "Not a bad half-hour's work," was her modest appraisal.

Vanessa gave her a hug while I beamed from ear to ear like any proud aunt at the birth of a bouncing baby gallery. Leon congratulated them, saying he considered himself lucky to be the next artist featured by the Discriminating Palette. I couldn't help wondering if he meant that as a compliment or he really needed a lucky break. That depended on how well his work was selling and if his coming exhibit was a new and sober foot back in the door. Still, Nessa wouldn't risk her fledgling gallery's reputation on a has-been. Leon might have changed his style, but from her enthusiasm I gathered it was an improvement. I even questioned what Jerrold Willet's impact might have been if he'd lived to say otherwise. True, he had given away his magazine to all and sundry, but if people had paid so much attention to his commentaries, how come there were so many artists still around whom he'd commented on?

After getting some final words of encouragement, including a few more from me, Leon left for his appointment with the minions of the law. Nessa felt relieved that I didn't consider him in danger of immediate arrest, but she crossed her fingers. "I hope they don't give him a hard time. Leon doesn't need any hassles in his life right now."

"Who does?" Ruth said with some asperity as she moved to greet a couple of potential art patrons coming in the door.

I put a hand on Vanessa's sleeve before she could follow. "By the way, just for the record, and I'm sure you won't mind, but I know what really happened between Leon and Jerrold Willet."

For a moment she did mind. "What do you mean 'really'? How could you . . . ?" Then she stopped and sighed. "What's the matter with me? It's no secret. Not from the police either, since someone reported all the details. But you did mean everything you said, Ellie? About Jerrold's murder being planned long in advance of Saturday night, and the person who killed him purposely bringing a gun to the party?"

"Unless he kept one stashed in his car. This is the Wild West. Don't people sometimes carry an equalizer in the glove compartment?"

Vanessa turned pale. "What are you saying? That Leon became so enraged he ran outside to get his trusty six-shooter? That's ridiculous. He came to the party sober and left sober. I know!"

"And if he dipped into the punch bowl you'd be suspecting him yourself?" Nessa looked so stricken, I immediately put my arm around her. "Listen to me. I am not, repeat, not casting Leon as the villain. I'm simply pointing out that it's much too soon for you to panic about whodunnit. If I thought Leon were a rash, impetuous killer who couldn't tell the difference between jest and just plain mean, I would not be taking off with him to his fabled pueblo, even with you there to protect me. You know how my sense of humor sounds to the uninitiated. I'm liable to transgress some tribal taboo by telling knock-knock jokes."

"You never tell knock-knock jokes," she smiled, "but if Leon doesn't laugh, it's only because he's heard them all. He likes to dress as if he hasn't stepped off the reservation since 1912, but he never stepped on it until after he graduated from U.C.L.A. His non-ancestral home is Los Angeles."

"Yes, I know that territory. But not this one. Want to point me in the right direction?"

Though the morning was half-gone, I still had plenty of time to shoot a roll of film at Santa Fe's police station. Vanessa's directions on how to get there were clear and concise. Three blocks to the left and five galleries over, but I had hardly reached the door of this one when Conchita came breezing through it.

"Ellie, you're just the person I want to see." She turned me right around. "Ruth, Vanessa, you too. Wait until you hear what I've endured this morning. You won't believe it. But first, how's business? Landslide, I hope."

Ruth poured her a cup of coffee from the pot they kept in the Queen Anne armoire. "We're doing great," she proclaimed with some truth, though the gallery was empty of customers at the moment. A good thing, too.

Conchita polished off the coffee as if it were eighty proof, then threw back her head dramatically. "That's some compensation. At least I'll be rich even if I am in prison." Having grabbed our undivided attention, she flung herself on the couch by the potted cactus. "I have just spent the most harrowing hour and a half of my life in the ugliest police station in the world," she announced in sweeping superlatives. "Ramon Chavez wanted to know if I used the bathroom here Saturday night, when I used it, for how long, and who could verify that I spent ten minutes powdering my nose. Since I didn't invite anybody in to watch me take a pee, I told him, he was going to have to figure out for himself if I went number one or number two or just sat there for the fun of it. Finally, I asked him why he was so interested in my movements, and he said the only kind he cared about was one that might have gotten me out to the patio. Is that unreal? The man really thinks I could be a murderer." Dressed in a painter's smock, cropped pants, and sandals, Conchita managed to look both indignant and self-satisfied, as if being the center of controversy suited her very well.

Apparently Ruth thought so too. "I can't imagine why you're surprised." She leaned on the edge of the desk. "Skeletons in the closet do have a way of rattling."

Conchita reared up. "You mean, nobody else had a better reason to pump Jerrold's stinking guts full of lead?"

"I didn't mean that at all. But Detective Chavez may have found out about the time neighbors called the police to break up one of your fights," Ruth reminded her.

"That was ages ago! If I didn't kill Jerrold in those days, why would I bother now?" Seeing the look on my face at that intriguing revelation, she pointed at me. "Don't tell me you haven't filled Ellie in on Santa Fe's juiciest gossip?"

Just then, a his and hers couple wearing matching khaki slacks and red polo shirts came in. The Ken version caroled a friendly howdy in a thick west Texas accent, while his female counterpart raised a bejeweled hand in greeting.

"You fill Ellie in," Nessa said under her breath. "Ruth and I will see what we can do about making you rich."

Conchita stood up and took my arm. "Come on, let's go

to the kitchen and talk. I can't whisper this story. Besides, I'm starved. Maybe we'll find something worth raiding in the refrigerator."

It didn't take much to satisfy Conchita. Some homespun cookies and milk, a sweet guileless ear, and out poured the past, passionate, and stormy affair between Melinda Morrison and Jerrold P. Willet.

Toying with one of the neon green hoops dangling from her ears, Conchita—or should I think of her as Melinda?—confided that theirs had been a love/hate affair right from the beginning. "We had fights that were absolute classics. Once he had to have eight stitches in his scalp because I threw a plate at him."

"Is that when the neighbors called the police?"

"Uh-uh. The night the police came is an even better story. It was over two years ago, just before we split up for the first time, when our relationship was in the pits. We went to a party, a wild bash. I got a little drunk and disappeared with a guy for a few minutes. Jerrold blew his stack and went home without me. No big deal, right? But when I got to the house and realized I didn't have my key, he wouldn't open the door, the bastard. A cold, snowy January night and he was leaving me outside to freeze to death. I screamed at him to let me in, but he told me to fuck off. So I got an ax from the garage and started chopping the door down, yelling at him pretty loud, I guess. It was three A.M. so I really can't blame the Ortegas for being upset, though Jerrold may have been the one who called the cops. I think he was worried I might take that ax to him."

"Forbearing of you not to," I murmured.

"Damn right. But I was committed to the Hari Krishna principles of nonviolence at the time."

I tried to keep a straight face, while visualizing Conchita with a shaved head and saffron robe. "Did you formally convert?"

"No, I just went to a few meetings, experimented with vegetarianism, sold flowers in the airport for a while. Actually I liked Zen better. You should have seen the art I produced at that stage of my growth—birds, trees, butterflies, Japanese watercolors. But they didn't sell either." She stuffed a cookie in her mouth. "You see, I was searching for the ultimate truth. All my paintings before then showed the dark side of life, portraits of twisted souls, scenes of orgies, cannibalism." She gave a bitter laugh. "Of course, in those days Jerrold considered my work pure genius, when no one appreciated it but him. But people don't want misery hanging on their living-room walls. They want light and happy, something that matches the couch."

"And doesn't scare the kids."

"Exactly." She tapped her Fig Newton on the table. "Optimism is the word, not that I got any from Jerrold." The Fig Newton split in half. "He didn't think the change in my outlook was uplifting or an improvement. He said I was sacrificing my talent at the altar of cartoon worship. Now tell me, does that say something about the guy or not?"

Only that he preferred Bosch to Disney, but this was not the moment to make theological comparisons. "I take it, then, the love affair ended when you adopted Eastern philosophies."

"Oh, I dropped them. Spiritually and artistically, they weren't doing me much good. There isn't a big market for Oriental pictures around here. Still, I consider the phase an important process in my development, even if Jerrold disagreed. But it was really Jesus who broke us up."

"Excuse me?"

"When I decided to try and find Jesus. You know, the Christian God," she explained, in case I was unfamiliar with the name. "That's when my work evolved into what it is now and Jerrold gave me his worst critique. 'Stinko,' he sneered. 'Seraphic claptrap.' " She jammed another cookie into her mouth as if it would sweeten the sour memory. "I might have believed him, too, except my work had really started to sell. That didn't mean I was ready to call it quits with him. I was still dumb enough to want his approval, and I kept hoping he'd change his mind. We'd argue, I'd walk out in a huff, stay gone a week, go back, fight with him again, then storm out a few days later swearing it was forever. Five times I did that. Can you believe anyone could be such a stupid shithead? But six months ago, when the card company offered me a contract and Jerrold insisted I turn it down, I finally got smart. It wasn't my art he despised so much, or the 'uncultivated masses' who encouraged my mistakes by buying them. He'd been the one encouraging my mistakes all along, and when I flouted his so-called expertise, became a success in spite of him, he resented it like hell. And for one reason only. It made him look stupid."

Yes, seeing his protégée rise above and beyond his "superior" wisdom would be a crushing blow to an intellectual snob like Jerrold Willet. But then, he could cover the egg on his face by calling it *Insight*, and hope no one would ever know he was taking a personal ego trip in cutting her down to size. The question was, had Conchita returned the slice, or just turned the other cheek?

"Finding the Lord certainly gave you inspiration," I said noncommittally.

"Oh, I haven't found Him yet," she answered, not too cast down by the delay. "I'm still trying, and it's been a lot easier since I left Jerrold for good. Lately, I've been making real headway. You know my painting 'Two Children on Horseback'? *Reader's Digest* bought the reprint rights for their back cover."

A true religious experience by Conchita's standards, I thought irreverently. Of course, she was still just trying. Who knew what heights she'd achieve in her quest for the "ultimate truth"? The front page of *Time* at least. Or would she consider that only halfway to heaven? Real Godliness probably hung in the Louvre, unless Conchita got a better offer in the meantime.

But if Conchita's search for a convenient deity, or one with the greatest profit margin, seemed more self-serving than pious, I kept that value judgment to myself. She didn't need an Ellie Gordon version of "Confucius says," though when she asked for my opinion, I nearly told her virtue was its own reward, until I realized she didn't want me to give her any wise words to paint by. She wanted secular guidance.

"What do you think? Will the police see all this as a motive for murder?"

Again I was being asked to second guess the local constabulary when they probably hadn't even made a first guess yet. If I had to choose my favorite suspect in the morning's lineup, I'd have to say it was a tie between Conchita and Leon Yepa. Willet's former lover took the lead when it came to length of grievance, but the potter had an edge in the impulse-killing department. Both had their strong points, and both reinforced the one aspect of this case that wasn't in doubt: Jerrold Willet's amazing luck in not being silenced before by the slings and arrows of those unfortunates he'd outraged for so long.

However, my sage counsel to Conchita was, "Well, they haven't arrested you yet."

"You're right." She nodded emphatically, as though I'd just quoted Scripture rather than made a personal observation. "If they question my integrity again, I'll show them 'Down the Straight and Narrow Donkey Path.' That painting will vouch for me. Unless Chavez wants more bathroom details," she said flippantly.

Before I could suggest she try a self-portrait of "Lady Powdering Her Nose for Ten Minutes," Vanessa popped her head in the doorway. "Sorry to interrupt, Ellie, but would you please come out to the gallery?"

"What is it?" I turned around. "Someone else want to make my acquaintance?"

"In a manner of speaking." She grinned. "Adam's here to see you."

Chapter

6

I held up a pair of navy cotton slacks and the matching striped knit shirt. "Too blue or too boring?"

Vanessa gave my latest suggestion a cursory glance. "It's fine. So's everything you've shown me. Jeans and that shirt would be perfect."

"Who showed you jeans? I didn't even bring any."

"Sorry."

"Me too. Should I go out and buy a pair?"

"Probably, but it's ten o'clock and the stores are closed."

After inspecting the navy pants to see if they could pass for unlabeled Calvin Kleins, I added them to the pile of rejects and waved my hand at the clothes strewn around the room. "Come on, pick something for me. Mix and match. If you were going out with Adam Montgomery tomorrow, what would you wear?"

"Jeans," she answered. "No, I'm kidding. Here, wear this." She held up my shortest shorts and halter top.

"Have you lost your mind?" I grabbed them from her hand. "They're for sunbathing in a twelve-foot-high walled patio where nobody can see the dimples in my thighs."

"Dimples are cute."

"On Adam's cheeks, yes. Not on my fat legs."

"Will you stop that. Your legs aren't fat. Even Jake commented what a great bod you have."

"What do you mean, even Jake? He's your criterion of good taste? The man doesn't own a shirt that's not wrinkled."

"Which ought to make him an expert on legs that are."

Vanessa collapsed on the bed giggling at her own witticism, but I didn't think it was so funny that Jake Siegel had seen some of my most vulnerable spots undraped. The lecher must have been ogling me for a full five minutes this afternoon before I realized he was standing at the kitchen door. Peeping Tom. When I rolled over on the chaise-longue and finally noticed him, he had had the audacity to suggest I try for an all-over tan.

"Okay, let's drop the subject." I wadded my offending shorts in a ball. "I'll decide on an outfit tomorrow morning after I see what the weather's like."

"Clear skies, mid-eighties, with a chance of showers in the higher elevations," she recited glibly. "Did you pack a hat and sweater, or did you leave them home to keep the jeans company?"

"I came prepared for every contingency except mountain climbing and sky diving. No hobnail boots or parachute in my suitcase either."

"How about a peek-a-boo nightgown?" she teased. "For indoor sports."

"No problem there. I brought the perfect wardrobe for that kind of recreation. None."

While Nessa prophesied Adam's eventual bedazzlement when he found a voluptuous sex goddess under my analytical mind, I hung my scattered clothes back in the closet. Prosaic, but practical if I wanted to use the bed for sleeping. Even then, I didn't crawl into it until much later, but that was because I had to do some homework first. Before I went sightseeing with a celebrated author, I wanted to see why he was celebrated. In preparation, I sat up half the night and read all three hundred pages of *Desert Intrigue*.

Intriguing, I yawned, finally closing the book at two A.M. If Nessa hadn't been snoring as I crept quietly into the bedroom, I would have asked if she also had guessed the identity of the villain four chapters before he was unmasked by the intrepid Sean O'Donnell. Not that it was easy for me, or Sean, with all the chase scenes, shootings, bombings, airplane crashes, and twenty-seven characters dashing from behind the Iron Curtain to between the sheets. I concentrated on the facts rather than the figures, unlike most male readers, and realized "the wet-lipped feline on the tiger-skin rug" was too smart to be caught with her claws down. Her negligee, yes. But that was a necessary part of the genre. Hard bodies and hardware made for hard-sell espionage tales.

Too bad "The Case of the Curtailed Critic" didn't have such strict guidelines for the police to follow but there were more than twenty-seven characters to chase in and out of kitchen doors. I might get to interview all of them at the rate Vanessa was bringing me pseudo-suspects who wondered if a police statement was a confession of guilt. Even then, I doubted if the murderer would come to me for advice, not that I didn't have plenty to give him. Never shoot anyone at an open house; too many possible witnesses. Always take the murder weapon with you; leaving it as a party favor reflects poorly on the hostess. And last, since you're going to lie on your police statement anyway, don't check with the Great Oracle from California to be sure you told the best lies; she won't know, doesn't care, and wouldn't let on if she did.

When Adam picked me up the next morning, the first thing I noticed were his Levis and hiking boots. I, on the other hand, was dressed in an outfit suitable for looking out the window of a Maserati, not climbing through it.

My handsome escort whistled appreciatively when he saw me in my slenderizing, color-coordinated culotte ensemble. Then he pointed to my pink canvas sandals. "Hot stuff. But can you walk in those?"

From car to tearoom, yes. "Of course," I claimed, showing him the crepe soles.

"They look kind of flimsy. All those straps. Maybe you should change into some tennis shoes with socks. I don't want you to get blisters or slip on the ladders at Bandelier."

"Ladders?"

"To climb up the cliffs and down into the kivas."

Forget the blue jeans and boots I didn't bring. The parachute sounded more appropriate. Dashing back to the bedroom, I hurriedly threw my Adidas in a bag, along with the sweater and hat Vanessa recommended, then wondered if I should hope for the promised showers in the higher elevations. "Canceled because of rain" sounded awfully good at the moment.

But only for a moment. By the time I slid into the leather seat of Adam's red racing car, my heart was racing too. Some of it was due to Vanessa's fond farewell. She came outside to see us off and felt obliged to offer a few words of advice.

"Take good care of Ellie," she instructed my escort. "Remember, you're breaking in a tenderfoot. Don't make her walk too many miles. Oh, and Adam," she called, stepping back from the curb as he turned on the ignition, "did you pack the snake-bite kit?"

"Would I forget anything that important?" He threw her a wave good-bye, shifted the car into first gear, and sent it shooting forward in a splatter of gravel before I could ask if that exchange was for real.

"What's this about a snake-bite kit? Nessa's little joke?" I tried to sound casual, but I should have realized someone named Adam wouldn't be taking me to a Garden of Eden that was serpent-free. When we slowed at the corner, he reached into the glove compartment and handed me a green plastic tube.

"I always travel prepared."

Needless to say, I didn't. But I read the directions with feigned composure and nodded in approval as if this wonder product would now be a permanent item in my carry-on luggage. "You're very wise to take precautions," I said lightly. "Tramping through rattler-infested territory isn't exactly a tiptoe through the tulips."

"Don't worry, I'll protect you." Apparently I didn't seem overly reassured. Adam took one look at my face and put a comforting hand on my knee. "No, you really don't have to worry. In the three and a half years I've been trekking the wilds of New Mexico, nary a rattler has crossed my path."

"Why, because as soon as one did, you turned around and went in the other direction?"

"Now you're getting the hang of it," he said, grinning.

Not quite, but I was getting the hang of Adam Montgomery. He had a sense of humor, didn't mind that I was no frontierswoman, and, like the rip-roaring hero of his books, he couldn't abide driving in the slow lane. As we inched our way through Santa Fe's picturesque center, creeping past the cathedral and getting caught in a traffic jam at the plaza, he complained that it would take us all day to get to Bandelier at this rate.

"How far away are we going?"

"Well into the past," he answered poetically. "To a twelfth century cliff dwelling that's now a national monument. Below there's a trail that runs along the Rito de los Frijoles. Bean Creek," he translated freely. "Not nearly as charming in English, is it? But you'll like the view. I thought we'd picnic by the waterfall."

"On beans, naturally."

"On cheese, breadsticks, stuffed artichoke hearts, and

wine." He flashed me one of his breath-halting smiles. "There's a full hamper in the trunk."

Seems this was another day to forget my diet. "My, you do travel prepared."

"For everything except this traffic." He revved the motor to pass a lumbering station wagon. "Normally, the trip doesn't take more than forty minutes."

"Then we'll be there in plenty of time for lunch," I said, thinking about the full hamper.

"No question about that." Adam patted the dashboard. "Rosinante hates to go under seventy miles an hour."

It would have implied distrust to buckle up at that instant, though I recalled those same words in chapter ten of Adam's opus and the hair-raising ride that followed in Sean O'Donnell's identically and inappropriately named steed. Granted, he had been chasing international terrorists at the time, while his creator was merely out to beat the clock, and the competition. Adam released the reins, jumped a green light, and charged past the station wagon to take an easy lead onto the highway. Groping for the seat belt, all I could think was, if the rattlers didn't do me in, getting to them might.

As the real Rosinante ate up the miles, I relaxed. Adam was a marvelously competent driver, in fact as well as fiction, though the true-life version would probably earn a ticket from a state trooper sometime today. He only slowed the car when he turned off the interstate and onto a two-lane highway that was marked LOS ALAMOS, 45 MILES.

"Oh good. In all the years Nessa lived there, I never paid her one visit, and I always wanted to see where the atomic bomb was built."

"To be honest, I wasn't planning on driving into town. But if you're interested, we can stop at the museum on our way home and inspect Frankenstein's monster."

"You mean it's actually on display? I thought the whole Manhattan Project was top secret."

"Forty years ago it was. Along with the location of Los Alamos. No road sign then. But what used to be a totally secluded camp for scientists is now a regular small town, with McDonald's, Kentucky Fried Chicken, and Burger King."

"Sort of lost something in the transition, didn't it?"

"Something," he agreed. "That's why I changed the description in *Countdown to Terror*. I made the laboratory surrounded by crack rifle experts with instructions to shoot at will."

Not wanting to confess that I hadn't gotten that far in my reading, I complimented him on his vivid imagination. "It's amazing the way you can dream up so many extraordinary plots."

"The daily paper is full of extraordinary plots, only most of them are too strange to use in a book. My books, anyway. I have to give some illusion of credibility, or who'd buy Sean as a fiction?"

"That's an interesting interpretation." I paused. "How would you make Jerrold Willet's murder credible if you were writing it as a story? A man shot four times next to a houseful of people. That was quite a risk."

"Elementary, my dear Ms. Watson. It's obvious that Willet was a spy for the KGB and his death was ordered before he could pass a classified piece of microfilm to the enemy."

"Great story line," I nodded, "but no microfilm was found on his body."

"Of course not. Our side retrieved it from his coat pocket and sent the film to Washington for analysis."

"Somehow I can't imagine one of our brilliant agents leaving his Beretta behind."

Adam looked at me quizzically. "You want to switch to reality, I see. Sorry, I'm at a disadvantage there, since I never met the victim. I didn't even notice him at the party."

"Probably because there was nothing very noticeable

about him, unless you had an eye out for a man with a toupee on his head and a cigar in his mouth. He was medium height, middle-aged, with a few homegrown strands of brown hair fringing the fake."

"Yes, I saw the picture in the paper. But you're the detective. What do you think, or haven't you stolen a march on the police yet?"

"No, and I don't expect to, even if everyone who makes a statement beats a track to my door before the ink is dry on his signature."

After that leading remark, I naturally had to tell Adam about my unsought role as chief confidante and allayer of anxieties. I didn't mention names or repeat any titillating gossip. I just gave him a summary of the facts or lack of any, most of which I gleaned from Monday's impromptu picture-taking session at the police station. There were no signs that anyone had climbed over the wall, no hint of who might have followed Willet outside, and no indication that it would take anything less than questioning every single person at the party to locate even one useful witness. The problem was an overabundance of suspects, though Frank Ott still led the pack. That had more to do with the theory of criminal repeater statistics than any evidence found. His gloves hadn't revealed any traces of gunpowder and his fingerprints weren't on the murder weapon. Neither were anyone else's. The Beretta was an unregistered, anonymous piece of disposable hardware that implicated no one and everyone.

"There weren't even any readable prints in the kitchen," I told Adam. "Everything on the wall around the door, the knob, and the light switch was smudged."

"For someone who claims involuntary participation, you must have done a lot of voluntary digging to get all those details. Whenever I ask the police for specific information, they refer me to their public relations department."

"Then you've met Billy Wayne Fisk," I said in a dry voice.

"On several occasions. And I didn't alter one 'gotta go by procedure' when I used him for the crooked cop in *Daggers Drawn*."

Vowing to read that one next, I described a few highlights from my interview with the cowboy detective, omitting the part where he confiscated my camera because I hadn't gotten permission from the "old man" to photograph the interior of the building. Otherwise, the rest of my synopsis was fairly accurate.

As Adam well knew, Billy Wayne was not a PR spokesman, just a stickler for the rules. By the same token, I was not an inveterate shutterbug when it came to police stations; just unable to resist the lure of being near this one without satisfying my curiosity. I thought I'd simply snap my way in the front door and on down to Ramon Chavez's office, where he could give me an update on his investigation. Unfortunately, he wasn't around to do that, or to vouch for my 35-mm Yashica. That's when I discovered the "old man" was really an honorific title for the middle-aged police chief, an enthusiastic camera buff who offered to check my light meter for me. He also suggested I get a picture of the unused, antique courtroom down the hall. It was a perfect period piece, authentically 1922, though the WPA mural had been added later. I thanked him for the tip and went to retrieve the wherewithal, permission slip in hand. But when I got there, Billy Wayne was sitting at his desk with an open file in front of him.

"So you're mixed up in the Willet case," he informed me as I entered his office. "I sorta thought your name sounded familiar."

"Yes, well, I'm not really mixed up in it, and my name is rather ordinary."

"When this goes to trial," he pointed at the file on his desk, "you might have to come back and testify."

Wondering if he meant as a witness or as a defendant and if that determined my getting my camera back, I smiled prettily. "With pleasure. I never shirk my civic duty, no matter what the jurisdiction."

"Says here you're a detective." He tapped the sheet of paper on top of the stack.

"Oh no, that's a mistake. Or rather, a figurative expression. On Vanessa Harper's statement, right?"

"What's figurative?" He eyed me suspiciously. "She swore it's the truth."

"And by her lights, it is." I pretended amusement. "But by your standards, I'm just a dabbler."

"Yeah?" He shifted his burly form as the swivel chair squeaked in protest. "A dabbler? What kinda detective is that?"

I was tempted to ask what "kinda" detective dressed like a rodeo rider while he was on duty. Plainclothes cops usually wore plain clothes, not yellow-plaid pearl-buttoned shirts and turquoise-studded bolo ties. But not wishing to antagonize him into charging Vanessa with a "metaphorically speaking" on her police statement, I explained that I worked in a law office where sometimes my job consisted of typing out crime reports and checking to make sure the facts were correct. Being unfamiliar with California legal procedure, he accepted that lame excuse, then closed the file on his desk, and finally returned my commandeered property—but only after inspecting all 35-mm for hidden contraband. A routine security measure, he told me.

"Nice case," he nodded as he exchanged my strip-searched Yashica for the blue release form. "The old man has one just like it."

"So he said," I replied coolly.

"You take any pictures Saturday night?"

Assuming his friendly overture sprang from guilt at having misjudged a perfectly innocent piece of photographic equipment, I relented. "Actually, I meant to, but I was so busy refilling food trays that I never got around to filling the camera."

"Too bad."

"Oh." I gazed at him in dawning enlightenment. "You were wondering if I got anything worth developing, like a picture of somebody who came to the reception and didn't sign the guest book. Or a party crasher. I wish I had. I'm sorry."

"Nah, it was a long shot."

"I know. But I might have gotten a long shot of Jerrold Willet with a group of people, maybe talking to someone who doesn't want to admit it. You had a very clever idea," I complimented.

"Coulda been a clever idea." He shrugged his massive shoulders.

Mistakenly interpreting this as a burgeoning esprit de corps, and guessing what lay behind his disappointment that I didn't have any candid camera angles, I shrugged too. "So the crime lab couldn't trace the gun to anyone. Tough break," I commiserated. "Even the serial number was filed off, huh?"

"How do you know?" He glanced at me sharply.

"Well, I don't actually know." I lowered my head with appropriate modesty. "I just made a logical deduction based on . . ."

"It ain't your business to deduct nothing." He loomed over me. "That's confidential evidence, restricted to police personnel."

Realizing my error, I took a step back. "Then you shouldn't have given me food for thought," I accused fairly. "It seems pretty clear you can't tie the murder weapon to anyone or you wouldn't be looking for another lead."

His jowls quivered. "I got all the leads I need."

He didn't have even one-tenth of all the statements he needed, I scoffed to myself. The case was only twenty-four hours old. Billy Wayne was just annoyed because he'd accidentally said too much in front of a person who had the ability to "deduct" things. Nevertheless, I apologized for jumping to the right conclusions. Only somewhat appeased, he hoisted his pants over his turquoise-belted potbelly and said that since this was my first offense, he'd just issue a warning. Dabbling might be a sanctioned occupation where I came from, but now that I'd crossed state lines, it would be wise of me to follow New Mexico regulations.

Yep, that there was a cowboy cop who went by the book, I concluded to Adam. Two books, actually. The police manual and *Wyatt Earp Revisited*. All the modern-day version lacked were spurs on his boots as he kicked his way down the sagebrush trail. Side arms came with the job.

We had a good laugh at Billy Wayne's expense, but my analytic powers so impressed Adam that he suggested I keep using them. I reaffirmed my vow of nonintervention in the case, reminding him that I was going to be in Santa Fe only another twelve days. But Adam said that with my uncanny ability to worm information out of total strangers *and* my understanding of police strategy, it wouldn't take half that time for me to solve the murder.

"Are you pulling my leg?" I looked at him from over the top of my sunglasses.

"A little," he teased. "But I could use an unusual mystery for my next book. If you figure out this one, and the answer isn't too unreasonable for fiction, I'll list you as my reference source, fully accredited and acknowledged."

"On the dedication page, I hope."

"Certainly."

I pushed my sunglasses back in place and sighed. "What

a temptation. To be immortalized. My name recorded in the annals of history."

"No, just in the Library of Congress." He smiled.

Adam was joking, but I could see some very appealing possibilities in a merger of our minds. For one thing, it would necessitate frequent get-togethers, and getting together with men four years my junior and twice as pretty couldn't happen too frequently. But more, a professional association with Adam Montgomery would give me entree into the world of letters. I'd be a popular guest on talk shows, a leading speaker at writers' conferences, a dropper of big literary names. If Adam didn't drop me first. *Whoa, Ellie, I reined in my galloping imagination. It's okay to fantasize, but don't hallucinate. What do you think, that Adam's going to win the Pulitzer Prize for this make-believe novel and introduce you as his inspiration? You'll be lucky if he remembers you as a footnote.*

Bringing myself back to reality, but not cutting off all options, I promised to keep Adam informed of any interesting developments, although there was only a slight chance we'd be able to collaborate on a bestseller, a relationship that now entitled me to fifty percent of the royalties. The author didn't accuse me of elevating my status from fact finder to accompanying artist. He just said that all material would be gratefully accepted. I gratefully let the subject drop and turned my attention to the scenery.

It was worth looking at. We'd been steadily climbing in altitude, leaving behind the brown, bare mesa for the green sun-dappled shade of a ponderosa pine forest. Unlike the old song, however, the best things in life weren't free, not national monuments anyway. When we entered Bandelier, Adam had to pay the ranger a cover charge for the privilege of seeing America first, although the steep descent into Frijoles Canyon did come with a floor show. The five-minute drive to the bottom was a fascinating corkscrew of hairpin turns, made even more exciting by the suicidal deer that bounded in front of the car. With the reflexes of Sean O'Donnell, his inventor applied the brakes and brought the Maserati to a smooth but sudden stop. Bambi scampered away unharmed, while I checked my pulse to make sure it was still there.

By the time we pulled into a parking place by the small museum, both my pulse and my poise were back to normal. I changed into my sensible walking shoes, and we strolled the asphalted path below the cliff dwellings before climbing the ladders and inspecting the ruins. They were miniature penthouse apartments, part cave and part masonry. Then Adam gave me another mystery to solve. With water available, plenty of trees for fuel, deer to hunt, and fertile soil on top of the surrounding mesa, this location had everything but Bloomingdale's. So why had the Indians abandoned it hundreds of years before the Spanish conquistadores arrived?

"Because the doorways are so short," I said, ducking through one.

"Fits your size, anyway, but that's not the accepted theory."

"What is?"

"Drought, marauding tribes from the north. No efficient crop rotation."

"I'll buy every one, but it's sad." I climbed back down the ladder.

We were almost through with our tour. Last stop was the remains of a kiva, or ceremonial chamber. Several of these circular pits were scattered on the floor of the canyon below the cliff dwellings.

Adam read aloud from his guidebook. "'The kivas were the center of clan and religious life, just as they are today in all the pueblos of the Rio Grande Valley. Round and windowless, they were entered only by a ladder projecting from a hole in the roof.'"

From there we roamed to the outskirts of the ruins, past a stream, and to the waterfall where Adam said we'd dine alfresco. While he went back to the car to collect our lunch, I snapped a few pictures of the canyon and the narrow ribbon of water plunging off the cliff. Then I insisted on taking a couple of him under a sign that warned DANGER, FALLING ROCKS. This was to prove he had nerves of steel. For that matter, so did I. When Adam found a large rock we could use as a seat, I didn't even check for snakes before sitting down.

While making a considerable dent on the glorious contents of the picnic hamper, our conversation became more personal. I told him a little about my history as wife, mother, displaced homemaker, and recently emerged office manager. While I toyed with an artichoke heart, Adam gave me a brief autobiography.

"By the time I was your son's age, I'd traveled all over the world. Saudi Arabia, Germany, Hawaii, Japan. But being an army brat isn't the same as jet-setting, though it gave me a permanent taste for travel. As a kid, I was jealous of people who got to stay in one town forever. Each place we went was interesting, but we'd get transferred every two years, long enough to make friends—not long enough to enjoy having them. Finally, I stopped trying to put down roots, and stuck to the pals I could pack in a suitcase. Robin Hood, Frodo the Hobbit, Holden Caulfield."

"I was a book freak at an early age, too. Only my heroes were heroines."

Adam smiled. "Wait. Let me guess. Jo March, Jane Eyre, and . . . Nancy Drew."

"Very perceptive. And were you also an English major in college?"

Adam's laugh was short. "Chemistry. Dad was already

unhappy that I picked Yale over West Point, so I chose a science. To prove something to him, probably. To prove something to myself, I started writing. Short stories for the college literary quarterly first, then for money. I went to work at Dow Chemical, writing nights and weekends, and when I had my first bestseller I dumped the job."

"In exchange for fame and fortune. Not a bad trade. Your father should be happy now that you didn't go to West Point."

"The general isn't one to hand out compliments." Adam poured us each another glass of wine. "He's the strong, silent type, and to keep him that way, I just use my first and second names for writing. I dropped Baker."

"Alphabetically speaking, *M* gets better shelf space than *B* at the bookstores. People tend to start looking at eye level," I said.

Adam laughed and wondered if that accounted for his phenomenal sales.

"Extremely glamorous," I agreed.

For the rest of the day, we visited the atomic museum in Los Alamos and talked at length on a hundred different subjects. Vanessa was right, we were on the same intellectual plane—or at least Adam treated me as if we were. In fact, we became so *en rapport* that when he dropped me off at the gallery a little after five and asked if he could take me to dinner Saturday night, I wasn't really surprised. For that matter, I wasn't slow in accepting the invitation, either.

Chapter 7

"**R**uth, got a minute to help with this skylight? Long as this thing measures right, might as well... Oh, didn't realize it was you, Miss Ellie."

Frank Ott was standing on a ladder in the middle of the workroom. Above his head was a hole in the ceiling, and above that an oblong Plexiglas dome now replaced a section of roof. He was holding the inside liner.

"Can I substitute for Ruth? The last I saw her, she was running a credit check on a customer who doesn't have any, and he was insisting that she let him buy a painting on the pay-as-you-can plan. What do you need? I'd be glad to help."

"Thanks."

Balancing the thin sheet of plastic on his palms like a tray of hors d'oeuvres, Frank slid one end into a ceiling bracket, then held the other side flat while he fitted a metal brace over it.

"A hammer'll do me fine. In that corner." He pointed with his chin.

The room was filled with construction supplies, from lumber to lathes to sawdust. I picked my way across the floor to the corner, but I didn't see any hammer. "It's not here."

"Try the toolbox. Sittin' by that bag of plaster."

I found the plaster and the toolbox, but no tool. "Got any other suggestions?" I glanced around vaguely.

"Coulda slipped under the tarp."

I lifted all the edges and felt underneath, but it wasn't there either, or in the bin of nuts and bolts. "I have a good idea. Why don't we trade jobs. I'll hold the skylight, and you search."

" 'Fraid you wouldn't be able to reach this high, even on a ladder." He smiled at me.

"Okay, then you can keep that pose for another ten minutes while I go to the hardware store and buy a new hammer."

"Maybe I better unhook this and . . ."

"Never mind. I just struck gold. Right under your foot and my nose." I picked it up from the bottom rung of the ladder. "And you thought I wasn't mechanical."

The rest Frank did by himself. He'd mastered the time-saving technique of spitting nails, and no sooner was one pounded into the bracket than the next was waiting between his lips. Before I could ask him about the dangers of lead poisoning, he was done. All that remained was the finishing work, trimming the borders with a wood molding, he told me.

Frank's remodeling blueprint was complete down to the last detail. It had been his energy-efficient idea to bring the light of day into the windowless workroom, where pictures were wrapped, matted, framed, and sometimes englassed . . . depending on the medium. Oils were never covered, while charcoals never went without. He'd already built storage shelves along the walls, and vertical slide-out racks underneath. After he made the cabinets in Ruth's bathroom, he was going to put a sink in here too, and add some ceiling wire so he could hang another fluorescent light.

"You're a marvel," I complimented. "A one-man construction team: electrician, plumber, carpenter. How did you learn to do all that yourself?"

"Different places." He stooped beside a pile of wood fittings on the floor. "Got me my carpentry skills at Leavenworth. They teach a mighty fine course there."

"Oh." I gulped. "Well, you have to give credit where credit's due."

"No question 'bout it." He selected several pieces of future molding and carried them over to the long worktable that was pushed against the wall. "Did a stint at Joliet in the machine shop. Then spent a year at Folsom learning what to do with conduit. Rewired the loudspeaker system in the yard." He crossed the room, fished through a box of tools for a small vise, then knelt at the end of the table to attach it. "Last time was metals. Making license plates, you know. That was here, at the joint. Santa Fe pen." He bent his blond head down to check bolts. "Yep, a fella can get himself a real education behind bars if he's a mind to."

Frank was certainly a mind to, but now that he explained his curriculum and listed all the boarding schools he'd attended, what was I supposed to say? Jail sounds so terrific, it's no wonder you kept going back?

"Guess I shocked you a little, huh?" He stood up and brushed off his hands.

"A little," I admitted. "But if you don't mind my asking, what kept you from enrolling in more courses?"

"You mean, how come I turned straight?" He shrugged. "'Cause somebody finally had the good sense to put me in a drug program."

Realizing that a leading line was no way to end a conversation, especially since his listener was obviously agog to hear more, Frank turned over an empty crate for me to sit on. Then he hoisted himself onto the edge of the table and told me how his past had become so checkered.

Like a lot of young men, Frank got hooked on drugs in

Vietnam, then came home to a politically split country that gave him less than a hero's welcome and an overcrowded veterans' hospital that was unequipped to deal with his problem. So it never got solved. It also became an expensive habit, which led Frank to supplement his income as a garage mechanic by moonlighting as a commercial burglar and auto thief. He worked his way across the plains and hills of America in this fashion until he worked his way into the New Mexico state pen. That's where he got the anchor tatooed on his hand. Not in a Shanghai shanty, but a thousand miles inland and four cellblocks over. Of all prison industries, body-etching and drug-trafficking were the most popular, he said.

To me, it seemed impossible that anything could be smuggled past chainlink fences, sliding steel doors, and armed guards. But Frank's former bunkie got his weekly cache of crack on visiting day, via a kiss hello from his wife, a method that gave a new meaning to mouth-to-mouth contact. Hidden next to her back molar was a small non-air filled balloon which she subtly transferred during their romantic clinch. None of this hiding of files in homemade cakes anymore. Today's methods were more tongue-in-cheek.

"Seems our penal system offers all kinds of vocational training," I commented.

"Yep. I picked up a few other tricks along the way, but I never was much good as a con man."

"Con man? What did you do? Sell sand dunes to Easterners in lieu of retirement homes? Or peddle a surefire cure for baldness?"

He laughed and slid off the table, ready to go back to work. "Those are business enterprises. Shady maybe, but I was talking about flimflam tricks, like the pigeon-drop."

"That's an old one," I said with a nod. "You convince somebody to put up good-faith money to share in some found loot, then you take off with both. Of course, he never asks where you got the loot or suggests turning it in. That's why the trick works. No matter how many times you read about it in the paper, the idea of something for nothing still hooks people. Must be the basic larceny in men's souls."

"Honest men," Frank qualified as he mitered the edge of the wood strip to a perfectly angled corner. "The kind of people that go for hanky-panky only cheat a little on their taxes."

"And don't notice if a grocery store clerk gives them too much change."

"Them's the ones."

I leaned forward and rested my chin in my hands. "Obviously, crime does pay if you're selective. And don't get caught," I added. "But you said you didn't go in for con games much. How much?"

"Well, there was this scam I used to pull with a buddy," he said, sliding the handsaw back and forth as he talked. "Him being the finer-spoken and the only one of us who owned a suit, he'd go into a bar, sit at the counter, and flash this big diamond ring around. Zircon," Frank explained kindly, in case I couldn't figure that for myself.

"Anyways, after a while, he'd mosey into the men's room, come out and finish his drink, and suddenly notice the ring was missing. Musta left it on the sink when he was washing his hands, he says real loud. But a' course, when he goes back to get it, his 'diamond's' gone. Then he'd kick up a fuss about how valuable the thing is, been in his family for years. After telling the bartender he'll give a reward of five hundred bucks to whoever finds it, he comes outside, slips me the ring from his pocket, and I follow his footsteps. Naturally, I find the fancy-looking doo-dad in the john, having a better eye than those folks who rushed in there the minute my pal left."

"Naturally," I murmured. "But I'm confused. How does the reward turn into a trap?"

"It don't." Frank grinned. "Like you said, the larceny in men's souls is the trap. You see, I'd pretend to want to keep my find, only the bartender's got this rich dude's telephone number and a chance to collect half a grand. So he offers to split the reward with me, fifty-fifty . . . a whole three hundred dollars divided two ways."

"The lousy cheat. And I get it now too. The bartender can't let you hear him make the call or you'll know he's bilking you, and he can't let you leave with the prize. So he pays your share on the spot in exchange for the ring . . . thinking he's going to claim more than triple that amount for himself. *Gonif.*" I frowned, as if two disreputable swindlers were more honest than one avaricious altruist.

"You sure do have a knack for flimflam," my instructor said with a glint of amusement in his eyes. "But careful there, Miss Ellie. You don't want to be favoring the lawless."

"Sometimes it's hard to see any difference between the bad guys and the good guys."

"Yeah," Frank granted, "'cept intent to defraud ain't viewed the same as trying to pick up a few extra bucks on the side."

"Depends on which side you look at, and, as my patron saint Will Shakespeare put it, there are those who 'wouldst not play false, and yet wouldst wrongly win.'"

"Sounds like a mighty smart fellow." Frank seconded my feelings on the matter, then returned to the more pressing business of attaching another piece of wood to the vise.

"And you're a mighty busy one," I acknowledged, sliding my front-row seat back against the wall where he could use it as a crate again. "So if you can manage without my mechanical assistance now that I found your hammer, I'll leave the carpenter to ply his trade undisturbed. And, Frank," I paused at the door, "thanks for the education."

"My pleasure." He nodded, then teased, "Just be sure you don't go showing off what you learned."

"Are you kidding? I'd never try to install a skylight without you."

The sound of his laughter followed me down the hall. As if I'd get away with hustling an innkeeper out of his semi-ill-gotten gains. With my innate klutziness, I'd probably wear a real diamond, actually leave it in the bathroom, then have to pay the reward myself to get it back. No thank you. If there was a sucker born every minute, I was one of the biggest.

My next thought was, *Did I just prove it?*

No, I decided firmly, going into the bedroom to get my camera and purse. The reason Frank Ott had been so candid with me was because I'd already shown myself to be non-judgmental, liberal, open-minded. I was a nice person, that's all.

Then why was I wondering whether he was a reformed renegade or still a countrified con? Maybe because I had just heard how he plied his "mighty fine" brand of simplicity on pluckable pigeons. *Don't be silly,* I told myself. Frank wasn't conning me, except when he said I had a knack for bunco games, and only an idiot like me would have considered that a compliment. Anyway, his record was no secret. And so what if drugs had led to his downfall. Frank had been clean for two years, thanks to someone's wisdom in putting him into a rehab program. Besides, even if he was still hooked on his favorite high, robbing stores to buy what they don't sell isn't quite the same as killing a man because of what he wouldn't pay. That's a more likely motive for someone who needs a tax loss and wants to make sure he gets it. Working people have more impecunious reasons for murder.

Apparently the police agreed. They hadn't hassled Frank at all in the last couple of days. Maybe they'd found a better suspect, which was their job anyway. Mine was to take a walking tour of Santa Fe, the only way to savor the city's full charm, Vanessa insisted. She provided me with a hand-drawn map, a list of don't-miss stops, and a proviso that I should spend Wednesday enjoying my vacation.

Two hours later what I needed was a vacation from my vacation. After museum-hopping, touring the historical Palace of the Governors, and seeing the chapel with the miraculous staircase, among other landmark visitors' attractions, I hit the retail establishments. Most of them were boutique shops and jewelry stores, which meant a high mark-up and a low return rate. Tourists don't come back to their vacation sites just to make an even exchange. I bought a jar of cactus jelly anyway, figuring that if I didn't like it, I could always paste it in my scrapbook as a souvenir.

Finally, out of film and almost out of money, most spent on gifts for the office staff back home, plus a silver belt buckle for my son, I headed for the gallery. Or would have if I'd known which way to turn. Santa Fe is a rabbit warren of twisting lanes leading back on themselves. What's more, every building, ancient and modern, has the same façade. By city ordinance, the entire town is stuccoed some shade of beige. It's a manifestation of the local obsession with adobe. When a certain picturesque wrought iron gate loomed into view for the third time, I had to admit I was lost.

The map was no help at all. Nessa had meant well, but the squiggles she'd drawn didn't correspond to anything in sight. Depending, like Blanche Dubois, on the kindness of strangers, I stopped a passerby and facetiously inquired the way to New Mexico's capital. He told me the Roundhouse was six blocks due south.

"You'll find the building an interesting example of a modern adaptation of Territorial-style architecture," he boasted.

That would teach me to joke with a native. My gentleman friend strode purposefully on, and I was left stranded between a fake adobe bank and a fake adobe gas station. What I needed was a fake adobe restaurant where I could rest my authentically weary bones and get something to drink.

Footsore and thirsty, I rounded a corner and found myself standing under a sign that said THE GOOD SHOP LOLLIPOP. Normally, I avoided cafés with cutesy names, one of the few dietary rules I maintained. They invariably thought that plagiarizing the hackneyed entitled them to charge twice as much for the same thing you could get in a place called Eats. Still, all I wanted was a cup of coffee and a chair, but when I looked in the window, there, shimmering in the glory of its three Génoise layers, was the most luscious chocolate Lutetia torte I'd ever seen.

I hated myself. Where was the courage of my convictions? Where were my standards of creative terminology? Where was my diet? But, more important, what was I going to choose from this array of culinary delights?

Stepping over the threshold was the easy part, though forcing myself not to look around took some discipline. But people who give in to unbridled epicureanism have to endure chairs with candy cane legs, heart-shaped tables, and lollipops festooning the walls. However, for all its plastic banality, the decor of the unParisian pastry shop didn't deter me. My keen eye and unerring nose led me straight to the counter where I found everything I'd always wanted to eat at one sitting but was afraid to consume in public.

In the end I did exercise some self-control, but only because I was going to be in town another week and a half. That gave me plenty of chances to come back here three times a day, or until I died of a chocolate overdose, as I told the happy proprietor. Surprisingly, he really was a Frenchman, *mais oui*, Monsieur Jacques. But what's in a name? I thought by then. His cakes said it all.

Using the logic that there was no need to limit myself to *one* pièce de résistance, since I was counting this meal as brunch, lunch, and mid-afternoon snack, I finally settled on a first course, when a voice whispered in my ear.

"I love you."

"What?" I looked up.

"I adore women who can't resist chocolate mousse. Either marry me or let me have a taste."

"Oh, it's you. Stop breathing on my neck, Jake." Then I noticed his plate. "You picked the hazelnut torte."

"I know, but I'm greedy. Come on. If you sit with me, I'll pay. I'll even buy you another one."

"Well," I said demurely. "I'm not sure I could eat two, but your offer is tempting."

I followed him to a heart-shaped table crowded in by the window, and no sooner had I asked the waitress to bring our cappuccinos *tout de suite* than his spoon was poised over my meal. "Stop," I ordered. "You're slobbering all over the place mat. Ugh. Shirley Temple's face." I covered the offending picture with a napkin.

"One bite," he said, leering at my dish.

"Okay. But just one," I stipulated.

"Don't be so stingy. I'll give you some of my torte."

That silenced me, until I realized he had taken three spoonfuls of my entrée as opposed to my one bite of his dessert. "Hey! You're cheating. Enough, you pig. Jake!" I finally had to push his hand away.

He licked his lips. "That mousse is sensational."

"Glad you like it. Now get back to your side of the table and do not take my bowl with you. Very good." I almost laughed at the lugubrious expression on his face. "Oh, all right. Here, we'll switch."

"No, I'm just teasing." He smiled, moving his chair back to its proper position. "You have the generous heart of a true chocolate freak."

"Thank you. But what brings the busy doctor into this

Eden of earthly delights? Shouldn't you be curing someone instead of taking office hours to feed your own mania?"

"As it happens, I just came from a session." He dug into his torte appreciatively. "Mmmm. Taste this."

"I tasted it already." Which didn't stop me from accepting a second sampling. "Wonderful," I agreed. "So that's why you're dressed with such unusual elegance, for the paying patients. An ironed shirt, long pants, even socks. Impressive. I thought perhaps you were in disguise, or the AMA ran periodic checks."

"First of all, I belong to the American Psychiatric Association. Secondly, I'm always elegant. Didn't you notice that even in my weekend attire, I have a commanding dignity?"

"Sorry. It escaped me somehow."

"Blind child. And thirdly," he pushed his empty plate next to my empty bowl, "on Wednesday and Friday mornings I go to the state penitentiary."

"Oh? And what do you do there? Coach the pastry chef?" Then I remembered. "Wait. Didn't Ruth tell me you're involved in some kind of prison reform?"

"I don't know if she told you, but I am in a way."

"What way? Do you put inmates in drug programs?" I asked, wondering if he was the one who had saved Frank Ott from himself.

Jake shook his head. "Not directly. Narcotics Anonymous and AA have volunteer programs in prisons already. I encourage substance abusers to join one of their groups, but that's not the thrust of my work." He scratched his beard. "Are you sure you want to hear? I warn you, once I get started, I'm hard to turn off."

"Do you have a patient waiting?"

"Nobody until two-thirty."

"Okay, Doctor. Since you insist, flag down the waitress and order another round of anything chocolate, then start talking."

He did, at length, just as he promised. But the target of his reformation wasn't just the penal code. It was the entire criminal justice system, accepted attitudes, misconceptions, and the economic insanity of building bigger and better jails instead of investing in keeping them empty.

Jake's investment was a halfway house. Aptly named the Turning Point, it was a port of re-entry and treatment center for newly released prison inmates with drug and alcohol addictions. The state provided basic funding, and there were some private donations, plenty from Jake's own pocket from what I surmised. But when he committed himself to something, he committed himself to the hilt.

"What I'm fighting is the way we mix apples and oranges." Jake leaned forward earnestly. "Substance abuse is a disease. It's a physical as well as an emotional dependency, and punishment doesn't cure a medical problem. We need to do more than just warehouse people in prison because they break the law. It gets them off the streets temporarily, but unless something is done about their addiction before they get out again, they'll march right back through that revolving door. The question isn't why, but what took so long."

"I know exactly what you mean," I nodded in agreement. "But law and medicine don't speak the same language. I work for a firm of lawyers, and they have an almost impossible time getting clients into rehab centers instead of jail. The current philosophy is: you were bad, go to your room and stay there for five years."

"Delaying the inevitable." Jake shook his head. "That's my argument. What good is it to lock up a user when you're only buying time by having him serve it? The few therapists or staff psychiatrists who work in a prison have to deal with an inmate population of over six hundred. That's about ten minutes a year treatment time for each one. You can't cure even an ingrown toenail in ten minutes, much less influence anyone's behavior or thinking patterns. That's why rehabilitation is such a joke. There is none. The system is spinning its wheels by attacking the effect instead of the cause."

"How does the halfway house change that?"

"By showing people they have choices. Giving them support. If they're willing to fight the battle, we help them win it. Only it's never easy." Jake rested his elbows on the table. "You have to remember two things, Ellie. A person usually abuses a chemical because he's in a lousy situation. It's his escape, at least in the short run. And then, whether he's drowning his sorrows or just trying to fit in with all the other kids on the block, after awhile it becomes a way of life. Even if he dries out in the pen, which may or may not happen, when he's released, there's his old life waiting for him. All the old crap plus plenty of new trouble. No job. A family that's ashamed of him. Sometimes a wife who's been hustling in the streets. Kids on welfare. You pick. And chances are, he's going to turn to the bottle or the needle to shut out the pain because he hasn't been taught another way to deal with his problems."

"Unless he gets to the Turning Point first. I think that's terrific, Dr. Siegel. And you still have time for a private practice?"

"I've got to do something to pay the bills." He glanced at the one in front of him. "Especially since you ordered the most expensive thing on the menu, Charlotte Basque, and you didn't even save me one bite."

I hardened my heart. "You were too busy talking."

"And you were too busy eating to listen."

"I heard every word. In fact, I was so fascinated that you may continue speaking while you drive me back to the gallery. Unless it's out of your way?"

Jake said not at all, and after paying for our accumulated extravagance he led me outside to his car. Or rather, he told me the Mercedes I was about to step into didn't belong to him. I should have known. A doctor with three ex-wives and a cause to support couldn't afford a car that ran on four cylinders. His had eight, he informed me. It was an ancient Ford Fairlane in dire need of a paint job and a set of matching tires. Two whitewalls and two black, without hubcaps, looked lopsided, I told him critically. But then so did half a steering wheel and radically different covers on front and back seats, he pointed out to me.

"Aren't you ashamed to go to the country club in this thing?"

"Now you know why I don't go." He jerked the car into first. "I've been meaning to get that fixed."

"Which particular flaw do you have in mind?"

"The clutch. I think it's slipping." He experimented with the gear shift for a minute, then pulled into traffic anyway. "I'll just drive slowly."

Jake might have been a fine humanitarian, but I thought the ride in Adam's car was a lot safer. To begin with, the Maserati had seatbelts, to say nothing of a more competent driver behind a fully circular wheel. Not that Jake was inept, but he talked with his hands as well as his mouth.

"Why don't you come with me to the prison next Wednesday? I'll take you on a tour of the place and show you why I try to make a dent in the process. They completely remodeled the old building after the riot, but it's still overcrowded and understaffed."

"What riot?"

"It happened a few years ago. Don't you read newspapers? The story made national headlines. The violence here was worse than at Attica."

"And you want to show me where they painted over the blood. No thanks."

Jake couldn't understand why the prospect of spending a morning behind bars didn't thrill me. As a bribe he offered to take me to his halfway house afterward. "You're in a

related line of work. Besides, you seemed interested while I
was plying you with chocolate."

Well practiced at defending myself from undeserved
guilt, I reminded the great crusader that he plied most of the
chocolate on himself. "And I am not in a related line of
work, if you're referring to my reputation as a crime solver.
I type for a living."

Jake looked at me. "What reputation as a crime solver?"

The only person in Santa Fe whom Vanessa had missed. I
briefly explained, then pointed at the dashboard. "Why does
that red light keep flashing on and off?"

"It's just the brakes." He waved away my concern. "The
light's been blinking all morning. Don't worry. The car
probably needs fluid again. These old crates burn oil like
crazy."

I advised him that motor oil and brake fluid were as different as his seat covers, but Jake said he didn't have time to
stop at a gas station now. He was taking the car to his garage
later to have the clutch fixed, and he'd have them check the
brakes then too. I didn't argue with him, though I did keep a
wary eye on the dashboard while he talked. Even so, it
wasn't until I noticed his hand had stopped moving that I
realized we'd driven an entire block in silence.

"What's the matter?"

"The brakes don't seem to be working."

"The brakes? I thought you said it was the clutch."

"What have you been watching all this time? A clutch
light?" he said in irritation.

Since we were cruising at a top speed of fifteen on a
semideserted street, I didn't see any reason to panic. "You
idiot," I said calmly. "Pull the emergency brake."

He reached under the dashboard and came up with a
black handle attached to a dangling cord. "I think it's broken."

My natural inclination to say that his head would soon be

in the same condition was superseded by the pressing necessity of deciding what to do next. At the corner was a stop
sign, which we obviously wouldn't obey, but no cars in
sight. Jake wanted to go straight, while I insisted it would be
smarter to go uphill. He took my advice and a second later
we were facing the wrong way on a one-way street.

"This is illegal," I protested.

"So is driving without brakes."

"That's not my fault."

"No, but if I hadn't listened to you, I wouldn't be driving
on this street."

Since the point was to come to a gliding standstill, prefer-
ably not into the rear end of another vehicle, the route of
least resistance was whatever route happened to be empty at
the moment. Fortunately, we didn't encounter any oncoming
traffic until we coasted to the Yield sign, where Jake yielded
to the inevitable and turned right before the Volvo pointed at
us reached point-blank range.

Then, he just kept making right-hand turns, ostensibly to
slow the car. Except this was Santa Fe, and some streets
sloped up, some streets sloped down. We were on a rectan-
gular course that was getting us nowhere.

Then we started going nowhere fast.

The last stupid turn put us at the top of a hill. As we
whizzed down, the speedometer needle whizzed up to a terrifying twenty-five miles per hour. Jake crouched forward
against the steering wheel as if he were headed around the
stretch of the Indy 500.

"Stop!" I ordered inanely.

"Gee, I wish I'd thought of that myself."

"Shut off the motor," I demanded.

"Then we'd have no control at all," he argued.

"You call this control?" I pointed at what was coming up
ahead. "What are you going to do?"

"I don't know yet."

No wonder. Less than a block away was a major intersection with four lanes of traffic zooming across our path. And the light was red. We could jump the curb and run over a couple of pedestrians, but Dr. Siegel wouldn't sacrifice an innocent life except for mine.

Jake leaned on the horn, stomped on the accelerator and charged straight through a gap between a school bus speeding east and a semi speeding west. I had a glimpse of the truck driver's horrified face as we whizzed by.

We made it. One more turn to the right and we were out of town. Instead of curbs and pedestrians, the roadside was lined with scrub cedar and rabbitbrush. As a van passed us impatiently, the driver shook his fist at us.

"Get out of the way, creep!"

"Not a bad idea." Jake guided his barely functioning jalopy onto the soft shoulder and shut off the engine. Now we just had to wait for the car to stop of its own accord. As it slowed, so did my heart.

"How could you drive this dilapidated heap?" I railed at him. "You should have decent transportation, if not to maintain your position in society, then for the preservation of mankind. We almost died back there."

"The car wasn't even scratched."

I crossed my arms and glowered at the barely moving scenery. When it stopped moving altogether, I opened the door and stepped out on a cactus. "I hate this car."

Jake got out on his side and carefully locked the door. "Then you won't mind walking home."

Chapter

8

Except for a jeans-clad young couple checking the price tag on *Cactus Capers,* one of Conchita's replacements for the growing number of bare spaces on the walls, the gallery was empty when I got back. Absently wondering why neither Nessa nor Ruth was on hand to give a pitch on art as a better investment than any IRA, I hurried down the hall. After a half-mile trudge on a dusty road with Jake and a ride in the back of a pickup truck, I certainly wasn't fit to be seen in public. What the wind had done to my hair was nothing compared to what sitting on bags of steer manure had done to my Liz Claiborne linen-blend skirt. But before beginning an extensive degriming session, I had to quench a raging thirst, which led me straight to the kitchen and into the middle of a heated family dispute.

"Dammit, Nessa, why wouldn't you pick up the phone? I've been worried sick ever since I heard about the murder. And not only didn't you call, you wouldn't even talk when I did. It's not as though I telephoned collect." Malcolm sounded deeply aggrieved that his generosity in offering to pay for the long-distance quarrel had gone unappreciated.

My untimely entrance into the war zone should have been followed by a timely exit. Only it was too late. The combatants had seen me, or more likely, smelled my presence. Two pairs of angry eyes met mine as I hovered uncertainly in the doorway. Then Malcolm's frosty blue gaze dropped to his feet, while Nessa bit her lip in chagrin. Caught between their embarrassment and my own, I did the only thing possible. I ignored both.

"Hi there, guys." I sailed into the room. "You're looking good, Malcolm. How are things going?" Silence accompanied me to the refrigerator, but I pretended not to hear it. "Boy, do I need a cold drink. It's a scorcher out there today. Ninety at least."

That brought Malcolm to life. "Ninety-two," he informed us, as if he'd just consulted his pocket thermometer.

Vanessa glared at him. "Ninety-one."

Sorry to have brought up such a touchy subject, I swallowed a glassful of lemonade in record speed, hoping to escape before they got into the barometric pressure. Already Malcolm's was at a dangerous level. His white shirt was still tucked neatly into his trousers, but he'd loosened his tie to an inch below his button-down collar, and for him that meant high turbulence.

"Well, I'm off to take a shower." I set my empty glass in the sink and waved an airy good-bye.

"Wait." Nessa stepped in front of me. "You haven't had lunch yet."

"I had the equivalent of three, all at the Good Shop Lollipop. But thanks." I started for the door, but she moved to the right and blocked me again.

"How about a salami sandwich?"

The desperate inanity of her question was only a ploy to keep me in the room. Obviously, Malcolm wouldn't reopen hostilities while a neutral observer was picnicking on the battlefield. If I remained as a UN "buffer" force, he might give up hand-to-hand combat and retreat to the telephone lines again.

But Vanessa miscalculated her opponent's endurance. He

was at the end of it. When she took my elbow and asked if I'd rather have tuna salad, Malcolm grunted impatiently. "Stop pestering her. She's not hungry."

"Not at all," I agreed with cowardly promptness.

"Yes, she is," Nessa contradicted. "And as my guest, Ellie comes first around here. You're the one who's outstayed his welcome, so you can leave the way you came in. With a sneer on your face."

Now Malcolm wanted an audience. He looked at me and pointed an accusing finger at his ex-wife. "Do you hear that? I try to give her some business advice and she calls it sneering."

"What do you know about business?" Nessa let go of my arm so she could wave hers. "All you've ever done is fill out a requisition sheet and the government hands you everything on a silver platter."

"Well, it's been nice, folks." I started backing toward the door, but Malcolm ordered me to stop.

"Don't leave, Ellie. Maybe you'll be able to knock some sense into your friend. She won't listen to me when I say she's headed for ruin."

"Yes. Stay, Ellie. I want you to hear how he enjoys undermining my confidence. Come on, Mr. High Finance. Tell her I've made a costly mistake and the gallery is doomed to failure."

Stung into dragging the knot in his tie down another fraction, Malcolm glowered at her through his horn-rimmed glasses. "Only an idiot refuses to face facts."

"Oh, so now I'm an idiot."

A scientist to the bone, he ignored the emotional implications of the term and set out to prove its technical validity. "Fact one: you're undercapitalized. Fact two: most galleries lose money the first five years. And fact three: a man was murdered on the premises last Saturday night, implicating you and your associates, as well as damaging the reputation of a business that hasn't even built one yet. You'll never survive that much trouble. The only sensible move is to sell out now before the bank auctions everything for you on the steps of the courthouse."

"Well, here are some facts to stick up your computer." Vanessa tossed her red hair scornfully. "The Discriminating Palette is not only surviving, we're over the top in sales. That's right. In less than a week, our undercapitalized gallery earned enough for two bank payments. And do you know why? Because I'm not the incompetent dingbat you like to think I am. I opened this place with a name artist to ensure sales from the beginning. And the murder doesn't change that. If anything, it's been a help." She stuck her nose in the air. "All the notoriety is attracting customers, not keeping them away."

"A temporary boom," he said curtly. "But when this seven-day wonder fades, so will your profit margin. Unless you plan to murder people on a weekly basis to maintain sales figures."

"Oh, good. Ellie gets to see you sneer. Charming, isn't it?" she asked rhetorically, since I had no intention of answering.

Malcolm didn't give me a chance anyway. "Dammit, Vanessa, why can't you accept that I care what happens to you? You don't really think I'm a heartless monster."

She raised her voice to match his decibel level. "I don't want you to care what happens to me. I don't want you checking up on my every move so you can protect me from myself. If I lose my share of the divorce settlement on the gallery or any other business, that's my problem. Not yours. And when I'm a bag lady, scrounging in garbage cans, sleeping in the streets, it still won't concern you. Please, do me a favor, Malcolm. If you see my body in a gutter, just step over it. Pretend you don't know me. And as an added favor, you can start right now."

Malcolm turned to me with a wounded expression on his long, thin face. "She acts like I can shut off my feelings with a snap of her fingers. I can't. How could I not be concerned when the police came to the lab and started asking questions about her? How could I not worry when I called to find out if she was all right, and Ruth said Nessa was lying down? For three evenings straight she's lying down and can't talk? Naturally, I assumed there was plenty wrong. After twenty years of marriage, you can bet I know how upset Vanessa gets. So I came by to see if she needed help. Is that a crime? Offering help?"

Before I could respond, as if either of them really wanted my opinion on the matter, Vanessa gave hers. "You could have assumed I didn't want to speak to you, which was the simple truth. And stop implying that a little stress makes me crazy. The only thing that makes me crazy is you."

"If you're going to misinterpret everything I say..." He rubbed his balding head with a helpless gesture. "Look, I didn't take off work to have another fight. Just send the lawyer's bill to me and I'll pay it."

"What lawyer?" Vanessa was impatient.

"You aren't getting legal advice about this situation? For crying out loud, Nessa. You act like a child sometimes."

She met my embarrassed gaze with a defiant shrug. "Now do you understand how he drives me insane?" Taking a deep breath, she pressed her hands together. "I'm not a murder suspect and I'm not filing for bankruptcy. Ergo, I do not need a lawyer. And if I ever do, I'll pay the bill myself. So go away, Malcolm. Just go away and leave me alone, with my corpses, my debts, and my life."

They stared at each other for a long moment, then his stooped shoulders slumped in defeat. "She doesn't want anything from me." He shook his head as if Vanessa's attitude were beyond his comprehension. "Why, Ellie, why?"

Now that there was an actual lull in the conversation, I

wished they'd start another salvo so I could sneak away under cover of the artillery fire. How could I answer Malcolm's lament? Reveal that most of Nessa's brusque words were motivated by sheer bravado? Of course, she was afraid of standing on her own two feet, scared that the slightest imbalance might send her falling back on him for all the wrong reasons. But exposing her Achilles' heel to a man who'd take advantage of it, even for the right reasons, was no way to treat an old friend. Even if I sympathized with Malcolm's hurt confusion, as long as Nessa had her defenses up, I wasn't going to tear them down.

"Sometimes the best thing we can do for people is leave them alone" was my unhelpful response.

Malcolm's expression turned sour with resentment. "Tell me about it. If Jake Siegel had stayed out of our lives, we wouldn't be in this mess," he said bitterly before unraveling his tie all the way and marching out of the room.

After a brief but awkward silence, Vanessa ran a trembling hand across her flushed cheeks. "I'm sorry, Ellie. I had no right to put you through that scene. I should have . . ." Then her eyes widened in horror, but not because she suddenly noticed that my yellow skirt had sprouted long brown streaks since this morning. "Oh my God! How long have we been back here? Nobody's minding the store."

We ran down the hall like two maniacs to find everything still intact. No one had stolen the art or the IBM Selectric. No one was there, either.

Mourning the loss of potential sales, Vanessa collapsed on the couch. "Ruth went shopping. I took Malcolm to the kitchen because I didn't want to have a scene in front of any customers. Then I forgot about everything else." She smoothed the ruffles on her white sundress as if it would smooth her own ruffled feelings. "But you saw how he transformed me into a witch right in front of your eyes." She shifted the blame neatly. "Maybe now you can understand why the divorce was inevitable. Jake had nothing to do with my decision, no matter what Malcolm thinks."

"Really?" I wasn't actually probing, though I was curious. This was the first time Nessa had even hinted that her relationship with Dr. Siegel was anything more than neighborly. It would be nice if she would come clean with me so that I wouldn't have to keep tiptoeing around the subject.

"Malcolm doesn't want to face the truth," she grumbled. "We were unhappy with each other for years. If he was so madly attached to me, why did he spend all his time at the lab? After I went to Jake for counseling . . . at Malcolm's insistence, by the way . . . and realized that our marriage was over in everything but name, suddenly Jake was a no-good quack who put ideas in my head."

And where was Malcolm's head all that time? Marriage counseling usually involved both partners, unless Nessa had wiped her ex-husband from her past as well as her present. Maybe she couldn't tolerate his memory any better than she could stand his company. Taking into account Nessa's biases, I figured that Dr. Jake Siegel hadn't made a very effective effort to reconcile the feuding couple.

Perhaps a certain skepticism showed on my face, because she said, "You don't like Jake either, do you?"

"Are you kidding? I'm nuts about the guy."

For some reason, she didn't believe me. "Just wait until you get to know him. Jake is the most honest person I've ever met. He made me confront myself, my fears. He taught me that it's wrong to stay in a destructive situation just because you're afraid to change."

"Vanessa," I pleaded in exasperation, "take a good look at me. Or maybe you should trade in those green contact lenses for some clear glasses first. I just spent the last two hours with Jake. Would anyone else but your marvelous marriage counselor do this to a perfectly innocent tourist?"

"Good Lord, Ellie." She finally gave me her undivided attention. "That didn't happen in the Good Shop Lollipop."

"Only the chocolate stains on my shirt."

Vanessa thought my adventure in absurdity was the funniest story she'd ever heard. When Ruth came in carrying a bag of groceries, I had to repeat the tale for her amusement, and Nessa said it was even more hilarious the second time around. "Isn't Jake a card? Don't you just adore him?" she interrupted my narrative several times. I agreed he was the joker in the deck, but I didn't go as far as adoration. Some emotions are simply too hard to feign.

However, a shower and a change into fresh clothing did put me in a more forgiving spirit. Nessa got over her pique too, though it was probably the three o'clock rush of customers that accounted for the wide smile on her face. I'd no sooner curled up in the windowseat with my required reading for the day than Nessa rushed in, looking pleased but flustered.

"Ellie, we need an extra salesperson. Would you mind volunteering?"

Putting a bookmark in *Daggers Drawn,* on the page where Sean O'Donnell is standing on a time bomb and doesn't know it, I followed Vanessa into the gallery to begin my career as an art maven.

Truthfully, I thought she'd station me at the desk, where only my ignorance of how to run a charge card through the machine would show. Instead, she told me to circulate. I warned her that if someone asked the technical difference between a serigraph and a litho, I couldn't explain. Vanessa said all I had to do was be friendly. Anybody who could recognize which was which already knew the answer.

To be on the safe side, or rather the safe side of the gallery, I went around the partition that existed simply to create more wall space. Maybe no one would notice me in the corner. The only customer there was a lady well past middle age who kept taking her spectacles off and putting them on as she surveyed one of Conchita's larger paintings. The poor dear was almost too short to get a good perspective. She'd step up, tilt her curly gray head to the side, then move back to see if it looked better from a distance. Her cherub cheeks were pursed in thought when she saw me.

"Excuse me, young woman. Do you work here? Good. I'd like your opinion. What do you think of this?" She nodded toward the sixteen-by-twenty oil of a smiling burro.

"Very nice," I said, which was as friendly as I dared get.

"Does it compare well to the one over there?" She pointed a chubby finger to the same burro without a smile.

"It depends on your viewpoint," I said, groping for a scholarly allusion. "Some people see a glass of water as half-full. Others see it as half-empty."

"How profound." She turned to me with new appreciation. "You have quite a penetrating eye."

Good grief, she was even friendlier than I was. Nevertheless, I accepted her tribute with the same sincerity as it was given. "Thank you very much. And may I say, you have quite an eye for fine art." This was stretching sincerity a little, but she seemed like a sweet lady.

Then she whipped out a pocket calculator from her purse. "Actually, I'm comparing values. This painting is larger by two inches all around, but that one is more expensive."

"There's probably more paint on it," I said in a business-like manner.

"Yes, I hadn't thought of it in those terms, but I'm sure you're right. That's why you're the expert, isn't it?" She beamed at me. "Very well. I'll take the picture marked twenty-five hundred dollars, and you can put it on my account."

"You have a charge account here already?"

"No, but I told Vanessa I'd be opening one. She assured me the gallery would be carrying nothing but the finest-quality merchandise, so naturally I plan to shop here regularly. Silly to write a check every time when I can pay on a monthly basis."

"Certainly," I agreed after realizing my mouth was hanging open. "You must have an incredible collection of merchandise . . . I mean art, if you buy so often."

"Yes, but I do try to be selective. As my late husband used to say, if something costs more, it must be better. So I always check price tags carefully before making a purchase. There's so much garbage on the market these days."

Obeying the motto that the customer is always right, no matter how eccentric, I remarked on her late husband's acumen. After all, he couldn't have been a complete fool if he had amassed the fortune his widow spent on art alone. That's when she told me she was "The" Mrs. Christian St. Laurent. Of strip-mining fame, she elucidated in case I had him confused with another Christian St. Laurent.

"He's been gone eight years this June, and his dying wish was for me to be happy." Her bright blue eyes sparkled with joy at the memory. "What a dear, dear man. And I didn't let my social life lapse for a minute. I retained every committee seat I had while he was alive, and kept up all my friendships. It's vital for a woman to stay active after a tragedy," she advised me with a tap on the arm. "I tell that to Vanessa all the time. Remind her of it."

"I think she's staying fairly active," I said as two more people wandered into the alcove. "In fact, she probably needs my help now. If you'll give me your address, I'll have the painting delivered to you."

"Vanessa knows where I live, but you must be a newcomer to Santa Fe if you're unaware that there are only two houses on Calle de Fuente. Mine and Adam Montgomery's. He's also famous," she conceded, rating bestselling authors somewhere below mining magnates, but granting Adam celebrity status anyway.

"He must be very proud to live next door to you," I couldn't resist saying.

I should have resisted. Lowering her voice so that the couple five feet away wouldn't overhear, Mrs. St. Laurent craned her neck and put her lips only inches from my ear. "His habits are very irregular," she whispered.

"Oh dear."

I didn't mean that to imply shock at her revelation, just regret at having opened a floodgate. Already she was poised on tiptoe for the second gush. If I walked away and left her in that position, she might topple forward. Besides, I wouldn't want to offend anyone capable of singlehandedly keeping the Discriminating Palette solvent.

"He comes and goes at the oddest hours," she confided. "And sometimes his lights stay on all night."

I wanted to ask if she lost much sleep checking up on him, but, more tactfully, I murmured something about writers working when the inspiration strikes.

"That may be," she allowed. "But he's very standoffish. Three times I asked him to speak at our ladies' club luncheon, and not once did he accept. My late husband never refused," she said by way of comparison.

"He must have been a mine of information," I punned unforgivably, noticing that the two customers who'd been there a moment ago had migrated to the busy end of the gallery. Eager to be there myself now, but seeing no escape route in sight, I invented one. "Oops, I think Ruth is signaling me. It's been a pleasure meeting you, Mrs. St. Laurent. Anytime you're in the neighborhood . . ."

She put a detaining hand on my arm. "My dear, you've been so kind, so helpful. Please let me express my gratitude by saying you needn't have any fears about working here.

I'm sure doubts have crossed your mind, what with Jerrold's dreadful murder and poor Vanessa's nervous breakdown. But I'm quite positive the rumor about Ruth Metcalf isn't true. You'll be perfectly safe."

"Safe?" I asked weakly.

"Absolutely." Her face lit with a benign smile. "She'd never poison you."

Chapter
9

My vacation was starting to get out of hand. I seriously considered sending myself a telegram demanding my immediate return to California. LAW OFFICE CAN'T FUNCTION WITHOUT YOU STOP SECRETARIES ON STRIKE STOP COFFEE MACHINE ON BLINK STOP COME BACK NOW STOP PROMISE DOUBLE YOUR SALARY PLUS INCREASED HEALTH BENEFITS STOP

But I stopped. Vanessa would be crushed if I left before my official two weeks were over. Not because she needed me here or wanted me here, but because she had invited me here. I didn't remember her being such a stickler for social obligations in the past. When she and Malcolm brought their two kids and stayed with us ten years ago, Nessa wasn't the least bit offended when I didn't want to go to Disneyland with them. She even brought me back a Mickey Mouse hat with ears. Granted, the situation was a little different this time. But just because my visit coincided with a murder, there wasn't any need for her to work it into my entertainment.

She woke me Thursday with what was becoming a familiar refrain. "I'm sorry Ellie. I feel terrible."

"Take two aspirin and call me in the morning," I said, yawning.

"It is morning. That's the problem. Leon's due here in less than an hour, and I can't go. Believe me, I want to. But it wouldn't be fair to take off and leave Ruth to mind the store by herself. Will you forgive me?"

"Sure. I wanted to sleep late anyway." I pulled the sheet over my head.

Nessa pulled it down. "Don't be silly. You're still going to Jemez. Leon specifically invited you to be his guest whether I tagged along or not. Come on, I thought you wanted to taste Indian bread."

"Not today. I'm finally starting my diet."

"Start tomorrow." She took the pillow off my face. "Honestly, Ellie, Leon's a doll. He'll love showing you around. Besides, he wants your advice."

"About pottery?"

"No, about the police investigation. We were talking the other day, and I told him you could answer all his questions."

"Thanks."

She slumped on the edge of the bed. "You hate me, don't you?"

"Yes." I rolled over.

"Come on, tell the truth."

"I did."

"You're just trying to spare my feelings. But I know what you really think, and you're right. Even without a murder to spoil everything, my timing was off. I never should have insisted you come for the gallery opening. It was stupid. Next month would have been a lot better. Things would have settled into a routine, and I could have been a decent hostess instead of pushing you off on strangers."

"I'm always pushing myself off on strangers," I consoled her. "How do you think I get my dates? Hey, smile, will you? That was a joke. I'm having a great time."

"No, you're not. I promised to show you New Mexico in

all its glory and I haven't taken you to one single place," she mourned.

"You took me out to dinner last night." That got me to a sitting position.

"You paid."

"I became an art expert yesterday under your tutelage." Now one leg dangled off the bed.

"I'm a beast. I forced you to work," she said tragically.

"Oh, my goodness, will you look at the clock?" I jumped to my feet. "Leon will be here any minute."

Nessa hugged me, with assurances that today would be a once-in-a-lifetime experience. Then, with her guilt absolved for another twenty-four hours, until an unprogrammed Friday set her off again, she shoved me toward the bathroom. "Don't forget. I want to hear every detail later."

Good, bad, and indifferent, I wondered, or an edited travelogue? Definitely edited, as if I hadn't been blue-penciling everything I said to her all week. It was only to protect her from unneeded stress, but my tongue was already full of teeth marks. No unflattering comments about Jake Siegel, which definitely cramped my style. I had to pretend Conchita was the greatest artist since Michaelangelo, even if their only similarity was having one name. And I couldn't mention Jerrold Willet in the same breath with anyone on Nessa's most-favored list unless it was to disassociate them. All this and she wanted me to have a wonderful holiday, which was presumably half the purpose of today's outing. I'd get to see an Indian reservation, and if I came back alive it proved Leon Yepa wasn't a murderer.

Actually, it proved nothing of the sort. The question of his guilt remained unanswered after I returned, along with how I got the scratches on my arm and bruises on my behind. Not that Leon tried to kill me, at least not intentionally. But my report to Vanessa that evening had more holes in it than yesterday's account of my tête à tête with Mrs. St. Laurent.

Of course, nothing that woman said was worth repeating anyway. She lived by the motto "if it's not true, it is very well invented." And she invented very well. But then why pass on gossip unless it's been embellished for entertainment value? How dull if Vanessa's divorce was caused by boredom instead of a nervous breakdown. And who wanted to hear about the man next door unless his movements could be described as furtive? Otherwise Adam was just a busy writer who typed at night and avoided his neighbor by day. Still, Mrs. St. Laurent did slip a little at the end, not that her Lucrezia Borgia parallel wasn't as thrilling as everything else she whispered in my ear. But even based on the rumor that Ruth Metcalf's former boss had keeled over during a dinner party at her house, it was a bit of a stretch for me to watch that she didn't drop cyanide pellets into my demitasse.

Naturally, I wouldn't spoil Vanessa's delight in my celebrated sale by telling her that pack of nonsense. After all, Mrs. St. Laurent might be a case of the customer always being wrong, but she did buy a painting. Maybe if I told her about my trip with Leon, she'd develop an interest in pottery.

He arrived at the gallery in high spirits, dressed in jeans and a T-shirt and wearing a smile. I thought it would disappear when Nessa broke the news that our threesome had been reduced to a duo. But Leon felt sorry for her only after she spent five minutes apologizing for the change of plan. He did suggest postponing the expedition to a mutually agreeable date, but Nessa said time was running out. I'd be leaving in another ten days and she didn't want to take the chance that I might miss seeing Jemez altogether, perish the thought.

Leon heartily agreed that that would be a shame. And so, despite Vanessa's defection, I climbed aboard his "cowboy

Cadillac," a fancy western phrase for a pickup truck, and we were off. Ahead of us was a long drive into the hinterlands. Maybe that was why, whatever advice Leon wanted from me, he wasn't in any rush to get it. We talked about cars, clothes, and the difference between what he termed "real," as opposed to California-style, chili. Then we got around to how I was spending my time while Vanessa tended the gallery.

"Are you enjoying yourself in Santa Fe?" he wanted to know.

"Absolutely. I've been hitting the museums, taking pictures of the local architecture. Pueblo-Revival, isn't it? To say nothing of shopping for souvenirs. I bought a gorgeous Navajo rug for fifty dollars."

"A rug for fifty dollars? You got a bargain."

"Well, it's really more the size of a place mat, but I wouldn't walk on it anyway."

He laughed. "And how's the detecting business? Keeping you busy?"

"What makes you think I've hung out a shingle?" As if I couldn't guess.

"Vanessa says you're sure to solve this murder. I just wish you'd hurry up. Then I'll be off the hook."

I was pretty sure Leon was joking. "That's some tall order. You do know she wildly overrates my abilities?"

"Well, she did promise you'd help me out." He checked the rearview mirror and passed a slow-moving horse trailer. "Listen, this is hard to explain . . ."

"You don't have to. Vanessa already explained." I sighed in resignation. "And I don't think you have to worry. The police may have more than one account of your argument with Jerrold Willet on Saturday night, but since you told them about it in your statement, they know you're not hiding anything."

"There's more to it." Leon's hands tightened on the steering wheel. "They've had me back in for questioning twice since Monday. You see, I've been in trouble with the police before." He took his eyes off the highway to shoot me an apologetic smile. "I used to have a drinking problem. It's licked now, but Billy Wayne keeps bringing up the past."

"Yes, he's quite an historian."

"He thinks I probably got drunk Saturday and lost control, if you know what I mean."

"I certainly do," I said, my liberal hackles rising, unpleasantly reminded of the way Detective Chavez had treated Frank Ott. What was it with cops? "If it's your sobriety that's the test, there must be plenty of witnesses who can vouch that you didn't guzzle champagne at the reception."

"Will you?"

"Me? I wish I could, but we didn't meet until Monday morning. Remember? I didn't even know who you were at the party. But Ruth was with you. Get her to tell Billy Wayne he's got bubbles up his nose."

"I'll ask her," Leon agreed, if less than enthusiastically.

For the last few miles the highway had been meandering through a narrow valley green with cottonwoods and lined by spectacular red cliffs. Now suddenly we had arrived. Though Vanessa had briefed me, Jemez Pueblo was a surprise. Not that I had expected tepees, but the sprinkling of normal suburban-type houses took me aback. Even when we drove into the maze of unpaved dusty lanes where small flat-roofed adobes leaned against one another for support, the twentieth century was clearly in evidence. A late-model truck was parked next to an outdoor oven called a *horno*, while television antennas sprouted from the oldest structures.

As Leon pulled up in front of one, he waved an expansive arm. "Now you know where Santa Fe got its 'unique architecture.' From us. Come on in and meet my Aunt Tita. We can have a cup of coffee before I start the ten-cent tour."

"There don't seem to be many people around." That was an understatement. The only living thing in sight was a dog, lazily scratching himself in the shade of a wall. I stepped down from the cab and stretched muscles stiff from sitting.

"Almost everyone commutes into Albuquerque to work. They farm a little too, but it's not like they can make a living from it."

I followed Leon through a bright blue door and into the front room of his aunt's house. It was cool and dim with a built-in bench running along one wall. Hanging near the beamed ceiling were baskets, woven dance kilts, and animal skins. There were also big colorful Mexican shawls, and on a couple of pegs, strand after strand of magnificent turquoise necklaces.

"For the ceremonial dances," Leon said, following my eyes. "Not everyday."

Just then a plump, white-haired woman bustled in from the kitchen. She was wearing a house dress with a cross-stitch–embroidered apron tied around her waist and orthopedic shoes on her feet. Aunt Tita took my hand and patted it, then welcomed me to her home and immediately offered food. I could have been at my grandmother's. Fresh-baked Indian bread, straight from the oven outside the door, replaced bagels, but there was an international language of *ess, mein kind* that I understood perfectly. Just like my *bubbe*, Aunt Tita beamed in approval as I matched Leon bite for bite. Healthy eaters are always beloved by little old ladies who want to see skin and bones covered with decent fat.

When I couldn't swallow another mouthful, Leon and Aunt Tita brought their pottery to the oil-cloth–covered kitchen table to show me. "This one I made." She handed me a graceful double-necked vessel. "It's a wedding vase."

"Lovely." I held it up to admire. "And the sienna and black pot with the gem turquoise set in?"

"Mine," Leon claimed proudly. "One of my latest pieces. You probably see the similarity between it and Aunt Tita's. She taught me the craft."

"I love the soft way the colors join."

"You like it? Willet didn't. He said my newer work lacked authenticity. The jerk didn't know what he was talking about. Look at it, Ellie. Can't you see how this design is a natural evolution from my aunt's?"

"That was his complaint? You changed the drawing on the front?"

"I didn't change it," Leon insisted. "I adapted it. This is more flowing. His other objection was that I used a firing technique developed at San Ildefonso. Each of the pueblos has its own characteristic style. But I am using Jemez traditions and ancient decorative motifs. Willet's so-called subjective expertise didn't qualify him to judge on this topic. I'm the Indian, and I know what's authentic." Leon sounded testy, as if he still resented the criticism even though Willet underground was never going to offend him again.

I agreed politely. Not that I could really see the connection between the two pieces, but if the art critic hadn't been entitled to judge, that went double for me.

Aunt Tita chimed in, "Leon's a good potter. For years I've been selling mine in Albuquerque and Santa Fe. To the tourists. But Leon sells in the galleries to the serious collectors. Much better for us."

I had no argument with that premise. Then Aunt Tita was pushing a couple of loaves of homemade bread into my arms to take back to Nessa.

"I'm so sorry she couldn't come today. Tell her I'll visit that gallery of hers real soon. Oh, Leon," she walked us to the door, "don't forget to show Ellie the new school and the tribal offices. They're completely up-to-date. We have a computer now. IBM," she reported proudly.

"Has anyone actually found a use for it?" Leon asked scornfully.

"I'm sure the pueblo governor has," she countered gently, while Leon shrugged, as if he thought a computer a silly acquisition.

After we thanked Aunt Tita and said good-bye, Leon took me around the sights. We peeked into the old Catholic church with its *santos* and candles, then wandered onto the plaza. It was just a dusty rectangle of bare beaten earth lined by shabby, seemingly deserted homes. No shops, no throngs, no trees or grass. How ironic that the plaza in Santa Fe was undoubtedly full of Indians today, sitting on the museum's portal, selling their beautiful jewelry, their pots and Indian bread, while the village lay empty in the hot July sun. But Leon defended the arrangement, saying that this plaza was used for ceremonial dances, not designed as a shopping mall.

He pointed out the kivas—sacred meeting places for the pueblo's secret societies—then said he was sorry I wouldn't be around for Jemez's saint day in August. "Everyone comes back then, if only for the Pecos bull dance. It's something special to our pueblo."

"Someday I'd love to see it." I squinted in the bright sunlight and imagined the barren space full of dancers in strange regalia, the walls lined with spectators, the silence exchanged for the sounds of drums and chants.

"Ready to get your hands dirty now?" Leon asked, smiling as if he had something up his dirty sleeve.

"You're the tour guide. 'Lead on, Macduff,'" I misquoted cheerfully.

I never dreamed that delving to the roots of Indian crafts would require a pick and shovel, but when Leon said we were going to dig into the past, he meant it literally. We went bucketing a mile or two down a rutted dirt road, past some fields of corn and over Jemez creek, then across the mesa on a barely discernible track. Leon pointed out the landmarks, plus a quick glimpse of my favorite cartoon character, the roadrunner hightailing it through the brush.

When we got to the potter's clay source, Leon swore me to secrecy. This was a special place, and no one outside his family was supposed to know about it. Not that he was really worried; a tenderfoot like me would never be able to find the place again on my own. After parking the truck at the foot of a red cliff, he took two shovels out of the back, handed me one, and invited me to help dig up a three months' supply of raw material. I asked if a pretty-please would get me a bulldozer, but Leon said that a little hard work was good for the soul.

I had to agree. There was a spiritual quality to the silent wilderness, though maybe I sensed it only because Leon did. Before starting, he sprinkled corn pollen on the ground, an ancient ritual that thanked the earth for its gifts. The small ceremony set the mood. We were dwarfed by the pine-clad Jemez Mountains to the east, and the vast dry tablelands stretching west. The pueblo had moved into the twentieth century, but not this harshly beautiful land. From here even the highway was out of sight, hidden in a fold of the hills. Leon swung his shovel around. All of this was his heritage.

An hour later, I had a pretty fair-sized heritage of my own. Leon's pile was bigger, but mine was neater, I bragged. As a pat on my weary back, he appointed me supervisor of sifting. I could pick the rock and gravel from the clay, while he collected some volcanic sand needed in the firing process. Then we just had to bag everything in old flour sacks and load up the truck.

I said after all that, he could bag me too. "Funny how this educational trip just happened to coincide with the day you needed slave labor."

"I thought you'd appreciate learning about the craft from the ground up," he answered straight-faced.

"Very funny. And I thought only white man speaks with forked tongue."

"Watch it, Ellie," he teased. "Between sunburn and red clay, you look like an official member of the tribe."

I took that as a compliment. Still, when we were finished, the fruits of our labor stowed in the truck's flat bed, I tried to wash off some of the dust. Leon had brought along a jug of water; and after I'd taken a big drink, I dampened a corner of the bandanna he lent me and wiped off the worst of the dirt.

Sitting in the shade, resting before starting the drive back, Leon started telling me about his background, how he'd grown up and gone to school in L.A. Some of the story I'd heard before from Vanessa, but not what it actually meant to him. His parents were both college teachers, his father the head of Native American studies, his mother teaching Spanish in the same small school. They weren't that atypical anymore, Leon said. After all, a lot of Indians had left the reservation to make a living. His folks had just gone further away than most, while their son longed to come back to his roots.

"I always meant to move here after college. I had a romantic idea, to use my art training to preserve the past. But nothing stands still. Look what's happening here. You saw it. People are moving out of the old houses, into new ones. They're brown stucco, made to look like adobe, but they're bad copies. Even Aunt Tita's kitchen isn't the same. She used to have a wood-burning stove."

"If you have such strong feelings about preserving the old ways, why are you modernizing your style of pottery?"

"Are you saying it's fake?"

"Of course not," I backed off quickly. "I think it's wonderful. But what's wrong with doing something different? Even Indian artists are entitled to experiment."

"I'm not experimenting," he flashed.

My mistake was in telling him he had every right to do so. "Look here, Leon. It doesn't matter what Jerrold Willet thought or anybody else says. You don't have to apologize for interpreting an art form in your own way. You know what you're doing. I understand exactly how you feel about your work."

"How can you understand?" he said belligerently. "You think spending a couple of hours with me makes you an expert? Maybe you saw a television documentary on Native American outcasts? Bullshit. I was surfing in the Pacific when I should have been learning about the desert. Coming back here, I had to let my hair grow long just to feel like an Indian again. You don't understand a fucking thing about me, lady. Don't kid yourself."

I'd done it now. With the very best of intentions, I'd opened up my big mouth and accidentally insulted a mixed-up artist who also happened to be a murder suspect. Only why did it have to be in the middle of a wilderness? Leon could expunge the blot on his family escutcheon, bury me in the clay pit without anyone noticing. It wasn't much consolation to think I'd reappear one day as an unusually shaped pot.

He stood up and wiped a sweaty hand across his face. "Don't pay any attention to me."

"Ditto." I scrambled to my feet.

"I just get . . . Never mind." He turned aside.

That incomplete comment didn't need an answer. Besides, if I claimed to understand anything else, Leon might make me walk home. I had presumed too much already. Breaking Indian bread with him did not make me a soul sister, any more than a little red dirt on my face was an initiation into the tribe. I kept my ready tongue still for a full fifteen minutes as we headed back toward Santa Fe. Leon didn't say anything either.

Silence might be golden, but there was nothing wonderful about this one. In fact, it was becoming extremely uncomfortable, though there was something else bothering me too. So when we drove into a little town called Jemez Springs, I finally spoke.

"Hey, there's a Chevron station. I'll pay for gas."

"No need. Anyway, you're my guest," he said civilly and kept on going.

I threw a despairing look over my shoulder, then another one ahead. We were almost out of town already, but there was a bar coming up on the left. Not the stop of choice, but any port in a storm. "Aren't you thirsty?" I asked hastily. "How about a Coke?"

He glanced at me, then pulled into the parking lot under the Coors sign. "Sorry to be so slow to catch on, Ellie. Why didn't you just say you had to use the john?"

When we walked into the beer-drenched darkness, I had to stand still for a minute and let my eyes adjust. When I could see, I headed directly for the arch in the back labeled BUCKS AND BUCKEROOS.

I picked ROOS on a guess. Lucky me, it was the ladies' room, only it was the kind that called for a protective layer of toilet paper, not just between the lady and the seat, but between the lady and the doorknob. Actually, places like that don't always have a doorknob, but they can be depended on to be out of paper. Good thing I had a travel pack of Kleenex in my purse.

When I came out, allowing myself a cautious breath through my nose again, all I wanted to do was get back to the gallery. I'd been a good sport and had my horizons widened, but enough was enough. Or so I thought.

Threading my way through the tables and chairs toward

the bar where Leon waited, I passed the only two other customers in the joint.

"Hey, sweetheart!" A wolf whistle. "Why don't you join
us?"

They weren't very drunk, just a little happy and a lot
grungy . . . a couple of cowboys who hadn't shaved or showered for quite some time. Out of work, I thought, since they
were boozing it up on a Thursday afternoon.

· I ignored them and sat down next to Leon. "Let's get out
of here," was my reasonable suggestion.

He pushed a glass of Coke toward me. The ice had
melted. "As soon as we finish our drinks."

A loud voice from the table interrupted. "How do you
like that, Orville? The little lady likes the redskin
better'n us. Don't it kinda make you sick at your stumick?"

I don't know how Orville felt, but I was definitely
queasy, mostly because of the way my companion was
reacting. "Don't pay any attention to them," I urged.

Instead of taking my advice, Leon turned on the barstool
and stared challengingly at the two. "You talking to us?" he
asked.

"Leon! Don't encourage them."

"Yeah, Le-on," Orville hiccuped, grinning. "Be a good
boy and mind the woman. Maybe she'll let you into her
pants, that way."

Leon stood up. "Apologize to the lady, you fucking assholes."

I grabbed Leon's elbow and tried to drag him toward the
door. "Let's go. Hey, it's getting late and I have to get back
to Santa Fe. Leon, please?"

My "please" was heartfelt. Orville and his good buddy
were on their feet and heading in our direction. They were
huge. And ugly. And mean. And even supposing Leon had
been almost as huge and ugly, he'd still be only half as
mean. But twice as dumb.

He pulled his arm from my grasp and faced our hecklers. "Come on, assholes, let's hear it. Tell the lady you're sorry."

"Who you think you're talking to, redskin?"

"Nobody," I piped. "He wasn't talking to anyone."

They kept coming.

It seemed obvious to me that the only sensible thing to do was leave . . . five minutes ago. I tugged on Leon's arm again, but he was intent on defending his honor and mine. He shook off my restraining grasp. "Tell her you're sorry, or I'll make you say it."

The man with the three-day beard, as opposed to Orville's one-day stubble, reached out a grimy hand and shoved Leon against the bar. "Oh yeah? You and who else, Indian?"

I guess there wasn't much choice about who else. The bartender was pretending he hadn't heard a thing, but I was still trying to avoid a fight. "Calm down," I suggested from the sidelines. "No need for anyone to get upset. We'll just mosey on out of here, right?" I looked to Leon for confirmation of this excellent plan.

Instead, my stalwart hero tried throwing a roundhouse punch. His fist connected, but without inflicting noticeable damage, though it did annoy the opposition. With a roar, the cowboy picked up Leon and threw him halfway across the room.

Shivering in my size-five shoes, I stepped smartly in front of my fallen comrade and spread my arms wide. Confronting the big bully eyeball to belly button, I used the force of moral superiority. "You back off and leave him alone or you're asking for trouble, mister."

The mouse that roared. I really wanted to scurry into a hole and hide, except I couldn't abandon Leon to his own folly. Anyway, I comforted myself, before either one of these brutes could slug me, I'd faint.

I never got a chance. Laughing, Orville lifted me in the air and set me on a table behind him. "Wait here, cutie. I'll get to you in a minute."

Now I was furious. For all he knew, this little cutie had a black belt in karate. The jerk was so positive I was utterly beneath his notice that that's where he put me. Out of sight.

In all honesty, I might have stayed there. It was the safest place to be at the moment. But Leon was enraged that one of them had dared to touch me. Struggling to his feet, he lunged forward and took another wild swing that got Orville right in the nose. This time Leon drew blood.

It was a brave move, but fatal under the circumstances. Orville pummeled Leon from one side while the other creep held his arms. I slithered off my perch and grabbed a chair.

I'd seen it in the movies a hundred times. You hoist a rickety barstool over your head and bring it down on your opponent's with just enough force to splinter the furniture. But John Wayne must have used a different system. When I landed the chair on Orville's skull, he landed on the floor.

"Gimme that!" The suddenly irate bartender seized his abused property. "If you broke it, lady, you're paying for a new one."

"Is he dead?" I looked down at my victim.

The barkeep cast a cursory eye on the body. "No, you just knocked him silly, but I want you out of here." He wiggled the legs of the chair to make sure they were still attached. "I don't let no women start no brawls in here."

Drawing myself erect, I stared at him coolly. "I don't start them. I finish them."

Too bad I didn't have a pair of pearl-handled six-shooters to twirl in a flashy display as I swaggered out. But my exit was spoiled anyway by having to scrape Leon off the floor and take him with me. He didn't appreciate the courtesy, but at least the score was even now. Rednecks 1. Redskins 1.

When we were safely in the truck I dabbed at his scraped knuckles with my last Kleenex while he complained. "You didn't have to interfere. I almost had them. Ouch! That stings!" He pulled away his hand.

"That's what you get for using your fists instead of your brains."

"Or the furniture." He winced as he put the key in the ignition. "Am I supposed to thank you for saving my bacon?"

"Only if you want to."

He looked at me unhappily. "Ellie, I'm sorry. But they started it. I didn't pick the fight."

"Oh, and you didn't overreact at all to a couple of witless boobs?"

"I couldn't let them insult you."

"Ah, the code of the West."

I was only joking, but Leon didn't see it that way.

"Okay, okay." He pounded his fists on the steering wheel. "I fucked up. I blew my lid. It was dumb and irresponsible and I admit it. Shit." He bowed his head. "I did it again."

I didn't ask what he had done again. Or whom he'd done it to before.

Chapter
10

I never thought I'd be calling a psychiatrist. More specifically, I never thought I'd be calling Dr. Jacob Siegel. The hardest part, as the authorities claim, was admitting I had a problem. Several, in fact, and I wrestled with all of them Thursday night before deciding to get professional help. The second difficulty was stretching the telephone cord from bedroom to bathroom, so I could talk to him from behind a locked door and with the shower running.

Jake would probably diagnose that as borderline neurotic. He'd be right. I could have spent a quarter for privacy and gone to the corner phone booth, but the route led through the gallery and past my social director, who'd never let me out the door without a daily itinerary in hand. At the very least, she would ask where I was going, and how could I say to arrange a secret rendezvous with her favorite shrink? The next question would be "What for?" followed by a heart-rending "What do you mean Leon Yepa has trouble with his alcoholism, his anger management, and his sociocultural conflicts?"

A long time ago when we were both students at Stanford, Vanessa and I had shared everything—not just boyfriends and sweaters but secrets too. Now I couldn't tell her anything. If she found out I had morning-after-the-day-before misgivings, she'd find out all those things I didn't tell her about the day before. And why worry her when I didn't know how much to worry myself?

Sure, I was sympathetic to Leon's problems; on the other hand, he'd nearly scared me to death. Trouble was, I didn't know whether yesterday's erratic behavior signaled a deep-seated psychosis or a routine case of delayed adolescence. Still, the grandstanding in the bar revealed a certain telltale refusal to deal with reality. Probably he intended to restage Custer's Last Stand. And typical of Leon, it was a modern adaptation of the original version.

What put him on the warpath anyway? The strain of coping with me all day, or not coping with the strain of our pit stop at the grubbiest watering hole in New Mexico? I'd taken a recovering alcoholic to a saloon and left him alone with temptation. For that sin alone, I deserved what I got: a chance to play Calamity Jane in a Wild West Show. It was wild, all right, a story to save for my grandchildren. They'd love hearing how sweet gray-haired Granny was once kicked out of a bar for brawling.

I hadn't intended any harm, but my trip to the ladies gave Leon time to fall off the wagon, presuming he even needed a stiff belt to start belting. According to his remorseful confessions during the ride home, anything was possible. He had been on the wagon for only a shaky month, not the year he claimed earlier. And when he fell off, it was, as usual, with a violent thud. Last time his attacking an unfriendly fire hydrant had earned him another overnight stay in the jail's dry-out cell. That didn't make him a psychopathic killer, but by his own admission, soused or sober, he had a hair-trigger temper. All the above added up to a confused young man with a "nobody understands me" complex, and maybe nobody did.

Maybe nobody had to, but as appealing as Leon could be, his actions could be a danger signal. Dangerous to whom and a signal of what, I had no idea. But then, I wouldn't recognize the symptoms of paranoid schizophrenia from a case of delayed adolescence. That's why I wanted to present the facts for Dr. Siegel's analysis. He was the expert on abnormal behavior; he'd know whether Leon's alarming tendencies warranted further investigation.

Sitting on the closed toilet seat with the shower going full blast beside me, I flipped through the phone book for Jake's home number. Naturally, he had followed medical protocol and hadn't listed it. Eight forty-five in the morning was a little early, but he might be at his couch already. I checked the Yellow Pages and dialed.

"Hello, Dr. Siegel's office. May I help you?"

"Yes. I'd like to speak to the doctor, please."

"He's not available at the moment, but if you'll leave your name and number, I'll have him return your call."

"No, that won't be possible. Can you put me on hold?"

"On hold?" the woman echoed. "I'm sorry. Please forgive me. We must have a bad connection. I can't hear you very well. But the doctor hasn't come into the office yet."

"Oh. What time do you expect him?"

"Fairly soon. Are you a patient?"

"No, but I need to consult him about a problem."

"Excuse me, could you speak up? The static on the line is terrible. It sounds like rain."

"I said," raising my voice over the sound of running water, "I need to consult the doctor about a problem."

"That can be arranged. Why don't you make a regular appointment with him. The doctor has an opening at three today."

"Thank you, that won't be necessary. I'll just wait."

"For anything in particular?" she asked, showing a well-trained ear for silent messages even if she had trouble hearing over the "rain."

"No. Just for Dr. Siegel to arrive."

"You can be sure he'll be here at three," she coaxed.

"That's very nice. But I won't be," I said firmly, hoping she'd pick up the note of finality in my voice.

She did. But it was the wrong note, an understandable mistake when someone calls a psychiatrist's office and announces a three o'clock deadline. Except I didn't mean on my life. Fortunately, before she could signal the rescue squad, crisis intervention came; Jake took the receiver.

"Dr. Siegel here."

"Thank goodness," I sighed in relief. "Your secretary is about to have nervous apoplexy because of me. Please tell her I'm not suicidal."

"Ellie's not suicidal," he said over the mouthpiece. "Anything else I can do for you?"

"Yes. I need to talk to you about a problem that's come up. No emergency. And Vanessa's fine," I added. "This is a situation that may be important, but I need a second opinion."

Jake was silent for a moment. "Where are you calling from, the shower?"

"Yes."

"Okay. Dry off and get dressed. I'll be by for you in twenty minutes."

There was a comforting insanity in not having mine questioned. But then, Jake was used to odd behavior, his own if no one else's, so why should my antics surprise him?

Apparently, they didn't. He picked me up and gave Nessa a wonderfully altruistic cover story for my sudden departure. "Ellie's volunteering this morning at the halfway house," he called through the car window as I hurried out of the gallery, Vanessa at my heels.

"When was this arranged?" She stopped me in the middle of the sidewalk.

"Oh, a while ago." Much more time with her would turn me into an accomplished liar.

"Really? You didn't say anything." She got a romantic gleam in her eye. "Does Adam know?"

"What do you mean, does Adam know? There's nothing to know."

"Don't be so positive." She gave me a smug grin before sending me toward the car with a gentle shove. "I think Jake likes you too."

Obviously. He'd gotten the brakes and the clutch fixed since our last romantic ride together. If he became any more attached to me, he might spring for new seat covers. Hopping into the car, I sank back on the old ones. "Thanks, Jake. I really appreciate this."

Putting the car into first gear, he pulled away from the curb, then took the stub of a cigar from the ashtray. "So what's the nonemergency? You have recurring dreams about murderers and want me to analyze why?"

"I already know why. I'm just not sure who's giving me nightmares. Or maybe I'm having delusions."

"Then you've come to the right man." He bit the tobacco remnant between his teeth and reached for the dashboard lighter.

"Why do you hang onto everything until it's past the point of garbage?"

"My shirt?"

"No. That smelly stub you're chewing." I waved the smoke away from my face. "That's not your breakfast, is it?"

"Nope. I had coffee first."

"Wonderful. The only medical man who thinks caffeine and nicotine have all the daily adult required vitamins."

He lowered the window on his side to purify the air, but kept smoking. "Ready to tell me what you were doing in the shower?"

"Yes, but first, promise you'll keep everything I say in the strictest confidence."

"Who took the Hippocratic oath? You or me?"

"Okay, I trust you. I just wanted to let you know I'm not

gossiping. Whatever you tell me will be held in strictest confidence too."

"Now that we've straightened that out, shoot," he said, nodding graciously.

"Is an alcoholic more dangerous when he's drunk? Or is he a menace all the time?"

Jake slowly turned his beard in my direction. "That's it? You just want me to boil down all the complexity of human nature into one simple sentence?"

I looked so disappointed that he tried. "Look, Ellie, despite the stereotypes, alcoholics don't fit into one neat pattern. Some have one drink a year and go off the deep end. Some survive on a two-martini lunch, and others go on a three-week binge. They don't have the same consumption rate or tolerance level. And yes, alcoholics are dangerous. To themselves, mostly. On the road, to everyone. That help you out?"

"Not really. What I'm trying to find out is if alcohol drives some people into uncontrolled rages. Or is that another stereotype? Surely, liquor does cause personality changes?"

Jake sighed in exasperation. Whether because we were temporarily stalled by a red light or because he didn't like my assumptions was unclear. "It can. It doesn't necessarily cause violent behavior. Sure, some people get drunk and beat up their spouses. Other people get drunk and pass out. But alcohol does not automatically produce pathological intoxication, and that's what you're assuming."

"Well, what about when an alcoholic stops drinking? Could he be unusually short-tempered, quarrelsome? Murderous, even?" There, I'd said it.

Jake shot me a satirical look. "Anyone can be murderous when he's not drinking. Why single out one special group?"

I gritted my teeth. How did he manage to make me sound so foolish? Maybe because I was. What a depressing thought.

"You must have one recovering alcoholic in mind. Someone you think killed Willet?" Jake went on more encouragingly.

Now it was my turn to sigh. "I'm not sure what to think. After spending all day with him yesterday, I'm wondering if he isn't unstable enough to have shot the carping critic just to shut his mouth. That's what I need you to tell me."

"Am I supposed to guess who you're talking about?"

"Leon Yepa. You know him?"

Jake didn't answer directly. "What's he done to rouse your suspicions?"

"All kinds of things. For a moment I thought he was going to kill me."

"You're still alive, right? By the way, is this a long story?"

" 'Fraid so."

Jake pulled into the parking lot of a shabby old motel and turned off the engine. "Then I'll have to hear the rest later. Well, what do you think?" he asked proudly.

Normally, I didn't give much thought to rehab centers for criminal offenders. In fact, the Turning Point wasn't even on my list of favorite tourist attractions, though by now I was interested in what Jake was doing; I even figured this was the very place to get some insight into Leon's chip-on-the-shoulder attitude. So despite the disappointment that we weren't continuing our conversation over chocolate-filled croissants at the Good Shop Lollipop, I didn't protest at all when Jake took me inside and told a cute blonde to put me to work.

"How do you do?" I extended my hand to Sugar Wilson. "I'd love to help, if I can."

"We'll find something for you, don't worry." Sugar was as sweet as her name. She linked her arm in mine and gave it an affectionate squeeze. "Are you just coming out?"

"Out?"

"Yeah. From the pen," she said with a warm glow in her eyes. "I'm on prerelease. As long as I stick with the program and keep the office going, I'll be a free woman in six more weeks. This place is great; just give it a chance."

Nobody had ever taken one look at me and assumed I was a convict before. But then, I'd been sure this lively twenty-year-old with the big teeth and cheerful smile was employed here. Which certainly goes to prove we all tend to see the world in our own image.

Jake left to conduct a therapy session in the rec room. As he disappeared down the hall, Sugar enthused, "He's a fantastic person, isn't he? Do you know how many hours he puts into this place? I just love him to pieces."

I learned plenty about Jake and the Turning Point in the next couple of hours. No wonder he drove a jalopy. This halfway house was an expensive hobby. It might be in a run-down motel in a very unposh part of Santa Fe, but the training programs and counseling were first-rate. Because there was a long waiting list of people needing help, wanting to get in, and not enough funding from the state to enlarge the facility, they were developing an income-producing furniture factory to be run by the residents. They already had a daycare center, used by working parents in the area. Its earnings helped pay for a new classroom wing, where volunteers taught the three Rs, plus life skills. That included how to deal with people, how to apply for and hold a job, and how to feel like a worthwhile person again. The last one was the hardest for most residents, Sugar confided.

"Why do ex-offenders make the most successful counselors?" I asked a little later, sitting with a couple of them and drinking my first cup of coffee of the morning.

"Because we understand all the cons, all the denials," Mark Richmond answered earnestly. He was in his thirties, beginning to go bald. "I went back to school, got my credentials, a degree in social work. But the real reason I can help is because I've been there myself. Hooked. Out of work. Desperate. Hey, it's tough enough to go from prison to the streets without freaking. If you're a junkie, forget it. Inside, they tell you when to get up, what to eat, what to wear. No decisions, right? Then, when you're really institutionalized, they put you back out in the real world and expect you to function. It's a miracle anybody ever makes it."

"Let me tell you something." The other counselor, Denis Romero, leaned on the edge of the table. "A rehab center like this isn't perfect, but it gives people support so they can kick their habit, get their heads together, you know? Before they have to deal with those mean streets on their own. Our graduates at least have a chance at making a successful reentry to society."

"Prisons ought to do more counseling. Then it wouldn't have to be done over again," I said, remembering what Jake had told me on Wednesday.

Mark shared a bitter smile with the other man. "Yeah. I wonder why that doesn't happen. Maybe because taxpayers don't want to spend money on subhumans."

"The counseling inside doesn't work," Sugar chimed in. "It's not real life. I was still doing some dope in the pen. It's not supposed to be like that, but everything's available . . . for a price. Anyway, the Turning Point is different. They care here. And they check your urine pretty often too."

"Easiest way to test for drug use." Mark nodded.

Denis laughed. "Yeah. We know all the tricks. And we tell our residents the straight scoop. 'So you paid your debt to society? That's the good news. The bad news is, society don't want to see your face. You're going to have to earn a place for yourself out here again. Nobody's gonna hand it to you on a silver platter; they'd just as soon see you back behind the walls, out of sight, out of mind.'"

That's how I got my assignment. Since I typed, I could help a few ex-cons take that first step toward self-sufficiency by putting their résumés together. But first I had to learn how to do them. Sugar took me to the office, installed me at what used to be a motel registration desk, and explained the guidelines. Writing "I was a disc jockey from 1972 to 1974, then a race-car driver from '80 to '81" made the telltale gap stand out like a sore thumb. It was better to say: "Radio announcer for two years and hot rodder until I came to my senses." And it wasn't illegal to omit where the resident had been between '74 and '80.

Of course, that didn't prevent the awful truth from coming out. Hiding a record gets complicated when you need to ask for time off to see your probation officer. Jake advised ex-offenders to volunteer the information right at the beginning, privately to the boss. Then, if he seemed prejudiced, he could be informed that the government gives tax credits for hiring ex-criminals. Not surprisingly, money talks louder than snitches.

What was surprising was how hopeful these people were, and how different from my expectations. Some of them had impressive work experience, and I did my darnedest to make them look good on paper.

I'd finished with my third client when a rumpus started out in the parking lot. The big windows from the old motel office gave me a ringside seat as a big man with tattooed biceps exploded with fury. Jake was the target, not two feet away and half a foot shorter.

"Goddamn you," the man shouted, waving a fist under the psychiatrist's nose. "All I took was a Percodan. That dirty urine ain't mine."

"Then you picked the wrong guy to cover for you. The lab tests show heroin in the sample you turned in."

"They mixed it up."

"Okay, go back inside and try again." Jake was as calm as if he were discussing the Cubs' chances for the pennant.

Not the other guy. He took a menacing step closer to the doctor. "You just want to put me back inside, don'cha? Tell 'em I violated parole?"

"Am I pressuring you, Harry? Narcotics Anonymous meetings too dull? Is that why you missed the last three? And what about the last group-counseling session?" Jake waved his hand in dismissal. "Don't waste my time. There are too many people waiting in line who want to get better. You don't like the rules here, go. But the pen isn't going to give you a two-room suite with maid service because you're such a good customer."

Harry yelled a few more profanities before making an obscene gesture and stalking off. Jake relit the stub of a cigar, then ambled in through the office door. "Ready for lunch?"

This morning, I'd expected Jake to answer all my questions over breakfast. But after two and a half hours at the Turning Point, I was looking forward to asking different ones.

The setting was different too: La Fonda Hotel, a relic from the days of the Santa Fe Railroad's glory and the famous Harvey Girls. It had real flagstone floors, massive vigas supporting high ceilings, and real antique furniture. I could tell it was authentic by the shabby upholstery. I could also tell by the prices that the menu had been updated.

After the waitress took our order, Jake listened to a condensed version of yesterday's trip to Jemez and then said, "So?"

"So—could Leon be guilty?"

"Could be, but not because he's an alcoholic."

"You're positive?" I raised my eyebrow.

"You want to solve a murder, go look for clues. I can't help you with forensic psychiatry."

"Too bad."

Over lunch Jake gave me some clinical background. He got a little technical at times, describing drug-induced psychosis and other emotional disorders caused by abuse, but I could see why Sugar was so devoted to him.

"There's a national epidemic of substance abuse in this country. I work with criminal offenders because they do the most damage to themselves and everybody else. Some of them are salvageable. Society can't afford to give up on these people."

"Then why did you give up on Harry?"

"Who?"

"The rough tough guy in the parking lot. He almost slugged you one in the kisser. I suggested calling the cops, but Sugar said you could handle it."

"Who gave up on him? I told him a few unpleasant facts. Sometimes it takes a confrontational approach to get through to a patient."

"Confrontational approach, huh? That would explain why it looked like pistols drawn at the not-so-okay corral."

Jake laughed. "The term really just means getting involved with patients, not just being a passive listener. They might get angry with me, but they have to face reality, start taking some responsibility for their own lives, their own mistakes." Jake's enchilada plate was long gone; he reached for a cherry tomato off my chef's salad. "Look, Ellie. I can offer help, but nothing ever changes until someone accepts treatment. If Harry won't, then he's got a three-year sentence to finish."

"What do you think he'll do?"

"I don't know. Come back tomorrow and see for yourself. Or are you going to be busy detecting again?" Jake was teasing me.

"I haven't really been detecting."

"Then you always call people from the shower."

"Don't make fun. I already told you why. Vanessa's got enough to worry about already."

"Why are you so protective of her?" Jake wanted to know.

"Because. By the way, was Frank Ott ever a resident at the Turning Point?"

Jake gave me the benefit of a long, studious gaze, probably analyzing my psyche and labeling it nosy. "What makes you think Frank needed curing?"

"Will you stop playing psychiatrist, answering every question with another question?" At least Jake didn't deny knowing him. But then, they could have met at the gallery. "Frank told me he went through a drug-rehab program and I wondered if it was yours."

"Would it make any difference?"

"I don't know. Would it?" I smiled smugly, giving the doctor a taste of his own medicine.

Jake didn't answer. He never got a chance. When the waitress set the bill on the table, we both grabbed for it.

"Let go, Jake. This is my treat. You went out of your way for me this morning, and the least I can do is buy you lunch as a thanks."

"You're right. It is the least you can do." He swiped the bill from my hand. "I expected you to go to bed with me."

"Be quiet." I glanced around the crowded restaurant. "Somebody might hear you."

"That's getting to be a phobia with you, isn't it? Don't worry. Just put yourself in my hands for one night, and your problems will be over."

"I don't have any problems—except for you."

"Aha." He rubbed his beard. "An irrational fear of sex. I recommend immediate treatment."

"I don't."

"Okay, if you don't suffer from acrophobia, how about a

ride in a hot-air balloon?" He tossed a twenty-dollar bill on the table, for lunch and waitress, then pulled out my chair for me.

"How did you make that leap so fast?" I stood up. "A second ago, you wanted my body."

"Just as I thought, a clear case of erotomania declaraumbaults syndrome."

"What's that?"

"When a woman believes a man of stature and prominence has evil designs on her and she must rebuke him publicly." He took my arm and led me through the crowded room.

I didn't say a word.

Chapter
11

Vanessa loved it. Jake Siegel had whisked me off for a romantic morning at his halfway house, and she couldn't wait to hear every salacious detail. The second I walked into the gallery, after holding the door open for two people maneuvering their bulky purchase outside, I was greeted with an all-encompassing "Well?"

"Yes, it went very well. Marvelous setup. Wonderful facilities." I breezed by her. "If there were more places like the Turning Point, we wouldn't need more places like the Turning Point."

"And men like Jake?" She pattered after me.

"Admirably suited to the task."

Ruth looked up from the desk where she was working. "Good try, Ellie, but Vanessa's heard that speech. You're not the only volunteer he's drafted for the cause. The issue is the length of time you've been with him. Not that we've kept track, but your field trip lasted five hours and . . ." she checked her watch, "thirty-seven minutes."

"Is that past my curfew?"

"No." Ruth smiled. "Just thirty-seven minutes past platonic."

"I can always tell when she's hiding something," Nessa

said to her partner. "See that innocent expression on her face? A dead giveaway."

"Then it's obvious." I started down the hall. "If I wasn't kidnapped by a band of roving social workers, I must be either engaged or pregnant."

"You're incorrigible." She laughed, trailing me all the way to the sitting room. "Okay, what's the scoop? Is Jake dazzled, captivated or totally besotted?"

"Has to be one of those categories, huh?" I slung my purse on the couch and followed it with my body. "Not just mildly grateful that I can type with both hands and chew gum at the same time?"

"Mild? After that amazing feat of dexterity?" Nessa shook her head. "Besides, I have it on good authority that your relationship is a lot juicier than Juicy Fruit. Maybe as spicy as an enchilada plate and beef burritos with rice." Her green eyes sparkled impishly. "Aren't you going to ask how I know?"

"How? The telltale thirty-seven minutes, or did I smear a telltale dab of chili on my innocent face?"

"Neither. The telltale Mrs. St. Laurent. You might as well confess, Ellie. She was here a little while ago and she told me everything, up to and including the fact that you and Jake were having such an intense conversation at La Fonda, neither one of you even noticed her."

"Which naturally inspired her to rush out of the restaurant and buy another painting. Funny, I thought I felt a lump under the table. Or was she behind the potted palm that kept banging into the back of my chair?" I patted the seat beside me. "Sit down, Nessa. Quit hovering over me like a self-satisfied Cupid. You know you can't swallow everything that old gossip says."

"Don't pick on her; she's my best customer." Vanessa slipped gracefully into her favorite cross-legged position on the floor. "Besides, she's also a great spy. You just won't admit the truth."

"What truth would you like me to admit?" I said lazily.

"The real reason Jake took you to La Fonda. I know him, and he doesn't stay at the Turning Point until noon and he always eats at McDonald's. What did he say?"

"Nothing much. Except he did invite me upstairs to one of the rooms in the hotel for a nooner."

"Come on, Ellie, stop joking. Be serious for once."

"Hey, you're the one who claimed he was besotted. You don't think my beauty could drive a man to mad, passionate desire in the middle of a crowded restaurant? Aha, now I know what you really think of me. My irresistible charms just can't compete with a salad bar."

"Can't you give me one straight answer?" She laughed.

"No, but I'll tell you something that will make you happy. Jake's taking me for a ride in his hot-air balloon on Sunday."

That she believed. I wasn't sure what made it seem more like something Jake would do. Either Vanessa thought his personal life was as snow-white as the lab coat he never wore or that he was just a slow worker. In any event, the enchantress she'd imported from California was given full honors for fatally charming two men in one week. That was an Olympic achievement for me.

At any rate, my elaborate subterfuge this morning had been completely ridiculous and totally unnecessary. If I had called Jake openly and said I wanted to do my share of community service, Nessa would have packed me a box lunch and told me not to bother the doctor while he was working.

Good advice. Asking the expert raised more questions than it answered. Should people with emotional problems be held responsible for their behavior? Why isn't drug and alcohol reliance treated as a disease instead of as a crime? Are people under the influence of whatever influences them capable of making a rational decision? Oh, Dr. Siegel had very definite opinions on all those larger social issues. But when it came to pinning a "Warning—High Explosive" tag on anyone who fit those categories, his only labels were "maybe," "possibly," and that old standby, "based on case studies."

There is no stereotypical killer profile. Clinically speaking, the doctor said unclinically, there was just as much chance that the butler did it. He never drank to excess, one reason why no one noticed the steadily diminishing supply in the wine cellar. He never abused the family silver, much less drugs. And he was so obsequiously polite that everyone assumed he was born to the polishing cloth rather than destined to wrap it around Mr. Thrupney-Throckmorton's skinflint neck.

I told Jake he read too many mysteries. He told me I should watch more McNeil-Lehrer Reports. Then I'd know alcoholics were not necessarily more dangerous than chocoholics. Even the violence level of drug users depends on the drug, the user, and if he is the type to hit first and apologize later. Leon Yepa definitely belonged in the high-risk group. For that matter Frank wasn't Mr. Calm When Accused either. But as murder suspects? Check out the butler first.

No thank you. I had nothing against butlers, and I had already jumped to enough unfounded conclusions. In fact, I'd done the same thing I accused the police of doing, making blanket judgments about a person's current behavior based on his past. There might be some validity in the adage that history repeats itself, but that motto wasn't going to be mine. The more I learned, the more confused I became. Besides, snooping into the murky corners of the human psyche was a terrible way to spend a vacation. From now on, I'd ask no more questions, forget about romantic charades, mind my own business.

Friday afternoon's empty calendar gave me a perfect opportunity to catch up on my recommended reading anyway. I couldn't let my favorite author take me out to dinner when I still had a hundred pages to finish in *Daggers Drawn*. Suppose he asked me a question? Something hard, like did I enjoy it? Besides, a few hours with Sean O'Donnell was the perfect cure for what ailed me. Unreality therapy. As soon as my hero landed the sabotaged helicopter, eliminated the bad guys, then stepped over their bodies to receive his reward from the rescued Saudi Arabian princess, I ran for another Diet Coke and dived into Sean's next caper.

Triggerfinger: "More terror and international intrigue as the debonair CIA agent shrugs his broad shoulders into a tailormade dinner jacket, downs a bottle of French champagne, beds another lush lovely, then saves the world." That was my version of what the book cover should say, with five stars for ideal escape reading. Vanessa came out to the patio a couple of times to make sure I hadn't completely disappeared into never-never land. But I was only going back to those thrilling days of yesteryear when "Let's Pretend" was on the radio every Saturday morning and I became the bewitching character on the other side of the dial. Cinderella. Snow White. Rapunzel. The Little Train That Could. Except that now I really knew who I wanted to be when I grew up: a long-limbed blonde with bright red fingernails that never break and full wet lips that don't need gloss.

"You have a magnificent body." Sean's eyes raked my . . . oops, I mean the cat lady's uncovered breasts before his hand removed the silk sheet that draped her sleek torso.

"Take me," she begged, quivering under his expert touch.

He stroked the tender inside of her thigh, then bent his head to the throbbing spot between her legs. As his tongue sent tremors of undulating passion through her veins, she tossed her lovely head from side to side on the tiger-skin pillow. "Now," she gasped. "Now."

In one fluid motion his unbuttoned shirt was on the floor,

but before his sharply creased gray trousers could follow, Vanessa interrupted.

"Ellie? Are you finished?"

"No." I put a marker in page 117 and closed the book.

"Sorry, but Conchita just called and she needs my station wagon. Do you mind taking it to her? Frank's not here."

Yes, I minded, and Frank would probably get back to the gallery before I got back to Sean. But what could I say? "No problem. Just let me take a cold shower first."

As it turned out, Conchita borrowed Vanessa's station wagon and her houseguest in lieu of a moving van and four longshoremen. She needed to retrieve her personal possessions from Jerrold Willet's house, a job she'd postponed for the last six months but suddenly couldn't put off another minute.

The explanation Conchita offered when I picked her up was simple, if characteristically dramatic. "I'd never set foot in that house again if he weren't dead."

The reason I was going along for the ride was equally simple: to do Vanessa a favor. Whatever natural curiosity I might have about Jerrold Willet, the man, the critic, and why he'd been murdered was purely coincidental. Super-psych Siegel might not believe that, but what kind of incriminating evidence could I find in a house already ransacked by the police? Even if they had left a psychological clue lying on the coffee table, I wouldn't know how to analyze it right. Anyway, I'd be happy to let Sean O'Donnell solve all the crimes around here for the next week as long as I could read about his exploits undisturbed. Which of course made me think of Adam and his flattering response when I said, "Guess where this little detective went yesterday?" Come on, Ellie, I chided myself. That's not how the scenario works. When you tell him all you did at Willet's house was carry crates, all he's going to say is that you have a magnificent body.

Conchita tossed some empty boxes in the back of the wagon then told me to scoot over, she'd drive. I relinquished the wheel gladly. I'd made it to her studio via one of Vanessa's close-to-indecipherable maps, but I circled the block three times before Conchita finally came outside and flagged me down. If she'd been standing on the corner in the first place, I wouldn't have missed the turn.

It was clear that we weren't going to Willet's house on a condolence call because Conchita was wearing every color but black. She had a hodgepodge of jangling bracelets on each arm, while mismatched earrings swung from the multiple holes in her earlobes.

"I dressed like this on purpose," she said, probably noticing that the glare from her outfit was making my eyes tear.

"Santa Fe style?"

"These are my exorcist clothes. They ought to scare any ghosts away." She glanced in the rearview mirror, possibly to check if one were chasing us, then floored the gas pedal.

"Ghosts of bad memories, you mean?" I sympathized.

"Hell no. Jerrold's ghost. I don't trust the bastard not to come back and haunt me. In person. Cigar and all."

I guessed this wasn't a spiritual holdover from one of the Eastern religions she frequently but briefly joined. "Haunt" was a funny word unless she felt guilty about something. Or was she just remorseful because she had waited until Jerrold was dead before stepping foot in "that house" again? It was hard to tell with Conchita. Melodrama was her forte.

"I'm an artist. I feel things, sense atmosphere. That place has bad vibes and I'm not taking any chances," she said.

I wanted to ask what kind of chances, but instead I said, "Of course," as if I understood.

"When I left Jerrold, I just threw some things in a suitcase and ran out the door." We sailed through a yellow traffic light with the same speed. "He wanted to talk, but I didn't. There wasn't any point. I had signed the contract with the greeting-card company, and who needed to hear him tell me what an idiot I was?"

Maybe Conchita hadn't needed to hear it, but she sure sounded defensive about not listening. "Did he try to patch things up with you later?"

"Are you kidding?" she snorted. "Jerrold unbend?"

"Then that was the last time you spoke to him. I mean, privately."

"Nothing we did was private." She shot me a sardonic glance. "The whole world knew when we had an argument. But if you're asking if I met him alone at the party, the answer's no. You heard everything we said to each other. I didn't talk to him again after that."

"I wasn't thinking about Saturday," I said half-truthfully. "I just wondered if you believed that last fight was going to be another temporary separation."

"Like the seventeen before?" She shook her head. "I don't know. Maybe at the beginning. But when he started writing those stinking reviews about my work, that corked it."

"Plus your new-found faith in the Lord."

"What? Oh, yeah. That too." She turned the corner in a jangle of bracelets.

A minute later, Conchita pulled up in front of a house that was so far from what I expected I almost asked if she had to make another stop first. Instead of a gingerbread mansion in the last stages of cobwebbed disrepair, the site of all the drama and enmity Conchita had described was a modest bungalow in a modest neighborhood. In fact, *chez* Willet was a beige stucco with the requisite shade tree in the front yard and a neatly clipped hedgerow along the driveway. I'm not sure what I pictured for a man who criticized unoriginality, but it certainly wasn't tract housing.

Actually, just every third house had an attached garage and minuscule porch, though Willet's didn't look any more haunted than the rest. There weren't even any ax marks in the door. When Conchita unlocked it and nothing jumped out and said "boo," I was almost disappointed.

"I'll start in the bedroom. Would you scout around and find my marble bookends? They might be in the studio." She took a box to fill and headed for the back of the house. "Oh, and Ellie," she called over her shoulder, "if you see any clues, feel free."

To do what? Clear her name as long as I was here? Browse around and look for a couple of other murder motives? What could I possibly find, a suspicious-looking ashtray? I took a spot check of the living room, but the only clue I saw was clear evidence that Jerrold Willet had liked modern Scandinavian furniture and antique clocks. He had eclectic tastes all right, but maybe that's why he felt entitled to criticize everything. The room held an interesting collection of old and new and wild. The oil painting over the sofa was a real shocker, black and brown and blues swirling like a maelstrom around pain-twisted faces.

"Did you find the bookends?" Conchita called.

"Not yet."

"See if my wicker wastebasket is there too."

Prodded into action, I went looking for the studio. It was part den, part workroom, and part greenhouse. A jungle of houseplants overflowed a small solarium built onto the south side of the house. The rubber tree was in great shape, ditto the giant philodendron, but the ferns and salmon red bougainvillea were turning brown. Evidently the heir to the Willet estate hadn't arrived on the scene as yet. Or maybe he didn't care if this part of his inheritance withered on the vine.

Bookends, I reminded myself, crossing the room to an alcove where Willet's desk had been left in disarray. I looked on, under, and behind the mess before opening the drawers to see if Conchita's property had been put away for safe-keeping.

The bill was in the third drawer down, clipped to a folder marked "House." The invoice was dated May 12 and item-ized an unpaid balance of $1,545.90 for construction of a passive solar addition to the studio. Scrawled across the bot-tom was a note: "Paint already flaking—windows not prop-erly caulked. Came back once May 21, left before noon. No payment until Ott makes all repairs to my satisfaction. J.W."

Aha, a clue! Not a very new one, though it did document Frank's story. As a motive for murder, an unpaid debt seemed awfully weak. On the other hand, fifteen hundred dollars might ignite passion in some, even in these inflation-ary times. I put the bill back in the folder and closed the drawer.

That's when I found the marble bookends . . . and the wicker wastebasket . . . and the layout of the August issue of *Insight,* the one that would never go to press. A good thing, too, I decided, scanning the contents.

"Back issues are in the file, in case you're interested." Conchita had come up behind me with a twelve-inch Sony TV under one arm and a cardboard carton full of wrinkled clothes under the other. She joined me at the pine library table and glanced at the camera-ready paste-up of the cover, then read aloud from page 2: "'Conchita ranks with the worst. Her latest showing makes the Sunday comic page look good.'"

She tossed her head in contempt, her earrings swinging wildly. "So he wrote the review before seeing my work. That figures."

"And you're not even surprised. I guess you knew what to expect from him."

For a moment there was a flicker of pain on her face, then she stared over my shoulder and her mouth tightened. "His fucking plants are dying."

Clutching her belongings, Conchita stalked out of the room while I followed with the bookends. The late afternoon sun that brightened the studio barely penetrated the narrow hall. Bronze shadows darkened the colors on the two eerie oils hanging side by side. They had the same quality as the six-by-four-foot painting in the living room and were signed with the same dramatic *M*.

"Melinda."

"What?"

How naturally she responded to that name. "These paintings are yours, aren't they?"

"Don't remind me." She shuddered, dumping her load by the door.

I looked at the oil over the sofa. "This is really a magnificent piece. Not the least bit like . . ."

"A smiling burro," she completed my thought. "That's okay. You're entitled to like what you want. Personally, I think this garbage stinks." Her eyes were drawn to the painting anyway. "You should have read the reviews Jerrold wrote in those days. According to him I was an unrecognized genius. He said it in print, for all the good it did me. I sold four pictures in three years."

"Are there more?"

"Jerrold insisted on saving a few. I burned most of them. Maybe he burned the rest."

"He kept three on prominent display."

"What are you trying to do? Make me feel guilty?"

"For what?"

"Nothing." She shrugged. "If you want to see if there are any other survivors, check in that closet. Jerrold used to keep them there along with the other local artwork he collected. Go ahead and look if you're curious."

She went back to the bedroom, muttering that the bastard had probably saved her shitty paintings and tossed her favorite raincoat. I opened the closet door. Stacks of canvases were crammed in every corner, and I almost gave up the project then and there. To find Melinda's, I was going to have to pull out every one.

Fifteen minutes later, arms tired, hands dusty, I had propped five more paintings by Melinda up and down the ill-lit hall. Now I knew why Willet had been so furious with her. It was also easy to see why Melinda had grown discouraged and reincarnated herself as Conchita. These gloomy oils might be masterpieces of emotional intensity, but they wouldn't appeal to many people. It took a Jerrold Willet to hang that much despair over the sofa. As much as I admired them, I wasn't sure I'd care to live with Conchita's blue period. But she had ten times more talent than I would have guessed, judging from the amusingly decorative work that was selling so briskly at the Discriminating Palette. She felt a pull toward these too. That's why I insisted that Conchita take Melinda with her.

"I'm not hauling that garbage home."

"Why not? You're hauling this garbage." I took a torn raincoat out of the cardboard box. "Is nostalgia going to keep you dry?"

"Give that back."

"And this." I tossed her another Hawaiian shirt. "You need a spare in case the one you're wearing falls completely apart?"

"It's only torn under the arm."

"Fine. You can use this one to patch it and have the only Hawaiian plaid on the mainland."

"Why is it so important that I take those pictures?" she argued, tossing the clothes into the box.

"It's not important, except you just spent five minutes crying over them. I assume you feel some attachment."

"So what? They remind me of my misspent youth. Besides, they're ugly. I must have been out of my mind to paint like that."

"Okay." I started to put the canvases back into the closet. "You want to leave them here, we'll leave them."

"No," she said in an abrupt turnaround. "I'll put them in the car. You bring the two hanging in the hall."

I lugged them out, and leaned them against the open tailgate.

"Is that it?" Conchita wanted to know, shoving another box into the loaded station wagon.

"Everything but the Tupperware."

On my way back from the kitchen, I made a quick side trip. After scooping up the layout of the August *Insight* off Willet's desk, I opened the file and took one copy each of the May, June, and July issues, tucking everything in my tote bag to look at later. In one of them Willet might have published the review that signed his death warrant. Fortunately, his ghost didn't materialize over my shoulder to protest that I was graverobbing. But why would he be angry? I was the living embodiment of the walking curse of the dead. I grabbed the box of Tupperware when I heard Conchita yelling.

"Keep your lousy hands off me!"

I got all the way to the front porch before seeing that it wasn't the wraith of Jerrold Willet that had set her off.

With his hand poised menacingly over his holster, the policeman standing beside her growled at me, "Hold it right there, sister."

I froze. "Certainly."

"How many more of you in the house?" he barked.

Conchita barked right back. "This asshole thinks we're burglars, but I told him we don't turn professional until after dark."

"There's just the two of us, Officer." I ignored her unhelpful explanation and tried to soothe his wounded feelings. "But we're not thieves. Really."

He gestured at the overflowing cartons and the television set sitting on the ground. "This stuff belong to you?"

"Well, not to me." I smiled uneasily and shifted the box in my arms. "To this lady. She used to live here. I'm only helping her move a few things."

"I told him," Conchita said belligerently, "but this pig won't believe me."

Trying to sound a little more conciliatory than my fellow crook, I explained, "I know the situation could be misinterpreted, but it's not what you think."

"You have any ID? A driver's license?"

Awkwardly, I put down the box and dug in my tote bag for my billfold. "Yes, but it's a California license. I'm just visiting Santa Fe." Did he think I'd come all this way to steal Conchita's old clothes? Or maybe her Tupperware. It, at least, was in good shape.

He took my license and eyed it suspiciously. "What about the Pontiac? You hold registration on it?"

"No," I admitted, clearly headed on a downward spiral. First burglary, then grand theft auto. "The station wagon belongs to a mutual friend, Vanessa Harper. You can ask her. She'll tell you she lent it to us for the evening."

"You borrowed it, huh?" He sounded as if he'd heard that one before. "Sit tight, ladies. I gotta do some checking." He walked to his patrol car to radio in for my criminal record.

Conchita sat down on the front step. "What lousy stinking luck," she complained.

"Don't panic. As soon as he finds out all my parking tickets are paid in full, he'll let us load up the car and leave."

"Maybe not."

"What do you mean?" I asked, not liking the sound of Conchita's tone.

"I mean, technically speaking, we're not supposed to be here."

"How technically? You do have permission from Willet's lawyer to get your things, don't you?"

"No."

"Then where did you get the key?" I asked, beginning to be really worried.

"It was mine. I kept it. But that's not the problem."

Oh yes it is, I wanted to say. Since we didn't have the estate's permission, we'd just committed a felony. Breaking and entering. But Conchita was explaining why even she thought we were in trouble.

As my heart sank lower and lower, almost to the soles of my white sandals, she gave me the bad news. After their last parting of ways, Jerrold Willet had gotten a restraining order, barring her from the premises. Conchita hadn't packed her suitcase and walked out as quietly as she had implied. On her way past the garage she'd broken a few window panes. And after she'd backed down the driveway, there were two dents in Willet's Buick, and the mailbox was no longer standing at the curb.

"Do you want me to tell you what makes this all worse?" she brooded darkly.

"I'd rather be spared the details."

"Those paintings you insisted on taking. I gave them to Jerrold. We're probably in possession of stolen property."

Not probably and not just we. The paintings were in Vanessa's car which we "borrowed" with a forged out-of-state driver's license. "Wonderful," I groaned, feeling the weight of the magazines in my tote bag. No doubt about those. I really had stolen them.

Two things saved our skin. The policeman returned our IDs for lack of evidence against us and let Conchita call a neighbor to vouch for her. Maybe Mrs. Martinez had witnessed too many shenanigans from her kitchen window to think highly of Conchita's character, but at least she recognized the *niña* who used to live next door. She also verified that the tattered raincoat was one Conchita used to wear. That was certification.

The policeman apologized for giving us a hard time. It seemed there'd been a rash of daytime break-ins recently, and since he knew the house was empty, he just wanted to check. "Sorry for the misunderstanding," he said.

When he left, Mrs. Martinez patted my partner in crime on the arm. "I know you feel bad about what happened to Mr. Willet. I wanted to go to the funeral myself, but I didn't have a ride. Was there a big crowd?"

"I don't know," Conchita said tersely. "I didn't go either."

Mrs. Martinez looked around in embarrassment. "Yes, well . . . you have a lot to do." Her eyes rested briefly on the splash of oil paintings leaning against the station wagon. "Oh, my, I left my iron on." She scuttled across the lawn.

Conchita watched her go into the house. "Pretty obvious, isn't it?"

"What?"

"She thinks I killed Jerrold."

"Don't be silly. She left her iron on."

"The policeman thinks I'm a thief."

"Not anymore. That's all been straightened out."

She smiled cynically. "And you think I'm crazy."

Chapter
12

"That slimy toad! That vicious fraud! If he weren't already dead, I'd kill him all over again."

When I opened my eyes, Vanessa was waving the mock-up of *Insight* over my head. "Did you read this piece of garbage? Do you know what Jerrold Willet said about us?" she raged.

"Yes, but how do you know? Where did you get that?"

"From your tote bag," she admitted unabashed. "I saw the corner sticking out so I took it. You weren't going to hide this from me, were you?"

Obviously not, if I left it in such a public place. While I dragged my tired body out of bed, Vanessa marched around the room in her nightgown, rattling pages and quoting. "'The Discriminating Palette, the newest so-called art gallery to spawn itself on Canyon Road, is neither discriminating nor palatable.' Can you believe that? Spawn!" She almost choked on the word. "As if we were salmon who didn't have the decency to swim upstream."

"Don't take it to heart," I advised her uselessly, going to the closet for my robe.

Vanessa stalked after me, spitting out the phrases I'd read the night before and decided not to show her. "'Its pretentiously cute name would more appropriately grace the golden arches of a fast-food chain.'" Her cheeks flushed with fury. "I spend weeks dreaming up a clever pun and he calls it 'pretentious.' That's a disgusting thing to say. Almost as bad as 'cute.' Ellie, do you think we should have called ourselves the Harper Metcalf Gallery of Modern Art?"

"Not at all," I said honestly, groping under the bed for my slippers and coming up one short.

Her eyes scanned to the bottom of the page. "Oh, God, will you listen to this. According to that lousy creep, we're also 'a tawdry tourist trap in another adobe cliché.'"

With one foot bare and one foot raised on a two-inch wedge, I hobbled across the room and tried unsuccessfully to take the papers from her clenched fist. "Nessa, you're getting all upset for no reason. None of this is going to be published, so why burst a blood vessel over an article no one will ever see?"

"It just makes me furious, that's all. He meant for all of Santa Fe to read it . . . to laugh at me," she said fiercely, her eyes too bright.

"Hey, this is nothing. You should see what he says about Conchita."

"Not that she's a synthetic imitation of a dime store shlock peddler." Vanessa pointed to the middle paragraph in outrage.

"No, but he says she's reduced 'art' to a three-letter word."

"Big deal. He calls the gallery a façade of a façade of a façcade." Her startlingly green eyes filled with angry tears.

"That is terribly overwritten," I consoled her. "And I'm sure he was going to edit it out. He put an extra 'c' in that last façade anyway."

"Don't defend him," she railed, smashing the pages into a ball and tossing it to the floor. "He wasn't going to change a word of this slander. It was ready to go to the printer. He wanted to ruin us."

"Take it easy. You told me yourself that inviting Jerrold Willet to the opening didn't guarantee a polite bread and butter thank-you note in his review. There's no reason to get hysterical because he came through the way you expected." I patted her shaking shoulders. "Besides, he couldn't have done the gallery any harm. Conchita was your ace in the hole, remember?"

Feverishly Vanessa wiped at her cheeks, but the tears kept raining down. "Ruth talked to him and he promised to be fair to us. She told me so! I was afraid he'd write something like this, just because he and Conchita hated each other."

From outside, there was the sound of hurried footsteps across the patio, then a knock at the curtained window. "Nessa? What's the matter? What are you crying about?"

"Willet lied to you. He was going to print the article the way you saw it," she answered on a sob, throwing herself on the unmade bed and bursting into a storm of weeping.

"Quiet!" Ruth said sharply. "I'm coming right in."

Wondering whether I should offer Vanessa some ice water or throw a glass of it on her, I temporized by collecting the scattered papers off the floor. Where could I put them? In the trash can this time? Not that it mattered now; the damage was done. Vanessa had read them; Ruth had had the pleasure already; and I'd probably have to break back into Jerrold Willet's house to return what I stole.

The three of us sitting around the bedroom in our nightgowns might have looked like an overage slumber party, but none of us were doing much kidding around. Instead, I was trying to justify becoming a sneak thief.

It was easier than I had expected. Conchita had given the gallery owners a dramatic account of yesterday's adventure, so they knew I'd been tricked into abetting her illegal search and seizure mission. My compounded felony was excused as readily as Conchita's peccadillo. I was a sleuth, after all, so whatever criminal acts I perpetrated on my own were routine skullduggery and for a good cause.

What I'd brought back from Willet's studio, however, wasn't so easily dismissed. I'd swiped all those copies of *Insight* as research material, but I said that only the earlier issues were significant. Not that they were any help in pinpointing an artist with a slur to avenge. In the past three months, Willet had insulted enough people to populate the entire left bank of the Rio Grande. Only Picasso earned a modicum of praise from the hard-to-please critic. But, as I pointed out cheeringly, unpublished diatribes didn't count. No one had seen the layout of the August issue before Jerrold Willet was shot. Or almost nobody. Ruth had had a peek when she paid him a visit four days before the gallery opening.

"What did he say?" I asked her.

"Nothing much," she answered noncommittally, laying a cold compress on her partner's aching head.

"But you told me . . ." Vanessa started.

Ruth interrupted her smoothly. "Hush, don't try to talk just yet. Rest a little while."

"Did he promise to change the review?" I pursued.

"He said he would reconsider carefully after evaluating the show. Maybe he did plan to rewrite the article. We'll never know now, will we?" Ruth glanced at me coolly.

What puzzled me was why Willet had let her read that devastating critique. Unless he wanted to prove to her she'd wasted a trip, that his mind was made up. "Did he say anything to you at the reception about making some editorial changes?"

"I didn't speak to him last Saturday." Ruth seemed annoyed that I was lingering on a topic Vanessa found distressing. "Not about that, anyway."

Really? I wondered why. It would have been good business to find out if the ill wind that blew in Conchita's direc-

tion was going to sideswipe the gallery. What I wanted to
ask, but couldn't, or wouldn't, or shouldn't, was if the two
women understood the implications. Hoping against hope
for a favorable review was one thing. But they knew in advance that Willet gave the gallery's address as the best place
on Canyon Road to buy justifiable refuse. Did they really
believe an egotistical perfectionist like Willet would play
"fair" with any gallery supporting the artist he loved to hate?
With a shrine to Melinda's squandered talents hanging on his
walls at home?

Probably Ruth had known from the time of her visit to the
man exactly what was in store. That would explain why she
didn't bother to discuss the problem with him the night of
the party; she knew there was no chance at all for a few
timely words of praise to appear in *Insight* next month. It
seemed equally logical to assume that she had postponed
telling Vanessa about the impending thunderbolt. Judging
from my friend's reaction this morning, Nessa badly needed
shielding from all such unpleasant news.

"I know what you're thinking," Ruth said. "I shouldn't
have trusted him." Her slippers clopped on the brick floor
as she returned from the bathroom with a glass of water
and two aspirin for Vanessa. "It was worth a try to ask
for his cooperation, though not getting a recommendation
wouldn't have been a matter of life and death."

Interesting choice of words. Even more interesting, Ruth
just contradicted what she had said a week ago. The way I
remembered it, both women had been very worried last Saturday night about how much damage Willet could do to the
fledgling gallery's reputation. I was the one who had insisted
that nobody pays attention to critics. Obviously, they had
disagreed if Ruth had gone to bargain with him beforehand,
which brought me back to the same old question with no
new answer. How much influence did a magazine like *In-*

sight carry? I still contended it was too little to kill for. But if I was right, why had Willet been murdered?

"How are you feeling, Nessa? Better now?" Ruth asked.

"Much."

"Good." Ruth stood up. "I'm going to get dressed, but you stay in bed until your headache's gone. And don't worry. Ellie and I will get our own breakfast." She gave me a tight smile before leaving the room.

"I'm sorry, Ellie." Vanessa's arm was flung over her face. "I didn't mean to go off the deep end. It just threw me for a loop, imagining how unbearable it would be if everyone in Santa Fe saw those miserable lies about the gallery."

"Reading is not believing." I pulled on a pair of slacks and a shirt.

"You just don't realize the power of the press," she said in a gloomy voice.

"Neither does anyone else. That's why so many newspapers are going out of business."

"That's not why." A wan smile tugged at her lips. "It's the price."

"A whole twenty-five cents?"

"No, the cost of higher wages. Replacing old equipment, unions. Newspapers can't afford it."

"And you think that proves the press has power?" I slapped on some blusher and lipstick.

"Okay, you made your point." She rolled over on her side to face me more cheerfully.

"Good. Now take a nap. The gallery doesn't open for another hour and Ruth can handle unlocking the door."

"What are you going to do?" she wanted to know.

"Finish my red-hot love affair with Sean O'Donnell. In the next chapter, I'll be enjoying a consummation devoutly to be wished."

"Afterward, why don't you take the car and go shopping," Vanessa suggested in a good imitation of her normal manner.

We'd talked about me needing a new dress for tonight's date with Adam, something a little more glamorous than anything I owned. But after all this raw emotion, a shopping trip was the farthest thing from my mind.

"What's wrong with my basic black? It makes me look thin."

She raised an eyebrow. "Because Adam already saw how thin you look in it, and black is boring. The Pampered Maiden on Water Street has a great selection of slinky stunners. You should go there."

"I will," I promised, "even though I think something called 'The Well-Preserved Matron' would be more my speed."

That feeble witticism won a full-fledged smile from the patient. "Don't be silly," she said.

As I shut the bedroom door quietly behind me, Frank loomed up in the hall. "Is Vanessa okay?" he asked anxiously.

"She's fine. All she needs is a little rest."

"What gave her the whim-whams anyway?"

"I did."

"Naw." He shook his head. "You never."

"Well, maybe I had a little help from Willet." I put a finger to my lips. "She's trying to sleep. Let's go in the kitchen."

Over a cup of coffee, I confessed my crime to Frank. After all, he'd confessed plenty to me.

"Stealing, Miss Ellie? I'm downright shocked."

"Me too. What a dumbo I was to leave those pages in plain sight where Vanessa would see them."

"You want to watch that kinda thinking. You're sorry you got caught, not sorry you did it."

"All I wanted to do was find out who had a motive for killing Willet . . . besides you," I defended myself.

Frank eyed me calmly. "You find anything?"

"A bill you sent him. But since the police didn't confiscate it as evidence, they must not think it has anything to do with the case. That make you feel better?"

He shrugged. "What would make me feel real good is getting paid for that work."

"You should demand the money from the estate. Take it to small claims court if necessary. What I don't understand is why Willet didn't pay you. Was he a cheapskate or just an all-around bastard?"

"Ornery, and stubborn to boot." Frank smiled cynically. "The guy hired me to add a greenhouse on the south side of the house. Said it'd cut his heating bills way down and give him a place to grow his flowers. He handed me the plans already drawn and I built it to his specs. That was in April. Then the warm weather hit us and he said it got too durn hot in there. His orchids were sunburnt or some such foolishness. Made him madder'n a wet hen. Now get this, Miss Ellie. He says it's my fault the plans didn't call for no overhang to shade all them windows from the sun. I'm the expert; I shoulda told him!"

"So he wouldn't give you a check until you installed an awning?"

Frank nodded. "Only I wasn't gonna do no more till I got what was owing me. He was already two months late settling up, and besides, I never laid title to being no architect."

"Didn't you talk to him about it? Ask for partial payment at least?"

"Oh, I tried reasoning with him. But there weren't no reason in him. Last time, he whooped and hollered till the neighbors came out-of-doors, craning their necks to see who was causing all the ruckus. I just got in the truck and drove off, with him still shouting and shaking his fist at me."

"You must be telling Ellie about your quarrel with Jerrold." Ruth closed the kitchen door behind her, then went to the counter to pour herself a cup of coffee. Her dark brown skirt and beige blouse were as nondescript as the bland expression on her face.

"When was this argument?" I asked Frank.

"A week ago Friday," he admitted. "But then, like I told Billy Wayne Fisk, the man gave everybody a fair chance to be riled at him."

"Did he ever." Ruth stood at the counter and sipped her coffee. "Even dead, he managed to upset Vanessa this morning. I don't know why I went to see him. Not that I pleaded for mercy, you understand. I just wanted to test the waters." She smiled dryly.

And found them too hot for comfort?

Frank went back to work and I mulled over my alternatives. Either I could try setting my mind at rest at the risk of sounding nosy, or I could stick my head firmly in the sand and pretend everything was fine, great, hunky-dory. No doubt which was the smart move, but I couldn't make up my mind to be smart. Not yet, anyway.

So I offered to make Ruth some breakfast, though worming information out of her proved a lot harder than frying French toast. She swallowed every bite and managed to keep her lips sealed at the same time. Quite a trick. I bet she won at poker too.

Finally I was reduced to asking point-blank if I could do anything for Vanessa. I was starting to worry about her.

Ruth wiped the maple syrup off her fingers. "She's tougher than you think. A little high-strung, but she'll be up and working in no time. Anyway, I can hold down the fort."

I never doubted it, but that was hardly the point.

Ruth pushed away her empty plate. "Don't underestimate your friend. She's pulling her weight. This gallery depends on her taste, her connections, her charm. What I supply is dull by comparison."

That was a lovely tribute and I admired Ruth's loyalty to her partner. "Hey, I'm not sitting in judgment. Anyone could get nervous starting a business and dealing with a murder in the backyard at the same time. To tell the truth, she's damn lucky to have you. Charm and connections are fine and dandy, but bookkeeping and common sense are even more necessary for commercial success. The two of you obviously make a great team."

Maybe it wasn't all beer and skittles being the practical half of the dynamic duo, but Ruth seemed embarrassed by my flattering words of praise. She never exhibited much emotion, but for once there was a trace of extra color in her cheeks. "Yes, we do. Still, it's been difficult putting the gallery on its feet under the circumstances."

Which circumstances? I wondered, hoping she didn't mean having a guest constantly underfoot.

"This can't have been a very entertaining week for you, either." She shook her head in sympathy. "Even if murder is your hobby," she added with an enigmatic smile.

Was Ruth hinting she wished me back in California? Or was that just another little something I was imagining?

Deciding to take all explanations at face value for the moment, I spent the rest of the morning in the patio with my nose buried in *Triggerfinger*. After I turned the last page, where Sean and his lady love stroll hand in hand into a Yugoslavian sunset, I wandered out to the gallery.

Vanessa seemed none the worse for her recent nerve storm. Her red hair gleamed with highlights while her white knit sleeveless dress skimmed her slender body attractively. Even the smudged blue shadows beneath her eyes simply made them seem more luminous than usual. When I asked how she was doing, she replied gaily that she felt marvelous and I had to go shopping.

So once again I took Nessa's car keys and ventured the byways of Santa Fe's tourist-clogged center. This time the Fates were kind. Vanessa's map was one straight line and two left turns; even *I* couldn't get lost. And, miracle of miracles, finding a parking place was almost as simple. A Winnebago full of Japanese tourists pulled away from a spot on Galisteo and I nabbed it, right out from under the nose of a blonde in a Saab. A good omen, I thought, slamming the car door shut and walking jauntily into the Pampered Maiden.

Once inside the boutique, I received the pampering promised. Two saleswomen converged on me from opposite sides of the room. The one with the measuring tape around her neck beat the other out by a hair, chirruping, "Can I help you?"

Glancing around at the tantalizing displays hanging from velvet posts and brass hooks, I was tempted to push my luck to the limit. "Do you have something that will make me look like a sex goddess on the right side of thirty?"

She made a circle with her thumb and forefinger. "Our most popular number." She led me to a rack and showed me three versions of the cat lady. One was a backless blue, one an almost frontless white. The third, a clingy red "can that be me?" model, I took back to the dressing room and tried on.

It was stunning all right, but there was one teensy problem. "When I lower my shoulder, the strap falls off and I . . . uh . . . fall out," I told the saleslady.

"What do you want? Sex goddess or girl next door?"

"I'm not sure." We both stared at me in the mirror.

"It doesn't need alterations," she said practically.

"Except for the strap."

"I'll throw in a safety pin, no extra charge."

"A bargain I can't refuse. Do you take Visa?"

Of course. Plus every other credit card known to mankind, making it horribly easy for a woman to spend more than she could possibly afford. Well, an occasional extravagance was excusable. After all, I had a reputation to live up to: the cat lady's. In this dress, I'd be as sultry and glamorous as she ever dared be.

What a fantasy! And what a thump coming back down to earth when I discovered that wonderful me had locked the keys inside Vanessa's station wagon. I tramped back into the dress shop with my purchase and asked if the sex goddess could use their telephone.

"Nessa? Could you bring over another set of car keys? That's dumb, not having a spare. About as dumb as locking them in the car. Listen, would it be easier if I just rented a dressing room here for the night? . . . Yes, I bought something and you'll love it. . . . Okay, tell Frank I'll be waiting outside. Thanks."

Ten minutes later, Frank's beat-up old truck rounded the corner and continued down the street. A few minutes later, it pulled around the corner again and kept going. I waited a little while, then saw Frank walking up the block toward me from the opposite direction.

"I didn't have any trouble finding a parking place," I greeted his scowl.

"Damn tourists," he muttered. "Sorry, Miss Ellie, no offense."

"That's all right. I might have bagged the best spot in town, only now I'm stuck in it."

"Not for long, you ain't." He put a key in the lock, fiddled with it for a second, then swung the door open.

"I thought Vanessa didn't have another set."

"She don't."

"Then what did you use?"

"A trick."

"Ah, something else you picked up along the way." Before he could ask what I was doing, I locked the door and closed it again. "Show me how the trick works."

Frank shook his head at me. "Okay, take a look. This here's a Pontiac so's any GM key'll fit in the slot. I slip mine in, jiggle it around a little, and the door's open faster than a fox can raid a chicken coop."

"That's fantastic. Then you hot-wire the car."

"Don't need to bother, not when somebody leaves the keys in the ignition." With a smile he took them out and dropped Vanessa's dangling chain into my palm.

Before he could ask what I was doing, I tossed it on the front seat, then pushed down the button and slammed the door shut. "Let me try."

It took me a lot longer than Frank to work the jiggling trick, but finally I heard the tumblers click back. "Not bad for a beginner, huh?" I handed him his truck key.

"You do show promise," he grinned. "Never did see anybody catch on so fast."

Now I was really impressed with myself. "Can you teach me how to pick a regular lock? On a house?"

"What for?" he asked suspiciously.

"For fun. As long as I have this native ability, why not develop its fullest potential?"

"I ain't so sure that's a good idea."

"Come on. Don't be a spoilsport. Everybody's entitled to have a hobby."

"Okay." His eyes glinted with amusement. "Meet you at the gallery in ten minutes."

It was only after he left that I realized the keys were locked in the car again.

Chapter
13

My mother always said practice makes perfect. Of course, she also said it would make me a concert pianist someday. Her little prodigy fell short of Carnegie Hall material; but when it came to picking locks, Van Cliburn couldn't share the same stage with me. His talent was on the keyboard. I didn't need keys. While Frank sat at the table as a captive audience, I burgled my way in and out of the kitchen door to the sound of my own applause.

"Another encore?" I insisted modestly.

"Ain't you gettin' tired of this yet?" He tried to stifle a yawn.

"Tired? On the eve of my debut when I'm giving such a stellar performance? How can you ask? Obviously, you've never heard that the show must go on and on and on?" I laughed at the expression on his face. "Perk up. I'm dedicating the next curtain call to you. My teacher and mentor," I bowed with a flourish, "who never lost faith in my inherent ability to manipulate a hair pin."

"No, you got a knack for doing the wrong thing." He tilted the chair back on two legs and crossed his arms behind his head.

"And this is just the beginning. There's a whole world waiting at my fingertips. Safes to be cracked, vaults to be opened, and we haven't even touched on combination locks yet."

"I ain't gonna give you none to touch neither," he said with a lazy smile. "You're a dangerous woman."

"Music to my ears. And a tribute to these hands." I held them out for special commendation. "Precision instruments. The tools of the trade. Along with a few pieces of helpful hardware," I acknowledged fairly. "But that just proves what the right kind of lessons will do. No, don't get up yet," I waved him back in the chair. "I want one last try at topping my own speed record. An illegal entry in under two minutes."

I didn't win a gold medal, but two minutes and fifty-seven seconds earned me the Frank Ott Good Housebreaking Seal Of Approval. Wait till I tell my mother. There were guys in the pen who couldn't do that well. Frank warned me against picking my way into a similiar position, but I assured him that my new-found talent for trouble would never be put to practical use unless I happened to lock myself out of the kitchen. Then I'd have to apply what he taught me or how could I get to the refrigerator?

At the thought of food, I realized it was nearly time to eat again. And how long my one-woman show had been running. No wonder I wasn't leaving my audience wanting more. I'd been burglarizing the door for over two hours, and Adam was due here in less than one. Now I really had a speed record to break. Be bathed, groomed and glamorous before a seven-thirty dinner reservation. Based on past performance, and because of this one, I'd miss the appetizer if I didn't step on it. Frank said that with my dedication to dishonesty, I shouldn't plan on such early suppers.

He was right. I should have planned on my hair looking awful. I attacked with mousse, styling gel, spray, wetting it and starting all over again, but nothing helped. Even the curling iron was a useless weapon. The only solution was to tie a scarf around my head and pretend it was the latest fashion in California evening wear.

I was still sitting at the vanity when Vanessa knocked on the bathroom door. "Are you nearly ready?" she peeked inside. "I guess not. Why do you keep changing your hair?"

"Because everything on the right side sticks up, the left droops down, and if I wear it like a punk rocker, I'll have to paint each side of my face a different color."

"Have you considered a compromise?"

"That's exactly what I'm considering. Shaving off all my hair and going bald. Do you think the style would look good on me?"

"Wonderful. It'll accent your sexy ears. But if you want Adam to whisper sweet nothings into them, you'd better get the rest of your body moving. He's here."

"He can't be," I moaned.

"You're right. It's his twin brother drinking my good Chablis. Should I expose him as a fraud or offer him a refill?"

"If it's Adam's identical twin, give him two refills." I flipped the hair dryer back on. "Make that three," I called as the bathroom door closed. "And some cheese and crackers."

Just because I was in a mad rush to be almost on time, almost everything went wrong. The same slippery fingers that opened locks so deftly let a bottle of moisturizer slip through them and not so deftly smeared mascara below one eye. The last snafu was losing my black jet earrings. I looked everywhere, but they weren't on the dresser, or under the bed, or in my sexy ears. Giving up, I went for pearl drops instead, and lying next to them in my jewelry case were the black jets.

Finally I was assembled and feeling guilty for making Adam wait so long. He probably missed the appetizer too by now, unless he'd left without me. I wouldn't blame him. Only dumb bunnies are late for very important dates, and aside from being idiotically overdue, I was unappreciative. Adam Montgomery had paid me the highest compliment a man can give a woman these days. He was taking me out for a second time when we hadn't even gone to bed together a first time.

Of course, I was being facetious. Adam was a gentleman, unlike some people who thought an enchilada plate was fair prelude to hopping in the sack. Adam admired my intelligence, my wit. He might not want to admire anything else either. After all, famous, handsome authors could have their pick of beautiful women; and even in my new red dress with no safety pin, I wasn't a glamor queen. Cute, maybe. No, upgrade that to strikingly attractive, I decided after one final glance in the mirror. With an abundance of chesty charms that verged on indecent exposure every time the shoulder strap slipped down. If I weren't careful, I might become a little too exposed for public dining. That didn't mean the view would rouse Adam to mad passionate desire in the middle of a crowded restaurant or that I was trying to compete with a salad bar. No reading the future in any lettuce leaves. Whatever came of this evening would be as au naturel as the damp curls frizzing on top of my head.

I grabbed my clutch purse and stuffed in some essentials. Lipstick, handkerchief, perfume atomizer, breath mints, then dashed down the hall to the gallery. Maybe it was an omen, but my entrance was highlighted by one bare shoulder.

Adam, or his identical twin, was still sipping Chablis, although the plate of Brie and Wheat Thins was empty. In an unhurried move, he set his wineglass on the table and rose to his feet. I bet he hadn't rushed into that pale gray suit without checking the creases first, and I was sure he'd had no trouble arranging his smooth black hair.

"Sorry I'm so late," I apologized as he watched me shove the errant strap back in place.

"No problem. Nessa's been telling me about your bad luck today, getting locked out of the car. Twice." His blue eyes crinkled in amusement.

It was sweet of Vanessa to provide an excuse with the snack, but it must have been some story if Adam thought the half-hour delay had taken me an entire afternoon to overcome. I hoped she hadn't made me seem too ditzy, though it was better than telling him that I'd been whiling away the hours honing my criminal skills.

"The Chablis was excellent," he thanked Vanessa. "And the Brie."

"I hope it didn't spoil your appetite," she said with a wink at me.

"Not at all. How's your appetite, Ellie?"

"Immense." I held out my silk stole to him.

With a smile Adam draped it around me, his hand lingering over my right shoulder. "Ready?"

"All set." I looked up at him.

After a slow start, the evening picked up in pace as Adam's Maserati zoomed us across town to one of Santa Fe's elegant eateries. We hadn't lost our reservations by default, though they'd probably hold a table indefinitely for a man of Adam's prominence. I followed the maître d' to a dim, candlelit corner, keeping my shoulders on the up and up.

Over escargots swimming in garlic butter, I told Adam how much I liked *Daggers Drawn,* and by now I could recite chapter and verse instead of nodding vaguely when specifics were mentioned. He was pleased by my compliments, and surprised that someone with a taste for belles-lettres would enjoy his rough and tumble kind of books so much.

"Let's face it, I write for popular appeal, not Shakespearean scholars."

"I told you I'm no scholar, Shakespearean or otherwise. That was Vanessa's advance billing. But you made Sean unusually literate for a man of action. After all, how could he fly a Lear jet blindfolded unless he'd been able to read the instrument panel beforehand?" I joked. "Besides, the CIA won't hire anyone without a college degree these days. Their requirements are very stiff."

"I know." Adam laughed at my analysis. "I once did a brief stint for them."

"You're kidding? You and Sean both went on secret missions behind enemy lines? No wonder he can escape the clutches of death so adroitly. All that derring-do comes from the man who dared to do it."

"Not quite. Sean's exploits aren't autobiographical, though I probably shouldn't spoil your illusions about me. But the closest I ever got to a secret mission was when I worked at Dow Chemical, and the government asked us to do some laboratory testing."

"On germ warfare, or is that classified information?"

"On plastic resins, and we published the results."

"Darn. And I bet you didn't do it in code either."

He poured me another glass of wine as consolation. "Don't be too disappointed. My dull scientific background comes in handy when I'm researching technical material for a book; but to redeem myself in your eyes, I promise to include personal experience next time. In fact, I'm developing a story line now that's based on the strategic space missile program, and I will definitely work plastic resins into the plot."

"And I will definitely tell everyone I was the first to know. Where are you going to put Sean? Undercover at Dow or in a space station?"

"Neither." Adam buttered a roll. "If you promise not to go bragging to the *National Enquirer,* I'll let you in on a deep, dark secret even my publisher doesn't know yet. I'm killing Sean off in the book I'm writing now. This will be his last caper."

That startled me into looking up from my baked baby salmon. "Why?"

"Ever the detective." He shook his head. "You want a motive."

"Well, it's none of my business," I hesitated, then gave in to curiosity, "but I presume there must be a literary reason for ending a string of bestsellers."

"No, a writer's reason. I'm tired of doing the same old thing. I'm ready to start a new string of bestsellers with a character who's more complex. Let's say a slightly more literate man of action." He smiled at me, sharing the inside joke. "Basically, I've run out of ideas on Sean's conventional tactics. For a fresh approach I need to go from supersonic to hypersonic, and he won't transfer. I can't change his time frame or his personality, or his capabilities. Sean O'Donnell doesn't have the scientific know-how for what I'm planning. He'd really be lost in space."

"Can't you send him back to college?"

"They don't even teach the courses I'll be writing about. He'd be the oldest freshman in the twenty-first century, maybe more into the future."

"Oh, then you're switching categories. Will your publisher object to leaving Sean behind?"

"Not as fast as he would if I tried to move a CIA agent into a different genre. From a business point of view, that's literary suicide." Adam cut into his steak, then pantomimed slicing the knife across his throat. "Writing for profit means catering to the public's tastes, and one man's meat is another's baked salmon. That's why books are aimed at very specific markets. People who like mysteries want mysteries, and a member of the science fiction book of the month club would cancel his subscription if the company slipped him an historical saga. By the same token, Sean's loyal following, who buy him as a semi-plausible espionage character, won't accept his sudden rebirth as Captain Marvel."

"Yes, I notice the way bookstores mark each section for their customers' convenience. T stands for thriller. R is romance. And you dial plain old M for murder."

"I detect a little spleen in that comment." He smiled and passed me the silver bread dish. "But don't feel too bad. Sean's residuals will live on. I'd never exterminate my royalties."

No, just his alter ego, I thought with a pang of regret. And just when I was getting attached. Still, I could understand Adam's itch to try something new. Sean O'Donnell did save the world with dependable regularity, and "every hero becomes a bore at last." Unless he can enter the fifth dimension.

"What are you going to do with the cat lady?" I asked, forgetting that was my private nickname for the sultry sexpot who lured the spy in from the cold to her warm bed.

Adam caught the analogy immediately. "I'm not sure about Oriana. We could have her kill Sean, or do you think that would be too cruel?"

"I'll say it's cruel, and you can leave me out of it. I'm not going to be an accessory to murder."

"You've solved enough of them. Why not get credit for planning one? Unless you changed your mind about being listed on the page of grateful acknowledgments," he enticed. "Your name recorded forever in the Library of Congress."

"I was depending on it, but I would like to state for the Congressional Record that I think it's highly unfair for you to bring the characters to life, then expect me to do them in."

"Who said writing's fair?" His eyes glinted in the candlelight.

I didn't need any more encouragement. "Very well, if you really want the benefit of my creative genius, as long as Sean is doomed anyway, let him go in a blaze of glory. Blow him up with explosives. Then have the body so badly burned that a positive identification is impossible. It'll torment his enemies, bring hope to his fans, and leave a poetic license that will never expire. If you or anyone else ever decide the poor guy wasn't so bad after all, he can be resurrected from the ashes."

"I hate to accuse you of plagiarism, but I think Conan Doyle used a similar trick with Sherlock Holmes."

"So? Who says writing's fair?"

Adam threw back his handsome head and let out a hoot of laughter. "You're priceless, Ellie. Blow Sean O'Donnell to kingdom come and leave his spirit for the ghostwriters. I love it."

"Did you say 'blow up'?" a familiar voice pealed cheerfully.

Either she'd been under the table all along or she had better hearing than most old ladies. "Quick," I whispered, clutching Adam's sleeve. "Let's make a run for it."

Too late. She came. She saw. She instantly invented a hundred variations of the story she'd tell tomorrow. "Why, Mr. Montgomery, what an unexpected pleasure." The delighted smile nearly split her face in half. "I didn't realize you were still in town. It's been so long since I've seen you."

Obviously, her binoculars had cracked since last week.

"Mrs. St. Laurent." Adam rose courteously. "I hope you've been well."

"I just had my blood pressure checked. One thirty-nine over ninety. Excellent for a woman my age. And there's Mrs. Gordon." She turned toward me in happy anticipation. "You seem to be flourishing beautifully." Her eyes flickered over Adam, then me again, then my dress, as if she knew all about the falling shoulder strap. "Still working at the gallery?"

At least she got my name right, but it wasn't worth the

effort to correct her about anything else. "They haven't fired me yet," I said agreeably.

"You haven't encountered any problems over there, I take it." Her voice throbbed with hidden meaning.

"Not a one. Except for the air conditioner," I confided. "Every once in a while it goes off for no reason."

"Well, as my late husband used to say, mechanical things can't be trusted too far. They wouldn't work at all without electricity."

Adam's hand twitched at his side, but his face remained politely inscrutable.

"I won't keep you from your dinner any longer, but this was such a delightful surprise." She beamed happily. "And such a coincidence." Her beam fell on me. "Isn't it interesting how I always seem to run across you at restaurants, Mrs. Gordon, though not always with the same escort. How is dear Dr. Siegel?"

"Just hunky-dory," I answered through gritted teeth.

"How nice. And so nice of him to take you ballooning tomorrow. I'm sure you'll have a marvelous experience."

I knew it. She was behind the potted palm at La Fonda. How else could she have found out, unless Jake ran an ad in the paper?

"My sister-in-law's doctor mentioned it," was her lame alibi. "He's another high-flyer." She tittered at her own joke. "Well, I'll be off myself now. You two enjoy yourselves. Mr. Montgomery." She bobbed her head.

"Mrs. St. Laurent."

"Mrs. Gordon."

"Mrs. St. Laurent."

When the name-calling was over, she pattered away in the rustle of taffeta rubbing against corset. "Abominable woman," I muttered, as Adam sat down again.

"Don't pay any attention to her. She's talkative but harmless."

"Except the way she twists things isn't so harmless. By Monday you'll be in the balloon, I'll be in therapy, and Ruth will be leaking cyanide into the air conditioning ducts."

I should have kept a better lid on my annoyance, athough my Freudian slip of the tongue about Ruth wouldn't have meant a thing under normal circumstances. After all, it was her gallery and she was responsible for the cooling system. But Adam wasn't a master of complicated plots for nothing. He picked up on a mystery when Mrs. St. Laurent asked if I was still working there. Her unsubtle hint of trouble afoot was the second clue, and my clever spate of sarcasm filled in the rest. He came to one wrong conclusion though. I was not dating Jake Siegel.

"Don't be embarrassed." Adam smiled at me. "I'm not surprised that we'd both be attracted to the same lovely woman. There's a very special quality about you, Ellie."

My shoulder strap? I wondered, tugging it back up again. "Thank you, Adam. But Dr. Siegel is Vanessa's friend. He just doesn't think anyone should come to New Mexico without seeing why it's the hot air balloon capital of the world."

"He's right, and Dr. Siegel is a very persistent man. You'll probably be seeing a lot more of him too before you leave. He'd be a fool not to try anyway."

Feeling slightly overwhelmed by the flattery, I denied that Jake had any romantic interest in me. Adam seemed about to disagree when we were interrupted by the waiter bearing a pastry cart. He rolled the laden trolley to the table and asked if we'd care to make a selection. I declined, but when Adam insisted I order the melon sorbet with raspberry sauce, I allowed him to persuade me. Ices hardly have any calories. That is, compared to a Lutetia torte.

Once we were alone again, I thought he'd return to the subject of Jake Siegel and my special if unspecified qualities. It was a little disappointing when he didn't, although I was fully prepared to explain Jake as a social aberration foisted on me by my hostess. Instead, Adam got back to the gist of the story; but rather than explaining Mrs. St. Laurent's gossip as an aberration foisted on me, he made two corrections. Ruth's former boss was really a former partner, and her *coup de grâce* was supposedly arsenic, not cyanide.

"Vanessa told me what happened." He tossed it off lightly. "There was some talk in Los Alamos at the time, and a couple of articles in the Santa Fe paper, but no case was ever established."

"You mean, there was an actual investigation?"

"Just an autopsy to determine cause of death," Adam corrected me again, "which was attributed to a massive coronary."

"Why did anyone believe it was foul play?"

"Circumstantial evidence. About six months earlier, Ruth and Ed Wallace had opened a small accounting firm. They'd each bought a life insurance policy naming the other as beneficiary. This is a standard practice so that if a death occurs, the survivor can use the proceeds to buy out a partner's interest in the business from his heirs. Wallace's family created the controversy because he had no history of heart problems, and they thought it was suspicious that he happened to drop dead at Ruth's dining room table."

"Purely circumstantial," I murmured.

"When no evidence was found, that was the end of it. But apparently rumors are still flying."

"Only on broomsticks," I answered, referring to one cherub-cheeked witch in particular. "What happened to the business?"

"The heirs bought Ruth out."

Which gave her double the proceeds to invest in a new venture. Not a bad deal. For the cost of one premium, she reaped the benefits of two. That tale didn't need embellishing, though I could see why Mrs. St. Laurent couldn't resist. However, I wasn't going to make the same mistake. So Ruth collected a little insurance money? That didn't mean she put poison in the soup.

"Some people enjoy assuming the worst," I said to Adam.

"Then you don't assume it. I thought perhaps this new information might put Ruth at the head of your suspect list," he teased.

"Certainly not. Besides, I don't have a list."

"No one is confiding in you anymore, or you haven't been back to pump Billy Wayne Fisk again?"

"Both. But I wouldn't confide in me either. All I've done is label every person at the party a viable suspect. In fact, I've even broadened the scope to include everybody in town who disliked Willet."

"What did you do, conduct a city-wide poll?" he asked in amusement.

"No, I conducted a private inquiry into the last three issues of *Insight* to find an artist with the greatest revenge motive."

"Good thinking. What did you find?"

"That I could have taken a city-wide poll. For one thing, the victims of Willet's most scathing reviews weren't even at the scene of the crime. Plus, that doesn't mean they were the most offended by his criticisms either. Some people fly into a rage at the slightest rebuff."

I was thinking of Leon, but Adam had Conchita in mind. As she had said to me, none of her quarrels with Jerrold Willet were private.

"She fits the bill," I agreed, "but why would Conchita want vengeance at this stage of her career? She became a success despite Willet's efforts to undermine her. Seems a little redundant to shoot him in cold blood when her cartoon characters are having the last laugh. Of course, the police might think it's funnier that she can't account for every minute she spent in the bathroom Saturday night. But then, how many people besides me can prove they never left the buffet? Can you?"

"Afraid not." Adam rubbed his jaw. "But maybe the murderer wasn't out to defend his artistic integrity. It could have been a money motive. Do you know of anyone who stood to gain financially from Willet's death?"

Indeed I did, but I wasn't going to incriminate one unknown nephew and a couple of gallery owners. Two held an advantage, though, especially if they pooled their resources. But who was the more resourceful? Would Vanessa have killed the critic in a fit of pique? Or had Ruth checked the profit and loss ledger then eliminated a debit?

"You know what I've decided?" I met Adam's too-perceptive gaze with a flippant smile. "Nobody killed Jerrold Willet. His murder is a hoax, like Sean's. A set-up. A fake."

"Have you been sipping the wine from your glass or guzzling from the bottle?"

"You're right. I'm babbling. Either order another dessert and coffee, or take me outside so I can walk off the one I've already had."

Instead, he took my hand and rubbed his thumb slowly across the palm while the strap of my dress almost shot off from sheer electricity. "We've been dwelling on a dreary topic of conversation, but I have a great way to make you feel better, and it isn't coffee."

"How much better?" I asked carefully.

The corners of his mouth curved upward. "That depends on you."

"Oh. Well, I'm really not that dependable."

"Just the kind of girl I've always wanted to take home to mother." His thumb moved to my wrist. "But since she lives in Washington, and there aren't any flights scheduled this late in the evening, why don't I take you home with me instead."

"That line can't be plagiarized. I've never heard anything like it before."

"If it doesn't work, I have another original. Don't you want to see where a famous author lives?"

"Adam," I smiled. "The first one was terrific. But the second is Pulitzer Prize caliber."

Not surprisingly, his house was prize-winning material too. Built on, into and atop a jutting crag in the foothills of the Sangre de Cristo Mountains, the place could have been featured as a full-page spread in *Architectural Digest*. From the outside, all I could see was size. When Adam opened the massive, carved oak front door, we stepped into an entry foyer that overlooked four separate levels and at least twice that many stairways connecting one to the other and back again.

It was spectacular. Modern, sleek and designed to accommodate the interesting mixture of leather, high-tech style furniture with unusual accent pieces. Japanese silkscreens, Navajo and Oriental rugs. I got the grand tour, emphasis on grand. As we wound a trail up and down and through the house, I admired the sauna, the weight room, the state-of-the-art kitchen, and finally the living room with its sixteen-foot beamed ceiling, fieldstone fireplace, and wide, undraped windows. On one side, the mountains rose in peaks, while opposite, the lights of the city twinkled below.

"It's magnificent. Everything, including the view." I turned my head from side to side. "How do you decide which way to look?"

"That's an easy choice with you here," he said handsomely. "But we're not finished."

"There's more?"

"The best is yet to come."

Eagerly anticipating I knew not what, I followed him down another short flight of stairs, where I almost turned around at the bottom and flew back up. Was this the best to come? A king-sized bedroom with a king-sized bed and a baby grand piano in one corner?

"Come on in," Adam invited. "Don't you want to see where the famous author writes his deathless prose?" He pointed to a ladder hanging against the wall. "To my loft."

"A loft?" I took a cautious step past the threshold. "Doesn't seem very unusual to me."

"That's the whole point."

I climbed up the rosewood ladder after him. At the top, he offered a strong hand and helped me over the ledge.

"Well, what do you think?"

"Very nice." I surveyed his private domain. "All the comforts of home and then some."

And then some more. Adam's aerie was a sharp contrast to the rest of the house. The tiny loft was a snug retreat, crammed with treasures and mementos along with a few modern touches. It was crowded with bookshelves, an antique oak desk, and a table covered by a computer and two printers.

"You hauled all this furniture up here by ladder, or had it dropped by helicopter?"

Adam said by ramp and pulley. The only window was a small round opening to the stars. I thought it was interesting that he preferred working in this cramped cubbyhole instead of the spacious den. But this was a boy's treehouse, a place to dream. Wasn't that what a writer did? Dream for a living? On his desk was a quaint, old-fashioned paperweight. Two ice skaters skimming across a frozen pond. Charmed by the scene, I picked up the paperweight then turned it over and back again. As the snow came tumbling down, so did my shoulder strap.

While I stood there like a nervous twit, wondering if I

was showing too much ear lobe, Adam crossed the short distance between us and slowly lowered the other strap. Now both sides matched. And I needed two safety pins. Of course, that had been the general idea. Push eventually had to come to shove. I'd bought a dress that was out of my league, then accepted the man's invitation to see his word processor. I shivered at my own audacity. Adam probably thought it was his touch.

That's not to say the sensation of his hand on my bare shoulder didn't have an effect. Or that his kiss didn't have my full cooperation. Breathless, we pulled apart and looked at each other. He was so gorgeous. Prettier than I and a lot more confident. Well, naturally. If he researched all the technical material for his books, why not the love scenes too?

"Standing isn't really very comfortable," he said in a husky voice as if he knew. "Let's go downstairs."

He didn't specify where, but I doubted if he meant to the kitchen or the hall closet. No. We descended the ladder and stayed in the room with the baby grand piano. Funny coincidence, but I'd always had a fantasy about draping myself across a Steinway and singing a torch song, the nightclub lights dimmed, the tinkle of glasses in the background. Only this wasn't a fantasy, and Adam would be stunned if I vaulted on top of his piano and broke into "Stormy Weather." What stunned me was how I got into his bedroom.

He slipped off his jacket and tossed it across a chair. His tie followed. I watched in fascination as he opened the top two buttons of his shirt, but that was the end of the strip for now. It was my turn next. Would Adam mind a short musical reprieve while I thought this over? Probably. It was a little late for me to start rationalizing about a relationship that had no future or to wonder if Adam would call me for a third date if we didn't make love on the second. Besides, I'd come to his house willingly, fully aware that his mother lived in Washington, and here I was. On the verge of a sweet midsummer's madness with Adam on the verge.

His lips brushed the hollow of my throat, nuzzled one of my sexy ears, then searched hungrily for my mouth. He pressed me close to him, and with his tongue sending a tingle of excitement through my body, I could feel the rising passion in both of us. But when he began backing toward the king-sized bed, I balked. No great intellectual decision, my legs just refused to move.

With his hands around my waist, his face inches from mine, he paused. "What's the matter? Aren't you going to spend the night?"

"I'm sorry. I can't." I stepped out of his embrace awkwardly, feeling stupid, silly and more than slightly embarrassed.

He backed off, shaking his head ruefully. "No, I'm sorry. I didn't mean to rush you. Forgive me, Ellie."

I shoved up both straps and said there was nothing to forgive. "I told you that I'm not very dependable." It was a lousy excuse, but Adam was magnanimous enough to provide me with a better one.

"Anyway, you have to get up early in the morning."

"What?" I looked at him blankly. "Oh, yes. That too."

Chapter
14

Jake said that hot air balloons hadn't changed much since the Montgolfier brothers went up in smoke. I did not find his comment reassuring, even after he explained that they were the intrepid pioneers who used a bed of smoldering charcoal in the first ascension of a linen bag. This was a scientific experiment, circa 1783, and the two Frenchmen wisely watched from below; but when their new-fangled flying machine stayed aloft for ten minutes, it proved hot air is lighter than cold air. I'm sure this was a brilliant advance in the field of aerodynamics, except Jake was right; things hadn't advanced much farther since then. Today's fuel system was a handy-dandy, smokeless tank of propane gas, but the original theory still applied. It took heat to get up, and staying up meant flying around with a real fire burning overhead. Maybe the continuing simplicity of the idea appealed to Jake; but when it came to siblings in aviation, I thought Orville and Wilber had a better idea.

In fact, the closer I got to my premier lift-off, the closer I came to cancelling my reservations. From the moment I woke up to countdown minus ten, I was the target of teasing, ridicule, bad puns, unfunny jokes, and the argument that next to polo, ballooning was the sport of kings. I always thought grouse hunting was the second favorite in royal circles, which still should have excluded me, but according to Vanessa I deserved regal status. Had I remembered how "uneasy lies the head that wears a crown," I would have abdicated the minute she dubbed me Queen of Hearts.

With stars in her eyes and visions of sugarplums dancing in her head, she snuggled under the covers, watching me get dressed and marveling at my romantic achievements. "You're amazing, Ellie. Dinner and who knows what else with a fabulous man last night and another one who wants to fly away with you this morning."

"Jake is taking me for a balloon ride, not to the heights of ecstasy. And you already know 'what else' happened last night. Nothing." I zipped up my navy pants.

"You're positive about nothing?" she asked for the sixth time even though I'd given her five variations of "we never went below the waist." "Weren't either of you consumed with a blazing passion?"

"Certainly, but it didn't get out of hand."

"Why not?"

"May I remind you, the reason you thought Adam and I would be such a perfect match was because we could meet on an intellectual plane. Would you reduce that fine ideal to a tawdry physical compulsion?"

"Sure. You drooled with lust the first minute you laid eyes on him."

"True. Crude but true." I looked for my watch on the dresser.

Vanessa tucked the pillow under her chin. "Oh well, if you actually went to Adam's house, climbed every flight of stairs with him peeking up your skirt, and still don't have one sordid detail to report, I'll just have to live with the disappointment."

"We all have our crosses to bear, but you're making me feel guilty. Do you really want the whole *megillah?* Sex, intrigue, flaming passion, duels in the sun?"

"Two out of four will do."

"No problem, then." I grabbed her heavy jacket from the bed. "You can read all about it in his next book."

Which wouldn't be based on any research with me, unless Adam wrote a scene where the cat lady turns into Chicken Little at the last minute and pulls up the strap of her dress. It seemed doubtful. She usually didn't have any straps to pull up, or a dress either for that matter.

At least Adam was polite about the disparity. When I flinched from his touch like a quivering virgin in a Gothic romance, he realized I was in the wrong novel. I, on the other hand, couldn't even read between the lines. Talk about confusing category fiction with uncategorical stupidity. When had I become a vamp? On page 117 of *Daggers Drawn?* I hardly made it to semi-sophisticate by the middle of *The Joys of Cooking in a Wok.* That didn't stop me though. I rushed out and bought a Saturday night special to knock Adam dead, and when he keeled over, I ran like hell before I got caught. Of course, I'd warned him in advance that I was the undependable girl-next-door-to-his-mother type. That's probably why he forgave me for leading him on then changing my mind. Just when I figured my brief literary career was finished, Adam's friendly goodnight kiss revived it. As we got out of the car, he asked if I'd keep Tuesday evening open for him. I said yes immediately, but I was going to do some serious thinking about what to wear.

After that fiasco, there was no place left for me to go but up. I was a lousy femme fatale, but maybe I'd show some promise as a sportswoman. I never had before, but Ruth was coming along to help me. Of all people, that feet-on-the-ground lady was an old pro at having her head in the clouds, and she accepted eagerly when Jake invited her to join the festivities. I crossed the patio and knocked on her door, but Ruth was bleary-eyed and still in her pajamas. She'd been doing some complicated bookkeeping until late last night,

and five A.M. had come around a little early in the day for
her. She was just too exhausted to go.

I told her to climb back in bed. I had to call Jake anyway
to make sure all systems were cleared for take-off, meaning
weather permitting, and he arranged alternate limo service.
A Dr. Fred Martin would swing by for me. He was one of
the people who shared Jake's hobby and the *Hobby Horse*.

There were five owners altogether. A psychiatrist, a surgeon, a dentist and a doctor of ornithology. Fred claimed he
wouldn't be any help in a medical emergency, but it never
hurt to have an accredited birdwatcher around to warn of
migrating geese. He was a funny, cheerful man with a re-
ceding hairline and a nose like a parrot's beak. In between
sneezes (he swore he had allergies and not something contagious), he turned on the car heater and said we were lucky to
have such unseasonably cool mornings this weekend.

Which gave me the opening I'd been waiting for. Why
were we starting out in the cold and the dark? Was this group
a bunch of insomniacs or people simply opposed to sleep on
principle?

When Fred stopped laughing, his answer was so logical
that I might have figured it out for myself eventually. A hot
air balloon works only when there's a significant difference
between the temperature outside and inside the envelope.
The burners can produce plenty of heat but not enough to
compensate when the atmosphere warms up. During the
summer months that usually limited flying time to early evening and the couple of hours right after dawn, which were
enough for some Sunday drivers to take turns piloting their
recreational vehicles.

This was the normal practice for multiple partnerships,
medical and otherwise, he explained. The entire route was
pre-planned, including stopovers where they'd land, refuel,
and change navigators. But not the navigation. Ballooning is
a one-way trip in whatever direction the wind happens to be

blowing, so the rest of the crew followed below in a chase truck to bring everything and everybody back home again.

"Don't worry." He dug an elbow into my rib. "We usually don't have to retrieve any fallen passengers along the way."

Another comedian. I hadn't thought of falling out until he said that. But then, I'd never considered any form of sky-diving until we got to the field, where I discovered I'd be traveling through space in something less than a LEM module.

The launching pad was a wide stretch of mesa to the west of town, occupied by sagebrush, jackrabbits, a familiar ja-lopy, and a four-wheel drive jeep with a U-Haul attached to the rear. The area was lit by several Coleman lanterns, and in the spotlight was the bottom half of the *Hobby Horse*. If words never do justice to a subject, neither had Jake. Or Ruth. Or anyone else. I had trash cans bigger than that wicker basket they called a gondola. Nobody told me that it was standing room for only two. Nobody mentioned that the sides scarcely reached waist high. And nobody offered me a parachute. Fred claimed I didn't need one. The balloon itself was a parachute that would float us down in the unlikely case of some malfunction. I couldn't see why it would spoil the fun to have a standby for personal use, but Jake came through in style. He said I'd be fine as long as I didn't lean over too far.

Daphne Borrows was more pragmatic. She poured me a cup of coffee from her Thermos and told them to blow all that hot air into the balloon. Everyone's scared the first time, she assured me. On her maiden voyage, she didn't even go.

"How did you like it the second time?" I asked.

"Marvelous. I didn't come to earth for a week. It was hell in the operating room, though."

Dr. Borrows was the cutest, shortest surgeon I'd ever met, which was at eye-level. Her brown hair was cut in just the style I'd tried to achieve the night before, and she was wearing the oddest assortment of army fatigues the U.S. government had ever made in her size. They were her peeling clothes, she told me. It was chilly now, but as the day warmed, she stripped. First the camouflage jacket came off, then the pants, and finally her jogging suit. Beneath were shorts and a T-shirt. I was tempted to ask if she ever had any trouble with shoulder straps.

Apparently not. She was happily married to the dentist, who couldn't come today. He had an emergency root canal at eight o'clock. "It's not a life-threatening situation," she laughed, "just too painful for Bob to ignore. He's a sweetheart."

He was also a dedicated dentist if he were willing to forgo a rare summer ride on his pleasure craft for the sake of a patient who'd obviously procrastinated too long. Mrs. St. Laurent's sister-in-law, no doubt. But losing him and Ruth left the crew short-handed, or would have if Daphne hadn't taken me under her tiny wing.

The sun was still hiding behind the mountains, but the sky had lightened considerably as we all pitched in to unload the balloon from the back of the trailer and spread the huge nylon envelope on the ground. While Fred and Jake hooked the coupling cables to the basket, Daphne showed me the rest of the ropes, from the drop line to the ground moorings. Dr. B. explained each stage of preparation as thoroughly as if I were assisting in a surgical procedure.

She interpreted the instrument panel in the gondola for me, altimeter, variometer, pyrometer, and compass, the only reading I understood without translation. The fuel pattern she called a plumber's nightmare. I didn't even try to understand that. It was a maze of hoses and valves that went from the propane tanks to the overhead burner. But I did learn that the number one tank was always on the right and the back-up tank stayed on the left. Daphne said the second was a redundant fuel system, although even in grammatical terms it wouldn't be repetitious if the first ten gallons ran dry sooner than expected. Besides, the rule came from the FAA, not the NEA.

Thank goodness there was one doctor in this crowd who had the right prescription. I felt a lot easier about going aloft after Daphne's briefing and her assurances that all the equipment had been checked and assembled last night before they packed everything into the U-Haul.

"Funny how we always use Jake's garage as the hangar," she smiled, "when we always use my Jeep to tow the trailer. But his old Ford can scarcely pull its own back fenders. You close to buying another car yet?" She razzed him. "Or are the alimony payments still competing with the..." She clamped her lips shut in exasperation and looked at me. "I'm sorry. That was tactless. You and Jake have something going and I..."

"No," I interrupted as fast as I could get my tongue over my teeth. "We don't. Honestly. I'm just visiting a friend of his and he's being," I groped for an appropriately bland word, "kind."

I wasn't sure Daphne believed me. But then, she knew Jake. And maybe all three ex-wives and the string of chippies who must have followed. I could just see him rubbing his unkempt beard and telling some gullible idiot that he could cure her sexual inhibitions. Like mine, for instance.

Before I could stage another round of protests, Daphne dragged me over to the two men and announced that I was now an official member of the crew. Thanks to her high level of instruction, I had graduated from intern to resident assistant co-pilot.

"Do a good job," Jake said, "and when we land, you get double the champagne."

"Champagne? You're actually going to toast my accomplishment with alcohol?"

"Nobody drinks anything," he grinned. "In the fine tradition of ballooning, first-timers get anointed with the bubbly."

"An external application, you mean."

"Poured right over the head." He was indecently pleased at the prospect of dumping a bottle just where it would do the most damage to my dignity.

"Here she blows," Fred called as he turned on the portable generator and the fan.

The blades began whirring, sending a stream of air past the balloon's reinforced rim, and the *Hobby Horse* slowly started to inflate. It was difficult to hear anything else over the noise of the machines; but in a short time the billowing canopy was almost full, though it still lay on the ground like a lazy giant. Jake and Fred lit the burner which was mounted on a frame above the basket, tilting it carefully so the flame pointed directly into the opening without touching the sides of the nylon bag. This was the tricky part, Daphne shouted in my ear. Getting the balloon on its feet. They had to put in enough hot air, but not too much too soon.

I watched in fascination as the *Hobby Horse* swelled to capacity, then finally tipped up to stand over the gondola. This was my first good look at the design on the balloon, and I saw why the name was so appropriate. Painted on the front was a picture of Pegasus, with a sixteen-foot wing span and rocking horse legs. Before I could do more than compliment them on a clever idea, it was time to climb aboard.

"Let's go, Ellie." Jake vaulted over the side of the basket as it strained against the crew's weight.

"How?" I asked, wishing there were a door, or a step stool, or that I had longer legs.

"Same way Daphne does." He grabbed my arms. "Give her a shove from behind, somebody."

It certainly wasn't a dignified arrival, but I was inside and right side up, though space was at a premium between two fuel tanks and Jake as traveling companions. Grabbing an overhead bar for support, I gazed into the bright interior of the balloon. The sun had finally topped the Sangre de Cristo Mountains, and the morning light shining through the translucent material made the colors of Pegasus's wings glow with a new intensity.

Jake squeezed my hand in encouragement. "Ready?"

I nodded, but before I had a chance to be frightened, we were off the ground. Daphne and Fred had let go of the basket and were waving good-bye as we ascended into the air, though it felt more as if the earth were dropping away from beneath us.

We rose slowly, lifting effortlessly nearly straight up. I could hear the faint sound of voices and laughter as the chase crew packed equipment into the trailer. When the propane burner briefly shut off, everything faded into quiet. Mesmerized, I watched our shadow move across the mesa.

"Jake, I love it."

"I told you."

"No, I really love it."

"I reálly told you."

Impossible to get the last word with him, but it didn't matter. Even mine were inadequate to describe the sensation I felt as we "slipped the surly bonds of earth." "'Let the world slide,'" I murmured.

"You want to see the world slide by, turn around and watch from this angle," he said. "We'll be right on top of Santa Fe in a minute, and you can really do some sightseeing from up here. Look," he pointed. "There's the Palace of the Governors."

"Lovely, but I've seen it already."

"Not from the roof."

"I'll admit, 'distance lends enchantment to the view,' but I'd rather look at the scenery."

"Remember the scenery at that intersection?"

"The bus and truck, you mean?" He pulled my attention to earth again when I was aspiring for higher. "What are you doing, Jake? Mapping the city for aerial tours?"

"My office is right over there. See that group of buildings?"

"Which one?" I asked.

"On the corner north of army recruiting headquarters, where the flag is."

"Handy," I said. "If we get any lower, we can climb down the pole and enlist."

"Okay." He reached for the blast valve. "You want height, the sky's the limit."

With the burner roaring on at frequent intervals, we ascended rapidly. The panorama was practically endless in all directions. As we soared slowly past the mountain peaks to the east, I could see where patches of snow still lingered above the tree line, even in July. Except for the intermittent thrusts of gas coming through the jets, the silence was as complete as the view. So was the cold. Even in Vanessa's warm jacket, I began to shiver. Daphne had told me that the temperature dropped three degrees for every one-thousand-foot increase in altitude. When we reached eight thousand feet, which was about twelve thousand above sea level, I would have been as frigid as the atmosphere if the sun hadn't warmed my back.

"Isn't this great?" Jake asked, his eyes gleaming with satisfaction as the hairs in his beard glittered gold from the sun's bright glare.

I no sooner agreed with him than the basket lurched to the side. "Another updraft?" I asked a little nervously.

"Right on." He adjusted the blast valve and the balloon settled. "You're doing very well." Then he looked at me. "Hey, we're still on course. In about twenty minutes we'll be landing in the cow pasture where Daphne and Fred will be waiting. Don't worry. I'm going to start our descent soon."

I wasn't worried, but the occasional turbulence we encountered took some getting used to. They weren't dangerous. Balloons don't fly in gale conditions, which for them is any air movement that exceeds ten miles an hour. But wind currents don't flow in the same direction at all elevations. Jake said something about a shift at seven thousand feet that would take us toward the mountains. He wanted to drop through it at a faster rate, then increase the drive to slow our descent again. Daphne hadn't gone that far with me yet, but I nodded in approval as if I understood escape velocity.

But when he tapped the fuel gauge and looked surprised, I knew enough to start worrying. We shouldn't be changing over to the redundant fuel system after only thirty minutes of flying time. Ten gallons was supposed to last for an hour.

"Anything wrong?"

"Not a thing. Sometimes the percentage gauge on the tanks won't register properly. They'll read full when it's two-thirds empty, but the instrument panel shows no pressure at all in this one. That's why we always have a back-up on board." He started to make the switchover when something went haywire.

There was a hiss, then a loud gush, and gas erupted from the burner above us, sending an avalanche of raw propane hailing down on our heads.

"Oh, my God! Jake! What did you do?" I threw my arms over my face as liquid gas sprayed in every direction.

"Close the tank," he shouted, using both hands at once to shut off the burner and blast valves.

Terrified, I groped for the round faucet handle and twisted frantically while Jake sealed the other end of the fuel line. After a final burst of ice-cold sprinkles, the propane shower spewed its last, leaving us enveloped in a cloud of white vapor.

Too stunned to think, I sank to the floor of the gondola and started to wipe the wet gook from my cheeks with the sleeve of Vanessa's jacket . . . her very flammable jacket, I realized suddenly. In fact, I was a combustible object from my sodden hair to my propane soaked shoes. So was Jake. So was the balloon, for that matter.

"Shouldn't we be engulfed in a sheet of flames by now?" I asked with remarkable calm.

"Don't panic." He pulled out his shirt tail and gave his face a swipe. "The balloon's not going to catch on fire."

"Why not?"

"We lost the pilot light."

Somewhere in this insane conversation, Jake lost me. Or maybe the fumes were addling my brain. "Since when does propane gas poured directly on a fire put it out?"

"It doesn't. Water douses fire. That's just plain H_2O dripping down your nose. The gas is already evaporating."

"Water?" I touched my nose gingerly to make sure.

"Condensation must have built up in the line." Leaving his shirt hanging over his pants, he bent to check the gauges on the second tank. "They register normal."

"Good. Then relight the pilot."

"I can't. There's a break somewhere under the blast valve, and even if I knew where it was, I couldn't disassemble the burner equipment up here."

"Dammit, Jake. Don't you own anything that works right? This thing's in worse condition than your car."

Naturally, I blamed the most obvious culprit. Jake logged more miles of vehicle nonmaintenance than the demolition derby. Except he wasn't in this derby alone. Left to his own devices, he might put off getting a clutch fixed or whatever was the equivalent in a blast valve. But his partners weren't careless slobs. Daphne had described their preflight inspection in detail, though the safety precautions apparently hadn't made any difference, I thought nervously as my numb began to wear off and panic set in.

I could feel it now. The steadily increasing drop. There wasn't a spark of fire on board to ignite anything, including me. But with no heat shooting into the envelope, we weren't lighter than air anymore. We were heavier than lead and falling out of the sky in a non-stop trip to earth.

As the balloon sailed down, my stomach churned in the opposite direction. We were losing altitude at five hundred feet a minute, Jake said to the top of my head. I hated him. While I huddled on the floor with my arms wrapped around myself, he stood in the middle of the gondola and gave me statistics.

"If I die, I'm suing you for malpractice," I told him, knowing full well there wouldn't be a penny left in his estate after the alimony settlements were deducted.

"Hold on." He looked at the altimeter reading on the instrument panel. "We're coming to the crossroads."

The wind shift hit us with the force of a battering ram. We were descending too fast to sail into it gently, but even Jake was unprepared for the impact. He fell to the side as the basket pitched violently to the left, while above us the balloon billowed inward for a terrifying instant before regaining its shape. If the nylon canopy had collapsed, we would have sunk to the ground like a rock instead of a ship of fools.

"Jake! You idiot! What are you doing?"

With the gondola swinging back and forth, he had one leg straddling the edge and was trying to climb over. Since I was still crouched on the floor, I couldn't see the rope that had been blown nearly out of reach by our wild gyrations. But when Jake grabbed it and half-jumped, half-fell back into the basket, I knew what he was planning.

"No, Jake. Don't."

Ignoring my protest, he spread his legs apart to keep his

balance, then peered up to the inside of the envelope and tugged on the rope. But this rein wouldn't slow the *Hobby Horse*. Pulling the deflation port line did just the opposite. It opened the vent at the top of the balloon, spilling out air, speeding our fall.

"You'll make a great little pilot someday, Ellie, but you better fly with a periscope if you want to see where you're going. Stand up and take a look. If I don't get us out of this wind lane quick, we'll head back on course just in time to hit that power station."

"Power station!" I jumped to my feet. "I thought you planned this route." Clutching the edge of the basket, I almost died of shock without getting near any electric poles. There must have been about a hundred high-voltage lines to the left of us, but straight ahead were the mountains and an entire national forest. That was my choice? To be fried alive or dive-bomb into a tree?

This was the most horrible experience of my life; I should live so long to make comparisons. The medical squad was nowhere in sight, and there wasn't a two-way radio on board to page Dr. Borrows. They couldn't follow us into a trackless wilderness anyway. We'd gone so far off course, even the National Aeronautics and Space Aviation Center couldn't have predicted where three prevailing wind currents and two malfunctioning propane tanks would take us.

Or rather, an empty tank. One that was mismarked. And no pilot light. Three untimely coincidences?

"Jake, do you know what I think?"

I never got a chance to tell him. Our downward swoop curved into a boomerang as a rush of air swept us in an updraft.

Jake let go of the rope. "That's it."

"The end?" I asked in a quavering voice.

"It's all over." He grabbed me and planted a kiss on my mouth. "I'm sorry this had to happen, Ellie, but we'll be fine, I promise." Then he shoved me back down in the corner. "Curl into a ball, grab your ankles and bend your head. Good. Stay in that position." He checked all the valves one more time to make sure everything was turned off. "Okay, tighten your seat belt. We're about to make a non-scheduled landing."

While Jake stood at the helm like a brave captain going down with his sinking ship, I cowered on the floor like a drowning rat. But instead of my life flashing before my closed eyes, I saw a picture of Ruth standing at the door in her pajamas and telling me she was too tired to go with us this morning.

"**A** re you alive?" Jake's arms were wrapped around me.

"No." I shivered.

"You could open your eyes and check." He rubbed his hands across my shaking back.

"What for? 'So wise, so young, they say, never do live long.'"

"I hate to tell you, but you're not so wise and you're not so young, but you are becoming a deadweight."

"Are you calling me fat and stupid?" I started to roll off him when Jake grabbed my wrists.

"How about looking at the scenery instead of falling into it. Come on, open your eyes already. I told you we'd be okay."

"No, you didn't. You said we were going to crash into the power station."

"I lied."

With Jake holding me steady, in case the view sent me toppling out of the basket in horror, I squinted enough to see blue sky. Then green trees. Then the sloping mountainside where the gondola was wedged between the trunk of a pine and the face of a huge lichen-covered rock. When I mustered the courage to pry my eyelids all the way apart, Jake and I were able to get our legs disentangled. Afraid a sudden movement might tip us out, I inched gingerly off Jake's chest. The *Hobby Horse* didn't even quiver.

"Great parking place," he sighed in relief after climbing to his feet and looking over the side.

I sat up and assessed the damage. Jake and I had survived all right, but the basket was splintered beyond repair.

"We'll be able to get down from here without too much trouble," Jake assured me.

"What about how we got up here?"

"I know how we got here. You're the one who wouldn't watch."

Jake Siegel was going to be the death of me, if not by land or air, then by sheer frustration. How do you argue with a man who denies the equipment failure was due to negligence on his part yet takes full responsibility? Wonderful. He lived up to the code of the owner's manual. Now that my eyes were open, I could bat my lashes in admiration. But the owner couldn't explain what happened except as a freak accident, and I couldn't convince him that I might have been the target of sabotage.

"What do you mean I'm suffering from a transient situational stress disorder? That's the dumbest thing I ever heard."

"Have you ever heard of it?"

"No, but it's still dumb."

Jake was squeezed down on the floor of the gondola with me again, keeping a therapeutic arm around my shoulders. "Listen to me, Ellie. You're going through a very normal reaction. Temporary shell shock, an anxiety attack. You're frightened and confused, and you're looking for an answer that fits."

"I know what fits. With all the clues I've discovered

about Jerrold Willet's murder, maybe I've stumbled onto the
truth and don't realize it."

"If you don't realize it, how could you be a danger to
anyone?"

"It's a matter of perception. I'm supposed to be a detective, and detectives are supposed to solve crimes."

"Have you solved this one?" he asked patiently.

"Of course not."

"Then maybe you're not a detective."

"Which naturally means nobody is trying to kill me."

"Feel better now?" He patted me on the back.

No, I felt worse. Not that Jake callously shrugged off
the possibility that my life might be in danger, but that I
was trying to prove a point with no proof and no point. I
didn't want to sound like an idiot by making a direct accusation, so I came across as "just because I'm paranoid
doesn't mean they're not out to get me." But was Ruth's
exhaustion this morning due to working late on the gallery
or working on the balloon? I ought to find out if Frank
taught her the jiggling trick before I suggested that she'd
used it on Jake's garage door. His lock was probably broken anyway.

Fortunately the chase crew arrived quickly. As promised
they had been following every mile of our erratic course.
When they realized the cow pasture wasn't going to be our
port of call, they changed direction and raced toward the
power station. Their final route was into the forest, driving
the jeep up an old logging road, then leaving the vehicle and
hiking the rest of the way. With all that, it took them fifteen
minutes from the time they saw us descend into the mountain greenery until they came charging through it, Daphne in
her camouflage clothes and Fred with his binoculars. I didn't
see her until after Fred spotted us.

Daphne and Fred were so relieved to find us unharmed
that the terrifying spectacle of our near-miss, or to be more

precise, near-hit, faded to joy that we were up a tree. So was the *Hobby Horse,* but its fate was sealed. Above our heads, Pegasus's wings lay in tattered splendor, impaled on the branches of a ponderosa pine.

I'd expected a little gloom over the one fatality, but the owners of the balloon were amazingly philosophical about its loss. The rescue team took one look at the *corpus delicti* and agreed that the coroner's report would have to wait until tomorrow when they could come back with some more helpers to schlepp the remains out to the road. No one even shed a tear, which wasn't so surprising after Fred explained that, of course they carried plenty of insurance.

And a good thing for me too. You'd assume that after surviving a tree-top crash, even a klutz could make it safely to the ground. But somehow, on the way down from our perch, I managed to twist my knee, scratch my hands, and totally trash Vanessa's jacket. It was just another episode in the vacationer's saga of "Why I Should Have Gone to Mazatlán Instead." Tourists came back from there with suntans instead of bruises. Not only had I gained a few more boo-boos to match the colorful souvenirs from my escapade with Leon, I had also earned a trip to St. Vincent's emergency room and a thigh to ankle leg brace just in case the x-rays missed something. All that for one little limp.

The three balloonists, though, had a bad case of collective guilt. Hadn't they lured me aloft and then almost done me in? In recompense, I got free medical care . . . whether needed or not. The psychiatrist labeled as paranoia my attempt to place the blame where it belonged; the surgeon prescribed a stop at the hospital; and the ornithologist apologized six times. Over my protests, Daphne insisted I wear the brace for a few days, at least. The crutches were just for decoration.

It was about noon when Jake helped me over the threshold of the gallery. I was greeted with all the pomp and circumstance due a wounded heroine back from the wars. What a dream. And so was the barrage of sympathy and questions from Vanessa and Ruth. Fortunately, Jake intervened and ordered immediate rest and quiet for the patient. And for once, I agreed with the doctor. I retreated to bed with a book for company and some aspirin for pain.

Sunlight was seeping through the curtains when I closed my eyes. When I opened them, it was dark. For a moment, I was confused. Groggily, I tried to move. Why was my leg tied to the bed, my knee the size of a football?

My aching body brought memory back in a rush—the vivid images of gushing fuel, and the marching pylons carrying those deadly wires over the hills to the power station.

The door to the bedroom creaked open and a figure stood silhouetted against the light in the sitting room.

I froze. "Who's there?"

"Ellie? How do you feel? Can I bring you some aspirin?" Ruth called softly.

I flipped on the bedside lamp. "I'd better get up. What time is it?"

"Nearly eight. Too bad this happened on your first flight." Ruth helped me to my feet.

"Beginner's luck," I said as casually as I could.

She suggested I just use one crutch and lean on her arm on the other side. "You were lucky. . . . Careful, watch that rug. Jake told us you could have been killed."

"He said that?"

"Yes, the electrical substation was directly in your wind path. I once saw a balloon hit a live wire. It gave us all a nervous few minutes."

"The people in the balloon must have been more than nervous when it caught on fire."

"But it didn't," she said as we crept our way to the bathroom door. "The balloon was ascending when the basket touched the wire and bounced off. The pilot just gave it a shot of fuel and they sailed right over."

"Why weren't they electrocuted?"

"You have to touch two wires, or a pole and a wire at the same time to be zapped. You've seen how birds perch on power lines? That's why they're perfectly okay up there," Ruth informed me knowledgeably.

After I took some more aspirin and washed my hands, I went out to the kitchen. Vanessa wanted to serve me supper in bed, but I said I'd rather join them. It gave the three of us a chance to discuss the major topic of interest.

Ruth was a fund of information concerning electric fields, but she wouldn't hazard a guess about why the blast valve had blown a gasket and started spewing gas. Or how water had gotten into the line. "There's sometimes a little moisture from condensation," she said matter-of-factly. "But not enough to douse the pilot light."

"So how do you suppose all that water got in there?"

Ruth didn't know. She even wondered if I wasn't mistaken. I hadn't taken any samples, but if Jake were sure, that was good enough for me.

Vanessa was puzzled. "But what happened? Was it a fuel leak or losing the pilot light that caused the accident?"

Ruth helped herself to another piece of chicken. "If Jake and Ellie hadn't been over difficult terrain, they wouldn't have been in any danger."

"Losing the fuel system is hardly safe," I argued.

"No, but it's not serious. Turning off the pilot light in mid-air is one of the procedures in balloon-training school." Ruth was awfully cool about it. But then she'd been on the ground when I was up in the air.

"Maybe so, but then you're expected to relight it. If we'd turned the valves on again and tried, we would have caught fire." Just the thought gave me cold prickles up and down my spine. In that scenario, there were no survivors.

"More coffee?" Ruth held out the pot.

"Yes, please," I answered absently, then quickly put my hand over my cup. "I mean no, thanks anyway."

I knew suspicions are easier to plant than uproot, but I couldn't help it. Suppose Ruth really was a poisoner of people and propane tanks. And suppose I did have a touch of transient situational stress disorder, after all.

It better be just as transient as the twenty-four-hour flu. Tomorrow morning, I intended to get up and bravely eat breakfast. Then I'd do a little investigating. Nothing too strenuous under the circumstances, since a bum leg was definitely hampering my movements. But why wait for an FAA-certified inspector to disassemble the plumber's nightmare when it was giving me nightmares now? I could make some inquiries and find out for myself what glitch in the works can make everything stop working at six thousand five hundred feet, even if I had to lock myself in the bathroom again to make the phone calls.

Monday morning I really did feel much better. I was still sure that someone had tried to get rid of me yesterday, but I was even further away from deciding who that someone could be. Today it seemed preposterous to single Ruth out for suspicion. Everybody knew that I was going up in Jake's balloon, thanks to Mrs. St. Laurent. And anyone could have gotten into Jake's garage and tampered with the *Hobby Horse* Saturday night. After all, even I could pick locks.

Crutches may look easy to use, but they're the very dickens to manage until you catch on to the balancing act. It took me ages to get up, washed and dressed. And by the time I hopped up and down all those little brick steps in Vanessa's adobe and out to the gallery it was already eleven o'clock. By then, I needed a rest and Vanessa needed a coffee break. After settling me on the couch, she poured us each a steaming cup and explained regretfully that she and Ruth had to go to the bank this afternoon. Would I mind watching the gallery for an hour or so? Frank would be available, of course, if I needed help.

I told them to run along and not to worry about me or the business. I was on crutches but perfectly capable of gallery-sitting.

The conversation ended abruptly when another group of art lovers entered the gallery. Vanessa and Ruth went back to work while I went back to the bedroom and read the section on propane from Vanessa's *Encyclopedia Britannica*. It said that the colorless, odorless, gaseous compound of carbon and hydrogen is readily liquefied under elevated pressures. Interesting, maybe, but it didn't seem particularly illuminating.

The two women finally left at one-thirty after helping me tenderly into a comfortable position behind the desk with my leg propped on a nest of cushions. Vanessa kept saying how sorry she was about their having to go. I was delighted. As the door closed behind them, I reached for the phone book.

"Yes, I'd like some information about a tank of propane gas."

"For a trailer park or a camper?"

"For a hot-air balloon."

"We don't handle those."

"Why not?"

" 'Cause we don't."

"Well, now that you've explained . . ."

"You gotta call Bute-Gas if you need a balloon tank filled. Want the number?"

Good thing I hadn't insulted him before he became so helpful. That was my second try and so far I'd gotten nowhere. Ruth and Vanessa wouldn't be at the bank forever and even though it had started raining, a customer might come in, if only to dry off. I shifted my sore leg to a more comfortable position and dialed again. Maybe three would be my lucky number.

"Hello. Is this Bute-Gas? Yes, you were highly recommended to me as a source of information on propane tanks for recreational vehicles."

"Motor home or camper?"

"Balloon," I sighed.

"You got a ten- or twenty-gallon tank?"

"Neither. I'd just like to know what goes in them."

"Hold it a minute." He turned his head away from the receiver. "Jerry, why the hell are you standin' around? Get that truck unloaded. So? Find Luis. I don't pay him to sit on the toilet. Tell him to get his ass out here." He got back to me. "Okay, what's your question?"

"If you're busy. . ."

"Sorry, we got two deliveries and I'm missing a man."

"Then I'll be as brief as possible. How does water get inside a tank of gas?"

"It don't."

"Well, for the sake of argument, let's say it did. Could you use a portable pressure pump of some kind to add it?"

"Beats me."

I tapped my pencil on the telephone book in irritation. "All right, I seem to be asking the wrong question. You're the pro. How would you sabotage a hot-air balloon?"

There was a brief silence on the other end of the line. "Who is this?"

"Nobody dangerous, I promise. I'm doing a survey on . . . on how to make a tank of propane gas serve as a fire extinguisher at the same time. I hear it's going to be a government safety regulation soon."

"Are you kidding?"

"Does the government kid around?"

"Well, it's a bum idea. They already put methanol with the gas to absorb any water that gets in there accidentally. You don't want nothing to wet that burner. It's a sonofabitch to relight after that."

"Yes, I . . ."

"You mind waiting another minute?" He set the receiver down. "Luis, if you don't get your butt out of there . . ." As his voice faded into the distance, I hung up.

"Damn," I grumbled, scratching off one more name before glaring at my strapped and tied leg in disgust.

"Need another pillow?" Frank had come out to the gallery to check on the invalid. Now he leaned over my shoulder and saw the open telephone book. I'd written some unflattering terms in the margin of the page. "You got trouble finding something?"

"Yes. A simple answer. Would you believe nobody can tell me why the balloon went down in a shower of water yesterday?"

"Thought you ran out of fuel."

"That was part of it. The first tank lasted all of thirty minutes, and the second not fifteen seconds. But according to the experts, the only way water could have gotten in there was by black magic."

"You can pour in a glass of milk if the tank's empty. It's just a canister. But once she's filled, you're talking 180 pounds of pressure. Ain't no way to add nothin' then. Takes a heck of a big machine to pump that much anyways, and you gotta have a special fitting. A DOL valve with left-handed threads."

"Oh," I said weakly.

"Sure you don't want another cushion for your knee? How about a cup of coffee? Okay, you give a whoop you want somethin'."

Nothing. Not even a glass of milk. Just two of Vanessa's Tylenols and a sheet to pull over my head. How would Jake analyze that? A phobic response to everyone who came near me? No, just to people who knew how to sabotage balloons and pick locks.

Logical enough. Now, if I could only figure out why one of them would go to so much trouble for sweet little me, I might even make sense to myself. Too bad Detective Chavez came calling just before I could relax in the fond delusion that my only problem was a persecution complex.

"What happened to you?"

I was about to ask the same question. He'd been on vacation for a week, and it seemed to have done him as much good as my holiday was doing me. He didn't hobble in on crutches, but his nose was peeling from sunburn and he had a Band-Aid on his hand.

He told me he'd been at Bluewater Lake all week. "It was fun, but I stayed out in the boat too long."

"And I didn't stay up in the balloon long enough."

That was the sum total of my explanation. We politely commiserated with each other, then he got down to business.

"Is Frank Ott around?"

"Yes, he's in the back. Let me get him for you." I started the laborious process of moving my leg from chair to floor, but Chavez stopped me.

"I want to talk to him privately."

"Anything I can help you with?" I asked.

"Nope. You just sit there and rest your leg."

I rested it until he went into the workroom. Then I tried to stand up. It would have been easier without the brace and if I hadn't left the crutches propped against the desk where I could knock them over. They clattered to the floor in a noisy heap, but when no one rushed into the gallery to see if I was lying next to them, I waited a few seconds, then limped quietly to the hall doorway.

". . . gonna believe some fucking snitch instead of me? It

ain't true! I told you cocksuckers yesterday when you came around to my house, that coke was a plant."

"Maybe it was, maybe it wasn't. And what about Willet? Were you his dealer? Did he owe you money for drugs, not just for remodeling his house?"

"Don't keep throwing that fucker's name at me. He owed me money, but it was legit." Frank was sullen.

"That's not what our informant said."

"Who's the shitface making up stories about me? That's what I want to know."

"It was a telephone call. Billy Wayne didn't get a name, just a tip."

"Well, the bastard is lying. I'm not dealing dope. Anyway, Willet didn't do hard stuff. Maybe he smoked pot a little."

"If you weren't selling the stuff to him, how do you know what drugs he did?" Chavez asked sharply.

"Talk. I heard talk, that's all." Now Frank was mumbling. He didn't sound nearly so sure of himself.

The policeman wasn't letting him off the hook. "Did you also hear that we found a big cache of cocaine at Willet's house when we searched it last week?"

"A set-up, like they put the bag of shit in my truck. You think I'd be dumb enough to leave something under the seat? Like I couldn't find no better place than that to hide it? Somebody's tryin' to frame me, Chavez, and you know it."

Yeah? Well, you're lucky I'm not taking you in today. Your P.O. says you're on the level; she thinks you're telling the truth. Plus, there weren't any prints on that stuff we found in your pickup yesterday. Not yours, not anybody's. So you might be right about it being a frame. But I'm going to be watching you, waiting for you to make one slip. You got that?"

A chunk of wood hit the floor as Frank hit the ceiling.

"You wanna violate me, is that it? Like you just can't believe a person could really go straight? I only got a year of probation left. Why would I fuck everything up again with a new charge?"

"No use asking me what I think, Ott. What I know is, kicking heroin is too tough for some of the toughest. Sure, a tip's only a tip. But drugs and murder, they go together often enough. So I'll be back to see you. Don't you go rushing off anywhere. You stick around town."

That was my signal to go rushing back to the desk. I didn't come near making it before the police detective emerged. As he walked past me, he said, "Be careful how you snoop. Wouldn't want you to get that other leg in a cast too." The front door shut firmly behind him.

I'd had every intention of talking to Chavez, asking a few questions about the case, but that remark threw me for a loop. I stumbled to my seat and sat down, pretending he had never said it. Carefully, I adjusted the pillow, raised my foot to the proper elevated position, when the front door swung open, then banged shut.

"Rain is bad enough, but does it have to blow sideways?" Conchita shook her wet head puppy-dog style, spraying everything around her. "Filthy weather. This was supposed to be the sunbelt, the last time I heard. Sometimes I . . . What in hell happened to you?"

"People have been asking me that all day. Probably because I'm overdressed for a minor knee injury. But this Velcro model is the latest fashion in medical haute couture."

"No kidding." Conchita inspected my leg shackle with keen interest. "How long do you have to wear it?"

"Oh, another hour and a half. Then I'm going to rip it off and flush it down the toilet."

"You're in a lot of pain, huh?"

"Now and then, if I forget to take aspirin. I'm due for one

now. Could you do me a favor and bring me something cold to drink from the kitchen?"

"Nessa and Ruth left you here all alone?" She took off her poncho and pushed her wet hair into shape. "That was crummy of them."

"Frank's here."

"Good, I have to see him. But I'll bring you a drink first." Instead, she went into the workroom and forgot about me.

I overheard the last part of their conversation, too. Not that I necessarily wanted to; she was yelling.

"Goddammit, Frank! Who asked you to stick out your neck and lie for me?"

His answer was unintelligible, but Conchita didn't give him time to talk anyway.

"You jerk! What do I care if everyone in the world knows about Jerrold's drug problem? You don't play games with Chavez. Stop worrying about me; I can take care of myself. Just get those pictures framed. You promised they'd be done yesterday."

On that dulcet note, she stormed back up the hall, and continued ranting. At me, now. "Can you believe it? That guy is this close to being arrested and he's trying to cover for me, the dumbo."

"What are you talking about, Conchita?" I interrupted.

She looked at me skeptically. "Come off it! You don't know what's going on? One of the original snoop sisters?" Then she shrugged, almost apologized. "Hey, don't mind me. I'm all shook up. Damn those cops. How come they have to pick on Frank? Okay, he used to have a drug problem, and Jerrold was hooked on nose candy. It's just a coincidence, right?"

"I just heard about the cocaine found at Willet's house, Conchita. And the matching bag in Frank's truck."

She pulled on her poncho. "What's that supposed to mean? You think Frank's guilty? Well, you're dead wrong. That's just the sort of dumb-ass attitude I'd expect from the police, not you. Look here, Ellie, why don't you stay out of this business if you can't do any better than that? Jee-sus." She slammed out of the gallery.

Chapter
16

After Conchita left, I scarcely had time enough to pour myself a cup of coffee and hobble to the couch before Vanessa stalked in, at least as gloomy as the gray clouds hanging over Santa Fe that day. Ruth trailed her, talking fast, and far too intent on what she was saying to stop on my account.

"Try to be sensible, Vanessa. We don't have a whole lot of options. I've gone over those books a dozen times and we have to renegotiate the loan. We have to!"

Vanessa banged her purse down on the desk. "Let's drop the subject, okay? You've done nothing but nag all the way home." She jerked her head slightly in my direction. No fighting in front of the company, she meant.

Ruth shot me an unfriendly glance before letting her mouth curve into a grudging smile. "How are you, Ellie?" she asked. "Make any terrific sales while we were gone?"

"There haven't been that many people in because of the rain. No customers, at any rate." Somehow, it didn't seem the right time to mention that Ramon Chavez didn't mind getting wet.

Vanessa rummaged in the desk drawer. "God, I have the worst headache," she complained. "Ellie, want to join me in a dose of painkillers? How's your leg doing?"

"It could use a couple of aspirin, if you can get to them."

She struggled with the cap on the Bayer. "Damn and blast these child-proof lids."

Ruth put the "closed" sign in the window, then poured herself a cup of coffee. Every movement was short, abrupt, as if whatever she was bottling up was dying to come spewing forth. "Nessa, we have to settle this now. It can't wait." Her tone was calm, matter-of-fact, and hard as nails.

Vanessa sighed. "You might as well know, Ellie. The bank refused to extend the loan."

Ruth's lips tightened. "That isn't exactly true. The loan officer was extremely cooperative. He agreed to give us whatever we needed. All we have to do is get Malcolm to cosign the note. Which leaves us with one little problem. Vanessa says she won't ask him."

The green eyes flashed. "You know I can't. Why are you bugging me?"

Two spots of color burned in Ruth's cheeks. She was sore, too. "You're just being stubborn. Can't you get it through your head that his signature is a formality, nothing more? You know we'll pay every penny back ourselves. It's not as if he were actually putting up any money."

"It's just the same as far as I'm concerned. How can I ask him for an enormous favor like that? The very last time I saw him I said I'd rather starve than let him help." Vanessa looked at me for support. "The whole situation is medieval. I can't believe it's possible these days for a bank to demand that a woman's ex-husband guarantee her loan. It's insulting, demeaning. They already gave us the money months ago. All we want to do is stretch the payments out a little."

Ruth cut in, "It's not that simple, Vanessa. The bank needs Malcolm's assets for collateral, to protect themselves."

"It's still not fair. We haven't been very extravagant,

Ellie. But the renovation of this house went way over estimate."

"Did Frank miscalculate?" I asked.

"It wasn't his fault," Ruth answered. "Frank tried to cut corners for us. But how could he guess the entire sewer line would need replacing? Now the swamp cooler keeps breaking down. We have to buy another unit, but it's foolish not to get refrigerated air-conditioning, at least for the gallery. Paintings should be kept at a cool, uniform temperature. Besides, the caliber of clientele we're trying to build expects some amount of pampering. They certainly don't want to swelter."

Vanessa's shoulders slumped in defeat. "We were going to put that expense off until next year. . . ."

"Doing it now will save money in the long run," Ruth argued impatiently, as if they'd played this tape over a few times between them.

With a harassed expression, Vanessa looked around for something to wash down her pills, then settled for swallowing them dry. She handed me two tablets. "I'll go get you a glass of water."

I didn't need it; there was still coffee in my mug. But before I could say that would do fine, she had left the room.

Ruth made sure she was out of earshot, then turned to me. "You could help us both. Tell her Malcolm owes her his support. She might just act practically for once."

My distaste for the ploy must have been written all over me. "Malcolm wanted me to intervene too. But his idea was for me to convince Nessa to close up shop. Even if she begs on bended knee, what makes you think he'll help keep the doors open?"

"Because I know Malcolm and he'll do anything for her. I understand how she feels," Ruth stuck out her jaw, "but it's nitty-gritty time and we're going to do whatever it takes to keep this place going. I, for one, am not about to let our investment get flushed down that very expensive sewer just to spare Vanessa's delicate feelings."

No, Ruth would trample all over them herself with Malcolm's help. Remembering the fight I'd witnessed last week, I too was sure he'd come through, if only to prove that Vanessa still needed him, that she had to be managed for her own good. Poor Nessa. It was tough to mix business and ex-husbands. Or partners and ex-husbands.

Just as Vanessa came back with my water, someone knocked on the front door. I knew who it was before she turned the latch, but I didn't think it was my place to tell Malcolm to run for his life.

"What are you doing here?" she snapped.

"I got your message." He walked in. "What's up?"

"I didn't send any message," she countered belligerently.

Ruth stepped between them, smiling widely at both of them as if that alone would defuse the situation. "I was the one who called. Come on in and sit down. I'm so glad you could make it."

Vanessa put the glass down on the desk blindly, sloshing water over the fine mahogany. She didn't even notice. "Ruth, how could you?"

"I had to." Ruth was much too stolid, too secure to be intimidated. "Now don't get upset, Nessa."

Her partner was already upset. "How dare you call Malcolm behind my back! When did you do it? And don't pretend you thought it wouldn't bother me. I forbid you to discuss the subject with him."

Maybe it wasn't exactly an abject apology, but Ruth did her best to explain. "I'm sorry. Really. I called him this morning before we left for the bank because I knew damn well they weren't going to extend that loan without more collateral. All I thought was, he could come down here tonight and sign the papers. If there had been anyone else to turn to . . . But there wasn't."

Malcolm had been listening to this exchange with growing perplexity. "What papers?" he naturally wanted to know. "Is the bank giving you trouble?"

"Just be quiet, will you?" Vanessa hissed at him. "This is between Ruth and me." Her red hair practically stood on end with rage. "So the bank is giving us a hard time. It's none of your business."

Malcolm was still putting two and two together and having trouble with the sum. "I don't get it. You told me last week that the gallery was doing so great you were ahead in your payments."

Ruth's eyes widened in astonishment; then she barked out a cynical laugh. "Nessa said that?"

This three-way brawl had nothing to do with me. I'd been trying to be invisible; now I tried to leave. I put my braced leg down and reached for my crutches, then wobbled to my feet. Except that now that I'd made a move, everyone suddenly remembered I was present.

Malcolm let out an exclamation. "Ellie! For God's sake, what happened to you?"

"It's not as bad as it looks," I said.

"A broken leg isn't bad? Since when? What's going on around here?"

I glanced at Ruth. "I . . . really, I don't know."

He shook his head, as if he'd had more than he could take. "Will somebody please fill me in? This is crazy. Does everything have to be a secret?"

Vanessa just wanted Malcolm to leave. "Nothing's going on," she insisted. "Ellie sprained her knee in a balloon accident, that's all. I appreciate you coming down from Los Alamos, but Ruth shouldn't have called you. Next time, she'll check with me first."

His expression turned stubborn. "Well, why did she call me? Vanessa? Ellie? You might as well tell me. I'm not leaving until I find out."

I resumed my slow progress toward the hallway, but Ruth was eager to talk. That is, until Vanessa glared her down.

"No you don't," she ordered.

Malcolm had taken all he could. Or maybe he just thought it was his turn to yell. "What's the secret that every-body gets to know but me? You need another loan from the bank? Or is it Ellie's leg that's bothering you?"

Thoroughly exasperated, Vanessa exploded. "You're my only problem, Malcolm, and you keep getting worse. Just when I think you're out of my hair, thanks to Ruth, you're back."

"I'm staying, too. Ruth wouldn't have called me for nothing. You need my help and you're too proud to admit it. God forbid your ex-husband should give you something."

"You're giving me a migraine and I'm not going to tell you a thing. Don't you understand, Malcolm? I don't want to talk to you now or ever."

"Sure. You won't talk to me but you'll divulge the most intimate, private . . ." he searched in frustration for another word, "embarrassing details of our life to sleazeballs, bums." He waved his hands. "Like that nut Conchita, and your pal the drunken potter. You still have that drug addict working here too, I bet."

"Don't you call my friends names," Vanessa shouted back.

"Friends? People you meet in a therapy group? What do you have in common except the same shrink? Ruth is the only normal person in your life."

Vanessa had turned pale. "You have no right to say things like that in front of Ellie. How dare you spill out secrets that aren't even yours!"

He looked surprised. "Ellie doesn't know? You didn't tell her about . . ."

"Shut up!" Vanessa had grabbed him by the arm and now she shook it. "Shut up!"

The cat was out of the proverbial bag. Though I didn't quite know everything yet, I could guess the rest. Too bad I couldn't disappear instantly since my presence was such an embarrassment.

If I couldn't think of anything to say, Malcolm was struck mute as well. But then he'd said too much already, while Vanessa looked ready to burst into tears. Fortunately, Ruth rose to the occasion. She put an arm around her partner's waist and made her sit down on the couch.

"There, there, what's it matter? You've got nothing to be ashamed of. Besides, he didn't mean to do it, Nessa. And I promise, if you don't want Malcolm to cosign the new loan, he won't. I don't know how we'll manage but we will . . . somehow."

It all came out in a comforting rush. Interesting how each time Ruth opened her mouth to soothe Vanessa, she managed to tell Malcolm what she wanted him to know. I was filled with admiration. Was she being devious or the opposite, simply laying the cards on the table?

He looked anxiously at Vanessa's bent head. "I'm sorry about talking out of turn. And I won't be back unless you want me. Good luck with the gallery . . . and the bank." It was a dignified exit line but Vanessa didn't let him get very far.

"Wait." She wiped her eyes.

"What for?"

"I'll walk you to the car."

Vanessa and Malcolm spent a long time together on the front porch while Ruth waited in the gallery hoping for the best. I took my aspirin, wiped up the spilled water, and went back to the bedroom to lie down. My head was aching now.

Surprisingly, I fell asleep, and it was nearly dark when I woke up. Nessa was standing over me.

"Hi," I said, my voice creaky with disuse.

"How do you feel?" She sat beside me on the edge of the bed.

"I was going to ask you the same question."

Her smile and shrug answered for her. "Want some supper? I'm afraid we've eaten; I didn't want to wake you."

"That was considerate. I must have been more tired than I realized."

"Ellie, I'm sorry. . ."

I interrupted, "Don't worry. I'll find something in the refrigerator."

"It's not supper I'm talking about." She gnawed at her lips. "But first I'd better tell you about what happened with Malcolm. I'm taking the money."

Of course she was. Vanessa couldn't fight both a partner and an ex-husband when they ganged up on her. Well, at least her financial problems were solved for the moment.

I squeezed her hand. "Good for you. As long as he was willing to cosign the note, why not take advantage?"

"I feel incredibly stupid." Vanessa's head was bent, the red hair a curtain hiding her face.

"Why? Because you refused his help and then changed your mind? It's a woman's prerogative. I do it every hour and a half."

She gave me a quick glance. "That isn't what I feel stupid about."

Having jumped the gun once already, I waited a moment before jumping it again. "Are you sure you want to discuss this with me? I don't have to know anything."

"Really?" she said skeptically. "Because you already know everything?"

"No, I didn't mean that at all," I protested.

"But you've figured out a lot in the last week, I'm sure. Ruth's probably dropped a hint or two that I'm not the most stable person in the world. Conchita's talked to you; Frank has too. Then Malcolm blabbed this afternoon." She shook her head. "I should have told you in the first place, but I didn't want you to despise me."

"Nessa, I could never despise you. For being in therapy? In California, no woman would be caught dead without a shrink of her very own. Anyway, Malcolm's the only blabbermouth. Your friends are the souls of discretion about you . . . and themselves."

"It's too late for discretion, I'm afraid." She laughed shortly. "Do you want to hear the long, sad, tragic tale of how I became a Valium addict?"

It was a story that reminded me that anyone can get caught in the trap, given the wrong set of circumstances. What if, after my divorce, I'd gone to a doctor who thought a tranquilizer was just what a woman needed when she was depressed, scared, and confused?

"I didn't know I was hooked, Ellie. Can you feature that? I actually thought I couldn't function without those little pills . . . when it was really the other way around. The damn pills were keeping me from coping with my life. Instead of dealing with my problems, my feelings, I hid from them behind a fog of chemicals. I even thought I wanted to die when all I really wanted was another kind of life."

"But you did realize the truth. You went to Jake to get off those pills."

She shook her head. "It wasn't like that." Nessa fell silent and I waited, not probing this time.

After getting up to switch on a light in a corner, she faced me painfully. "As much as I hate to admit it, Malcolm was the one who figured it out. He fussed at me about the Valium, saying it was dangerous. I wouldn't listen. Hadn't a doctor prescribed it? An M.D. had to know what he was doing. If he was giving the stuff to me, it must be safe, appropriate, needed. Damn him. Even now I get so mad.

What did that jerk of a G.P. think? He was keeping a raving lunatic quiet?"

"Didn't he see you were abusing his prescription?" I wondered.

"I think he was abusing me, shoving a tranq down my throat when he could have said 'see a counselor,' 'take up jogging,' or maybe even more honestly, 'you haven't got a medical problem, lady.'" She pushed her hair off her forehead and sighed again. "On the other hand, I was a dope, pun intended. It was my body, but I didn't take any responsibility for my own health."

Vanessa rubbed her eyes. "I was getting more and more dependent on the stuff, more and more down. Eventually I tried to kill myself, and that scared the bejesus out of my husband. Hell, it scared me. Malcolm did some research, came up with Jake's name, dragged me protesting all the way to his office here in Santa Fe."

"Oh, Nessa. I'm sorry. It must have been awful."

"It was. I still wouldn't admit I was an addict. Users were other people, not me. Not that nice lady I could see in the mirror. Valium is so middle-class, so safe, so legal. I wasn't stealing to support a habit, so how bad could it be? I was really dumb about it. That's what I can't forgive."

"I'll bet anything that Jake thinks you should. Give yourself credit. You're doing all right now."

"Oh, well, Jake." Her voice softened with affection. "I owe him so much. He gave me back my life. No exaggeration. It's amazing the way he can see right through people. I couldn't bullshit him ever. I had to get honest with myself. That was scary in the beginning."

"Tell me about the therapy group." It was the connection, the explanation for so many things I'd been puzzled about since I arrived. Like why Conchita chose an unknown, untried art gallery to show her work. Or why an ex-con like Frank Ott was treated as a member of the family. And even why the Discriminating Palette was showcasing Leon Yepa's as yet unfinished collection next month.

Vanessa straightened the collection of knickknacks on the dresser, then threw herself down into the chair in the corner. "You might call the group my maintenance program." She twisted a long lock of hair around her fingers. "We're at the stage where we don't need to see Jake individually anymore unless there's some great crisis going on in our lives. It works a lot like AA. We're getting very good at helping one another. There are just four of us and we've become close friends."

"Nobody from the Chamber Music Festival Board is there with you?" I asked.

"Of course not." Nessa seemed shocked I could even imagine such a thing.

"Okay. Just checking."

"Checking? On what?" Her eyes darkened.

"To see if everyone I've met in Santa Fe is one of Jake's patients," I half-joked.

Vanessa stared at me for a minute and then got up and moved restlessly around the room again. "What have you found out, Ellie?"

"About what?"

"About the murder. By the way, I didn't kill Jerrold Willet while I was having a backflash from Valium."

"I never dreamed you did."

"Kill Jerrold or take Valium?"

"If you're going to pin me down, neither one."

She pushed her hair back from her face with a nervous hand. "Are you sure about that? After all, I lied to you. That must make you suspicious."

"You didn't lie. You just didn't make a full confession of your sordid past. I want to hear about the two weeks you spent as a topless dancer at the Go-Go Club."

Vanessa didn't find my poor joke funny. "What about your sordid past, Ellie? Aren't you keeping a few things from me?"

I smiled guilelessly. "Of course. I never reveal my true age or real weight."

"Oh, you." Vanessa laughed at last.

Chapter
17

I couldn't exactly ignore the problem since it wasn't going away. If I had any sense, I would. Hopping on the next plane to L.A. wasn't what I would call a tactful departure, though it might be a lot safer than hanging around here. At this rate, I'd be the first murder victim in history who was ever bruised to death. On the bright side, now that I was immobile, the killer might feel secure enough to ignore me or emboldened enough to corner me and finish the job.

Maybe my stress syndrome was developing complications, but Malcolm's surprise revelation yesterday had added a new dimension to my worries. Instead of limiting myself to one murder suspect at a time, I was beginning to think in terms of a conspiracy. Not that a therapy group was a coven of would-be killers; but now that I knew the membership list, they seemed to have more in common than just being in treatment together. They shared a common enemy, though planning Willet's death as a joint effort would have taken remarkable hand and eye coordination, not to mention timing.

Somehow I couldn't picture Vanessa as the ringleader, scheduling a grand opening, a murder, and me on hand to solve the case the way she wanted all in the same weekend.

She wasn't that organized. Still, she might lie to protect someone else. She was sworn to secrecy about Frank's doings anyway, and Conchita's, and Leon's. On the other hand, if anyone in the friendship club were protecting another member, none of them would implicate Frank by planting a carry-out bag of cocaine in his truck. That would defeat their purpose, unless a maverick in the pack reneged on the unwritten code of loyalty.

I don't know why my mind leaped to Conchita. She had seemed sincere when she yelled at Frank for risking his safety to protect her. But she might have been putting on one of her innumerable acts. Her presence in the therapy group explained one thing I had never understood: why she was so hooked on Jerrold Willet. It wasn't his warm and caring disposition but his supply of coke that had her bouncing back like a Yo-Yo. That sidelight on her character also explained the recent transformation in her art. The dark, nightmarish pictures expressed her unhappiness as an addict, while the bright colors and smiling children symbolized her new life. Of course, she was still figuring out what new life she wanted. Possibly it took some extra effort . . . like eliminating the source of temptation.

As long as I was painting everyone in shades of black, gray, and blood red, I couldn't leave Ruth out of the picture. She might be conspiring against everyone, especially her partner. Considering her trick with Malcolm, maybe she was switching tactics from poisoning soup to poisoning minds. Or maybe she was the one who tried to frame Frank Ott, an appropriate crime in an art gallery.

But it wasn't appropriate to interpret relationships without any basis in fact. I had to stop being so unfair. Just because my leg ached was no reason to let it go to my head. I was overreacting. Panicking. Being silly. And suspicious.

At breakfast Tuesday, Vanessa hugged me, kissed me,

said I was a doll, and asked if the doll was still going home on Sunday. Ruth wanted to know if my leg hurt and would I be at the gallery all day. Even Frank hinted that my presence was *de trop*. When I limped past the workroom and asked if he wanted a hammer, I got a cool stare and a, "I don't need nothin'. From nobody."

I think I got the message. In fact, I was ready to leave a message with the travel agent and have him switch my flight home from Sunday to a half-hour from now. But then Adam called. He asked how I was doing and invited himself over for cocktails at five-thirty so he could check on my well-being in person. If I felt up to it, we'd go the chamber music concert as planned. If not, we'd stay home and visit. Vanessa was delighted. I was ecstatic. Even Ruth seemed pleased. Adam might not take me out, but he'd save the three of us from spending an evening making labored conversation to hide our real thoughts.

The drawing-room comedy took place in the sitting room. Ruth was in the wingback chair with her legs crossed decorously at the ankle, Nessa was curled on the sofa with her legs tucked underneath her, and I was enthroned on the loveseat with my gimpy foot propped on the ottoman. We looked as though we were gathered for the reading of the will. Adam even brought roses.

"Ellie, how are you? No, for heaven's sake, don't get up. Nessa will bring a vase for these."

I cradled the bouquet in my arms and breathed in the sweet scent before handing the roses to Nessa. "They're beautiful, Adam. Thank you so much."

He sat on the couch beside me and touched my bandaged knee. "Is it very painful?"

"Not really. The swelling's gone down quite a bit. As long as I keep my leg elevated part of the time, it doesn't hurt much."

Ruth brought each of us a margarita. "Ellie's a stoic. She never complains."

"Well, hardly ever," I amended modestly before taking a cautious sip of my drink. It tasted fine, but of course Ruth wouldn't poison me in front of Adam.

"You look wonderful." His warm smile approved me.

Nice words, and I treasured them. But then, I'd had all day to gild the lily. My nails were polished, my hair was curled and I was wearing a favorite dress. Not that I could match Adam when it came to beauty. He had on a white Matka silk sports coat worn over an open-necked blue shirt and pale beige trousers. On his tall, lean body, they were dynamite.

"I had a feeling it was a bad idea for you to go ballooning." His eyes met mine in a silent message that if I'd spent Saturday night with him, I'd have been too spent to get up at five on Sunday morning.

I had to agree, although there was no use crying over a missed opportunity. Adam probably wasn't, anyway.

"So tell me what happened." He leaned back and crossed his arms. "You didn't explain on the phone. How did you manage to crash when the weather was perfect? Was it pilot error?" he asked logically.

"The pilot never makes an error," Jake said from the doorway.

That's when the comedy started, although the scene came closer to satire. Jake bounded into the roomful of well-dressed company wearing a pair of khaki shorts and a KEEP AMERICA BEAUTIFUL T-shirt. No socks. Vanessa came into the room behind him. "Have a stuffed mushroom, Jake. They're Ruth's specialty."

Without checking to see if it were a toadstool, he popped one into his mouth. "How're you doing, Ellie?" he asked, still munching. "Adam, good to see you again." They shook hands. Then Jake spread himself on the sofa. "Want to hear what happened to the balloon?"

"Yes!" I almost jumped out of my seat, but the brace held me down.

"The O-ring under the blast valve broke."

"What's an O-ring?"

"A sealer, like a gasket." Adam draped his arm around the back of the loveseat, as if I needed protection from the news.

Jake explained the problem as a normal, run-of-the-mill defect, except that the flaw had come about because there was water in the propane tank. It froze when we hit six thousand feet, an oddity also helped by the wind-chill factor. When the icy particles shot through the hose, they cracked the seal and opened a floodgate.

"That's the story," Jake concluded. "No fire, no fuel, no controls."

"Are you sure there was water in the tank, or could there have been an unusual amount of condensation from the air?" Ruth asked.

"Did you fill the tank yourself?" Adam pursued. "Or add methanol to absorb any natural moisture?"

Jake looked from one to another, as if the inquisition were uncalled for, then answered anyway. "I picked up the tanks filled and ready to go, with methanol added beforehand."

"Then it must have been a case of Murphy's Law." Adam shrugged, dropping his hand to my shoulder.

It was childish, stupid, and totally unsophisticated, but I was embarrassed. The cat lady would have purred at Adam's proprietorial attitude, protecting me from the big, bad, careless Dr. Siegel. I wanted to crawl under the couch. If Jake said one word to match the expression on his face, I'd throw the plate of mushrooms at him. Instead, he took one on his own. Good. He couldn't talk with his mouth full. The look on Vanessa's face was making me nervous too. Only Ruth seemed unaware that my two supposed conquests shouldn't be in the same room together, especially with me in the middle. Not that they were fighting for supremacy like a couple of game cocks. Adam was more concerned about my injury, and Jake kept his attention on the mushrooms. When Ruth started talking about helium balloons, both men found that more fascinating than either my leg or the canapés. By the time Jake stood up to leave, they were making plans to continue their discussion of lighter-than-air vehicles.

"I want you to be more careful," Nessa admonished Jake as she followed him to the door. "Between the car and the balloon, you really seem to be accident-prone lately. Must be an astrological change." She smiled at him. "Venus crossing the path of Mars. Something weird, for sure."

Jake promised to take better care of himself and Ellie in the future. Adam squeezed my shoulder. Vanessa squeezed Jake's hand. I squeezed my lips together.

After Jake left, we made polite conversation for a few more minutes, then Adam stood up. "I still have the tickets for the Haydn concert tonight. It's the Guarneri Quartet. Do you feel up to coming, Ellie?"

"I'm sorry, really I am, but I just can't do it." I looked across the room. "Nessa, why don't you go instead?"

Adam was too much the gentleman to show a trace of disappointment. Or maybe he was as delighted with the suggestion as Vanessa was.

Her face lit up like a little kid's at the offer of a trip to the circus. "Oh, no . . ." she demurred at first. "Though if Adam doesn't mind . . ."

"Why should he mind?" Ruth butted in.

"She's right. You'd be doing a good deed, Nessa. Saving me from a lonely evening."

She touched her hair and smiled. "I'd love to come, then."

"Fine. I'll pick you up at seven-forty sharp. Take care of that foot, Ellie. So long, Ruth." He nodded good-bye, and Nessa walked out with him through the gallery.

By 7:45 I had the house to myself. Vanessa had hopped into the Maserati looking gorgeous and incredibly happy; Ruth had retreated to her apartment to watch a movie on HBO; and I had nothing to do but think.

A little later, my head was spinning. No matter how I added everything up, the total kept coming out weird, though that was Vanessa's assessment, not mine. I had to talk to Jake. I grabbed the phone book, then tossed it down, disgusted. He had an unlisted telephone number. On the other hand, he lived right around the corner. Once, Vanessa had even said where. If I recalled correctly, Dr. Siegel's house was on the next street, almost directly behind the gallery. So what if I didn't know the exact address? I'd recognize his jalopy anywhere. He wasn't the type to bother putting it in the garage on a summer's evening.

When I started walking, armed with a cane, the sunset was gold and pink in the west and Canyon Road was full of its soft light. It was pleasant to be outside after being cooped up for so long. Admittedly, the knee that had been too achy for an evening at a concert still hurt, but this suffering was in a good cause. Still, by the time I got to the corner of Cristo Rey, I was regretting not asking Ruth for Jake's phone number. I'd considered the option, then decided I didn't want her to know what I was up to.

Five minutes later, I was wondering what I was up to myself. Streets in Santa Fe were not a straightforward business. It seemed entirely possible that I had wound my way onto the wrong block as I limped onward, peering through ironwork gates and over adobe walls, almost coming nose to quivering nose with an hysterical doberman. Most of the one- and two-story houses were shaded by massive old cottonwoods, as if the neighborhood guarded its privacy, but there were names on the mailboxes by the road. I found one labeled Siegel eventually, and though his car was nowhere in sight, I took my chances and pushed open a blue painted wood gate, then struggled up the brick path and rang the doorbell. He'd better be home, because my leg wasn't in shape for the return trip, and besides, it was getting dark.

"Ellie! What are you doing here?"

"Oh, I was just taking a stroll. Aren't you going to invite me in?"

"You walked?" Jake swung the door open wider and made me lean on his arm. "Come on. Let's get your leg elevated right now."

The living room was furnished in a mixture of early American and early Sears catalog. It was homey and comfortable, despite being a bit dusty and cluttered. There were Indian pots shoved between books in the open cabinet, and kachina dolls hanging on the walls. Jake's easy chair was piled with a week's collection of newspapers. Instead of moving them, he led me to the sectional that was covered by a Mexican blanket, then pulled over a hassock for my braced leg.

"How's that?" he asked. "Can I get you something to drink? A glass of tea? A little seltzer?"

"I don't want anything, thanks." This was a difficult subject to broach, and when Jake sat down on the other end of the blanket, I just plunged in. "I came to talk to you about the balloon accident."

"I haven't got the cracked O-ring here, but if you want to see it . . ."

"No." I shook my head. "I believe it froze. I even believe water could have gotten into the fuel line and that one gas gauge registered improperly. But, as Vanessa said, putting all those accidents together, we have to include no clutch and no brakes."

"You think somebody tampered with my car to get to you?"

"No, to get to you."

Jake didn't say a word, but he didn't have to. I could read the expression on his face. He thought I was in an advanced stage of my situational stress syndrome.

I put up my hands. "Just listen. When I'm finished, you can poke as many holes as you want in my idea. Is it a deal?"

He thought it over for a moment, then sat back and lit a cigar in a Dr. Freud parody. "Absolutely, my dear."

"Okay, would you know if one of your patients wanted to kill you?"

"At certain stages of therapy, all of them do, but what are you getting at?"

"Hold your horses. I'm making a point. Vanessa said that when you were treating her . . . yes, she told me about her problem . . . she also said she couldn't fool you . . . and it wasn't always a comfortable sensation to be read so accurately. Wouldn't you say that other patients might feel the same way?"

"Probably."

"And if one of them were hiding something, or a group of them," I expanded, "wouldn't they want to keep you from spotting it?"

"They do all the time."

"What do you mean?"

Jake tipped an ash into the tray beside him. "I'm trained to see through masked disorders. I don't read minds. I read signs, and people have very set behavior patterns. A change from the norm can be nervous blinking, a sudden fit of eating, crying, or maybe unusual silence."

"What if someone were desperate to keep a terrible secret from you? Could he fool you by acting normally, as a sham?"

"Not very often, and not for very long."

"Can you tell if a patient had a temporary relapse? Used a drug or had a drink, then committed a crime?"

"The first two I can spot. The crime is usually discovered by the police." He looked at me through a cloud of smoke. "Is this supposed to parallel the theory that because you're viewed as a detective, your life's in danger? Only now, because I'm a psychiatrist, you think I was the intended victim?"

"That's it," I said in relief that he understood without my having to argue the point home.

"Have anybody in mind, or am I supposed to read your mind too?" he asked sarcastically, obviously not nearly as sold on the idea as I had assumed.

The moment for bluntness had arrived. "There are four murder suspects in your Wednesday-night therapy group. If any of them believe it's only a matter of time before 'the fringed curtain of thine eye advances,' you've only got a matter of time." I thought that was one of the most inventive things I'd ever said, and said so well. But Jake almost jumped down my throat.

"How the hell did you find out who goes to those sessions?" he demanded angrily. "Not from Vanessa."

"Of course not. From Malcolm."

"He's got a big mouth and you've got big ears. What did you do, worm the information out of him?"

"I resent that. He had a temper tantrum yesterday and aired his grievances right in front of me. I was just an innocent bystander."

Jake wasn't appeased. His cigar jutted belligerently from his clamped teeth. "Some innocent," he growled. "And I said you weren't a detective. So what else do you know that you shouldn't?"

"Does it matter? Look, I came to you with this idea. I haven't discussed it with anyone else, and I promise you the therapy group's secrets are safe with me. What worries me is whether you're safe with them."

"Worried about me, huh?" Jake sat back with a pleased smile on his face. "And you didn't talk this over with anybody. Not your boyfriend either?"

"Adam is not my boyfriend," I said coolly. "He's a wonderful person, and we have a very close relationship, but I wouldn't confide this kind of information to him or anyone else."

"So you came to me first. Good. Now it's my turn to poke holes in your story?" Clearly, Jake was looking forward to this stage in the proceedings.

I gave him *my* Dr. Freud imitation: "Absolutely, my dear."

He nodded sagely. "Just as I thought. You said 'my dear,' which confirms my diagnosis."

I was suspicious immediately. "Don't psychoanalyze me, Jake Siegel."

"I can't resist. You're so obvious."

"Oh, really?" I crossed my arms in front of my chest.

He sucked on his cigar, then blew out a smoke ring. "A classic case of reaction formation. Faced with the logic that no one would want to kill you, since in fact you know nothing about Jerrold Willet's murder, you devised a new theory. There's still a plot, but by necessity I'm now the supposed victim. To make a clinical assessment, I would say that after failing to gain the negative attention you wanted by claiming to be the target, you intend to win my interest another way."

"You must have a fancy label to fit my malady," I said dryly.

He raised one eyebrow. "An obsessive/compulsive desire for my body."

"That's sick."

"I know, but you can't help it," he said nobly. "I'm a constant intrusion in your thoughts. Transferring your fears onto me is the unconscious motivation that brought you here . . . late at night . . . wearing perfume and the prettiest dress I've seen you in."

"You're nuts." I shook my head in exasperation. "But then, I always heard psychiatrists are crazy."

"It's an occupational hazard," he agreed.

"What's that supposed to be, reverse psychology? You tell me how terrible you are, and I come to your defense?"

"See?" He grinned. "It's working already."

"Jake, be serious. Aren't you the slightest bit concerned about your safety?"

"No." He placed his cigar in the ashtray. "I'm only concerned about your leg. And your mouth."

"Jake . . . no . . ." My protest lasted until his lips shut me up. "What do you think you're doing?" I asked a little breathlessly.

"Conducting a clinical experiment." He put his arms around me. "Wait, let me check the results."

"Stop that." I started to laugh and push him away at the same time. "Leave my pulse alone."

"It's racing."

"It is not. Besides, I'm supposed to be suffering from a delusion, remember? If you really think I need curing, drive me home. Now."

"You don't really want to leave." He gazed soulfully into my eyes.

"Oh yeah? How do you know?"

"I can read your mind."

This time, my legs didn't balk. They didn't have a chance. Jake swung me off my feet and carried me into the bedroom.

Chapter
18

In the history of the world, and I mean the whole history, going all the way back to the very beginning, or at least to my aunt Sophie, there had never been a more stubborn, pigheaded, opinionated person than Jake Siegel. And I knew why he was put on this earth—to drive me crazy. First he said I was a drunk. Then he accused me of having an hysterical reaction to hot-air balloons. Now he claimed I was obsessed with murder. By the time he finished playing Name That Neurosis, the only problem I wouldn't have was erotomania declaraumbaults syndrome.

Never. I wouldn't tell a soul about last night, and certainly not to brag that a prominent doctor lusted after me . . . or that I lusted right back. I was furious with Jake. I was even more furious with myself for giving in to his idiotic blandishments. Whoever heard of going to bed with a man because he says it's good for your knee? Was that my criterion for award-winning come-hither lines? Inanity? All right, so ludicrous appeals to me. I've got a strange sense of humor. But I'd never forgive Jake for using my body and abusing my mind. Not because he scoffed at the idea that the saboteur was a frightened patient who realized the doctor was "a great observer of faults and could see clear through the deeds of men." It was when I finally saw through the deed and recognized the truth. Jake wouldn't believe that either.

I should have guessed how he'd react to a second theory when he had never bought the first one, except that Jake lulled me into a false sense of security. I assumed he respected my intelligence. Maybe I did need to have my head examined, but not by Dr. Siegel. He examined every other part of my anatomy, and when he got to the cerebrum he wasn't interested anymore. Damn. How could I let myself be seduced by a man who thought I was sexually repressed and mentally deficient? Okay, I was both, but on the wrong night and with the wrong man.

Unfortunately, that insight arrived only with the morning after. On Tuesday evening, for an hour or so, I actually deluded myself that nothing had ever been so right.

Lying on the rumpled bed in the dark, snuggled in the curve of Jake's arm, I felt at peace after we made love. No doubts then about what we had done; no nagging worries that I'd jumped too hastily into intimacy. Instead, I drifted contentedly in a mood of tender surprise that our bodies had found amazing comfort and pleasure together.

"How funny that we get along here so well," I murmured, twining my fingers through the mat of hair on his chest, and marveling at this unexpected shift in our relationship. Jake said that all the sparring we'd done was just foreplay.

"A subconscious attraction."

"Not really," he contradicted. "You fell into my arms the moment we met."

I propped myself on one elbow to look him in the eye. It was hard to see his expression in the dim light, but I could feel the smile on his face. "For your information, Doctor, I hated you at first sight."

"Is that so? I could have sworn you were throwing yourself at me." He planted a kiss in the hollow of my throat.

"Sheer clumsiness. I didn't notice those steps."

"It wasn't an accident." He nibbled at my breast.

"Fate?" I caught my breath. "Or you plotted my downfall?"

He lifted his head, his teeth gleaming at me. "Too much champagne."

"Propagandist." I pretended to swing at him, but he grasped my hand and pushed me back on the pillow.

"Let's just say we began our acquaintance with an embrace." He suited the action to the word.

"And all the battles in between?" I asked when he released me.

"Getting to know each other."

"Well, I will give you credit for originality. Our meetings haven't been mundane. No ordinary dates, where we asked ordinary questions, like is it really true you've been married three times?"

"Not according to my ex-wives." He rolled over and took a half-smoked cigar from the nightstand ashtray.

"What does that mean?"

"I was a lousy husband," he dismissed, relighting his stogie.

"What did you do that was so awful?" I watched the spiral of smoke drift toward the window. "Make the bedroom smell like a tobacco factory?"

"That was one complaint, but the three of them together had another common cause. And since I was outnumbered, I'll concede to majority opinion."

"Now you have to tell me," I coaxed. "My imagination is running rampant. How did you make a mockery of the sacred institution of marriage?"

"Technically, each of them left me. But as Phyllis explained to the judge, she walked out on an empty house. I never seemed to be there. Sharon claimed I was the one who abandoned the relationship. With minor variations, that's what happened with Joanie too."

"Why were you gone so much? You didn't realize wives need some attention?"

"I realized. I just thought other people needed me more. Don't get me wrong. I showed up regularly to sleep, shower, and change clothes. But when it came to parties, eating dinner at seven-thirty, or providing a little companionship on the weekends . . ." He laughed ruefully. "I like being a doctor, Ellie. I got used to putting in twenty-hour days when I was in medical school. I still do it sometimes."

"A very wise person once told me, seek not to be the redeemer or you too shall be crucified."

He grinned. "You mean 'no good deed goes unpunished.'"

"Something like that. It's a truism, Jake. You can't be everything to everybody."

"I like the halo effect you're giving me, but the general consensus is that I'm a selfish bastard. I do what I want."

"And I didn't say you deserved a halo. Selfish or selfless still divides your loyalties, and from your ex-wives' point of view, they should have come first . . . or second . . . or third. Why were you so persistent? Trying to reform yourself along with the world?"

"No." He shook his head. "I still expected to have a real family, with all the trimmings. Picnics, ball games, togetherness. Four kids and two dogs. The whole *megillah*. It just took me a while to realize that when it comes to making a choice between being home at six or seeing a patient, there's no contest."

"Then marriage is ruled out for your future. No kids or dogs. You're a confirmed workaholic."

"That's right. On the other hand, I'm not just piling up money or pushing pieces of paper. What I do really matters. And it takes all my energy, all my gifts. I'm not going to change; and I guess I'm never going to find someone who'll be content to share the time, the energy, I have left."

"The dribs and drabs of your life? The odd moments here and there? I think you've got the situation pretty well analyzed, Doctor. Maybe it's not even a problem. You don't feel guilty about it, do you?"

"I regret my mistakes, but I'm not into carrying a load of guilt around. Half my job as a therapist is getting people to dump that useless emotion."

"Useless?" I resettled my head more comfortably onto his shoulder. "Without guilt, no one would have any sense of responsibility."

"How do you figure that?" he asked, manifestly skeptical.

"You don't agree, but what does a psychiatrist know, anyway? A little guilt is necessary, Jake. Otherwise, children would grow up doing what they want to, instead of what they ought to. That's how I trained my son to take out the garbage every week. All I had to say was, 'You'd let your poor old mother lug a fifty-pound trash bag to the curb . . . in the rain . . . when she has a bad back?'"

"You don't have a bad back, and when it does rain in California, the bags still only weigh fifteen pounds."

"I know, but I was teaching him responsibility."

"You sound just like my second wife."

"Then she also must have been a woman of wit and charm and beauty."

"A woman with a big mouth."

"Good for her. Was she the paragon who kept throwing away your cigars?"

"You can talk about her in the present tense. I didn't kill her for it."

"Of course you didn't." In the warmth of the moment, even the sight and smell of his tobacco didn't annoy me. The ash tip glowed red. It almost hypnotized me.

Then I sat bolt upright. "Jake! I know what happened to Jerrold Willet."

"Again?"

"It's so obvious in the dark. Maybe that's why I didn't see it before."

Only Jake didn't see it—period. I argued, pleaded, reasoned, then got dressed and stormed out of the house, refusing to let him drive me around the corner. Jake told me to wear the leg brace if I was going to walk home in a huff. I told him to go to hell.

By the next day, I suffered all the consequences of last night's excesses. My knee ached, my misplaced concern for Jake's safety had increased, and my complaint to the police was dismissed by Billy Wayne's "gotta go by procedure."

"Is Detective Chavez here?"

"No." Billy Wayne put down the rest of his jelly doughnut and looked at me from behind a messy desk piled with papers. Obviously, he didn't remember me. Maybe it was the limp and the cane that threw him off. "What can I do for you, ma'am?"

"I've got some information to report . . . if you're still working on the Willet case?"

"Oh, yeah. You're the private eye from California. Got banged up, did you? Have a seat." He pointed gallantly at the extra chair in the office.

What did I expect? Real warmth in those beady little eyes? No doubt he assumed I was here to snitch. That deserved a welcome mat of sorts, but not the red carpet. I limped to the chair unassisted.

"So what have you got for me?" He leaned back in his seat, his hands crossed comfortably on his ample belly.

"Jerrold Willet was murdered by mistake."

Billy Wayne just scratched his jaw as if I'd announced nothing more momentous than the time of day. "Who goofed?"

That's what Jake asked when I had outlined the same

scenario for him. Billy Wayne's reaction wasn't much different.

"There musta been a hundred guys smoking stogies. You trying to tell me any of them could have been shot by mistake?"

Put that succinctly, it did sound like a sweeping generality, but I explained it logically. "Two men, both average height, average weight, both with cigars. From across a dark patio, someone very nervous might easily get confused. The killer saw the person he expected to see, not the man who was really there."

"You got any ideas why somebody'd want to off the doc?" Billy Wayne asked.

I didn't know the answer to that one either—a frustrating state of affairs when there were so many people who wanted to kill Willet, except the motives mostly evaporated on close inspection. As I had tried to tell Jake, no one really gained significantly from the critic's death. Jerrold Willet was a paper tiger, growling at Santa Fe's artistic community. An irritant, a gadfly, but he was ultimately powerless to hurt or to help anyone. I should have realized it immediately when Conchita said that his favorable reviews hadn't made her any sales, any more than his pans stopped her later phenomenal success.

My answer to Billy Wayne begged the question. "I can't say why. That's confidential information."

"Confidential?" The detective didn't like that.

I tried to remember the term Jake had used so I could twist it around for my own benefit. "Consentual validation," I came through with professional aplomb. "Part of the privileged doctor-patient relationship."

I don't think the policeman bought it, but he was used to milking facts from skittish witnesses. "You've got a suspicion against somebody but you're not talking. What the hell good is that to us?"

"If you can find out which of Dr. Siegel's patients attended the gallery opening, he'll be able to decide who poses a threat to him."

"Don't he know already?"

Good question. Last night, that had been Jake's major contention. Of course he'd know if one of his patients wanted him dead; that much hostility had to surface during therapy. And since Jake had noticed nothing of the kind, ipso facto, no hostility. In fact, the doctor totally rejected the basic proposition that anyone was trying to murder him. He admitted that the balloon accident involved some strange coincidences, and it was odd that both the power brakes and the emergency brake on his car would go out on him in the same week his balloon self-destructed. But that was as far as he would go.

I couldn't convince Jake, but I wasn't going to fail with Billy Wayne. I laid it on so thick, even I had trouble keeping up with me.

I leaned forward to make my point. "You've hit on the problem. It's very delicate, but then Dr. Siegel is ethically bound to silence, although he was able to tell me that the patient in question is probably someone who dropped out of treatment fairly recently. If we could verify that much, Dr. Siegel would agree to obey the Tarasoff case ruling."

"The what?"

Clearly Billy Wayne wasn't up on his law, so I summed up the court's interpretation for him. " 'A medical practitioner must inform the authorities or the object of possible harm when a patient presents a clear and present danger.' " Billy Wayne blinked, so I followed up my advantage instantly: "Since this isn't an open-and-shut case, Dr. Siegel is reluctant to name anyone just yet. You understand; he has to protect himself from a possible malpractice suit."

Maybe Billy Wayne wasn't quite as dull and inattentive as he seemed. "Well, Miz Gordon, seems to me that if you're right, and someone's gunning for him, the doc oughta be worrying more about that than some lawsuit." He rubbed his nose thoughtfully. "Why don't you just tell him to come see us hisself?"

That was a stumper. How was I going to double-talk my way around it? "Dr. Siegel is understandably reluctant. In the meantime, could you get a court order to look into his files? I'm sure the answer is there."

"Slow down a minute. You want to get a search warrant to see medical records when all the doc has to do is open a drawer and take a gander?"

Impatiently, I shook my head. "I told you, he won't reveal the information."

"Not even to save his own neck?" Now Billy Wayne Fisk really began to smell fish.

"Once you collect the evidence . . ."

He cut me off with a growl. "No judge is gonna buy that. I don't buy it myself. You can't get a court order to dig into a doctor's files against his will. Maybe I never heard of Tarasoff, but I know that much law. I gotta feeling you do too."

I was backed into a corner, but I came out swinging. "Okay, maybe you can't invade the patients' privacy, but you can get some names to cross-check with the guest list at the gallery opening. And the court will grant permission if you have probable cause that someone's life is in danger."

This was more frustrating than arguing with Jake. How could I say I just wanted to find a way to save the man from himself? Jake wouldn't listen to me, but maybe the police could make him reexamine the situation. Only, even to my own ears, my logic seemed weak.

Billy Wayne didn't believe a word I said. His little pig eyes narrowed with suspicion. "I think you're giving me the runaround. This sounds like one of Frank Ott's scams. Sure he didn't put you up to this?"

"I think you're right," Ramon Chavez said from behind me. "Ott, or else Leon Yepa convinced her. Maybe Conchita too." He strolled into the office and perched himself on the desk corner. "It would sure be nice for them if we started looking for some old patient of Dr. Siegel's . . . instead of a current one. Isn't that so, Mrs. Gordon?" He smiled down at me.

I asked the same question Jake had asked me. "Wait a minute. How do you know who his patients are?"

Chavez pulled up another chair, then turned it around so he was sitting with his arm resting on the back, facing me. "When people are suspects in a crime, one of the first things they tell the police is that they're under a doctor's care . . . especially when there's an arrest record in their past."

I didn't ask if Vanessa had confessed to him too. "Believe me, I didn't come here to defend anyone. What I want you to do is protect Jake Siegel. That's what's important now. If you don't do something, there's going to be another death."

Billy Wayne chuckled. "She says nobody meant to shoot Willet; he made the mistake of smoking a cigar." He tilted his swivel chair back and hooked his thumbs through his belt, looking disgustingly smug.

If I'd had two decent legs, I would have walked around that desk and stomped all over his cowboy boots. Maybe I should have poked him right in the belt buckle with my cane, but I had a feeling Chavez would come to his defense.

I also had a feeling it was a wasted effort, but I took Chavez back through the maze of logistic analysis. If anything, my explanation seemed even less convincing the third time around.

"So even though you were the only one hurt in the balloon accident, Dr. Siegel was the target," Chavez recapped.

"Yes, and that's what threw me off track at first. But once I realized the car accident couldn't have been plotted against me, since I hitched a ride by chance and no one knew I'd even see him that day, the rest fell into place."

"All except the motive, who had one, and proof that the accidents weren't just that." He and Billy Wayne exchanged looks. Then Chavez stood up. "Sorry, Mrs. Gordon, but we'll stick with the case we have."

"What case?"

"The one I've got a chance of proving. Somebody murdered Jerrold Willet. And don't worry; I'm going to find out who it was."

Defeated on all fronts, I limped away from the pink stucco police station, getting madder by the moment. Chavez wouldn't even agree to providing protection for Jake . . . not unless the doctor asked for it himself.

Couldn't those stupid cops see that they were going about solving the murder the wrong way around? But then, so was I. Jake Siegel didn't deserve my efforts, but he was going to get them anyway. If the police wouldn't help, I'd take the law into my own hands. Literally.

Chapter
19

Vanessa frowned. "You won't be bored, will you? I feel bad about leaving you all alone two nights in a row."

"Me, bored? I love my own company. You know what an entertaining person I am. In ten minutes I'll be falling off the couch laughing at my own jokes."

"Are you sure? You've been in a funny mood all afternoon and I don't mean ha-ha funny."

"It's my leg." I feigned acute discomfort. "Too much walking today."

"I told you not to overdo it."

"And I'm telling you to leave."

"If you get tired of your own jokes, you can see if Ruth knows any. She'd be happy for you to visit her," Nessa added unconvincingly.

I shook my head. "Please, go to the session. You missed last week because of me. You shouldn't miss again, and I know you want to go."

She had the car keys in her hand, but still she lingered. "I'll be home by ten at the latest. Oh, and Conchita's telephone number is in my red address book if you need me."

"Good-bye." I pushed her toward the door.

By the time the station wagon pulled out of the driveway,

I was in the bedroom changing clothes, donning what would let me slink inconspicuously around corners and down dark alleys. Running shoes would be nice too, if only my leg were up to running. With luck, I wouldn't have to make a quick getaway.

Settling for a pair of sturdy brown sandals with crepe soles, I put on my trusty navy blue pants (again) and a black long-sleeved T-shirt rummaged out of Vanessa's dresser drawer. It was the perfect ensemble, nondescript and wonderfully ugly. When I tied a dark scarf over my head, it was even uglier. Great. In this disguise, nobody would want to look at me, much less remember what I looked like.

Then I dived for the phone and called a cab.

"How long will it take you to get here?" I asked.

"Ten minutes, maybe twenty," the radio dispatcher drawled. Unlike me, she wasn't in a rush.

"Thanks." I was only slightly sarcastic. "Try for fifteen, won't you?"

Earlier that evening, while Vanessa showered, I'd packed part of what I needed into a plastic bag from Safeway. A tacky touch, but there weren't sacks from Neiman-Marcus handy. Now I added a roll of masking tape, a small flashlight, and a couple of those little skewers that you use to truss a turkey. Should I take a grapefruit knife? What the heck. Why not? I had two credit cards for good measure in case one broke, and some money in my pocket in case I was allowed to make one phone call. No purse; it would just be in the way. At the last minute, I remembered a notebook and pencil. Then I dashed out to the portal and waited for the cab.

It took a while, which gave me time to worry about what I was planning, then whether I ought to do it. Casing the joint that afternoon on my way home from the police station, I had figured the caper was just feasible. The main doors to the office complex would be open since the Tibetan Tai Chi

Center in Suite F was holding classes there tonight. Dressed
like this, I fitted right in with the students, a definite plus.
On the minus side, people wandering into the building increased the chances of being seen and questioned, maybe
even stopped.

I think if the cab had been even a minute later, I might
have abandoned the whole project and gone in to watch "Dy-
nasty" reruns. But it wasn't and I didn't. Instead, I stepped
off the curb and into the taxi.

"Where to?"

"Three-fifteen South State Street."

"You got it."

From the backseat the cabbie seemed young, dark-haired,
and jug-eared. He was also relaxed, a fact I deduced from
the way we were cruising down Canyon Road.

"Would you mind stepping on it?"

"Your car on the fritz?" He sped up slightly.

"I don't have one here. I'm just visiting."

He adjusted the rearview mirror to take a glance at me.
"Could have fooled me. I thought you were local."

Obviously, I was wearing the Santa Fe look. "Have you
lived here long?"

"Yeah, it's been three years already. You should've seen
the city then, before they ruined it."

"Who's they?"

"The newcomers." He snorted like a true native. "Santa
Fe used to be fantastic, let me tell you. Great ambience,
great air. People were laid-back and friendly. Now the devel-
opers are turning it into California, you know what I mean?
They keep building more houses, more condos, or they take
some funky old adobe and remodel it to death. Or make it
into another fancy restaurant. This town's all restaurants
anymore."

"You're right. It's getting to be just like California. We
have McDonald's too." I came to the defense of my ma-

ligned Golden State. "But tourists have to eat somewhere. You haven't got anything against us, I hope."

"Hey, tourists are cool. You come, spend some money, call a cab. Can't complain about that. It's the trendy types who've shown up lately grabbing for a slice of the action that get my goat. There used to be something real about this place. Now it's full of jerks trying to cash in on the media hype."

"You want to put up a sign that says anybody who moved here within the last three years has to move out?"

"Maybe you got a point," he conceded good-naturedly.

I leaned back, satisfied that I'd straightened out some sloppy thinking.

"You're going to the tai chi class, huh? You realize it started at eight?"

"You know about that . . . my class?"

"My girl friend takes it . . . a big blonde with long hair. Tell her Ron said hi. You'll see her in there, can't miss her."

What I could see was that it had been a big mistake to take a cab to the scene of the crime, probably a bigger mistake to talk to the driver. Even if I didn't get caught red-handed, Ron might be able to give the police a fairly good description of me. He couldn't tell the color of my hair under the scarf, but housebreaker from the Coast was my known M.O.

When the cabbie let me off, he offered to come back at nine. "The class gets out then. I can run you home."

"I'm hoping to bum a ride," I said evasively, wondering if it might not be a wise idea to have a getaway taxi later. But how would I explain not having seen a two-hundred-pound blonde?

"Thanks." He pocketed his money. "Enjoy yourself."

Somehow doubting I would, I took my Safeway bag and pushed through the big double doors. The accountants in Suite A were gone for the night, and no one was working late at the travel agency in Suite B either. Even Dr. Borrows hadn't been delayed by an emergency root canal. I continued out the matching doors on the other side and into the patio.

The one-story office complex, like a lot of others built to withstand neighborhood vandalism, presented a blank face to the street. Perfect for criminals. We had to go through an inner courtyard where it was easy to avoid a couple of spotlights, not to mention cruising patrol cars. This afternoon, the garden had seemed a pleasant place, with its fountain and landscaping. Now, it reminded me uncomfortably of the patio at the gallery where Willet had died. This one was much bigger, and it wasn't a simple rectangle either. Each suite of offices jutted into the center area, leaving irregularly shaped spaces for trees, bushes, and rustic benches in between. Visually appealing, except tonight those shadowy corners seemed full of menace. I tried taking a crook's point of view: shadows made great hiding places if someone came along.

No one did. I scooted down the dimly lit walkway, checking over my shoulder to make sure the students of Tibetan tai chi were all inside, focusing mind and body into a graceful weapon of self-defense. I tried focusing my mind and body, but apparently I hadn't taken enough lessons. Feeling horribly exposed standing there on the doorstep of Suite D, I swallowed nervously and reached into my bag for a turkey skewer.

It was the wrong tool, and the Yale lock was a little too high for me to manipulate easily. I switched to a nail file, then a paring knife. When my hands began shaking, I stopped for a moment and squinted at the luminous dial on my watch. No speed records broken this time. I'd been jiggling an unfamiliar lock for six minutes. I'd try for another five and then be sensible and give up. I had to allow time for my other illegal activities. No way could I let Vanessa beat me home.

Before the self-imposed deadline passed, the latch clicked back and the door opened. Torn between pride and terror, I hesitated on the step, debating my next move. Then I switched on the flashlight and tiptoed into the dark, empty waiting room.

Ordinarily, I'm a very law-abiding person: I park between the yellow lines, report all my income to the IRS, and always return books to the library promptly. So what was I doing breaking into Jake Siegel's office?

I admit it was a felony. But I wasn't going to steal anything or hurt anyone. And since there wasn't much chance of getting caught, it didn't seem too risky. Jake claimed to be a workaholic, but he was working at Conchita's this evening, counseling the therapy group. They preferred meeting in one another's homes, Vanessa said. It was less formal, and more comfortable than the doctor's office.

Which left Suite D empty and available to me.

Having read a few mysteries in my time, I remembered to plan an escape route before needing one, just in case of trouble. I found the back door in Dr. Siegel's consulting room: a private exit that led to the parking lot. The door was equipped with a deadbolt, its key in place. Below was what Frank called a storeroom lock—a turn of the knob on the inside and you're outside. That sort of convenient arrangement is standard in a psychiatrist's office. Patients come in one way and leave by another route, thus avoiding potentially embarrassing meetings in the soothing, blandly beige waiting room. Emotional problems are not something people compare, like the size of an appendix scar.

Jake's medical records were in his secretary's office, locked in a three-drawer filing cabinet. I had a little difficulty pushing up the slide bolts, but I switched from tweezers to a small screwdriver and sprung them loose at a rate of a drawer per minute. Damn, I was getting good at this.

After all that wonderfulness, I hit a snag. There was no Conchita under C, no Harper under H.

Working with just a pencil flashlight might be the best security, but it was slowing me down too much. I closed the drapes at the window, then turned on the desk lamp. The tai chi students might notice that someone was in the office as they walked through the courtyard, but at least they wouldn't see the unauthorized intruder.

The missing persons showed up at last in a separate section devoted to groups. The entire Wednesday-night gang had been filed together, including Morrison under M. Interesting. Conchita used her real name. I pulled out the folders and stacked them on top of the cabinet. But before cross-matching the names, I wanted to check a few other possibilities.

Disappointingly, there was no Ruth Metcalf under *M*, not in the group or in the individual patient folders . . . or even the "inactive" drawer where the records of ex-patients were stored. There was no Montgomery either, not that I expected to find Adam's name. And though I was sure she needed help, Mrs. St. Laurent had never come to Jake for treatment. Well, negative information was important too.

The process of elimination seemed to take forever. I was using the guest book, which the police had returned to the gallery, but I should have asked for a photostat copy of their list. The signatures weren't easy to decipher, and sometimes I had to work backward from Jake's files. Halfway through the names, I still had zilch, which in a way was better. My goal was to narrow down the number of suspects, not find more. Besides, everyone who attended the grand opening couldn't be in counseling, unless they were all seeing different shrinks.

Twice, I thought I had a match. But the Baker, A. turned out to be a scribbled Avery Benton. And the Lakewood, K. T.

Jake had in treatment was not the Valerie Lakewood who had bought one of Conchita's oils.

I was too engrossed to notice the sound of footsteps on the walk outside, but the sound of someone fumbling with the door had me on my feet in a second. Panicking, I doused the lamp and dashed for my escape route.

That's when I learned why Frank, and a few other talented burglars, took so many vocational education courses. It's easy to get lost in the dark. When Jake switched on the overhead lights, I was scrambling to open the door to the broom closet.

"Goddammit, Ellie! What the hell are you doing?" he bellowed.

It should have been obvious, unless Jake thought I had stopped by to borrow a mop. At least, he lowered the tire iron in his hand, if not his voice. "I saw the light in Mary's office and came in here expecting to catch some hopped-up kid looking for Quaaludes. Instead, it's you . . . dressed like . . . some . . ." At a loss to describe my appearance, he just yelled louder. "Why are you wearing that stupid scarf on your head?"

I ignored the slur on my disguise and addressed the more pertinent issue. "Don't tell me about stupid. If I were some hopped-up kid, do you realize how dumb you were to walk through that door by yourself? Any sensible person would have called the police and let them handle it," I charged. "You could have been attacked."

"And you could have been decked." He took a threatening step toward me, as if he were going to do it anyway, then laid the tire iron on a chair. "How did you get in?"

"I picked the lock."

"Dammit! Why?"

"Because I thought the coast would be clear. Vanessa said you were spending all evening with her."

The expression on his face was unrelentingly grim. "We

finished ten minutes ago. I didn't stay for coffee because I had some work to do. Now you can explain what you think you're doing."

Instead of smiling winsomely and going for the borrowed-mop story, I told the truth, which he would discover anyway as soon as he looked in the next room. "If you must know, I was checking your files, since you're too pigheaded to do it yourself."

"What?" he yelped, and dashed into his secretary's office. When he saw the folders out, he exploded. Picking them up, he waved them under my nose. "This is a breach of ethics, illegal," he roared. "I could have you arrested for breaking and entering, and tampering with confidential medical records."

I shrugged with pretended bravado. "Technically, you're correct, so you probably should call the cops. However, I was only trying to save your life. You don't owe me anything."

He slammed down the folders. "For the last time, none of my patients is trying to kill me. Why are you so bound and determined to conduct this witch hunt against people who used to take drugs or used to drink? And what's the obsession with Vanessa's group? Dammit, Ellie. You're a bigot on this subject, do you realize that?"

"I am not," I defended myself hotly. "Every one of those people was at the party when Willet was murdered, and they all have a connection to you. That's a fact, not a prejudice. And an investigation is not a witch hunt."

Jake glared at me. "Then why are you hunting here? If you're so anxious to find out who murdered Jerrold Willet, by mistake or not, why does it have to be one of my patients?"

"It doesn't," I argued. "But you're the only link, and the only thing I'm sure of is that too many accidents have happened to you. Is it biased to look for a motive in the most obvious place?"

"Yes. If someone does want me dead, which I in no way admit, why can't it be for a solid rational reason? Why assume the killer is a deranged nutcase, as you obviously label anyone who comes to me for counseling? Or would a touch of sanity upset your cockamamie theory?"

"Not at all. You could drive anyone to murder." I crossed my arms and glared back at him. "In fact, when I got to the *S*'s, I was going to check and see if any of your ex-wives came to the opening."

"Leave my ex-wives out of it," he growled. "They wouldn't kill me if only because that would mean the end of their alimony payments."

"Aha. I bet that really makes you feel wanted, doesn't it?"

"Don't play games," he ordered. "Nothing justifies your prying into my records. You're not even supposed to know the names of these people, much less what's in their case histories."

"Don't worry. I didn't read them. I didn't even peek, though I should have. At least I could examine the information with an open mind, which is more than you're willing to do."

That did it. Even his beard bristled with fury. "What in hell makes you think you have the knowledge or ability to evaluate my notes and make a better judgment than a trained professional? That's not chutzpah, that's ridiculous."

"No, it's not, and I'm sick and tired of being patronized by a so-called professional. You won't even consider that someone from the halfway house might have it in for you. Like Harry. Maybe your implosive therapy is making him explode."

"Where the shit did you get a degree in psychiatry? You've got your own personal copy of *I'm Okay, You're*

Okay? Or did you once read an article on 'How to Make Body Language Talk for You'? I know what'll make Harry explode, and you can't even guess. But that won't stop you, though, will it? Paperback psychology comes in cereal boxes these days. Mail in the enclosed coupon with two box tops as proof of purchase and get a free copy of Dr. Buffy's generic analysis chart, along with a plastic whistle in the color of your choice. Allow six weeks for handling and delivery. Anybody who doesn't want to wait that long can receive accreditation from a radio talk show. Is that where you learned everything, Ellie? Listening to on-the-air counseling? People call in with their neurosis and get a forty-five-second cure between commercial breaks."

"Don't condescend to me, Jake." I was so mad, I wanted to punch him. "I am not stupid. I do have the ability to think and reason."

"And rattle off all the lingo. Transference, hidden agendas, denial," he ranted.

"If you've finished sneering, can a mere mortal point out that 'a learned fool is more foolish than an ignorant fool'? But I suppose that insight doesn't count since Shakespeare didn't have a Ph.D. I'll put it another way. You're going to claim with all undue authority that no psychiatrist, expensively trained, brilliantly intelligent, has ever misread a patient? Ever missed a clue somebody else might see?"

"The somebody isn't you, Ellie. You've got murder on the brain. You think you can waltz into town and in one week decide what's real and what's not. You're not even a good crook. I caught you."

"You won't next time," I said with haughty disdain.

"I better not, or you'll end up in jail."

"You wouldn't like that, Jake. You'd have to rehabilitate me at the Turning Point and I'm obviously unreformable."

"I wouldn't say that. You have your good points," he conceded.

I banged the Safeway bag on his desk. "What are they, Jake? Mental or physical? Is there anything I say that interests you, or am I just good for a roll in the hay? The sex is great, but the minute I want to discuss anything seriously, I'm dismissed as an idiot with a bee in her bonnet. Oh, it's all dressed up in the latest psychobabble, but the bottom line is, you don't respect me. I'm just a sex goddess to you."

"What the . . . ?"

"Okay, you've had your one-night stand. Go ahead and die. I won't be bothering you anymore. I won't even say 'I told you so' . . . or make a donation to the Freud Foundation in your memory. Does that make you happy?"

"Don't overreact," he said, as if his condemnation of my character and intelligence was normal flattery. "Just forget about this detective nonsense."

"I already forgot it." I swung the Safeway bag over my shoulder with self-righteous dignity. "I'm leaving this very minute, and I hope our paths never cross again." I got as far as the door and stopped.

"Change your mind?" he asked.

"No, I need you to call me a cab."

——— *Chapter* ———
20

I was totally cured, completely rehabilitated. My life of crime was over. I was turning in my paring knife, my hairpins, my entire collection of kitchen cutlery, and going straight. With the stolen copies of *Insight* still in my suitcase and a charge of illegal invasion of medical mysteries pending against me, it was time to take up the piano again. At least no one could arrest me for butchering Beethoven.

My only excuse for last night was "Jake made me do it." Typical criminal thinking—shift the blame. If he had listened to me, I wouldn't have been forced to break in to his office. Of course, I could always blame Frank for teaching me how, though he had warned me that my talent for trouble would lead to plenty of it. After all, I was fighting for truth, justice, and the American Way. I had integrity on my side, to say nothing of a brilliant scheme that would definitely pinpoint the killer at last. No proof, though, or official approval. Just Ellie Gordon's Secret Theory that the police didn't buy any more than Jake did. The dumbest part was imagining I could change the doctor's mind. But even if I gave him a neatly typed cross-index of people who might want him dead, Jake would still be angry that I knew the names of his patients.

Okay, if he died, he died. The burden was off my shoulders. I'd done everything I could, by fair means and foul, and since Jake didn't appreciate my efforts, I quit. My conscience was clear and I could retire a champ, with a speed record for picking the lock on a file cabinet at an impressive three minutes and nine seconds.

It was a short step from felonies to food. All I wanted to do the next morning was stuff my face. I heard voices coming from the gallery when I crossed the hall to the kitchen, but Nessa must have started work without her daily dose of orange juice. The full glass was standing on the counter, untouched. I drank it for her. Then I wondered what I could eat for her. Deciding an omelet would take too long and cereal was boring, I checked in the cabinet for something interesting. Peanut butter and jelly or smoked oysters? The can of oysters was in my hand when I switched. Peanut butter had more calories.

The jar was almost empty when Vanessa came into the kitchen. She opened the door just wide enough to squeeze through, then closed it behind her. "Ellie, we've got a problem."

"I know. We're almost out of tortillas." I continued spreading grape jam on my second one.

"Shh. Not so loud." She threw a cautious look over her shoulder, as if even the appliances couldn't be trusted, then tiptoed across the brick floor to the table. "Keep your voice down. Leon's in the bedroom."

Very quietly, I folded my breakfast burrito into a big fat peanut butter and jelly roll. "What did he do? Drop by to take a nap?"

"No, to hide from the police."

"Sounds like Leon. Is he under your bed or mine?"

"Ellie!" She shook my arm. "This is serious. I told him to wait in there for me because Ruth's going to be opening the gallery in a minute, and I didn't want him pressing his ear to the sitting-room door trying to overhear us."

She sat down in the chair next to mine and leaned forward so we were within whispering distance of each other. Apparently I had drunk her juice prematurely. She wasn't dressed for work yet. Her crinkle-cotton jumpsuit was minus its striped sash, and without the green contact lenses her gray eyes were unfocused.

"Ellie, you remember reading about the outdoor art festival at Bosque Park?"

"Where Jerrold Willet was supposed to be a judge." I nodded.

"Yes, and where Leon has a booth. He's even been nominated for one of the prizes. Anyway, yesterday afternoon Detective Chavez paid him a visit."

"Not to buy a pot, I presume."

"You presume right. Chavez not only asked a lot more questions, he hinted he had some new information linking Leon to the murder. Now the poor guy's desperate to find out what you told the police."

Lucky I didn't have my mouth full of food, or I would have choked. As it was, jelly oozed over my fingers while Vanessa caught the tortilla before it landed in my lap. She grabbed a wad of napkins for both of us and started wiping.

"I'm sorry. I didn't mean to spring this on you. It's just that Leon is so worried. I wouldn't have mentioned it otherwise." Vanessa tossed the napkins into the trash with an overhand throw. "It's your business if you went to see Billy Wayne yesterday. Still, whatever you said to him has Leon in a panic."

"Seems I committed all kinds of sins against humanity in the last twenty-four hours." I licked a dab of jam off my thumb.

She tucked a strand of red hair behind her ear. "I haven't been checking up on you, Ellie, but I'm not totally self-absorbed. No matter how busy I was sobbing into a hanky all week, it was obvious you weren't telling me everything. That's okay. I asked you to sleuth, and private eyes have to keep things private."

"Damned if I do and damned if I don't," I muttered.

"I understand. You must have suspected me too. Only I hoped you knew me well enough . . ." She shrugged apologetically.

"I never suspected you."

"What a fib. The way I carried on about that review in *Insight* had to look terrible. Besides, if you'd trusted me, you would have told me about your adventure on the trip home from Jemez."

"It wasn't a question of trust. I just didn't want to worry you. Anyway, how did you find out?"

She smiled for the first time that morning. "Leon gave me a blow-by-blow account a few days ago, along with the bill for the barstool you smashed. I told him the least he could do was pay for it himself. Who would have thought you could hold your own in a brawl? You are really something, Ellie."

"Something weird, probably. So now you and Leon are both mad at me?"

"Just Leon. I didn't take it personally when you opted not to confide in me. You figured that even if I hadn't committed the murder, I might be protecting the person who did. You *had* to keep secrets from me."

"Will you stop being so noble?" I grumbled. "I can't stand it."

"Ellie," she took my hand, "I asked you to investigate Willet's murder to help my friends . . . to help me. But that was wrong; I realize that now. I shouldn't have expected you to compromise your principles. Listen to me, I don't care what you reported to those detectives yesterday. I don't even want to know what new evidence you found. Please, just go in there and lie to Leon. Tell him you never mentioned his name to the cops."

"Dammit." I abandoned all attempts to keep my voice down. "Is the whole world against me or am I doing everything backward? I talked to Ramon Chavez and Billy Wayne Fisk, but not—repeat, *not*—about Leon, or Ruth, or you."

"You suspected Ruth too?" Vanessa's eyes widened in surprise.

"Might as well add Conchita/Melinda and Frank to the lineup. I work on the family plan. With six you get egg on your face."

"Five," Nessa corrected me. "Conchita/Melinda is one person. Sometimes." She sighed. "Oh, Ellie, this must have been impossible for you."

"Impossible is right and I'm finished with it. I've tried my best to prove the murderer is not in your therapy group. But when I told my wonderful idea to the police, they must have thought I was trying to put one over on them. All my clever, underhanded, illegal, and unethical tactics backfired."

"You've got a theory about who did it?" Vanessa's eyes sparkled with interest.

"Of course I do. Only nobody will believe me."

"I believe you. Tell me right this instant. Oh, God, this is so exciting."

"No, it isn't," I denied, going to the refrigerator for a glass of milk.

Then Leon proved me wrong by bursting into the kitchen. "You said Ellie wasn't here," he accused loudly, "and then I hear you both talking. About me, I bet." He crossed his arms across his chest and struck a pose: Noble red man betrayed by fork-tongued palefaces.

Vanessa leaped up guiltily and put a soothing hand on the

potter's shoulder. "Leon, it's okay. Ellie didn't tell the police anything. I mean, nothing against you."

He pointedly addressed Vanessa as if I weren't even there. "Huh. That's what she says now. But she must have done something. I ask her to put in a good word for me at the station house, and the next thing, Chavez starts hassling me in public."

I slammed the milk carton back on the shelf and turned on Leon. "Did he actually say I named you as the murderer? Did he?"

Leon stuck out his jaw. "Not that bluntly, but he wouldn't. Chavez likes to protect his snitches. What he said was, you put up a smokescreen, but he knew who you were driving at all right."

"Oh, it's clear as a bell now. I make an ass of myself with the police in a double play that points indirectly around the corner and up the stairs at you."

Leon began to have doubts. "How do I . . ."

I pushed a finger against his chest and backed him up to the sink. "How do you know for sure? Because I wouldn't have to use words to incriminate you. This would do it." I held up the fading bruise on my elbow. "And this." I showed him the long scab on my wrist. "I'm living, limping testimony that you tried to murder me."

"Hey, I didn't do that to your leg," he said, aggrieved at the unfair accusation.

"Good. Then you can't be the killer. You just exonerated yourself."

Both Vanessa and Leon stared at my damaged limb.

"Fuck, man." He had just caught all the implications. "I thought that wreck was an accident. Somebody really tried to kill you?"

"No, no. I didn't mean that." Damn, I talked too much.

Vanessa eyed me wrathfully. "Oh, she means it, Leon. But Ellie would rather have a nice quiet unassuming funeral where people shake their heads and wonder what happened. 'Could she have been dying of natural causes all along? Gee, she looked healthy.' " Her voice dripped sarcasm.

"Who did it?" Leon demanded to know. "Who's the guy you're covering for? You tell me his name, and I'll take care of the bastard."

This was turning into a complete farce.

"Leon, do me a favor," I said quietly.

"Anything you say." A minute before, he'd been furious with me. Now he looked at me with puppy-dog goodwill, waiting for the command to sic 'em.

"Don't worry; I'll be just fine. And don't worry about yourself, either. Chavez is spinning his wheels. I don't think he's got any kind of case against you at all. Just go back to the art show, sell some more pots, and win a blue ribbon."

He looked disappointed. "You won't say who killed Willet? Vanessa, did she tell you?"

Nessa shook her head.

"I don't know who it is," I said impatiently.

"You need any help," Leon jabbed a thumb at his own manly chest, "you call me."

"Thanks. I appreciate the thought." I finally got him out of the room.

Disposing of Vanessa was more difficult. She wasn't satisfied until I told her the whole story, all the way through last night's disaster. The crazy part was, she thought my deductions were right on the money; she even claimed I was a genius.

"That settles it," Nessa said when I finished. "You have to keep on digging."

"No, I don't. Jake very firmly told me to stay off his turf and out of his files."

"Ellie, you can't leave us all as suspects in the wrong murder investigation. Besides, if Jake's life is in danger, we have to do something."

"What do you mean, 'we'?" I looked at her warily.

"As in 'you and me.' We'll solve the case together," she said, as if it were the easiest thing in the world. "I want to make everything up to you. You almost got killed while I was leaving you to your own devices. It was crummy of me, letting other people entertain you because I was too overcome by emotional stress to be a decent hostess . . . a decent friend. You just wait. The next three days will be entirely different. Ruth can take care of the gallery while we're busy. I'm not leaving you alone for a minute, and there won't be an inch of this town we won't cover."

"Good. We'll go sightseeing."

"Up yours. We're going to catch a murderer."

I tried to convince her that there wasn't much of a chance we'd succeed, but she argued that with her knowledge of Santa Fe and my knowledge of crime, we were an unbeatable team . . . or at least the most unusual.

Vanessa's idea of being a detective was right out of a high-concept television series where lovely lady sleuths wear Dior originals and sip French champagne while they track down desperados. We did it Santa Fe style. Vanessa wore white linen and sunglasses; her sidekick followed along in seersucker, camera at the ready. We were disguised as local resident and tourist.

The investigation began at the Palace Bakery with us nibbling fresh-baked croissants, drinking café au lait, and watching for suspicious-looking celebrities. When nobody there acted the least bit guilty, we moved on with relentless thoroughness to hit every art gallery in town. Vanessa introduced me to several people who'd been at the infamous party, then stood back and let me do the interrogating. By mid-afternoon, we were still clueless.

It was time for a break, she decreed, ushering me into a little frame house on Marcy Street for a late lunch of blue-corn enchiladas. There were no celebrities there either, unless we counted Billy Wayne. To keep him from guessing we were hot on the trail of the killer, Vanessa paused at his table to discuss the apricot pie he was devouring. He recommended it highly, so we ate some too, just to throw him off the scent.

It was a coincidence that Nessa had tickets for the Santa Fe Opera that evening. She had bought them the week before, but no glamorous gumshoe would miss that natural spot for hunting down leads. We could enjoy the music, she allowed, as long as we spent the intermissions circulating, meeting people, asking questions. The entire audience, and possibly the cast too, were grist for her mill. Amazingly, Vanessa didn't come up empty-handed either. She managed to meet a Texas oilman who collected Western art. Despite the current hard times in the energy business, he wanted to come by the Discriminating Palette to see Conchita's show.

When I finally crawled into bed around two A.M. I was bushed. But not my friend. She was bright-eyed and bushy-tailed and she wanted to talk.

"Wasn't it great?" She pulled on her nightgown. *"The Magic Flute* was never more magical. I love sitting out under the stars, listening to Mozart. You weren't cold, were you?"

"Mmm-uh."

"Meeting that Texan was a stroke of luck too. I bet he'll buy something." She sat on the edge of my bed, ready to discuss business. "So, what did we discover today?"

"That you should have your own television show," I said with my eyes closed. Getting my mouth open was almost too much of a strain.

"Do you think Faye Oberland is worth checking into? Hey, Ellie, wake up." Nessa shook my arm.

"I am awake. Who writes checks?"

"Faye, the woman who kept staring at you through her opera glasses during the second act. Don't you remember?"

"Yes. She used to be Jake's secretary until he fired her for taking forty-five-minute coffee breaks."

"That was Ramona," Nessa said in exasperation. "Faye Oberland owns a couple of ranches in Colorado."

"And she wants to kill Jake because he wouldn't take one of her checks for the halfway house," I mumbled into the pillow.

Vanessa sighed. "Why do I get the feeling you're not really concentrating?"

"Because you can hear my snores, probably."

Nessa poked me in the shoulder. "Don't fall asleep yet. Just tell me if we should start fresh tomorrow or go back to the same people. That's how the police do it. They keep asking questions until somebody contradicts himself."

"How do you know that?"

"You told me."

"Oh."

"So what should we do? Ellie?" She poked me again. "Go back or . . . ?"

"Start fresh, start fresh," I said quickly.

The next morning, she thought the best place to begin anew was at the Pecos Trail Riding Stables. I didn't know if we were sleuthing or rehearsing for a television show, but Vanessa could have won an Emmy for producing, directing, costume design, and best actress. She cast herself as Dale Evans and I tagged along as the faithful Gabby Hayes. While she took the breakfast ride with six other horse-women, I sat on the corral fence and chewed on a stalk of hay to stay in character until she got back.

I didn't expect results from her trip down the bridle path but she was very smug as she dismounted with practiced ease and told me it was the "bridal" path. Jake's third wife, Phyllis, was in town, and if we went to Edsel's tonight, we could probably find her there.

"So what?" I shrugged.

"So," Vanessa gave a triumphant look, "Phyllis is a psychologist and worked with Jake until about six months ago."

"Even if she could guess which ex-patient has turned murderous, she wouldn't tell us."

"We can't know that until we ask."

Edsel's, named for the car nobody wanted until twenty years after they stopped making it, was the hot new night-spot in town for the over-twenty-five but not over-the-hill set. It was a study in fifties nostalgia. Pink and white neon coils rimmed the ceiling over the packed dance floor where couples bounced to the beat of "Rock Around the Clock." The bar was a linoleum-covered drugstore counter with swivel stools, while the sign by the cash register read: GET YOUR CHERRY PHOSPHATE HERE.

I thought that was cute, but not as cute as the waitresses. Dressed in cheerleader costumes, complete with bobby sox, they jumped on the bar every hour to lead the crowd in a ritual dance routine to that golden oldie—"Let's All Do the Twist." It was as enthusiastically awaited as the popcorn-throwing scene in *The Rocky Horror Picture Show*. Everyone knew the steps and gyrated with gusto.

We were lucky enough to have a table next to the rear bumper of the actual Edsel parked in one corner of the room. From there Vanessa was almost sure she'd be able to spot Phyllis when she came in, though it might be tough. The place was filling up fast with the regular TGIF crowd.

"This is fun," she said. Whether she was talking about the ambience or our mission, there was no mistaking the gleam in Vanessa's eye. She was taking to this like a swan to water.

"Do you come here often?" I asked.

She shook her head. "Never. It's a pickup place, you know."

I looked around. "It's nice. The age rule keeps us oldies

from having to compete with the college crowd, and making us show our ID at the door is brilliant. Planned flattery always works with me."

"I suppose you've gone to a lot of clubs like this since your divorce." Vanessa took a sip of her margarita.

"Actually, no. I'm not opposed on principle. I've just never found a place where I had to show my ID."

"You've never just gone to a bar on your own and picked up a date?"

"No. Have you?"

Vanessa shook her head. "I wouldn't know how to."

I laughed. "You want to dance? Just make eye contact with that guy at the bar who's looking at us."

She glanced over her shoulder, then ducked her head in case she'd accidentally triggered an invitation. "Which one? The man in the sports jacket with the sleeves pushed up? Or the cowboy with the handlebar mustache?"

"I think you can have your pick. But remember, first the eye contact, then a cool smile. No eagerness."

"You first. Let me watch once. Then, maybe six months from now, I'll try it."

"Not me. We're here on business. Remember?"

Vanessa sighed. "Solving this case is a lot tougher than I thought it would be."

"But you've been terrific." I looked at her with affection. "These last two days . . . I don't want to sound gushy . . . but I think *magnificent* is the only word to describe you."

"I'm glad you think so now." Vanessa's slender finger rubbed the salt from the rim of her glass. "Last week you must have been terribly disappointed in me. No . . ." she anticipated my protest, "don't deny it. You thought I should be calmer, braver, more together than I've been most of these two weeks. That's okay; I wish I were more capable too. But the great thing is, I haven't fallen apart. Despite the opening, despite the murder, and the money worries, look at me.

I'm functioning. You don't realize what a miracle that is. A year ago, I would have said it would be impossible for me to get through this much stress without checking into a rubber room."

Or hiding behind a shield of tranquilizers. Was it any wonder that facing the world with all nerves bared frightened her as much as it excited her? I almost rushed in with a bunch of soothing platitudes, the kind of reassuring pep talk I'd fed her since the murder. Instead, I looked her square in the eye and told her the truth.

"Disappointed in you? Of course not. I was just scared to be open and honest. It was lousy of me, but I was trying to protect you—just like Malcolm does. It was a mistake. You don't need it. And the proof is, these last two days you've been taking care of me. Believe me, without you, I would have fallen apart."

"That has to be the nicest thing anybody's ever said to me," she said, smiling mistily.

"It's all gospel. I adore you just the way you are. You can just forget about keeping a stiff upper lip. Leave that for the phlegmatic types like Ruth. Now that you have red hair, you can have all the temperament you want. That's your flamboyant style, your charm." I raised my glass in a salute.

Vanessa looked embarrassed but pleased. "I hope you mean all that crap, because I'm never going to be the calmest person in the world. But I am proud of myself. Remember how upset I was about asking Malcolm to cosign the bank loan for the gallery? Believe it or not, letting him help me was the most mature thing I've done since the divorce. It seems like a paradox, but admitting you need support is the first step to recovery. Does that make any sense to you?"

"Yes, now that you explained it to me."

"You do understand." She was relieved. "I only started coping without the Valium after I accepted Jake's help.

Somehow, that was allowed. But until the other day, I wouldn't let Malcolm do a thing for me."

She was explaining this to herself as well as to me. "I've been lying to everyone, saying he was to blame for what was wrong with our relationship. That was less than half-true, of course. We were both at fault. Just admitting that makes it possible to forgive him. I can even begin to forgive myself. You don't know how good that feels."

Before I could tell her I knew exactly what she meant, she had jumped out of her chair to wave at a group of women coming in the door.

Vanessa had to do some fast talking but she snagged Phyllis Siegel and brought her over to our table to introduce me. In a minute, I was admiring Jake's taste in wives. She was warm, caring, and obviously intelligent. When we filled her in on the situation, Phyllis didn't scoff or even ask what we wanted from her. She was sharp; she knew.

"I can't give you any names. You realize that? What I will do is think this over carefully, then tell Jake my conclusions when I see him Sunday. He's stubborn, but he'll listen to me."

Vanessa smiled from ear to ear in relief. "That makes me feel about a million times better."

Phyllis was sympathetic. "You've done your part; let me do the rest. One thing makes me optimistic: the killer's feelings are extremely ambivalent. Three unsuccessful attempts on Jake's life? That's significant. Bungling like that is no accident."

When she left to rejoin her friends, Vanessa eyed me speculatively. "Well? Are you satisfied, even though we didn't catch the killer?"

"Yes, I guess I am. We gave it the old college try. At least Jake will be on his guard now."

Vanessa knew me very well. "But you're still worried."

"Not really." I shrugged. "Maybe I'm just frustrated to be

leaving Santa Fe with everything still up in the air. Promise me you'll call if something develops. If Chavez makes an arrest, for instance. Or anything happens to Jake."

She put her head to one side and looked at me with slitted eyes. "Oh, Ellie . . . you fell for him?"

"Of course not. Whatever gave you that *meshugge* idea?" I denied crossly.

She went on just as if I hadn't said a word. "You're both so vital, so determined. And you certainly strike sparks off each other. I bet, if you weren't going away, you and Jake would work something out."

"No, we wouldn't," I said mulishly. "He's the most irritating man I've ever met. I don't like the way he looks, or dresses; I can't stand his beard or his cigars. There's not even one thing about him that appeals to me."

She had the nerve to laugh. "That's why you're worried? Because you can't stand him?"

"Nessa!" I reproved. "The only thing he's got going for him is his sense of humor."

"And his intelligence, his dedication, his integrity?" she pushed.

"I'd take those qualities into consideration if he were running for elected office," I conceded grudgingly.

"Well, I think you're more attracted than you want to admit."

As we got up to leave, Johnny Mathis was singing "Chances Are."

Chapter
21

Late Saturday morning, packing my clothes, getting ready to leave Santa Fe, I kept thinking about Vanessa. The day I arrived, it had seemed to me she was someone I could almost envy. She had independence, great looks, fascinating friends, and, best of all, her very own business instead of a nine-to-five job. And then I'd begun to pity her, thought she was a flake, even wondered if she could be protecting a murderer . . . if she weren't actually the killer herself. I'd been wrong both times, but at least now I knew the truth about Nessa.

If my perception of the person I knew best had been so mistaken, I wondered how much I could trust my impressions of the people I'd met recently. It was hard to read character when everyone was so busy playing roles. Who could see beyond all those façades in a mere two weeks? I tried to tell myself not to worry. I'd be home in Casa Grande tomorrow and I could forget about all of them. Except that behind one of those masks was a murderer . . . who intended to kill again.

Dammit, there I went, trudging around the same old circle. No matter how much I distracted myself, the puzzle kept nagging away at me. What a waste of energy, as if I were going to solve the mystery at the last minute. Why couldn't I just put away my delusions about being a detective?

I nearly succeeded. Who had time to detect? Not only did I have to pack, I had to go shopping for my mother. It would be totally heartless to spend two weeks on vacation and not bring her some *tsatske* typical of this exotic locale. A present was a time-honored ritual, and she'd be terribly hurt if I didn't buy her something she would undoubtedly hate.

As if those two jobs weren't enough to keep me busy, everybody wanted some time with me today to say goodbye. Correction—not quite everybody. Jake I hadn't heard from, which was fine with me. What did we have to say to each other, after all? But Adam and I had a date for a farewell drink at six, and after that Ruth and Vanessa were taking me out for a last feast of New Mexican chili, which was why my suitcases were lying around the bedroom this morning.

But before I'd done more than make a start at packing, Conchita came by to bring me a gift. With her long dark hair hanging down her back, she looked very young. No neon-pink earrings, no outrageous clothes today, but then it was hard to see much of her at first, because she was almost hidden by the oversized package in her arms.

"I want you to have this," she said, thrusting it at me.

"Oh, Conchita. How sweet of you." I tore open the wrapping paper.

It was one of the paintings by Melinda that I'd praised at Willet's house. "Thank you. I'm going to treasure this." I propped it up against the dresser, wondering how in the world I was going to take a twenty-seven-by-forty-inch oil home on the plane. Would they let me carry it on board?

"I call it *The Opium-Eater*. Can you tell it's a self-portrait? Though, thank God, I don't look strung out like that these days," she said.

The girl in the picture had haunted eyes and the bony

hands that propped up the weary head seemed nothing like Conchita's. There really wasn't much resemblance. "The symbolism of the red poppies I understand. But tell me what those faces floating in the background mean," I asked.

"They're my dream people; I imagined that they were very sad for me. A Chagall touch." Conchita shrugged. "It's really terribly trite and obvious, but you said you liked it. Look, you don't have to take the fucking thing if you don't want to. I know it's crap."

"Will you stop knocking my present?" I exclaimed. "Your friend Jerrold Willet was right about one thing. Melinda had a lot of talent. *The Opium-Eater* is full of passion, and I want it."

"A print of *Donkey Serenade* would look a lot better over your sofa," she said, not quite straight-faced. "It's worth more, too. Might even appreciate in value. Want to change your mind?"

"No."

But she still seemed dissatisfied. "When you look at this garbage, you will remember that I'm not like that anymore? Vanessa said Malcolm told you about our little group of ex-junkies. Jake's our guru. He's such a hard-ass. Any backsliding and he's right there, telling us to shape up, no excuses accepted." She made a face. "Vanessa thinks he walks on water, but he can be a pain in the butt. Now don't tell her I said that."

"I'm with you. He can be difficult to take."

Conchita clearly thought only she was entitled to criticize. "So? He's special. My God, he goes around saving the world. Haven't you noticed?"

Jake and Gandhi . . . and Sean O'Donnell. Saving the world was definitely a dangerous mission. But I didn't say that to Conchita. We dropped the subject and she left after wishing me bon voyage. I wished her good luck, then got a drink of iced tea and went back to packing.

I won't say a light bulb went off in my head. It was far less clear than that . . . more like a painful groping toward a faint glow in the dark. But I did see one reason for my difficulty. I was hung up on motive. If "why" couldn't help me, maybe the "how" of things would.

I began again at the beginning, tossing out all preconceived notions. No playing favorites with the suspects, either. In the first place, the murderer had to have some connection with Jake, but not necessarily one I knew about. The next most obvious point was that whoever it was had to have been present at that grand-opening party. Willet's death had put me on the wrong track for quite a while. Even after I figured Jake was the intended target, the method had misled me. A shot in the dark was so straightforward, it might have been done on impulse.

But the sabotage of Jake's car brakes and the hot-air balloon revealed the killer in a new light. A sudden rage couldn't explain those actions. They took a sort of malevolent patience. Looking back on the murder with the usual 20/20 hindsight, I decided that that crime was planned carefully too. It had been no coincidence that the sound of the Beretta being fired was covered by an evening's worth of fireworks.

But there was another angle to consider. With much less chance of success, the later, staged accidents could have proved fatal to a lot of people besides Jake. Me, for instance, or even a busload of children. Someone that callous, that careless of human life, had to be a fairly sick individual. But I pushed the thought away and concentrated on another verifiable fact. The murderer definitely possessed considerable mechanical aptitude. He had to be handy with a monkey wrench, at least. Tampering with the car brakes didn't take too much specialized knowledge or skill, but bringing off a balloon accident took plenty.

Once those things were taken into consideration, I could

take a few names off my list. Leon, for instance, just didn't make a good suspect anymore. He'd use the monkey wrench more directly; say, to deliver a hard blow to the base of Jake's skull. The potter was too impulsive, too angry to concoct such elaborate schemes. Ditto for Vanessa. Even if I could imagine that her apparent devotion to Jake was a complete sham, I doubted that she would be willing to crawl under a dirty old car and mess with its brake line. My elegant, willowy friend in her fancy clothes? As for Conchita, she might have the strength to move propane tanks. She was young and vigorous if not particularly athletic. And she wouldn't mind crawling under a car, either. But, like Leon and Vanessa, she just wasn't the type to arrange death at long distance. No. When she was enraged, she picked up an ax and started swinging it.

Psychologically, Ruth made a more believable plotter, assuming she was as cool and calculating as I thought. She even knew a heck of a lot about balloons. But Ruth was also nearly fifty and distinctly out of shape. It was hard to picture her being able to muscle two propane tanks out of the *Hobby Horse*'s basket, and hoist two more in. Granted, she knew exactly how to reconnect them, but how could she lift that much deadweight without help? If she wanted Jake to die, wouldn't she have chosen an easier modus operandi? Say, a little cyanide in his stuffed mushroom?

Judging from methodology, I thought that a plan involving so much physical effort would be concocted by a strong, fit man. Which left me with one very obvious candidate and one not so obvious.

What about Malcolm? He'd been there at the gallery the night of the party, and he certainly had reason to hate his wife's therapist, the man who had encouraged Vanessa to demand a divorce. Sabotage would have its advantages for someone who lived and worked out of town, too. Malcolm could have driven down to Santa Fe late at night and let himself into Jake's garage without anyone knowing. As for learning about the fuel system in a hot-air balloon, that would be a piece of cake for him. The physicist was a specialist at research.

Nice and neat, and yet . . . from the very beginning, Frank Ott had been the most likely villain. The list of his qualifications made him a shoo-in for the job. He was definitely out on the patio the night Willet was killed; he was also one of Jake's patients, and he certainly knew how to pick the lock on the garage. If that weren't enough to convict him, add the fact that a former auto mechanic would be able to damage a car's brakes without any trouble. Frank had even explained to me the best way to put water into a propane tank. As for motive, I could dream up one. Maybe Chavez's informant was correct and Frank was dealing drugs. Who was more likely to find out than his psychiatrist, the man Vanessa said could practically read minds?

A lovely, long chain of ratiocination, and the result was that I'd narrowed down the possibilities to two pretty good maybes. Terrific. I couldn't even convince myself. There was absolutely no evidence that either of my theories was correct. Though one thing was sure: they both couldn't be.

Well, I'd made some progress. My bags were packed— all except for Mother's present.

I found Vanessa in the workroom. She was busy wrapping one of Conchita's prints for mailing, one of the services offered to out-of-state buyers.

"Hi." I stuck my head in the door. "I'm going shopping now. Need anything? Milk? Stamps?"

She looked up and brushed a wayward strand of hair out of her eyes. "Not a thing. You do remember that Adam is coming by at six to take you out? And you're not dressed." Obviously she thought walking shorts and a T-shirt weren't elegant enough for a drink with a successful author. Well, neither did I.

"I won't be long. What time is it?"

"After three anyhow." She glanced around vaguely. "Frank's taken the clock in here apart." He certainly had. The gutted timepiece lay on the table, its insides gone.

"Where is Frank?" I asked. "I haven't said good-bye yet."

"He's driving Jake to the garage to pick up his car. The old Ford is fixed . . . for now at least."

"Wait a minute. His jalopy was on the fritz again? Jake wasn't in another accident, was he?"

She shook her head. "No, of course not. It was something simple. The starter, I think."

There I went, overreacting again. I'd better watch that. "I'll be back in an hour or so. Can I borrow the wagon?"

She dug the keys out of her purse and handed them over. "Where are you going?"

"Where would you suggest?" I countered.

"Depends what your mother likes."

I shrugged. "I was thinking about getting her some sterling silver hair combs, with turquoise on them. Does that sound nice?"

"Great idea. You can probably buy some from the Indian craftsmen on the plaza."

I grinned. "Of course she'll never wear them."

Vanessa laughed. "You're so hard on her. She's a darling."

"I know. See you later."

If the traffic around the plaza is terrible most of the time, it's impossible on Saturdays. Eventually I found a parking spot only four blocks away from my destination. A mere half an hour after I left the gallery I was pricing genuine handmade native American silverwork. The wares of each craftsman were laid out on bright blankets, and I had to squat or stoop to examine the beauties. The first six jewelers had earrings, concho belts, necklaces, and rings by the

gross, but no combs. Then, two blankets down, I found a
pair that were perfect until I asked the price. Forty-five dollars seemed a lot to spend for something my darling mother
would keep in the bottom dresser drawer.

I kept on looking, but nothing appealed. Or maybe I just
wasn't concentrating. I bought a chocolate ice cream cone
from a vendor and sat down on a park bench on the plaza,
hoping for inspiration. If I didn't get her silver combs, what
then?

What I really needed was a little help from Sean O'Donnell. *If he were only here beside me, he'd know exactly what
to buy mother*, I thought. *Even better, Sean could help me
with my other problem and make mincemeat out of our
inept, local assassin.* Whoever he was, he had screwed up
from day one. How incredibly stupid to shoot the wrong
man. Now why was that? Because the killer had made a date
with Jake in the patio and then saw what he expected to see:
an average-sized man smoking a cigar? That would explain
the mistake. If so, asking one question might solve the
whole thing. And Jake could answer it.

At the first phone booth the telephone directory had all its
pages ripped out. At the second, I stepped into a wad of
bubblegum, but I did get Jake's answering service. The
woman at the other end of the line told me the office was
closed. What did I expect on Saturday afternoon? When I
asked where the doctor could be reached, she claimed that
was classified information. However, if I would leave my
name and number, he would return my call.

While I stood on a street corner and waited? I had a
better idea. I'd ring Vanessa. She'd have Jake's home number.

Of course, when I did, Vanessa wanted to know why I
needed it.

"I have to ask him a question about the night of Willet's
murder. It's important, Nessa."

But she reminded me he probably wasn't home anyway. "Frank isn't back yet. Maybe they're both still at the garage. Go straight over. It's the Chevron station on the corner of Old Pecos Trail and Alameda. Oh, Ellie, do you really think you're on the right track?"

"Maybe. Wait a minute, don't hang up. In case I miss him, what about Phyllis? Where can I reach her?"

"I'll find out. Go on, get moving. Call me back if you need some help. Promise?"

Of course I did. And of course, when I got to the Chevron station, there was no sign of either Jake's decrepit Ford or Frank's equally shabby old truck. I pulled up to the full-service pumps and asked the guy in an oil-stained coverall if Dr. Siegel had come for his car yet.

The young man spat some tobacco juice thoughtfully onto the concrete and reckoned he didn't rightly know.

"Ben, did the doc take off already?" he turned and shouted into the shadowy cavern of the garage.

No answer.

The young man shrugged. "Fill 'er up?"

I stuck a fiver in his hand and went hunting for Ben.

All I could see were his legs protruding from under a blue Volvo. When I bent over and asked my question again, he obligingly slid out to answer me.

"He left here . . . oh, five minutes ago maybe."

"Did he say where he was going?"

"Nope."

What did I expect, miracles? I asked to use the phone. Why did I feel like time was running out? Maybe because somewhere a clock was ticking?

That's when I knew who had done it and how he was going to kill again. The "when" was probably coming up fast. As for why, might as well ask why I had been so slow putting this together. Just because I liked the man he couldn't be guilty? What a dumbo I was.

When I dialed the Turning Point, Sugar was sweet as ever. "Dr. Siegel? He's not here, but I think he's coming by tonight. He usually stops in sometime Saturday. Hang on a minute, Ellie, let me check."

She put the phone down and went away. I looked at my watch. It was four-fifty-five. I tapped my foot in an agony of impatience.

Then she was back. "Ray says Jake is due here later, after he sees someone. A patient, Ray thinks, but he's not sure. Maybe you ought to try Jake's house. He could be there."

"Okay, thanks. I will."

I hung up and looked at my watch again. I could swing by on the way back to the gallery, but who was I kidding? He could be anywhere. Maybe even at his office, if he was seeing a patient. It was worth a try.

But the hurrieder I went, the behinder I got. First I lost State Street. Then, after I stopped for instructions, I hit every red light in town.

Eventually I made it . . . and sighed in relief. Jake's Ford was in the almost-deserted parking lot. It had to be his; there couldn't be two cars that ugly. I parked Vanessa's station wagon beside his heap, then walked around to the front of the building.

In the lobby, a very fit-looking Korean was locking the door to the tai chi club. He smiled and I smiled back absently. The travel agency was already closed, and Dr. Borrows had filled his last tooth and departed for the weekend. Naturally. Jake was the only workaholic in the building.

I pushed open the big double doors and crossed the deserted patio to Suite D. Jake had told me never to darken his door again, and here I was, back at the scene of my crime. If he was with a patient, I'd have to wait. That wouldn't be so bad. It would give me time to come up with just the right words. All the way over, I'd tried to marshal my arguments. He wouldn't want to believe what I had to tell him.

What if he refused to even listen? He'd been furious the last time we talked, but I hoped he hadn't actually taken out a restraining order to keep me from the premises. Still, I was trespassing as I stepped into the waiting room. It would have been a lot easier if I could have brought Phyllis along as a character reference. How in the world was I going to convince Jake of the truth? By asking him to check his patient files while I kept my back turned? It sounded so melodramatic to say that he and Sean O'Donnell were going to be blown to kingdom come by Mr. Baker.

When I didn't hear any voices, I started down the hall toward his office. Jake must be alone after all, I thought, since the door was ajar. I was on the point of calling out when the patient moved into view. He sat down on the chair in front of Jake's desk and said something about balloons. Turning on my heel, I tiptoed back the way I had come. There was no time to lose. No time for long drawn-out explanations to Ramon Chavez, either. I'd just report an assault in progress at 315 South State Street and hope the police would come with sirens blaring before Adam Montgomery detonated the bomb.

Chapter

22

"Ellie, is that you? Where are you going?" Adam called through the open office door to my retreating back.

I was going to the police, but that plan had just fizzled. There were only two ways to leave now—either have a heart attack and be carried out on a stretcher or have a nervous breakdown. Since that seemed more natural under the circumstances, I did.

I turned around and faced him with a sickly smile. "Oh, hi, Adam. You two were talking about balloons and I can't listen. My situational stress syndrome flares up at the very mention of hot air."

Adam stepped through the doorway and took my arm. "Come on in and relax. We'll change the subject, won't we, Jake?"

Pulling away, I stammered, "I can't relax. I don't have time to relax. I'm only here because," now I turned a glare on Jake, "you told Vanessa you needed a ride home. Couldn't you have called back and said you already had one with Adam? I don't have time for this crap. I still haven't bought a gift for my mother and you drag me out of my way for no reason. The stores close in half an hour and she's impossible to shop for."

"What the hell..." Jake began, but I cut him off at the pass.

"I don't want to hear your apologies or your excuses," I snapped, moving away from the door. "Adam, you're a sweetheart to do this for Jake. Can you believe he just gets his car from the garage and the clutch is slipping again?"

Jake got up from behind his desk, probably analyzing my breakdown as serious. "What are you babbling about? You're acting like an idiot."

True. My performance was disintegrating quickly. Vanessa would have handled this much better. I was sidling along the wall like a frightened crab, but there was method to my idiocy. Every inch brought me closer to the exit.

"You can't stop me, Jake. I'm going to Trumbull's. They carry half-sizes in nightgowns. That's all I ever buy her. Nightgowns. But what do you get for a finicky old lady who says 'you shouldn't have' in the same breath that she says 'it's the wrong color'?" Silently I begged my mother's forgiveness. She wasn't that old, just picky.

Jake looked disgusted. "So what's keeping you? Go already."

I wanted to, but on second thought, how could I leave him here with a crazed killer? Obviously Jake didn't know about Adam, or he would offer to come shopping with me. Which gave me a brilliant idea.

"Sure. That's easy for you to say, but I don't know how to get there. I keep getting lost. Santa Fe is so confusing with its quaint, meandering streets. And besides, if I ever do find Trumbull's, I won't know what color to choose." I put a hand out toward Adam without quite touching him. "You've got such great taste. Go to the store with me. We can let Jake find his own way home."

Now the doctor was really exasperated. "Ellie, get out of here. Go buy your mother a sweater. Pink. Old ladies like pink." He grabbed my arm and pulled me down the hall.

This was even better than taking Adam with me. In a minute, Jake would have me out the door, and then I'd yank him after me.

But not with Adam holding a gun on us.

He stood at the top of the hall looking calm, cool, collected, and deadly. "Sorry, Ellie," he said politely. "I'm afraid you'll have to forget about going anywhere today." He motioned with the automatic. "Both of you, put your hands on top of your heads and walk single file back into the office."

I should have had the heart attack. I was having a real one right now anyway. Then Jake made it worse.

"Give me the gun. You're not going to use it," he said brusquely, taking a quick step toward Adam and holding out his hand for the weapon.

Adam smiled coldly. "Don't be a fool." Poised in the stance of a trained marksman with both hands on the gun, he aimed it directly at Jake's chest.

"Do what he says," I hissed under my breath. My arms were already in the proper position.

Adam gave me an approving nod. "Ellie understands. You will too. Now move."

Slowly Jake raised his hands and started walking to the office as Adam backed across the room, keeping the gun pointed steadily at us.

I could see the muscles tensing in Jake's shoulders as he contemplated jumping his former patient. But Sean's creator was not about to make an amateur's mistake. He kept his distance.

When we were both in the office, Adam forced us to sit on the floor with our backs to the wall of built-in bookshelves. "Not so close together, and keep your hands on the back of your neck. That's right. Now, cross your legs."

"My knee won't bend," I said, wondering if he'd treat me

like a prize mare with a bad leg and put me out of my misery.

But Adam was, as ever, courteous. "It hurts? I'm so sorry. Tuck the good one under, then." He unplugged the phone and tossed it out into the hall. Next to the chair he'd been sitting in was a small blue workout bag. Adam picked it up carefully and placed it gently outside the door to the office.

My arms were already tired and blood was pounding in my ears, but inside I began to feel an icy calm to match Adam's. My act hadn't worked. But no matter what I said, Adam wouldn't have let me go. Once I'd seen him here, he couldn't kill Jake without killing me too.

The blue eyes smiled at me. His mouth curved in the same way I'd thought so dazzling, so charming. He looked marvelous, incredibly well-groomed and handsome in a tropical-weight suit. He must have intended to go straight from Jake's office to the gallery. We did have a date at six. Probably he would be there right on time. Vanessa would give him a drink while he waited for me. Typically, I'd be late.

"I didn't want to kill the cat lady," he said regretfully, "just Sean."

"He's not such a bad guy. Are you sure you don't want to change your mind?" My voice was casual, as if I didn't have a vested interest in his decision one way or the other.

"No." His eyes slid to Jake. "Sean has to go."

Jake broke into this off-the-wall conversation with a barrage of sanity. "Adam, look at me. Take a good look. I'm not Sean."

"Don't be so modest."

"I'm flattered by the comparison, but you know my name. Part of you is still in touch with reality. Hang on to that. Besides, killing me won't kill Sean. He'll still be there in your head where he always was."

"That's where he's supposed to be," Adam said with a chilling calm. "But he's been getting out."

Now Jake tried a risky kind of bribery. "I can help you get rid of him, Adam. Why don't you let me?"

Adam's face was impassive. "Don't make promises you can't keep, Doctor. I know all your games, all your mind trips. You taught me well. Now I can do them better than you can. Did you imagine I was one of those stupid drug addicts that you manipulate so easily? I haven't blown my mind on LSD and coke."

"I'm not trying to manipulate you," Jake went on in a soothing voice. "I'm trying to help you face your problem. You know you're sick and that you need therapy. That's why you came to me."

Maybe the doctor would dispense an instant cure. I crossed my fingers behind my neck. But Adam wasn't listening.

He gestured for silence with the gun, though his face was still expressionless. "Shut up. Your tricks are boring. The truth is, I went to you with a very minor problem—writer's block. I asked for a behavior-modification program." Adam's lip curled with disdain. "But you're just like my father. You think you know what's good for me, what I should do. You're into power, Doctor. You wanted to take over my life. You're still trying."

"No, that's what you think your father does. But I'm not your father, I'm your doctor."

Adam shook his head. "You're my enemy. And I've beaten you." No reality could penetrate the writer's defenses. His imaginary world had taken over.

He went on, his voice pleasant. "It's been rather interesting, this hide-and-seek we've been playing together. You're very hard to kill, you know that? I should have expected it. I wrote you that way. In *Desert Intrigue*, Sean landed the sabotaged helicopter, so of course you walked away from the balloon accident." Adam cocked his head to one side, looking puzzled. "But sending out Willet to die in your place? I never thought you would do such a thing. You're supposed to be a good person, Doctor. That's not the way a hero should behave."

"I didn't send Willet to his death. Why would I?" Jake was talking sense when only nonsense applied. "I went outside to meet you as we arranged. You never came."

"That can't be. I was there, on the patio, waiting a long time," Adam denied.

"I was sitting on the bench in front. Isn't that where we were supposed to meet?"

"No, I said out back." Adam shrugged. "Lucky mistake for you. But then Sean always has been lucky. There was always a chance the car brakes, the balloon accident wouldn't work. This time, though, there'll be no slip-up."

It was chilling to hear Adam sound so normal, yet to know that underneath he was lost in a make-believe world of madness. Jake had tried his brand of psychology and failed; maybe I would have better luck if I entered Adam's fantasy. After all, he and I had planned this scenario together.

"How did you make the bomb so quickly?" I asked him. "I'm really impressed. It is in the workout bag, isn't it?"

As always, he responded well to a pat on the ego. "You forget, I'm a trained chemist. I know a dozen ways to make an effective device. With a little research at the library, even you could, Ellie. Perhaps not the best, but something that would work quite well. Besides, these days it's easy enough to get hold of plastic explosives. They can be molded into any shape, and they're absolutely stable until detonated. Any fool can handle the stuff. That's why the terrorists use it routinely."

"But you're not a terrorist. Why bother with a bomb?" Jake asked. "That's a waste. You've got a gun in your hand

and there's no one around to hear. Why don't you want to shoot us?"

Wonderful, I thought. *Give him more ideas. That's just what we need*. Didn't Jake realize we had a chance as long as Adam didn't decide to use that gun? A very slim chance.

"The bomb was Ellie's idea." Adam smiled, giving credit where credit was due. "Don't worry," he said to me. "I won't forget to put your name on the list of resource people. I might even dedicate the book to you."

Thanks a lot. My name would be recorded in history, my body donated to science fiction. "I may have made a small suggestion, but you actually carried it through," I said admiringly, putting him back on center stage where he liked to be. "It was also very clever of you to get Jake to meet you here now when no one else was around. How did you manage it?"

He leaned against the wall and raised one eyebrow. "When you understand human nature the way I do, Ellie, it becomes ridiculously easy to push someone's buttons. The doctor imagines that he saves people. All I had to do was play to that. I told him I wanted to talk about my emotional problems. He didn't even think there was anything peculiar about meeting at five on Saturday. I claimed it was convenient because I'd be in his building this afternoon, taking a tai chi class. When he arrived, I was here, with my workout bag. Simple, isn't it, when you do your homework? The doctor remembered that I studied martial arts. What he forgot was that I went to Japan and learned from a master. I could give lessons."

Jake snorted. "Sean's a black belt. Not you."

Damn him, didn't he see that the way to handle Adam was to join his fantasies, not destroy them? I grimaced, terrified that Jake would push Adam into an uncontrolled rage.

He almost did. "Adam, listen to me. If you think you're so smart, take a look in that backward mirror of yours.

You've developed a systemized pattern of delusions. Wake up and smell the coffee."

Adam's face mirrored his confusion, then his regret, and finally the recognition that Jake was correct. But in an instant Adam had pushed the truth out of his consciousness again.

"It's getting late. I'd better be going." He looked at his watch, then stepped to the private exit from the office, the door that led to the parking lot. After checking that the bolt was locked, he pocketed the key and turned to Jake. "Throw me yours, Doctor. Careful. Use just one hand."

Jake fished in his pocket and brought the ring out, a steel hoop with a dozen keys on it. I tensed, afraid he was going to do something foolish, throw it in Adam's face, then make a wild leap and try to wrest the gun from him. That would have been fatal. Jake couldn't have gotten up from the floor and across the room before Adam fired at him. Jake added up the odds and evidently agreed with me. The keys landed with soft jingle on the rug at Adam's feet. Keeping the gun leveled at us, he picked them up.

"I'll explain this to you once," he said calmly, almost as if he were giving us a military briefing. "The bomb is on a timer set to explode at precisely eighteen hundred hours. That's four minutes and," he consulted his gold watch again, "forty-three seconds from now."

"That's a dumb, stupid move. Get the bag and turn it off right now," Jake ordered, sitting on the floor with his hands on his head. Somehow his words lacked authority.

Adam totally ignored him. Never interrupt a mad scientist in the midst of his experiment. Can't let all that research go to waste.

"I'm locking you in here," Adam continued, "because this room has no windows. There are two doors and you might be able to break down the one to the hall. It's fairly flimsy, but let me warn you, I'm placing the workout bag against it. The bomb inside is booby-trapped. If it's jarred, or even pushed gently, it will explode instantly. If you don't believe me, you can test my veracity for yourselves." A self-satisfied smile flitted briefly across his face. "Just let me add that I've calculated the force of the explosion quite carefully. It will totally destroy your offices, Doctor, including all patient files. You'll be pleased to hear that it will inflict only minor damage on the neighboring offices."

He paused. "Any last words? No? Then I'll be off. Don't worry. Your deaths should be quite painless." He backed out, closing and locking the hall door. A second later, we heard the outer door close behind him too.

Jake and I scrambled to our feet. "Could it possibly be a bluff?" I asked. "Is the bomb booby-trapped?"

"I don't know. And I don't know if there's really a bomb."

"You're the psychiatrist. How crazy is he?"

Jake rubbed at his face. "Looks like he's got a full-blown psychosis. I knew Adam had dropped out of therapy at a bad point. I just had no idea how far his illness had progressed. Maybe the bomb is a figment of his imagination. It's clear he hallucinates."

So did I. I should have known Adam was too good to be true, but not until an hour ago did I begin penetrating my own myths. That was when the evidence had started spelling out Adam Montgomery Baker, the writer who didn't use his last name . . . except when he was seeing a psychiatrist. I had found his folder in Jake's inactive file but I was checking against the guest book and Adam had signed the register with his nom de plume. Once I remembered—and Adam had told me at Bandelier that he made his father happy by not using the family name—everything fell into place. A gutted clock that made me think of bombs, and why the police hadn't arrested Frank for possession of cocaine . . . even why Sean had to die rather than fade into literary obscurity.

"He may hallucinate," I argued with Jake, "but we didn't dream Willet's death, and that balloon ride was a nightmare." I started scrambling in my purse. No turkey skewers and one cracked emery board instead of a nail file. "Have you got a pocket knife?"

"Why? Are you going to dig an escape tunnel like the Count of Monte Cristo?"

When I looked up he was walking toward the door. "Stop, Jake. Don't open it."

"I'm not." He leaned his ear against the panel. "I don't hear any ticking."

"You idiot. Bombs haven't ticked since 1963. They don't use clocks anymore," I said with authority, having read that fact in *Countdown to Terror*. "What's in the desk? I need something sharp, unless you have a spare key for that dead bolt." I pulled open the top drawer.

Jake shook his head. "There's one in Mary's desk. Mine was on the keychain. You're not going to try to pick the lock?"

He was awfully sarcastic for a person who didn't have any better suggestion. I twisted a couple of paper clips into a straight wire and slipped it into the slot of the dead bolt. "How much time do we have?" I asked tensely.

"Three minutes eleven seconds, according to my watch. Presuming we trust Adam's word."

"Well, I do. Which is what you should have done with me. If you had, we wouldn't be in this position. I hope you realize we're both going to die and it's all your fault. Try the skylight," I ordered desperately. "We might be able to break out through it."

"Okay. Anything is better than standing around listening to you." He shoved the desk into position and climbed up on it. "The molding is nailed in place and I don't have a crowbar. Any more brilliant ideas?"

"Dammit." I almost sobbed as one of the paper clips bent

in my hands. "You're a great help. You're a dud, Doctor. Your confrontational approach didn't work, and now you can't even take apart a skylight. Break it, for God's sake. That panel is plastic."

"How do you know?"

"I've installed them."

"Okay. I'll try."

But you can't break plastic with plastic. Everything on his desk was lightweight, flimsy. The heaviest piece of metal we had was a stapler and it was four inches long. Jake finally made a dent in the Plexiglas with the Scotch Tape dispenser.

"How much time is left?" I asked over my shoulder.

"Forty-five seconds," he said, banging away at his roof. "How's the great burglar coming down there? I hope you're doing better than I am."

"Not noticeably. This is a new kind of lock for me. I only went as far as Breaking and Entering 101." Damn, it was hard to move the tumblers. They weren't spring-loaded.

"Time's up." Jake jumped off the desk. "It's now ten seconds past eighteen hundred and we're not dead yet. Hurry up, Ellie. Adam's not Sean, but he can't have messed up too much. It's going to blow soon." He sounded anxious.

I wished there was time to wallow in the satisfaction of having Dr. Siegel admit I was right. But the paper clip was bending. If it cracked in half, it would be stuck in the lock and we'd be stuck in here. I held my breath and forced the last metal tumbler clear. The bolt slid back. I grabbed the doorknob with my sweaty hands.

"Jake, hurry!" I screamed. We scrambled out into the parking lot and ran for our lives.

The explosion was thirty-five seconds late.

Epilogue

Casa Grande, CA
July 30

Dear Vanessa,

My compliments to the hostess who made my vacation as exciting as promised. I enjoyed every hair-raising minute of it. Your report on a business boom isn't surprising, but great news anyway. Please congratulate Leon on his blue ribbon, and tell Conchita the wall over my couch never looked better. I can't believe that Frank is worried about me. Please tell him that he has my eternal gratitude and my promise to go through doors the easy way from now on: with a key.

As for the rest, I predicted Dr. Siegel would come through at the competency hearing. Who else but Superpsych would testify in behalf of the man who tried to kill him? Adam's lucky that he's unfit to stand trial, even if he's in no shape to appreciate that right now.

Give my love to the gang, and to Ruth. Malcolm, too, when you see him again. Which reminds me, I am not getting together with Jake when he comes to L.A. for his conference, even if that does break your romantic little heart. Take care and keep those green eyes flashing.

Love,
Ellie

P.S. Of course, I might change my mind about Jake.

Mystery . . . Intrigue
. . . Suspense

__BAD COMPANY
by Liza Cody   *(B30-738, $2.95)*

Liza Cody's first mystery, DUPE, won the John Creasey Award in England and was nominated for the Edgar Award in 1981. Private detective Anna Lee, the novel's heroine, was hailed by Michele Slung of National Public Radio as "the first worthy successor to Cordelia Gray in a decade." Anna Lee returns in BAD COMPANY, another fine mystery in the P.D. James tradition.

__DUPE
by Liza Cody   *(B32-241, $2.95)*

Anna Lee is the private investigator called in to placate the parents of Dierdre Jackson. Dierdre could not have died as the result of an accident on an icy road. She had driven race cars; the stretch of road was too easy. In search of simple corroborating evidence, Anna finds motives and murder as she probes the unsavory world of the London film industry where Dierdre sought glamour and found duplicity . . . and death.